# THE SECRET OF GANDALARA

"Do you understand me, my friends?" said Zanek. "Through the All-Mind I saw the death of Gandalara." He leaned forward, elbows on knees, to stare into the candle flame. "But when I saw this new danger, I knew I was helpless to stop it. Only you have the knowledge that is needed."

"All the pieces are here, somewhere," I said. "Why can't we see how they fit together?"

"There must be something that you two—and no one else—knows. . . . What is it, my friends?"

I had caught Zanek's hand without realizing it. I was looking at him, but what I was seeing was something else. Hazy images were crystallizing, pieces falling into place. A volcano. Salty deserts. A map . . .

"No!" I shouted. "That can't be it!" I turned my eyes to Tarani, who was watching me in alarm.

"You know, don't you?" Zanek asked softly. "Is it so horrible? Can it be changed?"

"Rikardon, *tell* us," Tarani pleaded, sliding down from her chair to kneel beside me. . . .

### *THE RIVER WALL*

The awesome conclusion to
*The Gandalara Cycle*

Bantam Spectra Books by Randall Garrett and Vicki Ann Heydron
Ask your bookseller for the titles you have missed.

THE GANDALARA CYCLE I:
  THE STEEL OF RAITHSKAR
  THE GLASS OF DYSKORNIS
  THE BRONZE OF EDDARTA
THE GANDALARA CYCLE II:
  THE WELL OF DARKNESS
  RETURN TO EDDARTA
  THE SEARCH FOR KÄ
THE RIVER WALL

# THE RIVER WALL

RANDALL GARRETT and VICKI ANN HEYDRON

**BANTAM BOOKS**
TORONTO · NEW YORK · LONDON · SYDNEY · AUCKLAND

To Randall...

I hope I've done well.

THE RIVER WALL
A Bantam Spectra Book / June 1986

ISBN 0-553-25565-7

Bantam Books are published by Bantam Books, Inc. Its trademark,
consisting of the words "Bantam Books" and the portrayal of a
rooster, is Registered in U.S. Patent and Trademark Office and in
other countries. Marca Registrada. Bantam Books, Inc., 666 Fifth
Avenue, New York, New York 10103.

PRINTED IN THE UNITED STATES OF AMERICA
KR       0 9 8 7 6 5 4 3

To Randall—
    I hope I have done well.
               —Vicki

# THE RIVER WALL

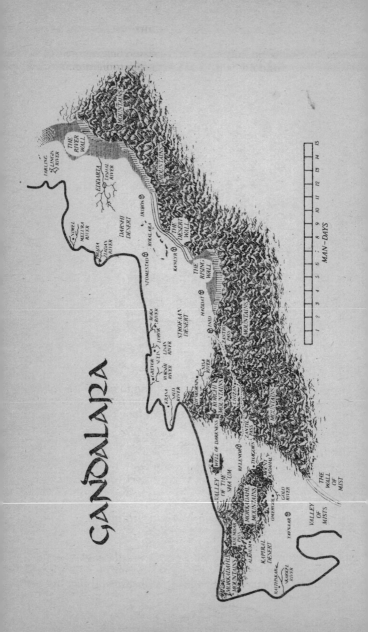

# PRELIMINARY PROCEEDINGS:
# INPUT SESSION SEVEN

—Good morning, Recorder.

—Welcome. All is prepared?

—Everything has been done according to your instruction, Recorder. Attendants will await our return from the All-Mind. We will not be disturbed, no matter how long this session lasts.

—Has something upset you?

—No. Yes. That is—yes. Our plans for this session were strongly opposed.

—I believe you expected that.

—I expected the opposition. What surprised me was the way I felt when I faced it.

—Were you angry?

—Not so much angry as indignant. I felt offended, as if the concern of my friends were an insult. . . .

—Yes? Continue.

—As if contradiction of my wishes were the highest crime.

—I see. Then I shall not ease your turmoil, for I must add my caution to theirs, and remind you, once again, that there is danger in this.

1

—Then I can only repeat what I've told you before, Recorder: there is more danger in not doing it this way. Every day that passes, the memories are more distant. It becomes more difficult to reconstruct the details of thought and action. And in spite of my commitment to the completion of the Record, I come to it ever more reluctantly.

—Do you refer to the intensity of experience in reliving the time of the Record? Surely that is familiar to you by now.

—Of course it is, Recorder. I do not expect this session to be entirely pleasant, but there is nothing here worse than the terrible grief that beset me when Keeshah closed off our mindlink, or when one of his cubs was killed by the vineh.

—What is it that you fear, then?

—The Record has a mirror quality that lets me see myself with unsettling clarity. I have the feeling that I have edited my memory of this time, and that the act of Recording will uncover what has been concealed. I may not like the man I find in the Record.

—You are not speaking the truth.

—You have no right to challenge my word! . . . Forgive me, Recorder.

—The hidden truth disturbs you. Speak it, that we may achieve the calmness with which to join our minds to the All-Mind.

—I have hidden it even from myself, Recorder. The truth is, I know that meeting the past man will help me see the present man more clearly. I'm afraid I won't like the way I have changed. . . . Why are you silent, Recorder? Are you afraid to say that you see the changes more clearly, and that you disapprove?

—I hesitate in order to consider whether I may answer you. I think I may not, as this is a matter concerning the Record.

—I see. You may not judge as a Recorder. But can't you speak only for yourself, as an individual?

—I can, and will do so when the Record is complete.

—By then, I will have seen the truth for myself.

—Truth is sometimes a matter of perception. You fear that yours has been clouded by the passage of time and events; I have the same fear. When we have shared the memory of actual events, we will share our refreshed perceptions, and thus build a stronger truth.

—*Very well, Recorder. Anytime you're ready.*

—*Rest a moment. Allow yourself to become totally calm and relaxed. Now make your mind one with mine, as I have made mine one with the All-Mind . . .*

*WE BEGIN!*

# 1

Tarani and I were walking the wide, stone-paved avenue through Lord City, dressed for the desert trail in loose-fitting trousers and tunics. Travel packs—leather pouches laced together in pairs—were slung across our shoulders. We had gathered a small following of children from the seven extended families of the Lords of Eddarta. They hung back, skittered after us, whispered.

Minutes earlier, Tarani had told only three people that their new High Lord was leaving Eddarta again: Indomel, Tarani's brother and enemy; Zefra, Tarani's mother and uncertain friend; and Hollin, the Lord in whom Tarani had vested her power for the duration of her absence.

*I wish I felt better about leaving Indomel and Zefra loose in Lord City,* I thought. *Still, Tarani seems satisfied that they won't make trouble, and she trusts Hollin. I like him, too, and I think he could handle either Indomel or Zefra alone. Tarani thinks they hate each other too much to cooperate against her, and she may be right.*

*Zefra, in fact, is still enjoying Indomel's defeat too much to notice that she hasn't collected any power for herself as a result of Tarani's accession as High Lord. But Indomel? As soon as Zefra shows the slightest discontent, he'll try to convince her that Tarani has abandoned her, and that they should work together and use their mindgifts to destroy the government Tarani has set up.*

*Should I tell Tarani I'm worried?* I wondered.

I looked around and noticed that we were approaching the arched stone gateway, the only entrance to Lord City except for the meandering branch of the Tashal River that paralleled the avenue to our left. Two guards, standing inside the gate, straightened into alertness as we approached. They were

members of the High Guard, the security force maintained by
the family of the High Lord.

Each of the Lord families maintained a Guard of ten to fifty
men inside the city and a somewhat larger force at the copper
mine run by each family. The city guards served as a symbol of
each family's independence inside Lord City, and acted as
perimeter guards around each family area. Their real function
was watching slaves, preventing theft, and, occasionally, acting
as a deterrent to open conflict between the families. The High
Guard, the largest in Lord City, also posted watch along the
wall around the city itself, and at its gate.

One of the gate guards was a burly, competent-looking man,
and he nodded slightly as we came abreast of him. It was
Naddam, the man who had been in charge of the Lingis mine
just before my own stint in his position. He had shown all the
compassion allowed him by the rules toward the slaves placed
in his care. I had come to admire and like the man, and I had
seen him again only the day before. Seeing him now helped
me decide not to voice my fears about Indomel to Tarani.

*Naddam promised to send word directly to Raithskar, if
anything goes wrong here*, I remembered. I nodded and
smiled as we passed, and wished for the opportunity to speak a
friendly word, but Tarani did not hesitate, and I kept pace with
her long stride.

*She's the High Lord*, I thought. *If she's content to leave
things this way, then I won't stir up any doubt. Besides, now
that she's agreed to go back to Raithskar with me, I think she's
as eager as I am to be out of here. We ought to be able to slip
away quietly. . . .*

We stepped through the thick stone archway, and stopped.

There must have been five hundred people outside the gate.
They clumped and milled over most of the grassy slope
between the walled city of the Lords and the sprawling, busy
streets of Lower Eddarta. When Tarani and I appeared, the
crowd focused and shifted toward us, the general murmur
coalescing into a louder sound.

I saw Tarani's shoulders twitch, and I believe I knew what
she was feeling. It was all I could do to keep my hand from the
hilt of Rika, the steel sword that hung from my baldric. The
noise of the crowd was unnerving, but as yet it was neither
friendly nor angry, and I had no desire to tilt the scales to the
negative side.

The mass of people surged up the slope like a strange kind of tide.

The crowd arced around us from the nearer bank of the Tashal to the wall of Lord City, leaving us in an opening that was shaped like a circle's quadrant. To our left, people were pressed to the very edge of the riverbank. To our right, the wall of mortared stone met a wall of people.

The leading edge of the crowd swept toward us, then seemed to grow shy about twenty feet away. When Tarani, moving with grace and without any sign of fear, stepped out into the open space, the people in front dug in their heels and struggled to move back against the pressure of the bodies behind them. In spite of their efforts, our space was shrinking, and I felt a touch of claustrophobic panic.

*Need help?*

*Keeshah!* I answered the mindvoice. *You're the reason for the crowd, aren't you? As soon as they saw you, the Eddartans knew something was up.*

*You said come,* the sha'um answered, with a note of irritation. *Here since light. Don't want people.*

*I'm not blaming you,* I soothed him, thinking: This crowd has been gathering since dawn, too, but nobody inside Lord City took any notice. Tarani's right—the Lords have been isolated from Eddarta too long.

The crowd was settling down some, but not enough to quell the panic I felt.

*We could use some room, Keeshah,* I said. I sensed restlessness and eagerness from him, and hurriedly added: *Don't hurt anyone, okay? Just bring the family through to us; the people will make room for you.*

Keeshah's rumbling growl sounded behind the outermost ranks pressed against the wall of Lord City. The edge of the mass shrank back from the wall, opening a passage for the sha'um. The big cats walked down the freshly opened pathway and into the pie wedge of open space that Tarani and I occupied. They fairly filled it up: two adult sha'um, nearly man-tall and the length of a man's trunk between shoulder and hip; and two cubs, still only a few months old but already the size of full-grown tigers.

As if by magic, the pie wedge grew to twice the size.

Keeshah came to me, and turned to face the crowd. Yayshah took a similar place beside Tarani. The cubs approached the

nearest people curiously, and Yayshah growled a warning to
the cubs. I would not have understood the message from the
female sha'um on my own, but I heard it loud and clear
through my link with the cubs.

Koshah, the young male who was a startling duplicate of his
father, roared a complaint and shook his head, fluffing his mane
at his mother. At the same time, he spoke to me.

*No fun,* he said, and I crunched down on my impulse to
laugh.

Yayshah lunged away from Tarani, and the people in front
went into full retreat, banging into and climbing over the
people behind them.

"Wait," Tarani called, her vibrant voice sounding clearly
above the sudden uproar. The noise subsided slightly. "Please
be calm," Tarani urged. "Yayshah will not harm you, but you
may injure each other."

The struggling stopped, and some of the folks in back
boosted themselves on others' shoulders to watch as Yayshah
herded the cubs—Koshah resisting to the last—away from the
people and back toward us.

When Yayshah had rejoined us, Tarani put her hand on the
female's side. Yayshah crouched; Tarani mounted; Yayshah
stood; Tarani sat up straight. From her sitting height, Tarani
had a fair view of the crowd, and most of the people could see
her.

The movement quieted almost instantly, and all the faces
turned toward Tarani.

*These people are curious, not angry,* I thought, surprised. *If
six people had just decided who had the final word for
thousands of people, and if that person were an absolute
stranger to me and my city and my way of life, I think I'd be a
little ticked off.*

I tried to see Tarani through the eyes of an Eddartan,
conscious that it was as difficult for Markasset, the native
Gandalaran, as it was for Ricardo, the stranger to all Gandalaran society and custom. Markasset's home city was ruled by a
small group of people, but the Supervisors of Raithskar had
nothing like the absolute power wielded by the Lords of
Eddarta. The Supervisors were administrators who served
their city out of dedication and a sense of privilege.

The Lords had decided, for themselves and for the populous
city at the foot of the slope, that Tarani was now the High

Lord, the leader of Lord City and, by default, the ruler of Lower Eddarta. The appointment had been made not from respect for her leadership skills—though I believe she had won that, after the fact, from the other Lords—but because she happened to have the right parents and seemed a less dangerous choice than her brother.

Yesterday, Lord City had held a Celebration Dance in Tarani's honor. I found myself wondering if the lower city had been celebrating with as much fervor.

Tarani's special, powerful voice rang out again across the quiet. "The sha'um will not harm you," she repeated. She reached down and drew her hand along the jaw of the female she rode, unconsciously slipping into the tradition of the Sharith—another society she had joined smoothly. "This is Yayshah, and the young ones are Koshah and Yoshah. I have asked Yayshah if her cubs may greet you. Please move slowly around them, and touch them only gently."

Tarani glanced at me, and I took the cue.

*Your mother has agreed,* I said, speaking to both the cubs, *to let you say hello to the folks. Koshah, go toward the river and walk back toward the center. Yoshah, you start at the wall. They may want to touch you, but they don't want to hurt you. If someone does hurt you, don't react; just come back over here. Understand?*

*Yes,* said Yoshah, a sense of excitement trembling through the contact.

*Now? Soon? Hurry?* was Koshah's answer. He was shifting his weight back and forth, twisting his neck to look around at me.

*Go slowly,* I emphasized, as the cubs moved out in different directions.

There were times when I could blend with the minds of the sha'um. Those times involved a special, intense sharing of emotions and sensations. It had happened with Keeshah when our survival depended on our united action. It had happened with the cubs unpredictably, at first, and usually as a result of the wild emotional swings common to the young of all species. During the long, tiring trip across Gandalara to Eddarta, I had worked with the cubs to bring that ability to blend under some control.

I reached out to each of them now, only briefly, to get a glimpse of what they were feeling as hand after hand reached out from the wall of bodies to touch them. The crowd had seemed fairly quiet to me, but to the keener hearing of Koshah, each voice was separate and distinct. It was like hearing the individual notes of a symphony. Yoshah was concentrating on the odors—not just the scent of the people, but of their clothes, their work, what they had eaten for breakfast.

At the first touch, Koshah tensed up and Yoshah's mind flinched. But the touch was light and rather pleasant, and it took only a moment for the cubs to relax and enjoy the attention.

The cubs—the first young sha'um ever to be born outside the isolated Valley of the Sha'um—had been a sensation everywhere, but never like this. In Raithskar, they had won the hearts of people mostly because Keeshah was their "resident sha'um" and the cubs were his children. In Thagorn, the Riders had been awed by more than the unique birth. Their feelings had been tied up with recognition of the historical significance of the entire situation: a female sha'um had chosen to leave the Valley; a Rider had formed the unique mind-to-mind bond with a sha'um while both were already adults; and the Rider in this case was a woman.

In both cities, the people had held a daily awareness of sha'um in some form or another. In Eddarta, sha'um were little more than a legend. In addition to being charming young animals, the cubs were almost mythic figures to the people of Eddarta.

When the cubs met in the center of our little clear space, I called them away from the crowd. They came, but only reluctantly.

"We're spoiling them," I said to myself, but Tarani heard and smiled back at me.

"In good cause," she whispered, and turned back toward the waiting people.

The crowd was silent now, everyone watching Tarani expectantly.

"Forgive me, people of Eddarta, for not speaking to you before now. There has been much to do in a very short time. You know I am High Lord, but you do not yet know me. I give you this as a beginning: I shall always give the truth, and I demand it in return."

She looked over the sea of faces.

"I would wish to speak to each of you individually, but that will not be possible. Is there one among you who will speak for all?"

The crowd rippled near the river, and a very old woman forced her way out into the clearing. She was nearly bald, and the skin of her face had shrunk up to emphasize the prominence of her supraorbital ridge. She was missing a couple of lower teeth, but the wide tusks—placed in the Gandalaran jaw where canine teeth grew in humans—were white and gleaming against her brownish skin. The old woman walked forward with a slow dignity, her back rounded, one hand lifting the hem of her long yellow tunic to keep it out from underfoot.

She walked to a spot halfway between the crowd and Tarani, and spoke up in a clear voice. "You may speak to me, High Lord," she said, meeting Tarani's gaze boldly. "But be warned that I will test your commitment to the truth. I am Shedo, the baker. The son of my brother is called Volitar, and I ask for news of my kinsman."

A ripple of muscle up Tarani's back was the only sign she gave of her surprise. The people in the crowd were less subtle—the news of who had stepped forward traveled backward in a wave of whispers.

After a moment of tense silence, Tarani said: "Volitar is dead now, Shedo. He died protecting me."

*And trying to make sure Tarani never set foot in Eddarta,* I thought. *That memory must be hard for Tarani right now.*

The old woman nodded as if she had expected that answer. The crowd murmured, responding as much to Tarani's obvious grief as to her announcement.

"We have been told," Shedo said, "that you are Pylomel's daughter. Now that I see you, I doubt it less."

"Yet you do have some doubt," Tarani said, "and justly. Physically, I am, indeed, the daughter of Pylomel. Zefra has sworn before the Lords that when she left Eddarta with Volitar, she already carried Pylomel's child." Tarani's voice went flat and bitter. "Your former High Lord, my father, was fair in one respect: he would not accept rejection from *any* woman, Lord or Eddartan. Zefra hated Pylomel and opposed the marriage which he had arranged through the death of her father and uncle. In punishment for her dislike, Pylomel used his mindpower to force Zefra to his bed—before their marriage, and against her will."

The crowd buzzed briefly, caught by the phrase "against her will." In Gandalara, where there were no moral objections or health hazards attached to sex between mutually consenting adults, rape was more rare and even more abhorred than in Ricardo's world. These people must have guessed at the fate of the women occasionally "chosen" from Eddarta as special servants to the High Lord. Tarani had just confirmed that suspicion, and her obvious distress forged a bond of empathy between her and Eddarta.

"In every other way, Shedo, Volitar *was* my father. He called himself my uncle, but he was the only parent I knew. It was he who taught me what all children must learn: what is right; what is wrong.

"Volitar and I lived quietly in Dyskornis, and I knew nothing of Zefra until less than a year ago. When I first learned her name, I believed as you do, that I had been born of Volitar and Zefra. That belief brought me both comfort—that the man who had raised me with such love and goodness was truly my father—and mystery—why should he have claimed otherwise? It was partially in quest of the answer to that mystery that I first came to Eddarta."

*Only partially*, I thought, beginning to panic slightly. *She's not going to tell them about the Ra'ira, is she? Of course not,* I assured myself. *I'm just uncomfortable because I'm useless. It's not the first time I've felt this way since we came to Eddarta. I'll have to remember to apologize to Tarani for never understanding, before now, what it's like to follow someone in blind faith, with no idea of what will happen next.*

It was no comfort that Shedo's words seemed to come directly from my own frightened thoughts.

"Only partially?" Shedo asked. She took a step closer, bending back her head to look up at Tarani. "What of the rest of the answer, High Lord? Why *have* you come back to Eddarta?"

# 2

Koshah pressed his nose into the back of my right thigh, making the knee bend and nearly bringing me down. *Can't play right now,* I told him, and absently reached down to scratch behind an ear. Yoshah came up on my left, and the cubs leaned against me, their heads tilted to get maximum benefit from the scratching.

I hardly knew what I was doing; like the rest of the people there, I was focused on Tarani. She had taken a deep breath, and was looking out over the crowd—not at the mass of them, but into individual faces. The people waited for her answer.

"Volitar," she said at last, "did more than merely hate the Lords. He acted for change. Never mind that the effect of the change was small at the time—the nearly momentary disruption of Pylomel's plans. When the opportunity appeared, he *acted*.

"He took action, too, in everything he taught me. He never mentioned Eddarta in the way one might think he would—to feed and perpetuate his hatred. He taught me what he believed in—that power is merely a tool, and nothing to be feared in itself. I did not learn to hate the Lords, but I learned to despise the misuse of power. Volitar knew that I would have a strong mindgift. In this way, he *acted* to change the way one born Lord viewed her own power.

"In a way, my becoming High Lord is Volitar's final action toward change. When I came to Eddarta, my vision was not warped by hatred or a lifetime of fear. I saw good and bad people on both sides of these walls," she said, waving her arm toward the stone wall behind me.

"The power in Lord City is obvious and visible, and Pylomel wore his corruption with pride. Yet I see power in Eddarta, too, my friends—power which is no less corrupt because its misuse lies in its idleness."

Tarani's voice had begun to tremble slightly. I stopped

petting the cubs and listened more closely. Tarani was saying things to the crowd she had never been able to say to me.

"Think of *me* as Lord City," Tarani said, "and of Yayshah, this sha'um, as Eddarta. I choose a destination, and she carries me there. Yet we travel *together*. She carries me *willingly*. If she has needs that conflict with my wishes, she tells me, and I alter my plans in consideration of those needs. The alternative is leaving her and traveling alone—possible, but a dismal prospect, after having known her friendship.

"For generations, the Lords have been riding Eddarta further into corruption. Yet Eddarta has made no effort to divert them."

A cry of protest began in the front ranks of the crowd and swelled. Tarani let it build for a moment, then raised her hand for attention again. Silence came quickly.

"Each of you sees power in the individual Lord to whom you pay tribute. You look, then, at yourself and see helplessness. Think—is there only one Lord who has built Lord City? No. It is their power *as a group* that rules Eddarta. And in Eddartans *as a group* lies the power to resist the demands of the Lords, and to guide the future, not only of Eddarta, but of Lord City.

"Eddarta's power has never been used, and for one excellent reason. Until now, it has not been needed. While the demands of the Lords were reasonable, and they returned benefit to Eddarta through more profitable work and guided growth, Eddarta and Lord City moved willingly, and together, in the same direction. When the power was needed, Eddartans were trapped in the habit, built up over generations, of unquestioning cooperation with the Lords.

"That Volitar was a man of vision is proved by the fact that he saw beyond the habit and recognized the unfairness of what his Lord asked of him. Yet even he did not see the hidden power." She smiled. "If he had seen it, you would have heard from him, years ago, what I have said today. He chose to act individually because Volitar, too, believed that he had no choice.

"I came to Eddarta with no history among you, no habits, no preconceptions. It was not my purpose to bring change to Eddarta or Lord City, but events made me the agent of change. It was not by my hand that Pylomel died, but partially on my account—and I felt regret only in the knowledge that Indomel exceeded our father in greed and corruption."

Tarani paused to let the crowd accept what amounted to a confession. In that moment, she turned her head slightly, so that she could see me out of the corner of her eye.

I brought my hand close to my chest and brought thumb and index finger together in the "OK" sign from Ricardo's world. The corner of Tarani's mouth twitched upward, but that was all the evidence I needed to know that she had seen it.

"I knew that I had been the instrument of installing Indomel as High Lord," Tarani said. "I knew, too, that Eddarta would suffer further at his hands. Finally, I accepted that I could be the instrument of freeing Eddarta from his oppression, that *I could act for change*. In me you see a bridge, my friends. I am bound to Lord City by blood, and to Eddarta by my love for Volitar. I came back as High Lord, Shedo," Tarani said, looking down at the old woman again, "to speak for Eddarta's power before the Lords, and to set the balance right again. Eddarta and Lord City are partners in the business of living; it is my purpose to speak that truth at every opportunity."

Shedo squinted and tilted her head. "I'm too old not to be blunt," she said. "What you're telling us—do the Lords know it?"

Tarani laughed. "I have not stated it so clearly for them," she admitted. "But then, they have not asked me, either."

That brought a few laughs, and Tarani waited for the sounds to die away.

"The Lords are not fools," Tarani said. "They have seen Eddarta's discontent, and have felt its effect in small ways— less artful workmanship, less prompt response, subtle disrespect. They have done nothing because Lord City is as trapped by habit as Eddarta. They have accepted me because they recognize that my vision is more true for being impartial.

"Do not expect sudden or radical differences, my friends. You will not waken tomorrow to find yourselves treated like Lords. The oppression you resent arrived only gradually; it cannot be removed any less gradually, and still guarantee the survival of anyone, Lord or Eddartan. But the process has already begun, with the gradual elimination of slavery in the copper mines." The crowd gasped.

"Details of the process will be announced formally in a few days," Tarani continued. "The Lords are making an effort to recognize and reward your worth. I ask that you accept their effort with dignity and patience."

Tarani sighed and pulled her shoulders straighter. Yayshah sidestepped restlessly.

*It's about over,* I thought. *Keeshah, it's almost time to go.*

*Good,* Keeshah grunted, and crouched down to let me mount. *Too many people.*

When Keeshah surged to his feet, the attention of the crowd shifted to us. Tarani followed the shift, smiled at me, and waved me forward. At my direction, Keeshah took a few steps and stopped beside Yayshah. The two sha'um dipped their heads toward one another, brushing the tips of their ears together.

Tarani lifted her hand to reclaim the attention of the people, then extended it to me. I took it, impressed as always by the strength in her long, fine-boned fingers.

"If I owe Volitar for teaching me to deplore the misuse of power," Tarani said, "I owe this man, Rikardon, for teaching me the proper use of power."

I kept my body from registering the shock I felt, but I could not hide it from Keeshah. His head lifted suddenly, and he shifted his weight. At the risk of falling, I kept hold of Tarani's hand until he had moved back to his original place.

"Rikardon is the Captain of the Sharith," Tarani was saying. "His power is not born of mindgift, or of wealth, or even of the strength of his sha'um. His power lies in the way he lives his life—in the example he sets and to which those who know him aspire. He is an honest man, and fair, and he looks beyond his own needs toward a greater good. He is a leader, and it is only his teaching that gave me the confidence to claim my birthright."

*She sees everything I've done to her as helping her?* I wondered incredulously. *I'd call that a very tolerant and forgiving attitude.* I could not look at her, because I knew my face would give away my amazement, and disrupt her farewell message to Eddarta.

"Rikardon and I are committed to a complex and arduous task which we believe contributes to the good of all Gandalara," Tarani continued. "It was this task, unrelated to my connection to the Lords, that first brought me to Eddarta. It remains unfinished, and its incompleteness prevents me from committing myself, freely and totally, to my purpose as High Lord.

"I must leave, now, to finish this duty. I have the promise of the Lords that they will begin to implement the plans on which we have agreed. I want your promise to give them room and time, and to cooperate patiently, to let the change begin gradually, as it must. Will you give me your word, that I may leave Eddarta with a lighter heart?"

In contrast to other reactions, this time the crowd was utterly silent. It was Shedo who finally spoke up.

"Tarani," she said. "I claim kin-right to call you by name, and—" She paused and looked around. "—By virtue of the fact that no one else is talking, I claim the right to speak for Eddarta. In all our history, no High Lord has sought the approval or cooperation of anyone outside Lord City. You've talked with us, justified yourself, and expressed a commitment to change. You've asked us to join in that commitment. Now you tell us you have to fulfill some secret duty elsewhere."

Shedo moved closer to Tarani and placed her hand on the girl's thigh.

"You've chosen a duty here, too, Tarani, and you're leaving it unfinished. You have convinced me that you were, indeed, raised by the Volitar I knew. So I will not ask you *if* you will return to Eddarta; only tell us *when* you will be back."

With no warning, Tarani swung her right leg over Yayshah's head and dropped down to the ground. Shedo had drawn back in alarm at the sudden movement, so that Tarani landed in the narrow space between her and the female sha'um.

Tarani gathered the old woman into her arms and held her for a long moment. "I cannot give you a day," Tarani said, "but there is no power in Gandalara except death that can prevent my return."

The old woman pulled away, obviously shaken and touched by Tarani's sudden impulse. Tarani whirled toward Yayshah, who crouched just in time to accept Tarani's weight. When Yayshah stood up, the private moment had ended, and Tarani and Shedo were once again representatives, rather than individuals.

"You have our promise, High Lord," Shedo said solemnly. "Eddarta will be the partner, and not the opponent, of Lord City. We wish you safety, success in your duty, and swift return."

"I hope that I shall always be worthy of your trust, my

friends," Tarani said, then smiled down at the old woman, "And of your kin-claim, Great-aunt."

I had envisioned a quick getaway eastward along the wall, but Tarani guided Yayshah to the south, along the road that led through Lower Eddarta. I brought Keeshah up beside the female, and called the cubs to walk at either side of the two adults. The crowd parted in front of us, but closed in on our flanks as people reached out to touch the young sha'um.

I kept my attention on the cubs as we moved down the slope and through Eddarta. Now, as before, they were enjoying the attention, but I watched for signs of impatience or anger, and made sure they kept up with Yayshah and Keeshah. If they were to slow down and find themselves surrounded and separated from their parents, they might panic. *It would hardly do*, I thought, *to spoil the mood of trust with a sha'um attack*.

The crowd had grown while Tarani had talked. The people at the foot of the slope could not possibly have heard Tarani's voice. Yet when we reached them, they were shouting support for Tarani and her goals. The news had been passed downslope and into the city, for I saw different faces in the tide of people that swirled around us in the relatively cramped area of the city streets. They had the same things to say, though: hurray for Tarani, have a good trip, come back soon—and don't forget the sha'um.

Even the cubs were getting a little tired of it all by the time we reached the southern edge of the city. The main street gave way, here, to divergent roadways that brought people and trade into the city. There was still a crowd, but Tarani had decided, apparently, that she had done enough for her public image. I called Keeshah and the cubs to a halt when Yayshah stopped, and followed Tarani's example of swinging the rope-linked travel bags off my shoulder and across my thighs. The nearest people got the idea, and started backing away.

"We travel west," Tarani said, and the roadway in that direction slowly cleared of people. She lifted her hand again, then lay forward on Yayshah's back. I stretched out, too, delighting in the feel of Keeshah's fur against my cheek, and asked the cubs to move between the adults. They had barely taken that position when Tarani looked at me and nodded slightly.

*Run, kids,* I told the cubs. *Keeshah, keep pace with the cubs; we have to stay together.*

All four sha'um jumped forward together, and Tarani and I left Eddarta once more.

# 3

I felt—and shared—the relief of three of the sha'um, as they left the smothering crowd for the open air of the countryside. The roadway lay beside a branch of the river, moving generally westward as it followed the gentle twisting of the riverbed. The sha'um ignored the road and set off across a grassy, open area. The majority of Eddarta's farming was done farther north, in a fertile delta formed by several branches of the Tashal. But this area south of the most westward branch saw some cultivation, and our run carried us across scattered fields of grain and through an occasional orchard of dakathrenil.

Dakathrenil trees grew wild all over Gandalara, and their nutty fruit comprised the primary diet of a great many species of small animals. In cultivation, the kinked and twisting trunks were trained so that the leaf- and fruit-bearing branches formed a spreading umbrella barely higher than a man's head. The dakathrenil provided Gandalarans more than its fruit. As the short-lived trees died, their wood was harvested for craftsmen who had learned to laminate long, narrow slices of the twisting wood into almost any utilitarian object, and to combine smaller pieces into intricate and decorative parquetry.

The passage of four sha'um did little good to the grainfields, and the lowest branches of the dakathrenil were a definite hazard to the heads of the riders. An hour out from Eddarta, I asked Keeshah to find the road and follow it. Tarani, roused from her rapport with Yayshah, saw my intent and directed Yayshah to follow us.

Once on the packed dirt of the roadway, Tarani and I slowed the sha'um to a walk. They were "formed up" as they had been when we left Eddarta—Yayshah and Keeshah on the outside, the cubs between them. Tarani leaned to her right a little, reaching to stroke Yoshah's head. Instantly, Koshah was shouldering his sister aside, pushing his head under Tarani's hand. I laughed and leaned to my left, diverting Yoshah's anger by petting her myself.

As I watched Tarani's hand wander through the ruff of tan fur behind the young male's head, I noticed—with some alarm—how thin her hand was, the pale skin pulled so tightly across her knuckles that I seemed to see the bone in fact as well as in outline.

Suddenly, I was angry—intensely, righteously, furiously angry.

It wasn't that Ricardo Carillo and Antonia Alderuccio had been snatched away from their own world and reborn in Gandalaran bodies. Those people had been dying in their own world, and we could only be grateful for our new lives as Rikardon and Tarani.

Nor was I angry because Tarani and I could not merely settle down and enjoy our extended lives. We had discussed this on several occasions, and I think we both felt that our commitment to removing the threat of the Ra'ira was fair, a service in trade for a priceless gift.

What bothered me now was the way we had been forced to fulfill that commitment, with the rules changing every step of the way. I thought of how much time, travel, stress, exhaustion, and pain we might have been saved, had we known at the beginning what we had only days ago learned: that the gemstone stolen from Raithskar had been a fake, an excellent glass imitation made by the same Volitar of whom Tarani had spoken with such respect. Gharlas, an ambitious and bitter relative of Pylomel, had blackmailed Volitar into making two copies of the Ra'ira. In Raithskar, Gharlas had lost one, then unwittingly had stolen it back, thinking it to be the true Ra'ira. *That* was the stone for which Tarani and I had crossed the length of Gandalara three times.

Our enemy was not Gharlas, but the man who controlled him, someone who knew and could use the true and long-hidden power of the odd blue stone.

Many Gandalarans had talents known as mindgifts, which allowed people to affect the minds of other creatures. Some could superimpose a mental image over another's normal vision. *Maufel*, Gandalaran bird-handlers, used a technique like that to direct their message-carrying birds to the correct location. Tarani had used that skill liberally in her entertainment troupe, and had won unique recognition as an "illusionist."

Stronger and more dangerous was the mindgift of "compulsion," in which the gifted (or more strongly gifted) individual controlled the behavior of another person. That skill could extend to autonomous physical functions, like breathing. Compulsion could kill.

The Ra'ira acted as an amplifier to make all those gifts even more effective. It also granted a mindgift totally unknown without it—the ability for one person to actually see and control the thoughts of another person. That power had been used well by Zanek, the First King of Gandalara. It had been used in less beneficial ways by his successors, until Zanek had returned in Serkajon's body to steal the Ra'ira from Harthim, the Last King.

The stone had been kept idle and securely guarded in Raithskar, until some enterprising Supervisor had discovered that most of the menial labor in the city could be accomplished by the apelike vineh, under the control of a Supervisor using the Ra'ira. The stone's power had found use again, and the people of Raithskar, all unwittingly, had become dependent on that power.

This was not the first time I had felt angry about the teasing way the truth had unfolded itself. But until now I had been able only to rail at "fate" or "destiny" or "chance." Now I knew that the mistakes, the misdirections, the pressures . . . the thinness of Tarani's hand—all these had been caused, in the final analysis, by the intricate scheming and deception of one man.

It was through the All-Mind that Tarani and I had finally recognized our enemy. With Tarani as Recorder, she and I had shared the thoughts and emotions and experience of an ancestor of Gharlas's. There we had learned of a strongly mindgifted Lord named Tinis, who had proved to be dangerous and who had excellent reason to crave vengeance against the Lords of Eddarta.

Later, we had discovered a sketch of Tinis. The sketch traveled with us, riding in Tarani's travel pack. The man who had been called Tinis as a boy was now known in Raithskar as

Ferrathyn. He was the Chief Supervisor of the Council of Supervisors. He *seemed* a kindly, caring old man.

Ferrathyn was practicing a double deception. The people of Raithskar thought the vineh had gone wild because of a new and uncontrolled illness. The Supervisors thought they were merely reacting to freedom from the Ra'ira's control. Neither was true.

The Ra'ira had never left Raithskar, and most of the vineh were still under its control. A red fury swept over me as I thought of it. The terror and devastation in Raithskar was being inflicted deliberately, and not by the vineh. They were merely agents. People were being hurt and killed because of the ambition of one man.

Tinis of Rusal.

Ferrathyn.

Our enemy.

*Let go,* Keeshah told me, a note of complaint in his mindvoice.

I was lying on the big cat's back, leaning over to the left to scratch at Yoshah's head. My other arm was laid out in front of me, the hand braced around Keeshah's shoulder to anchor me. In physical reaction to the strong emotion, that hand had clenched, pinching fur and skin.

*I'm sorry, Keeshah,* I said, and relaxed my hand.

I gave Yoshah's head one final pat, and heaved myself upward to balance more naturally on her father's back. The cub's displeasure at my quitting reached me through our link. Yoshah shook her head and dropped back briefly as she brought one hind foot forward to scratch her ear one more time. Then she trotted out ahead of us and began to nose along the tall growth that lined the riverbank.

"Go. Follow your sister," Tarani said to Koshah, and took her hand away.

The male cub was already on his way. He caught up with Yoshah and nipped lightly at her flank, eliciting a yowl and a swat. Then both of them began to prowl the edge of the bamboolike growth, occasionally poking a head through the reeds briefly before trotting on to a new place, farther along the road.

When the cubs left, Yayshah and Keeshah moved closer together, and for a while Tarani and I rode in a quiet, close silence. Then I said: "Thank you for coming back with me."

Tarani stared at me for a moment, her dark eyes lustrous against the paleness of her skin. "It was a difficult decision," she admitted. "I truly feel as if I have abandoned my own children, at their time of greatest need."

"What you have started will continue while you are gone," I assured her, with more confidence than I felt. "And your coming back to Raithskar with me is as much for Eddarta as for Raithskar."

"I hope so," she said, her voice sounding odd.

"What do you mean?"

"I mean," she said, smiling a little sadly, "that I hope my choice was real—the reasons logical and right—and that I did not deceive myself."

"Deceive yourself?" I echoed, confused. "How?"

"By telling myself that my 'destiny' lies with you," she answered quietly, "when it is only my love, and fear of being without you, that brought me out of Eddarta."

"Fear? Of being without me?" I stammered. "But you— didn't you—you're the one who suggested I go back alone."

"I suggested it," she admitted. "I did not say I would enjoy it."

I reached across the distance between us, but Tarani was too fast for me. With a laugh, she threw herself forward into the true riding position, and Yayshah leaped ahead.

*Catch her, Keeshah,* I said—begging, rather than ordering. Keeshah responded with a surge of speed that nearly unseated me, and a feeling of joy that was a mixture of his own pleasure in the chase and amusement at the turmoil of emotions he must have felt from me.

I caught a glimpse of the cubs, looking around in surprise as their parents barreled past them. The rounded points of their ears aimed backward as they quested, with mind and nose, for some source of danger.

*It's all right,* I reassured them. *Follow at your own speed; we'll wait for you to catch up.*

*Can keep up,* Koshah insisted, and started to run after us.

*No,* I said sharply, then spared my full attention to reach out to both of them with a mental hug. *Take your time, and follow when you feel like it. We won't be far.*

I suffered a momentary uneasiness about leaving the cubs on their own. *Don't be stupid*, I scolded myself. *There's no question of them getting lost—their sense of smell is as keen as*

*Keeshah's. If nothing else, I can guide them to us through our mindlink. And I can't believe I'd be worried about them getting hurt. Who's going to mess with kittens with that much tooth and claw?*

While Yayshah followed the road, Keeshah's marginally longer stride narrowed the female's lead. When Yayshah's dark tail seemed to float in the air beside Keeshah's head, Tarani directed the female to veer off into a dakathrenil orchard, where Yayshah's slightly smaller size yielded a distinct advantage in maneuverability.

I noticed that the fur along Yayshah's tail was fluffed slightly, and I took it for a sign of Tarani's mood. My reaction probably translated through Keeshah's mind to fluff his tail, as well.

Yayshah dodged among the trees, keeping Tarani just out of my reach. Tarani's back skimmed beneath branches that might have given me a concussion, if Keeshah had not been watchful of my safety. As it was, I had to protect my head and face with my arms, until the sleeves of my tunic were redolent with the nutty odor of the trees.

I took an extra risk and lifted my head to look around. Through the whipping branches, I saw that this orchard followed the pattern of most others I had seen.

Most orchards had a system of groves, or fields, in which the trees were planted in successive years, so that one field would reach maturity each year. The sha'um were in one of the older fields; we had run across an open space that marked the area where the trees had already been harvested. To the north was the next field, with less mature trees.

At my direction, Keeshah began to herd Yayshah northward. The division between the fields was obvious, and Tarani gave a small cry as Yayshah carried her into an area where both of us had to go around, rather than under, the trees. Blocked from retreat to the older trees by Keeshah's body, Yayshah whirled and plunged into a corridor between the rows. I slipped off Keeshah's back and sent him after Yayshah with instructions to catch up and drive the female eastward. Then I started running northeast, listening to the progress of the sha'um and adjusting the angle of my run.

When I caught sight of the sha'um, Yayshah was still resisting Keeshah's drive, moving eastward slowly but feinting frequently toward the north. I was half-surprised to see Tarani still with Yayshah.

*Tarani has to have figured out what I'm doing*, I thought, as I ran up a corridor toward the group, and I slowed down, wary for her next move.

It came quickly. Tarani caught sight of me and laughed. Yayshah whirled away from Keeshah and pounded down the corridor, straight toward me. I backed up a little, waited until it was obvious Yayshah was not going to stop short of running right over me, then launched myself backward and to the left. My back came up against the young dakathrenil I had spotted. The resilient trunk bent backward, then righted itself, catapulting me back toward Yayshah, who had nearly passed me. I grabbed Tarani's leg and pulled her down with me as I fell in Yayshah's wake.

"Gotcha!" I yelled, noting in passing that I had actually used Ricardo's slang instead of some Gandaresh equivalent.

Tarani laughed and struggled for a moment, then abandoned pretense and put her arms around me.

"Who shall judge which of us is the prisoner?" she asked softly.

# 4

The orchards, grainfields, and berry patches became more scarce, then disappeared entirely before nightfall. We paused for a meal, but all of us agreed to push on to the Refreshment House at Iribos before stopping.

The moon's light, diffused through the cloud cover that seemed to be a permanent feature of Gandalara, cast the desert in a silvery glow. Though Keeshah's fur and muscle and motion made him real to me, the other sha'um seemed to be merely shadows, and the only sounds were their powerful breathing and the amazingly soft thudding of their feet.

There was little sand here, only dry ground and stubborn bushes. Salty sand was a feature of what I had come to think of as the "inner deserts"—the Kapiral, south and east of Raithskar, the Darshi, of which we were now skirting the southern border, and the Strofaan, largest and most severe of the three.

It was after midnight when the sha'um halted, panting, before the barrier of heavy fabric that marked the entrance to Iribos. I called the formula softly, so as not to waken the whole compound: "Two are here who request shelter and water."

There was a moment's delay and the sound of a yawn. Tarani and I exchanged smiles. We waited on foot, with the cubs between us and the adult sha'um at either side.

After a moment, the barrier dropped from between the man-high walls of salt blocks, and two boys appeared in the opening. The smaller one held one end of the rope which, when tied, pulled up one high corner of the fabric. The other boy was bigger, and stood a few feet behind the center of the gateway, his back stiff with pride. He was already speaking as the barrier fell.

"I speak for Charol, Respected Elder of Iribos," the boy said with stiff pride. "No quarrel s—shall . . ."

He gaped at the six of us for an awkward moment, then recovered and spoke to the wide-eyed boy beside him. "Bring a skin of water to the gate," he said. The little boy stared at him. "Hurry," the bigger boy whispered. The younger one dropped the end of the rope and ran away from the circle of light cast by the lamp, toward the single door on the left that marked the entrance to the living quarters of Charol's family.

The boy straightened his shoulders, and restarted the formula greeting. "No quarrel shall enter here," he said. "Put aside your weapons, and be welcome to any service we may provide." He took a step toward us, his sandaled feet nearly treading on the slack barrier. Through the ritual, he had spoken with a kind of nervous dignity that betrayed his youth. Now his formality slipped in favor of sincerity.

"I regret we cannot invite your sha'um into the compound," he said, with a small bow toward each of us. "The *vleks*—their noise would rouse the other visitors."

The lamp held by the boy cast little light inside the compound, but the inner walls were set with lamps. Against the far wall of the open space we faced was a huge, lumpy shadow—twenty-five or thirty vleks, sleeping all clumped together and seeming to lean, *en masse*, on the compound wall. It was pure luck that they had not already scented the sha'um. The slightest shift in the direction of air movement—there were few places in Gandalara where it could be called a breeze—would set them to bawling and stamping.

"I regret we have brought them close enough to create that danger," I said. "It was thoughtless."

The little boy came back, staggering under the burden of a huge water pouch. It was made of tanned hide from the haunch of a *glith*, the deer-sized meat animal. Sewn and sealed at the large end and along the side, the neck was tied with a hide thong. I pulled out my sword and dagger and handed them to the bigger boy, then lifted the heavy skin from the little boy's shoulders.

"I will give the sha'um only a little water now, and send them away until morning," I said. "Please make the lady Tarani comfortable."

The older boy bowed deeply. "The High Lord honors us," he said, and accepted the sword and dagger she held out to him. Tarani did not look back as she walked through the gateway, but I could guess what she was thinking.

*The Fa'aldu claim to be uninvolved in the world, totally neutral,* I thought. *But they seem to know everything that goes on. They're sworn to aid anyone in survival-type need, but they've helped us far beyond that oath. What do they think of Tarani becoming High Lord? How do they view their own role in that?*

These thoughts ran through my head as I poured water from the pouch into one of the troughs built against the outer wall of the compound. The troughs were made of nested semicylindrical tiles, supported by small salt blocks the size of large bricks. The main watering troughs were inside the walls, down the center of the large open space between the family residence and the line of cubicles that served as overnight lodging for travelers. These on the outside were provided for the use of caravans so large that both vleks and people could not be accommodated inside.

I petted all the sha'um once more, as they drank, and told my three to put some distance between them and the Refreshment House before they settled down. After Keeshah finished drinking, he rubbed the top of his head across my midsection, then waited to lead his family away.

When I returned to the gate, the older boy was waiting for me. To my surprise, he bowed and said: "The Captain of the Sharith honors us."

"What is your name?" I asked him.

"I am called Thuren, sir," he said, a little uncertainly.

"I expect to speak with Charol tomorrow, Thuren. I will tell him how responsibly and graciously you represented him tonight."

The boy led me to one of the cubicles on the "visitor" side of the compound. "The High Lord refused to let me rouse anyone else, in order to offer you Fa'aldu shelter," he explained in a whisper. He pulled aside the fabric curtain that hung across the doorway. Light spilled out, and he avoided looking inside. "Rest well, Captain," he said.

I wished him good night and stepped inside, letting the fabric fall behind me. The cubicle was lined with three large salt blocks which, covered with thin pads, served as sleeping ledges. Tarani was already stretched out on one, and the sight of her nearly asleep made my own eyelids feel heavy. I lifted the glass chimney from the lamp which stood in a niche in the wall, sighted the ledge I had chosen for my bed, and blew out the candle's flame.

The vleks woke us just past dawn, when their handlers stirred and began packing the caravan to move out. The vleks could draw small carts or carry baskets which were tied into a brace and rested across their backs.

I sat up, rubbing my eyes, then stretched. Across from me, Tarani's eyes opened. She smiled.

"It is a good sound, is it not, when we are not causing it?" She sat up. "I cannot claim that I have ever led an easy life," she said, "but those days disguised as a vlek handler, always smelling of the beasts, always struggling with them, are ones I would not care to relive. I always had the fear that I would come to think like them, to be stupid and stubborn and nasty."

I laughed. "Well, that's one thing I didn't have to fear," I said, picking up the belt and baldric I had laid aside sometime during the night. "I started out that way."

"I shall not deny that," she said, and for a moment her eyes held mine.

I wondered what she was thinking. *She could be remembering any of a hundred painful moments,* I thought, *when my words struck at her from distrust and jealousy, when my silence limited her knowledge of herself, when my needs took precedence—not gently—over hers and Yayshah's.*

Suddenly she took her eyes away and dragged her saddlebags up from where they had lain on the floor into her lap. She opened one and began digging in it carefully with her hands. "We have grown a great deal, each of us," she said, and looked up, smiling again. "I had nothing to teach you of gentleness except how to express it. And you have made me see my own strength." She shrugged. "As for stubbornness," she said, "what else could have driven us so far through a shifting bog of questions and secrets?"

"And stupidity?" I prompted. "And nastiness?"

She had found what she was searching for, a folded piece of thin leather. She stood up, pushing aside her packs, and offered her hand.

"I believe neither of us is guilty of the first," she said. "As for the second, we both fear we have it, and that serves to drive it away. Shall we refresh ourselves, and think of the day ahead?"

I took her hand, and we stepped out under the spectacular Gandalaran sunrise. Across the courtyard, Thuren appeared at the single doorway and hurried across to us. He was followed by an older man who limped, but carried himself with the same quiet pride I had seen in every one of the Elders I had met.

"Greetings, Respected Elder," Tarani and I said, almost in one voice.

"Welcome, my friends," the old man said, touching our hands lightly with his own. "Thuren told me of your arrival as soon as I woke. One of the household apartments is, of course, available to you. After you have refreshed yourselves, I would ask your presence in the inner courtyard. A judgment is necessary, and it has awaited your arrival."

"A judgment?" Tarani echoed, and looked at me. I shrugged, and we both looked at Charol.

"One among us has broken Fa'aldu law," the old man said. "He must speak and be judged before the family. He asked for delay until you could be present. The delay was granted."

"Who is being judged?" I asked. "What for? How are we involved?"

"It is Veron who faces judgment," Charol said. "I may say nothing of the lawbreaking. If you please, Thuren will show you to your apartment now."

Tarani started to say something, but I squeezed her hand to signal silence.

"We will join you as quickly as we can," I assured the Elder, and we followed the straight-backed boy.

Thuren led us through the doorway, down a shadowy

corridor, and out into a bright courtyard which lay at the center of the family area. This inner courtyard was much larger than the one in which the vleks had bedded down. Around it were arranged rooms and suites in which resided the members of this House, who were all kin of some kind and were led by the Elder.

After Thuren had conducted us to a large apartment and left us there, Tarani demanded: "How did they find out Veron has been helping slaves escape from the copper mines?"

"The sooner we get out there," I said, "the sooner we'll know."

We washed at a ceramic basin and quickly changed to fresh tunics and trousers. Although I had been ravenously hungry when I had awakened, I left the fruit and bread and cheese untouched. I noticed Tarani made no attempt to eat, either, and wondered if her stomach had turned queasy too. We glanced at each other, and stepped out into the courtyard.

The entire family was assembled. Though they did not form ranks but sat on the hard-packed ground in an uneven semicircle, there was the air of parade formality about the assembly. There were fifty or more people in the courtyard. After Tarani and I had sat down at the back of the crowd, the Elder was the only person standing, until he said: "The judgment begins."

Toward the front of the crowd, a young man stood up, moved forward and turned to face his family. He was slim and pale.

"Veron," the Elder said, "tell the family of Iribos why you are to be judged."

"I have broken the law of neutrality," the young man said in a loud if somewhat shaky voice.

Silence greeted that announcement. The young man took a deep breath and continued.

"I sought to help Eddarta's slaves escape to freedom," he said, then his voice turned bitter. "Recently I learned that my good wishes only led the slaves of the copper mines into a different kind of slavery, or into death."

This time, the family reacted. Heads turned and a whispering sound rose from the seated people.

"For endangering the neutrality of the Fa'aldu, I offer no apology," Veron said, defiance ringing in his strident voice. "My views in that area are well known. I ask to be judged"—

his voice faltered—"for allowing those views to endanger the lives of others."

"Judgment cannot rest merely on the result and not on the act itself," Charol said, speaking with a careful formality. "Judgment cannot touch you at all, if you alone seek it. Who of the family will confirm your lawbreaking?"

"I acted alone," Veron said, "but many knew, and kept silent because they approved. I required their word-bond to continue silent, lest they, too, be called to judgment. There are two here who *can* speak, however. They are outside our laws, but honored by the family. I ask that the Fa'aldu accept the voices of Rikardon and Tarani as our own."

Heads turned toward us, and the family waited expectantly. Nobody—except us—seemed very surprised.

*Now what the hell do I say?* I wondered. *I don't want to wind up convicting this kid, but he's right—with all good intentions, he channeled slaves toward their deaths. Good intentions,* I repeated to myself. *Not what happened, but what he wanted to happen. He worked for what he thought was right, and nobody is going to convince me that can ever be a crime.*

I climbed to my feet. Beside me, Tarani rose in the graceful single movement I admired but could never quite master.

"When Harredon proposed the establishment of the Refreshment Houses," I said, letting some of my anger show, "the Fa'aldu chose to be loyal to the Kingdom. In spite of what your law says, that marked the end, not the beginning, of Fa'aldu neutrality." A shocked gasp swept through the crowd. Even Veron gaped at me. Only Charol maintained an aloof composure.

"The raiders and scavengers and barbarians who hoarded their water," I continued, "*they* were truly neutral because they cared for no one but themselves. The Fa'aldu who abandoned that life in favor of peace and service made a commitment to the value of the individual—a commitment reflected in Veron's opposition to Eddartan slavery."

It took a moment for everyone to realize I was finished. Then attention shifted to the woman standing beside me.

"I will speak," Tarani said, "to the results which have tormented our friend into asking judgment. It is true that the house in Chizan which Veron believed to be a safe place, the beginning of new life for the slaves he helped, was in the hands of a roguelord who enslaved them again or killed them. Compared to the promise of freedom, that is a bitter fate. But compare it to continued service in the copper mines, and it seems again to be relief. Who is to say that the former slaves were not still grateful to Veron, even in Chizan?

"I ask you to remember, as well, that Veron's system worked in both directions. Had the way out of Eddarta not been so carefully organized, Veron would have been unable to help us when we wanted to enter Eddarta in secret. He acted as blindly with us as with the slaves, wanting only to help and having no knowledge or control over the result. If you argue that Veron caused the slaves to die, then you must also grant that Veron caused me to be High Lord. As High Lord, I have set in motion the end of Eddarta slavery.

"Weigh the lives he has destroyed—indirectly—against those he has saved—indirectly—and I believe you will find Veron more worthy of honor than of condemnation."

There was a shocked silence after Tarani finished, then Charol stirred. I forestalled whatever he had planned to say.

"You invited us to help you judge one of your own for breaking the law," I said. "Instead, we ask you to judge the rightness of his actions and the reality of the law. We make this request not merely for Veron's sake, but because the 'neutrality' of the Fa'aldu may soon be tested. When that time comes, we hope you will remember that the Fa'aldu have always favored those who care for and value the individual."

I sat down. Tarani had caught the beginning of my movement, and she sat at the same time.

There was a general shifting as the faces which had watched us turned back toward the other end of the courtyard. Charol pulled at his long white tunic, rearranging it slightly, then looked up and spoke to the family.

"It seems clear that Veron has broken the law as it has been practiced," he said, "and deserves to be forbidden the shelter of the Fa'aldu."

A kind of sigh issued from the audience, acknowledgment of the severity of the penalty. *To Fa'aldu*, I thought, *that sort of banishment must be tantamount to being stripped of identity.*

"Yet our guests," Charol continued, "remind us of the law as it was designed. In that light, Veron's aid to the slaves seems little different from a gift of water to the traveler in need."

A louder sigh rose up, somehow carrying a message of agreement.

"As Elder of Iribos, I may judge alone *within* the law," Charol said, "but I may not *question* it alone. I call for a family statement. Veron: condemn?"

Charol extended his arm to the right, the hand tensed into a fist. No one in the courtyard moved. Then he dropped his right arm and extended his left.

"Forgive?"

Everyone in the courtyard leaned to the right. A sound came from Veron—half sob, half laughter.

"Veron is of Iribos," Charol said, with an intonation that made it a formal pardon. "To those who may feel he yet deserves a lesser punishment, I say that the fate of those he attempted to help will continue to torment him. To those who would challenge our law, I say that the questions raised today will be reported to the other Elders, and considered seriously.

"The judgment ends."

## 5

The people stood up and scattered in all directions, vanishing through the multitude of doors that lined the perimeter of the courtyard. Veron bowed deeply to Charol, who stood straight and still as a statue, then came toward us and bowed again, aimed at a point between us but slightly closer to Tarani.

"I am grateful for your words," he said. "I am blamed, now, by no one—except myself."

I gripped Veron's shoulder until his gaze left the ground and rested on my face. "If you respect your family, Veron," I said, "you have to respect their judgment too."

"Your guilt," Tarani added gently, "does you even less honor than your misguided efforts."

Veron thought about that a moment, looking from Tarani to me and back again, and finally nodded. "I will try to—to forgive myself. What you said about ending slavery in Eddarta, High Lord, that is true?"

"It is true," Tarani said. "I dared not make such a sweeping change immediately, but the process has begun. A person who is sent to the mines for punishment will remain for a length of time that is assigned in proportion to his offense. He will be free to return to his former occupation at the end of that period, but if he worked well, he may be offered employment at the mine.

"Those who are serving as slaves now will be examined for health problems. The severely ill will be released immediately; the remainder will be treated, assigned a service time of approximately one-fourth their remaining life span, and will continue their service with decent rations and adequate rest. They, too, may be offered payment for their continued service.

"The Lords have agreed to this program as a test for the next five years. I have predicted that people who are allowed fair treatment and a sense of the worth of their effort will become sufficiently more productive to allow the mines more profit, even while payment is given for labor which once was free. If my prediction proves true—as I am sure it will—the Lords will consider abandoning the most dangerous mine, and establishing the entire mining operation on an employment basis."

*It can't have hurt her chances for acceptance of this plan,* I thought, *that the dangerous mine she proposes to close down belongs to her own family, the Harthim.*

I remembered the time I had spent at the Lingis mine—not as a slave but as one of their guards. It had suited Indomel's humor to keep Tarani and me apart, each of us hostage for the good behavior of the other. The Lingis mine was a surface mine with deposits of copper ore that occurred near the surface of the hilly area, and the duty of the slaves there had been harsh enough. The Harthim mine had followed the ore lode straight into the side of a mountain, so that the slaves were essentially working in an unsupported tunnel mine. Between the collapsing walls and the congested air, the slaves had little hope of survival.

Ricardo Carillo—the man I had been before my personality arrived in Gandalara—had accumulated an amazing assortment of unrelated information during his long life, and I had not lost his habit of examining and comparing information in order to find meaning in facts. It had hampered neither

Ricardo nor Rikardon that I often peered out at those facts from inside an empty well of ignorance—very often, the level of water in the well rose in the course of such an exercise.

It occurred to me now to speculate on the geologic trauma that could create an area as large as Gandalara with rich deposits of copper and tin, but almost no iron. The only iron in Gandalara seemed to be mined from the remains of a meteor that had crashed into the wall above Raithskar, thousands of years ago.

*There is no native iron,* I thought, *but plentiful native copper. No, wait, there's another way of looking at that. Copper has been found only in the hills—at a lower level, I think, than the iron near Raithskar, but nonetheless above the floor of Gandalara. You could say that neither one is truly native to Gandalara. The green marble that is quarried in Omergol is also pulled out of a hillside. If you define Gandalara as the flat area between the "walls" (considering that in most areas, mountain ranges are called "walls" as a Gandalaran convention), then the only thing truly native to Gandalara is salt.*

Something nibbled at the edge of my consciousness, a frustrating half-image, like the face of someone whose name is familiar but will not come to mind. I reached for it, almost had it—then Charol's voice drew me back from my thoughts.

Veron was walking away from us, toward a doorway on the opposite side of the courtyard from the visitors' area. Tarani and Charol were both staring at me, Charol with concern written clearly in his expression, Tarani with faint amusement and a touch of impatience.

"I'm sorry," I said, laughing. "I was thinking. Do I owe Veron an apology for being rude?"

"Not at all," Charol said. "It is clear to him, as to me, that you are concerned with grave matters. You spoke of a coming choice, Captain. May I hazard a guess that it has something to do with the theft of the Ra'ira?"

Tarani jumped, and Charol smiled.

"The Fa'aldu have never believed that *knowing* about the affairs of the world is the same as *meddling* in them, High Lord." His smile faded. "Normally we choose to learn of such things indirectly, but I feel this situation warrants the ill manners of direct inquiry. Captain? The choice?"

"I hope it never comes, Respected Elder, but—yes, the Ra'ira is involved. I would say more, but . . ."

I glanced at Tarani, who hesitated only a moment before speaking.

"Rikardon hesitates out of consideration for me," she said. "We share a truth which has been hidden for centuries. I give him my consent to share it with you, as well, Charol, but I give you a warning: in accepting this knowledge, you are making that choice."

*I hadn't considered it in those terms, but of course Tarani's right,* I thought. *We would not merely be warning the Fa'aldu about Ferrathyn, we would be asking their support against him, should it come to that—all in the same breath.*

Tarani and I waited, while Charol thought about it. Slowly, he grew calm—and a little grim.

"The Fa'aldu," Charol said, "have been following your activities since Balgokh's first report of meeting you, Rikardon. He spoke then of sensing a difference in you, and foretold that you would have a profound effect on the future of Gandalara. I had thought we had already seen that effect in your becoming Captain of the Sharith, in the appearance of Yayshah and the birth of her cubs, certainly in the acclamation of Tarani as High Lord of Eddarta.

"But now I feel that these are meaningless, that the knowledge you offer me will reveal what Balgokh would not even attempt to guess."

Charol paused expectantly. I was stunned to learn of Balgokh's assessment of me, based as it was on a very brief encounter. Tarani seemed to sense my confusion and stepped into the silence.

"No one knows what Balgokh foresaw," Tarani said, "and I would not call 'meaningless' the changes you cite. I would say, rather, that they have been preparatory to the purpose contained in the knowledge."

The man nodded vigorously, as if he regarded Tarani's answer as total and direct confirmation of his statement. "It would be cowardly, then, to retreat to ignorance now. I choose to learn what you would tell me."

"Then let's go inside," I said, "where we can be comfortable." To myself, I added: *And private.* "It's a long story."

Instead of returning to our suite, Charol led us into his own quarters, where he invited us to share a luxury rare among the

Fa'aldu—armchairs made of wood and fabric, instead of the backless salt blocks used for most other furniture. Even after we were all physically comfortable, however, an awkwardness remained.

"Perhaps it will help," Charol said, "if I summarize the present knowledge of this matter among the Fa'aldu?"

"That seems as good a way as any to start," I agreed gratefully.

"Balgokh has kept us informed of the state of things in Raithskar," the Elder said. "He told us of the theft of the Ra'ira originally, of course, and of your pursuit of the thief. It seems to be widely known in the city that an Eddartan stole the gem, and feeling runs high against Eddarta. Most of the rumors make a quite ridiculous connection between the theft of the gem and the illness of the vineh, so that the city's fear of its former servants is turning to anger toward Eddarta."

Tarani and I exchanged glances.

"How bad is it in Raithskar now?" I asked.

Charol shook his head. "I only know that the people from the outlying communities and farms have been called to dwell within the city walls, and Balgokh has seen fewer and fewer caravans dare the journey from Yafnaar to Raithskar."

Fear clutched at my chest and stomach. *Thanasset and Milda are in Raithskar,* I thought. Markasset's father and aunt had accepted me as a replacement for their son. Ricardo Carillo had acquired Markasset's body, as far as I could tell, at the very moment of the boy's death. Ricardo had acquired Markasset's memory, and become the human-Gandalaran blend of Rikardon, on accepting the steel sword which I had surrendered on entering this Refreshment House. *They're my family now, and they're locked up with a madman in a city that's getting hysterical.*

# 6

*Associating the loss of the Ra'ira with the onset of danger from the vineh is ridiculous to Charol*, I thought, *because he's native to Gandalara and has never been exposed to the irrationality of superstition. These people have fewer mysteries than humans because they believe they understand and are part of the All-Mind, a concept humans might treat as a god. They respect the All-Mind, but are not in awe of it.*

Even as the thought was formed, another was contradicting it.

*Except*, I reminded myself, *when they talk about Visitors, personalities of dead people which reappear in the body of another person. Gandalarans believe such Visitors have spent the time since their death as part of the All-Mind, and fully share its knowledge—the total memory and learning of every member of this race, since it began the mutation toward its present form.*

*To the people of Raithskar, the Ra'ira has been a symbol of pride and history. For all they know, the loss of the gem and the rebellion of the vineh are only coincidentally linked. I'll bet anything that the same reason those events are not a coincidence is the cause for that attitude. Ferrathyn whispers here, mindpushes there, and bingo!—suddenly Gandalara achieves the concept of a lucky charm.*

"You had confided in Balgokh that Gharlas was the thief," Charol continued. "And it seems clear that, even though Gharlas died during your first visit to Eddarta, you were not able to recover the Ra'ira. Now Tarani is High Lord and you are both leaving Eddarta. I assume that you now have possession of the Ra'ira and are taking it back to Raithskar."

He stopped and looked from Tarani to me expectantly. It seemed to be our turn.

Tarani opened a leather pouch which hung from her belt, and dumped its contents into her hand. Charol gasped. Tarani leaned forward and put the blue stone on the small table around which the three of us were seated.

It was a beautiful thing, two fingers high, smooth and rounded, shaped amorphously but saved from looking lumpish by faintly crystalline lines that radiated unevenly toward the darker blue at the heart of the stone.

"That," Charol said with a gasp, "is the Ra'ira?"

"That," I answered, "is a glass copy of the Ra'ira, which was made by Volitar."

"I have heard that name—" Charol began.

"The man who left Eddarta with Zefra," Tarani said. "He raised me as his niece. For a time, I thought he was my father."

Charol reached out, paused to look at us for permission, then picked up the piece of glass at Tarani's nod.

"I have never seen the Ra'ira," he said, turning the blue thing in his hand and peering into it. "Is this a good image of the real stone?"

I had to answer that, drawing from Markasset's memory.

"It's a nearly perfect duplicate," I said.

Charol's brow creased, wrinkling the skin between his widow's peak of darkening headfur and the prominent supraorbital ridge that was a characteristic of Gandalaran appearance.

"Then—forgive me, I do not question the truth of your statement, I am merely curious—how do you know that this one is not the real one?"

"The answer to that," I said, "begins with Zanek."

"The First King?" Charol said.

"Yes, and the first to discover that the Ra'ira allows someone who is already mindgifted the power to actually read the thoughts of another person."

Charol glanced at Tarani, who shook her head. "It is not the same thing as the ways in which I—and other Lords—can use the natural mindgift without aid," she said, and frowned. "I find it hard to describe the difference, but I shall try. To cast an illusion, or to compel another's behavior, is like . . . like . . ." She groped for words. "Like struggling to open a shutter to look inside a dwelling. With practice, the effort becomes less, the task easier.

"With the Ra'ira, however, it is as if all the windows in the house are paned with glass, and there is no struggle—one merely has to look in through the glass."

Charol was staring at Tarani. "You . . . you have used the gem's power, then?"

"Not I, personally," she said. "I have shared the experience of its use with Zanek, the First King."

Charol opened his mouth, closed it again. I felt sorry for him; this was a lot to take in all at once.

"You knew me first," Tarani explained gently, "as the dancer and illusionist. But I was trained as a Recorder. During our search for the second steel sword"—unconsciously, her hand moved to where the hilt of that sword would have rested, had she been wearing it—"Rikardon and I witnessed the fall of the Kingdom through the lifememory of Serkajon."

Charol leaned forward then, the stone still cupped in his hands but seeming forgotten in the face of his fascination with what Tarani was saying.

"You—you both—met Serkajon? And Zanek—did you actually know Zanek?"

"I met him, alone, at a different time," I said, not bothering to explain that 'met' was not the right concept at all. *This is complicated enough without arguing about vocabulary*, I thought. "Another Recorder helped me share Zanek's lifememory at the time he began the Kingdom. Tarani and I, together, met him when he appeared in Serkajon's body to put an end to Harthim's Kingdom."

"*Zanek* stole the Ra'ira?" Charol stammered. "Not Serkajon?"

"Well, both of them, if it comes to that," I said. "I believe that Serkajon would have done precisely the same thing, if he had known about the Ra'ira's power. As it was, he knew *something* was strange, and very wrong; and he wanted to help."

"I think," Tarani said suddenly, "that Zanek appeared as a Visitor because Serkajon's distress and desire to change things was very strong in the All-Mind. The only thing which *could* help him understand was the knowledge of someone who had used the Ra'ira."

"And," I added, "someone committed to the *proper* use of its power—for the benefit of Gandalara, not the comfort of the Kings. Zanek had used the Ra'ira's power to find out what people *really* needed, what they were *really* arguing about, so that he could find solutions that contributed to peace and harmony. Through the reign of the Kings, however, the use of the stone had shifted.

"By Harthim's time, the entire city of Kä was isolated in the desert, and was being maintained by slaves so that the Kings could live in luxury. Harthim was using the Ra'ira to find rebellion and stop it, to enforce a nonproductive slave system."

Charol seemed to remember that he was holding the duplicate Ra'ira. He held it out to Tarani who took it and replaced it in her belt pouch.

"If this only *begins* your story, my friends," Charol said, sitting back and clapping his hands, "we shall need refreshment to sustain us."

A young girl appeared in the doorway, her face turned toward Charol but her eyes sliding in our direction. The Elder asked her to bring *faen* (the Gandalaran equivalent of beer) and some food, which she did promptly.

We did not talk while we waited for the girl to bring our food. Charol stared at the wall, obviously trying to absorb the information we had already given him.

I had never been through what Charol was undergoing now, because, in spite of the integration of Markasset's memories of Gandalara, I had always seen this culture and its history from the viewpoint of an outsider. When I had learned about the true nature of the Ra'ira, it had come to me simply as another fact.

Tarani's experience had been closer to Charol's, for the news had come to her before the integration of Tarani with Antonia, while the Gandalaran personality was consciously unaware of the human one. For her, however, this fact had been only one of many—some of them far more personal—that she had been required to absorb at once.

Then, too, acceptance had been forced on us by the circumstances. Gharlas had been demonstrating a tremendous power of compulsion when he told us the truth about the Ra'ira, and Tarani and I had been given little time or opportunity to doubt that the Ra'ira was the source of some of that power. Of course, *then* we had thought that Gharlas was using it directly. *Now* we knew the greatest part of that compulsive force had come *through* him, from Ferrathyn/Tinis, who had been using the real Ra'ira in Raithskar.

Neither I nor Tarani had ever been told something, calmly and rationally, that changed our perspective of a history we had known and trusted all our lives.

Charol's thoughts must have been following similar lines, for after the girl had brought in a plate of sliced bread, ceramic mugs, and a pitcher filled with faen, he said: "This is how you learned about the Ra'ira's power? Through your meeting with Zanek in the All-Mind?"

"When I left Raithskar in pursuit of Gharlas," I said, "I did *not* know the truth. Gharlas told us the truth when we caught up with him in Dyskornis. He thought he *had* the real stone; we thought he did, too, and followed him to Eddarta, where he died trying to hold on to a worthless duplicate Ra'ira."

"Even then"—Tarani picked up the story—"we believed that this was the real stone. We gave another glass duplicate, also made by Volitar, to my brother, Indomel, and escaped with *this* stone. By the time we were recaptured, Indomel had discovered that the stone he had was useless."

"He made the same mistake we did," I said. "Because he knew one was not real, he assumed the other one *was* real. And he had, seemingly, seen proof of the stone's reality in the ease with which Tarani read the Bronze."

"The Bronze?" Charol repeated.

"It is a document engraved on a large bronze plaque," Tarani said, "a message, really, from Zanek. After the scribe had engraved the message—in the old writing, of course, with the lines placed very precisely—Zanek had him add all the other lines to make each figure the master character."

"But how could one read a message so totally concealed?" Charol asked.

"During my first meeting with Zanek," I interrupted, "I watched him plan and order the Bronze. I think he just knew it would work, and didn't question it, but I believe I understand the logic he didn't bother with. Everyone is connected to the All-Mind, with a greater or lesser *awareness* of that link. By extension, everyone is also connected to everyone else— *through* the All-Mind. Normally," I said, "each Gandalaran can only reach the *past* All-Mind—the lifememories of those who are already dead. Those who have a special sort of mindgift *can* follow the connection through—or maybe *along* is a better word—the past and into the present, to *affect* the minds of their contemporaries.

"What I think the Ra'ira does, is it makes all those connections effortless. Zanek had planned to test possible candidates for King with the Bronze. He would be present, of course, and have the Ra'ira with him. A mindgifted boy would use the Ra'ira without realizing it, and reach back to connect with the lifememory of the man who had done the engraving, and would be able to read the message.

"Meanwhile, of course, Zanek (or the later Kings) would be using the Ra'ira consciously to see the boy's true reaction to the words."

"What—I mean, if I may know—what is the message written on the Bronze?"

Tarani smiled. "If we have revealed the truth about the Ra'ira, which speaks now of danger, why should we conceal Zanek's message, which told of his goodness and hope? The Bronze carries these words . . ."

Tarani closed her eyes and, from memory, recited Zanek's message:

> *I greet thee in the name of the new Kingdom.*
>
> > *From chaos have we created order.*
> > *From strife have we enabled peace.*
> > *From greed have we encouraged sharing.*
>
> *Not I alone, but the Sharith have done this.*
> *Not we alone, but the Ra'ira has done this.*
>
> > *THESE ARE THE WEAPONS*
> > *OF WHICH I GIVE THEE CHARGE*
> > *AND WARNING:*
>
> *The Sharith are our visible strength—*
>
> > *Offer them respect;*
> > *Be ever worthy of their loyalty.*
>
> *The Ra'ira is our secret wisdom—*
>
> > *Seek out the discontented;*
> > *Give them answer, not penalty.*
>
> > *THIS IS THE TASK I GIVE THEE*
> > *AS FIRST DUTY:*

*As you read the scholar's meaning*
*Within the craftsman's skill,*
*So read within yourself*
*Your commitment*

> *To guide*
> *To lead*
> *To learn*
> *To protect.*

*If you lack a high need*
*To improve life for all men,*
*Then turn aside now,*
*For you would fail the Kingdom.*

*I greet thee in the name of the new Kingdom,*
*And I charge thee: care for it well.*

> *I am Zanek,*
> *King of Gandalara*

Charol sat motionless as Tarani's vibrant voice spoke the words which the First King had left for all of his successors. When Tarani opened her eyes and smiled shakily, obviously moved as deeply by this memory as when she had first read those words, Charol twitched as if he were rousing from a trance.

"I—forgive me for my slowness, but I see contradiction in this. You have said that the message could be read only with the aid of the Ra'ira, and you have also said that the true Ra'ira was never *in* Eddarta to aid the High Lord?"

I felt that welcome sense of confidence that comes at the end of a struggle for understanding of a worrisome problem. Charol was verbalizing a lot of the same questions I had been suppressing or dealing with on the subconscious level. As we had talked, the questions—and some unrecognized answers— had surfaced to the conscious level.

"I think," I said slowly, "that the specific mindgift discipline of the Recorder was developed long after Zanek's time. Because of her Recorder training, Tarani has a very strong link with the All-Mind. I believe that her skills were functioning on an unconscious level, and they guided her and connected her to the craftsman's memory.

"The Bronze has continued to be a test for mindgift—but the boys who have been tested since the fall of the Kingdom have been able to get only a few words, without the benefit of either the Ra'ira or Recorder training."

"The words," Charol said, with a deep sigh. "How could the Kings have turned against those wonderful words?"

"That," I answered, "could be a matter of perspective. Once the Kingdom was well established, and all of Gandalara dependent on the Kings for leadership, it would have been an easy and logical step to begin to believe that the 'highest benefit to all men' lay in the comfort and security of the Kings."

"So," Charol said, "Zanek returned as Serkajon and took the Ra'ira away from the Kings. Having heard his message, I see why he would want to deprive them of its power, but—well, if it had been my choice, and I had seen my—well, my vision so corrupted, I believe I would have destroyed the gem."

*Good for you,* I cheered silently. *You just climbed a few points on my scale of good people, Charol—and removed any doubts I might have had about telling you all this.*

"Zanek did try to destroy the Ra'ira," I told the Elder. "The stone seems to be indestructible. So he did the next best thing; he used the Ra'ira one more time to choose twelve honorable men. He entrusted the secret of the stone to them, and charged them with keeping it safe from misuse."

"The Council of Supervisors?" Charol asked.

"It seems to me," Tarani said, "that Zanek would have made a deliberate choice *against* the mindgifted, so that the Supervisors themselves could not be tempted by the Ra'ira's power."

"That makes sense," I said, "but it does make me wonder about the vineh."

She looked thoughtful for a moment.

"Could the mindgift of controlling the vineh be a different *quality* of mindpower? Something like that used by the maufel in directing their message birds? Perhaps the Supervisors were not on guard against that sort of gift—or could not recognize it."

"Or it may be," I added, "that the Ra'ira has different levels of function—that the mindgifted can affect other people, but those with no natural gift—or one that has been unrecognized until the Supervisor screening—could learn to use the Ra'ira on animals."

I glanced at Charol and realized that Tarani and I had left him behind. "I'm sorry, Charol—what you don't know is that sometime in the centuries since Serkajon—in a fairly recent time, I believe—the Supervisors began using the Ra'ira again to train and control the vineh, and put them to work in the city."

The Elder's eyes widened. "Then there was no illness among the vineh in Raithskar? The removal of the Ra'ira merely let them revert to natural behavior?"

I squirmed in my chair. *Now we get down to the nitty-gritty,* I thought.

"Not exactly. You see, the Ra'ira never left Raithskar. The vineh are *still* being controlled."

Charol was quick to pick up the implication, and it clearly horrified him. "Do you mean to say that the disruption in Raithskar, the danger from the vineh—that these are the result of someone's *deliberate* action? Who?" he demanded. "Who would do such a thing, and why?"

"We have told you," Tarani said, "what we *know* of this, and some opinion which has been derived from that knowledge. We *are* reasonably sure that the Ra'ira is indeed finding use, still, in the vineh activity around Raithskar.

"The identity of the man who is doing this—and his reasons—are the subjects of less certain speculation." Tarani glanced at me, and I nodded. "Yet we are confident of our conclusions. One of the Supervisors in Raithskar once lived in Eddarta under the name of Tinis—"

Charol gasped, and Tarani nodded to confirm his guess.

"I see why you have guarded this knowledge so carefully," Charol said, standing up and beginning to pace in an erratic circle. "I am grateful for your trust, and quite convinced of the danger. As a boy, I heard the stories of Tinis—of his arrogance, his power, and his fury.

"I will not," Charol continued, "ask how Tinis attained leadership among men committed to guarding against this very thing. Nor will I inquire about the manner in which the supposed theft was contrived. My mind is reeling now; I shall not burden it further with nonessential details."

He stood up straight.

"You spoke of a choice, and I believe I am now in the position of making that choice on behalf of all Fa'aldu. Speaking not as Elder of Iribos but for all Elders, I do need to know three things before I can make that choice:

"First, what does Tinis—or Ferrathyn—want?

"Second, what do you—the High Lord of Eddarta and the Captain of the Sharith—want?

"Lastly, how will the Fa'aldu be involved in what you want?"

"Those are fair questions," Tarani said. She stood up and walked to the open window, lowered her hip to the sill and looked out at the inner courtyard. I could just see past her; children were building fires in the ovens, and women were mixing dough. "Easily asked," she said musingly, "but less easily answered."

"I believe," I spoke up, "that Ferrathyn wants *power*—not the kind he has in Raithskar, covert and unacknowledged—but the outright power of a ruler. I also believe," I added, recalling the terror in the lifememory of Gharlas's ancestor, "that he especially wants to wield that kind of power in Eddarta, over the Lords who scorned, exiled, and probably tried to kill him."

Tarani turned back to us, braced her hands on her knees, and leaned forward.

"*We* want to stop him," she said, "to remove the Ra'ira from his reach. As to what we would ask of the Fa'aldu in support of that effort . . ." She shrugged. "We have no idea of what Ferrathyn plans, and therefore can compose no strategy to counteract his plans. Although Rikardon and I have had no opportunity to discuss this, I believe I may assure you that we would prefer to deal, singly and alone, with Ferrathyn."

She glanced at me, and I nodded.

"That's why we're on our way back to Raithskar now," I said. "We're afraid that if we can't stop him there, he'll drive an army of men and vineh all the way to Eddarta. If that happens . . ."

"A choice will be forced on everyone," Charol said angrily. "I see it in what I know of Tinis. He will brook no neutrality. Those who do not support him will be destroyed."

"Or," Tarani said quietly, "*persuaded* to join him."

The old man's face paled, and a muscle flexed in his neck. "The law of the Fa'aldu allows one Elder to speak for all," he said. "Balgokh asked the Families for friendship for his friend

Rikardon. Short of bearing arms or denying water, the service of the Fa'aldu is pledged to the Captain and the High Lord. How may we help?"

I stood up. At the judgment, I had spoken impulsively, with no conscious purpose other than to sway the decision in Veron's favor. Now I saw a deeper, unrecognized purpose.

"With the Ra'ira, Ferrathyn can learn what's going on anywhere in Gandalara," I said. "I doubt he exercises it often, but he has the capability, and we don't—not alone."

Charol frowned. "You have our willingness to share with you any and all information which comes to us," he said. "But our maufel are trained only for their local areas."

It was a feature of the bird-handlers' gift that they could direct their maufa only to places which they had visited personally. I thought Charol meant that information might not reach us quickly enough to be of any use, and I began to think aloud.

"Say we're in Omergol," I said. "You would have to send the message to Kanlyr, Haddat, Inid, Relenor, then Yafnaar, before it could be directed to Omergol, right?"

"Yes, that's right," Charol said, "but—"

"Considering the speed of the birds," I interrupted, "I think that's not a problem."

"Rikardon," Tarani said, "I believe you are missing the point. There is no problem if we are in Omergol. There *is* a problem if we are in Thagorn. Is that not what you meant, Charol?"

The Elder nodded, and his face formed itself into an unreadable mask. "No Fa'aldu has ever visited the stronghold of the Sharith."

I had met many differing views of the Sharith, from ignorance to contempt to fear to the awe associated with legends, but the Fa'aldu held the prize for ambivalence. On the one hand, the aloof isolation of the Riders was an uncomfortable reminder to the Fa'aldu of their own history. On the other, they were as subject as city dwellers to fascination with the sha'um and the men for whom they were willing to abandon their own kind. The Sharith were very conscious of the privilege granted them by their sha'um partners, and made no attempt to conceal their pride on the occasions when they mingled with people outside Thagorn. Their attitude grated on the equally proud Fa'aldu, so that most of the contact between the two groups had occurred on a very impersonal, formal level. In their dealing with me, the Fa'aldu had been forced to deal with an individual, rather than a stereotype, but Charol's sudden remoteness was evidence that the conflict lingered.

"I believe I can help, if the maufel will allow it. May I speak with him?" Tarani asked as she stood up.

"Her," Charol corrected. "Lesara is young, but very capable. Her father became ill, and died suddenly, less than a year ago. Come, we will see her now."

*So there is disease in Gandalara,* I thought, as we left Charol's apartment and crossed the inner courtyard. *All the "early" deaths Markasset had heard of were violent, or the result of some definable cause—like the lung corruption caused by spending time in the copper mines. There are human illnesses I know these people don't share, but I guess they have some of their own. At least they seem to be comfortingly rare.*

In the northeast corner of the complex, we stepped through a doorway and found ourselves in a small, empty room. A second doorway, fully covered by a tapestry hanging, faced us. After a moment, a slight figure pushed the curtain aside and stepped into the room. The young girl, whom I presumed to be Lesara, was dressed in an ankle-length white robe not unlike Charol's, indicating her special standing among the Fa'aldu. I tried to mask my surprise when I saw her face; it was disturbingly off-center. Instead of forming a precise widow's peak at the center of her forehead, her thick, gold-brown headfur reached down to the widow's point somewhat left of center, then swept off to the girl's left in a ragged line. The left brow ridge, usually a smooth arc, looked bumpy, as if it had been broken at one time and healed imperfectly. Under it, her eye and the corner of her mouth pulled together slightly. Her head rode slightly leftward on her body, as well.

Lesara bowed to Charol, then held back the curtain while we entered the inner area. I was surprised to be in a small courtyard, open to the sky, with a pair of salt-block benches in its center. A large cage, built of dried reeds lashed together, lined one wall. On the opposite wall was another tapestry-draped door which was, I assumed, Lesara's sleeping quarters.

The girl led us to the benches, a shorter stride with her left leg giving the effect of a limp. She sat down on one of the

benches, and gestured wordlessly that we were to sit opposite
her, which we did. She looked at her hands, clasped with
careful calm in her lap, as she spoke.

"How may I serve the Family, Respected Elder?"

"Lesara, I present Rikardon and Tarani. You know who they
are?" Charol asked gently.

Lesara looked up then. Her eyes were exceptionally dark,
and they focused on Tarani's face with a brief, intense, and
unreadable gaze. Then her head dropped again.

"They honor me with their presence," she said.

"They have asked the Fa'aldu for aid, my child, and I have
promised them your cooperation and that of all maufel among
the Families. I believe there is an obstacle, however—"

He told her about the need to communicate with Thagorn.
As he spoke, her hands tensed together, and her shoulders
hunched forward. When he finished, she whispered: "It
cannot be done." Suddenly her face came up and she looked at
Tarani with an anguish that was painful to see.

"Even had my Elder not asked it of me, I would wish to help
you, High Lord. I—I—"

Tarani left our bench to sit beside the girl. Tarani was so tall,
and the girl so slight, that Lesara looked even younger—I
guessed she was about fourteen.

"There may be a solution to the problem."

The girl's face brightened into a shy smile, but she shook her
head sadly.

"You know of me?" Tarani asked. "Of my history?"

"I—" she began, then hesitated. Suddenly, words poured
out of her in a breathless, eager rush. "Yes, High Lord, I heard
of you even before you came to Iribos. I seldom speak to
travelers, but those Fa'aldu who serve them shared with me
their tales of a beautiful woman who danced with fire." The
girl's expression softened, her gaze seeing *past* the Tarani
sitting beside her. "The stories made me long to see such a
dance, High Lord. No—truth—they made me long to *be* such
a dancer."

Tarani stood up, and offered her hands to the girl.

"Come then, and dance with me," she said.

Stunned beyond any thought of refusal, Lesara put her
hands in Tarani's and allowed the High Lord to draw her into
the largest open space in the room, the corner between the
benches and the wall that held the entry door. Charol and I

stood up and moved to the opposite wall. The maufa, disturbed by our nearness, fluttered and chirped inside their cage.

"I know the High Lord means well," Charol whispered to me, "but I fear she will only leave Lesara more aware than ever of her . . ."

"Difference?" I supplied, and the Elder nodded uncomfortably. "Tarani would not do this," I assured him, "if she thought harm would come of it. Besides," I added, "Lesara may not be as 'different' as you think." I nodded toward the two women, and Charol looked at them in surprise.

Tarani had executed a turn, arms lifted and back arched. She stopped and waited, and Lesara's face suddenly beamed. The girl tried the turn and, though she stopped too soon, her movements and body position were an exact imitation of Tarani's model. Tarani spoke to her, encouraged her to try it again, and Lesara did it perfectly the second time.

They worked together for several minutes, Tarani performing a movement and then watching Lesara. They were simple steps, designed with a syncopation that blended well with Lesara's slightly left-favoring gait. Lesara was a quick study, and one thing soon became clear: she had a natural grace almost the equal of Tarani's. And she *wanted* what was happening, wanted it so tangibly that I felt afraid to breathe, lest it break the spell that bound the two women together.

Tarani began to repeat the steps in different combinations, and Lesara imitated them exactly. Lesara's long white robe was slit to above the knee, and did not hamper her in the leaping or kneeling steps. It swirled to good effect in the turns, reminding me of the gown Tarani had worn in her performances.

Finally, Tarani combined all the steps into a single, fluid dance. When she finished, Lesara took a deep breath and then, her face absolutely shining with joy, Lesara performed the dance.

Tarani turned to us.

"Gentlemen," she said, "if you will please take you seats?"

Charol and I moved forward to sit on the salt-block bench that Tarani and Lesara had occupied. Tarani turned back to Lesara, whose joy faltered as she became aware of her audience.

"Together," Tarani said, and though her voice was not harsh,

no refusal of its tone was possible. Lesara snapped back into
the almost-trance of obedience, and she and Tarani executed
the dance together, matching one another's movements and
timing exactly. Though each step had seemed simple, the
combination was complex and impressive. Tarani had choreo-
graphed the dance to take advantage of every square inch of
available space, without making the "stage" seem crowded or
cramped.

Beside me, I felt the tension in Charol's body. When the
dance ended, I knew he was on the verge of shouting his
pleasure and congratulations. I put my hand on his arm to
delay his outburst, because I had finally figured out what
Tarani was doing.

Charol looked at me questioningly, but I only nodded
toward the "stage." Tarani took Lesara's arm and led her back
to the starting point of their dance. Both women were
breathing heavily; since I knew Tarani's tolerance, I suspected
her fatigue was partly faked for the sake of Lesara's self-image.

Tarani faced the girl, and lifted her arms above her.

Her hands caught fire.

Charol gasped.

Lesara took a step backward, with a little cry of surprise.

Tarani brought her flaming hands down and offered them to
Lesara.

The girl stared at Tarani's hands, their outlines barely visible
within the flames. She looked up at Tarani's face, and a look of
resolution came into her own face.

Lesara stepped foward, closed her eyes, and placed her
hands in Tarani's. She opened her eyes and stepped back again;
four hands now seemed to burn.

Tarani and Lesara danced again, their burning hands leaving
fiery trails in the air as they turned and bent and leaped about
the room.

The dance was faultless.

The dance was beautiful.

Lesara was beautiful.

When they froze in the final pose, a kneeling bow, it was
evident that Lesara had reached the end of her endurance.
She was panting heavily, but the glow in her face outshone the
brightness of her hands. They stood. They faced each other.
Their hands touched, and the flames went out. Still holding
the girl's hands, Tarani leaned down to kiss Lesara's cheek.

"Thank you," she said, "for giving me a reason to dance again."

Charol could contain himself no longer. He jumped up from the bench and rushed over to them. Heedless now of what he perceived to be Tarani's "rank," he put his arms around both women and hugged them fiercely, so overcome that his voice was raspy and barely understandable.

"That was beautiful . . . so special . . . I feel privileged . . . I have never seen anything so remarkable. . . ."

He released them at last, and regained his composure. I gave him credit for not showing the least embarrassment over his impulsive gesture. "Lesara, it would be selfish of me to keep this memory for myself alone. It would please me greatly if you will dance before the family—at a time of your choosing, of course."

The glow of triumph faded from Lesara's face.

"The High Lord must leave soon," the girl said. "I would not ask her to perform, and I—I cannot make the flame. That is her gift."

"With great respect for the High Lord," Charol said, "I have not asked her to perform, and the flame is not the sole—nor even the greatest—beauty of that dance. You have allowed me to see a Lesara who is hidden from us, my daughter. I ask you to share her with the rest of the family."

"I—I will consider it, Respected Elder," Lesara said.

Charol nodded, then said to Tarani: "This performance was a treasured gift, High Lord. But we have yet to discuss the solution to your problem."

"On the contrary," Tarani said. "Lesara and I have demonstrated that a solution is possible. Through an illusion, she can see the places *I* have visited, and share that vision with her maufa."

Lesara frowned.

"Will that not work?" Tarani asked her.

"It may, High Lord," Lesara said. "But —I find this hard to explain—a maufa cannot *learn* in the same way you and I can. It must *know*. It knows where to go because I know, from my own experience, where it must go. I fear that my learning, through you, will not have that same sense of . . . sureness."

"I have some skill with animals," Tarani said slowly. "Nothing so great as the skill of a maufel, but I once shared a bond with . . . a bird."

A look of pain flashed across Tarani's face as she thought of Lonna, now dead; the look quickly passed.

"Perhaps," she suggested, "if I share my vision with you *while* you are bonded to a maufa . . . ?"

"Yes," Lesara said, suddenly excited. "That might work—shall we try?"

The two women moved toward the cage, as deeply absorbed in this new project as they had been entranced by the dance a few moments earlier. Charol looked at me and gestured toward the door. I nodded and followed him out, leaving the illusionist and the bird-handler to their task.

## 7

We ate dinner with the family that evening, and served the Fa'aldu's hunger for news with stories about the sha'um cubs. For a time, the crisis and the purpose were forgotten. They came back, full force, though, when we entered our apartment and I let the door tapestry fall into place behind us. "We have their help, now," I said. "But to do what?" I sighed. "I still don't know where to start."

Tarani came to me and hugged me, pressing the warmth and shape and strength of her body all along mine. It was inexpressibly comforting, and I held on and tried to return the comfort. After a moment, she pulled away.

"I would share this burden if I could, Rikardon," she said. "But though we are both committed to the need, only you have the knowledge to guide us."

"That's part of the problem," I said. "I know Raithskar because Markasset grew up there. I know something of the Ra'ira because of my contact with Zanek in the All-Mind. But Markasset didn't know Ferrathyn, except as a presence that drifted in and out of his father's house." I grimaced. "I might have suspected something wrong with Ferrathyn right from the first, if I'd had full access to Markasset's memories immediately. The Chief Supervisor came to Thanasset's house and spent a good deal of time talking to Markasset. Before he became Chief Supervisor, I doubt he'd said a total of ten words to the boy."

"You have access to Markasset's memories now," Tarani said. "Did he know anything at all of Ferrathyn before he became a Supervisor?"

I closed my eyes and tried to search the Gandalaran half of the blended individual I had become when Thanasset had given me Serkajon's sword. After a few seconds, I opened them again, shaking my head.

"Nothing," I said. "Even as a Supervisor, Ferrathyn was only a name. Markasset never met the man until he had become Chief Supervisor. *Damn!*" I swore. "How I wish I could talk to Thanasset. He *must* have known Ferrathyn outside the Council."

"Why is that important?" Tarani asked. "We must deal with the man as he is now, not as he was then."

"True," I agreed. I shrugged my shoulders and smiled grimly. "We have a goal, Tarani—to get the Ra'ira away from Ferrathyn—but no real plan. In the absence of anything more definite, I'm thinking along very basic strategy lines. What it comes down to is: 'Know thine enemy.'"

"Forgive me for saying it," she said, a trifle sarcastically, "but given the situation in Raithskar, reaching Thanasset to discuss Ferrathyn's history may be as difficult as reaching Ferrathyn, and rather too late to be of much help."

"Absolutely true," I agreed. "Yet Markasset doesn't know of anyone else who has long-term knowledge of Ferrathyn. No, wait, that's wrong," I said, frowning at an elusive memory that had just floated by. "Zaddorn? Talking to him would probably help, too—Ferrathyn and Zaddorn have been at odds for most of Zaddorn's tenure as Chief of Peace and Security. But Zaddorn's in Raithskar, too, and anyway, I think he's too young—"

"Ligor!" I nearly shouted, whirling on Tarani with a fierceness that made her jump.

"He was Chief of Peace and Security before Zaddorn. He left, in fact, because of conflict with Ferrathyn. And he is *not* in Thagorn; he's in Krasa."

"To visit Krasa now," Tarani said, pacing about and staring at the floor, "would cost us several days of precious time. We might shorten the time by crossing the desert, but I would prefer not to expose Koshah and Yoshah to that hardship,

much less to the danger of the wild vineh that live along the
Wall in that area."

I could tell when the logical solution hit her. She stopped
pacing and displayed a sudden interest in a wall hanging—a
yellow-brown weaving that conveyed the impression of a
desert scene.

I could tell when she accepted it. The outline of her body
shifted, the stiff tension relaxing.

"Will there ever be an end to these partings?" she asked
quietly. "A time when we can share one another in peace,
without the interference of duty and destiny?"

I approached her and put my hands on her shoulders, not
knowing what to say. But words came anyway, from that same
odd sense that had often given me glimpses of truth in the
puzzle that was Gandalara.

"Maybe," I said, "we can hope for a pleasant duty and a
peaceful destiny."

## 8

Tarani and I took our leave of Charol and the Iribos Fa'aldu
early the next morning. Aware that we planned to split up at
some point, they had packed the supplies they provided us in
two lots and, although Tarani would be traveling with Yayshah
and the cubs and therefore had more mouths to feed, I had the
larger share of ready food and water.

We stayed together as long as we could, going so far west
that we were both taken slightly out of our way. We reached
the foot of Rikalara, a huge island of stone that rose abruptly
from the desert floor and disappeared into the cloud cover
above us. From here, Tarani would turn south, and follow the
dry, rocky southern trail around Rikalara and then continue
west toward the Chizan passage. Hers was the route most
frequently traveled by caravans, and it was studded with
Refreshment Houses.

Keeshah and I would turn north until I reached the
northeastern side of the—I had to think of Rikalara as a

mountain. Then I would head northwest, straight across the most uncomfortable desert I had yet seen in Gandalara. Most of the dry areas in Gandalara were held together by stubborn, scrubby bushes. They were given some contour and relief by an occasional rocky pattern. The Strofaan, however, was only fine, salty sand coating an up-and-down ground pattern that was totally monotonous and thoroughly tiring. Every step drove up a cloud of sand that stung the eyes and coated the lungs. Crossing the Strofaan was like walking across the bottom of a bowl filled with lumpy sugar.

I wasn't looking forward to the trip.

When the ground around the base of Rikalara became too rocky and steep for comfort, we called the sha'um to a halt side by side. Tarani leaned over and stroked Keeshah's neckfur. He made a soft sound, like a sigh, and shifted his weight, moving a little closer to Yayshah.

*Sorry to leave,* he said to me. *Why?*

The question echoed in the minds of the cubs. Yoshah came up beside Keeshah and rubbed her side along my leg.

The question surprised me a little. Through our mindlink, Keeshah was usually more aware than I of my own motivations. Then I realized that he was still showing the same kind of insight. My consciousness had determined the need for this parting, but a large part of me hated it a whole lot.

*When I called to you from the Well of Darkness, you left Yayshah to come to me,* I said to Keeshah. *Why?*

*Needed me,* came Keeshah's answer, without any hesitation.

*As I do now, and always will,* I said, feeling the warm tightness that always came over me when I thought of the bond that Keeshah and I shared. *I have to make that same kind of choice here, Keeshah,* I said. *I want to stay with Tarani and Yayshah and the cubs, but there is something I have to do that is more important than what I want.*

He was struggling to understand, even as he turned his head to nuzzle Yayshah's jaw.

*You want to stay,* he said at last. *You want to go?*

*I think that lives may be saved by my leaving Tarani now,* I said. *It's not the same kind of wanting, but—yes, I want to go.*

He gave a kind of mental shrug and said: *We go.*

Koshah was not linked directly to Keeshah, but he sensed

his father's assent from his link with me. *Go with!* he demanded, coming around his mother and jumping to the top of a rocky rise to face me nearly at eye level. His eyes were like Keeshah's—green, flecked with gold—and the posture of his body would have expressed his determination, even without benefit of the mindlink.

*You must stay with Yayshah and Yoshah,* I said firmly.

*Why?* he asked.

I started to answer him, but his mindvoice interrupted.

*I will keep up,* he said defensively. Like his father, he was able to see some of my thoughts before I expressed them.

*That's only part of the reason, Koshah,* I told the cub. *I need you to stay with Tarani and help protect her.*

The cub's tail twitched, and he shifted position, the neckful of fur that had lifted settling down slightly as he considered that.

*Truth?* he asked.

*You know it's true,* I said, scolding gently.

*I stay,* he finally agreed, and he jumped down in front of Yayshah. He lifted his head, and they touched noses briefly.

Tarani had been watching with interest. She did not have the benefit of the direct link I shared with the cubs, but she could see them from Yayshah's perception as well as her own, and she seldom had trouble divining the content of any conversation I had with the cubs.

"How did you convince him to stay with us?" she asked.

"I told him that you need him more than I do," I said. "And it's true, darling. Of the two of us, you and your mindgift are the greater threat to Ferrathyn. If there is anything Ferrathyn *can* do between here and Raithskar to stop us, and he has to choose which one of us to stop, he'll go after you. Be very careful, Tarani."

"I shall be cautious," she agreed. "Guard yourself well, too, Rikardon—and be watchful. Danger can come from any direction, and not solely from Ferrathyn."

"Keeshah and I will be all right," I assured her. "But we'll miss you terribly."

I leaned over to kiss her. Her hand found and held my shoulder, so that the kiss lasted a moment longer than I had intended. When I pulled away, she smiled shakily.

"You choose to travel alone for the sake of speed," she said. "Prove your point by coming soon to Thagorn, my love."

"As soon as possible," I promised. Keeshah nuzzled each of the cubs, and rubbed his cheek along Yayshah's once, then turned northward and started running.

The trip was relatively easy for a while; we stopped at the Refreshment House of Stomestad in the late afternoon, and rested there briefly, then set out northwest across the Strofaan, sent on our way with the good wishes and unsatisfied puzzlement of the Stomestad Fa'aldu.

Travelers normally traveled directly north from Stomestad, heading for the hills that formed the beginning of the northern Wall on this end of Gandalara. There, the traveler would turn west or east, and follow the hills to the nearest town—to the west, Lorok, to the east, Prozia. I had never visited either town, but they were clearly marked on maps. It was a long haul to either town, but their locations marked the only sizable sources of water in the area and following the Wall was safer for most Gandalarans.

I had already discovered that following the Wall to the west was *not* the safer choice for a man traveling with a sha'um. Beyond Lorok was Sulis, and beyond that, Grevor. Between Grevor and Sulis lay a section of green, hilly land that housed at least one colony of wild vineh. *People* could pass through that territory without molestation; the vineh had learned to coexist with the towns. On our previous trip through that area, however, the sha'um had triggered the aggression of the vineh. Thymas, Tarani, and I, with Keeshah and Ronar, had barely managed to escape their attack.

Compared to the possibility of another such attack, the desert crossing seemed much more attractive. It was made easier by the nature of this traveling party. With Thymas and Ronar, badly injured, we had been forced to travel slowly, people walking beside sha'um, and so had been trapped in the sandy clouds that puffed up around us. I was riding Keeshah this time, and he set himself to a steady, loping run. The pads of his paws were spread flat against the sand, the long claws extended for traction. He kicked up a storm of the fine-particled sand, but his speed kept us ahead of it most of the time.

After all our experience together in deserts, we had developed an effective travel pattern. Keeshah ran until he felt slightly fatigued, then we both rested briefly before going on. Night was no deterrence to us; even when the moon did not share its silvering light, Keeshah had an unerring sense of direction, and sufficient night vision to guide him across the subtle hilliness of the flat-seeming ground.

The journey was monotonous and tiring, but Keeshah and I had some comfort in it through my link with the cubs. I spoke to them frequently, and shared the progress of their journey with Keeshah. By the time Keeshah and I sighted the grayish bushes that marked the beginning of land with soil instead of dust, Tarani and the sha'um with her had left the Refreshment House at Haddat and were on the final leg of their approach to the Chizan passage. They would stop once more at the Refreshment House at Inid, then brave the harsh, high-altitude mountain crossing.

I entered Krasa with my scarf wrapped around my face so that only my eyes were showing. I received curious glances from the merchants from whom I purchased water and meat (in several small portions) for Keeshah, but no one asked questions. It was not the fact that my face was covered that intrigued them. People often used that style as they crossed the desert, and I was still wearing enough Strofaan sand to make the scarf totally in character. Rather, it was rare for anyone to arrive at Krasa with recent desert experience so evident.

I left them to their curiosity and returned to the grass-covered pocket Keeshah and I had found in the hills above the city. He had been lying on his side; he got up slowly when I arrived—hardly the same reaction someone he did not know might have expected.

I removed the small meat pieces from their oiled paper, and set them out for him, then cleaned off the surface of a nearby rock and filled the shallow depression with water. He had followed me to the rock, and now waited for me to pour a swallow of water into my hand and offer it to him. He lapped at it lightly, and his raspy tongue took an extra swipe across the palm of my hand. Only then did he turn to the rock and drink to his satisfaction. I refilled the depression after he had begun to eat.

*I have to go back to town,* I said. *When I come back, I'll bring you more meat.*

*No,* he said, his mind full of fatigue and the beginnings of new energy brought on by the taste of the meat. *I will rest, then hunt. When go?*

*Probably not until tomorrow morning,* I answered, thinking that I could do with a full night's sleep myself. I wanted to touch him, but was reluctant to disturb his meal. *Thank you for carrying me across the desert, Keeshah. Rest well.*

# 9

When I reached town, I decided to have a meal before beginning my search for Ligor. It was midevening, and the little diner was nearly deserted. I had just sat down at a table when Ligor came into the room. I started to call out to him, but he looked my way, stopped at the serving bar for the mug of faen, which was poured for him the instant he appeared in the doorway, and walked over. He put his mug down on the tiled top of the small table, and lowered himself slowly into the chair without speaking, his eyes on me the entire time.

"Boy," he said at last, "you look like you just walked across the Strofaan."

"Not this time," I said. "I rode."

His scarred face was unreadable as he took a long drink of faen. "'Not this time?'" he quoted. "You make that a habit?"

"I've done it once or twice," I said. "And only when I had no choice."

He finished the faen and said quietly: "Well, son, that's no more surprise to me than seeing you here at all, still breathing. I figured Worfit woulda collected that sword of yours a long time before now."

"He's tried hard enough," I said. "Thanks for the reminder; I had almost forgotten about him."

That finally shook the old man's composure.

"Almost forgotten—" he began, then interrupted himself to wave away the server who was bringing him a refill. "Son, you got problems bigger'n Worfit, we got no business discussing 'em in public." He stood up. "My place ain't no Supervisor's house, but it'll sleep two people, as long as they're friends. C'mon."

Without waiting for me to agree, he started out of the diner. I took a little longer, and he was looking around impatiently when I finally stepped out into the street, a stoppered ceramic jug in one hand.

Ligor grinned widely enough to show that some of his back teeth were missing. "I like the way you think, son," he said.

I had thought Ligor to be joking about the size of his home, but it *was* tiny—little more than a sitting room with an attached sleeping area, which was barely big enough for one sleeping mat. If I stayed, the floor of the sitting room would be my bed. The small house was one of several surrounding a larger building that contained, according to Ligor, the best bathhouse and the worst food in Krasa.

"So now you know why the folks at the diner know me so well," he said. "I stay here because it's clean and—ahem—Profa, the lady who owns the place, has other talents I value higher'n good cooking."

Ligor started rummaging on a littered shelf, and finally turned back to me with two chipped clay bowls in his hands. His face darkened when he saw me smiling. I put up my hands to forestall whatever he might say.

"Ligor, I mean neither you nor the lady any disrespect, believe me. I'm only glad for you."

"Not amazed that somebody would find this ugly face attractive?" he asked, still embarrassed.

"Not amazed at all," I said sincerely. He waited a moment, and then nodded. He held out the drinking bowls; I pulled the wooden stopper out of the jug and poured faen into both bowls. We drank together, then sat down on the benches that jutted out from the wall in one corner. With two blocky chairs, they formed the seating accommodations for a dining-style table. It had once borne a smooth mosaic of small tiles, but now its surface was uneven and pocked where pieces had come loose. I noticed that although the room was understandably cluttered, it was clean. I set my bowl on the table and refilled it.

"I want you to tell me everything you know about Ferrathyn," I told Ligor. He nearly dropped the bowl he was offering for a refill.

"Well now, you're full of surprises, aren't you? That's probably the last thing I'd expect you to ask, son. 'Where's

Worfit?' 'I need money.' 'Send a message for me.' Those I might expect. But Ferrathyn? What in Zanek's name—"

"Please, Ligor," I interrupted him. "I'll explain later. Right now, I just need to know about him. When did he come to Raithskar? When did he become a Supervisor? Whom did he replace? When did he become the Chief Supervisor? I know you quit shortly after that. You've already told me that it was basically because of Ferrathyn. I want to know the details. I *need* to know—*before* I tell you what it's all about."

*Smart move,* I scolded myself. *You've only been wondering for days whether to take Ligor into your confidence, and now you're committed to it without thinking it through. Still,* I considered, looking at the rough man who had been Markasset's friend and who had accepted the differences in me with an attitude of minding his own business, *I could do worse than trust Ligor. I would probably have decided to tell him, anyway.*

Ligor shrugged, kicked one of the chairs around and put his feet up on it, and leaned back against the wall.

"All right, son—Rikardon, as you're called now. First you gotta know about me. My daddy was a vlek handler, and I grew up hating the sight and sound and smell of the beasts, and knowin' that was not the way I wanted to spend my life. Still, I was caravan-born, and the caravans were all I really knew."

I understood what he meant. During the short stint Tarani and I had spent working as vlek handlers, we had encountered almost an elite spirit among them, and something of the parent-to-child tradition maintained in most of Gandalara's other skill areas. But even knowing that it was often true, it was entirely beyond my capacity to envision a kid growing up with *ambition* to be a vlek handler.

"I was bigger'n some," Ligor said, "and not afraid of a fight. I started working as a guard, I was young, and cocky, and I guess you see where that led. The other guards taught me *how* to fight—the hard way." He stretched. "All the time my dad and I had been working caravans, we never crossed the Chizan passage. Well, I took it into my head to see the other side of the world for a change. We heard the stories, you know— about how every caravan hired hundreds of guards to see them through past the Sharith." He snorted. "Hogwash, of course. But jobs were scarce just about then, and I was young. I was downright fed up with doin' nothing most of the time. When I did catch some sneakthief tryin' to make off with part of the goods, half the time the thief was one of my folk."

I noticed his phrasing and thought: *I guess your beginnings are always with you.*

"So I waited for a caravan going to Chizan, then caught one in Chizan going to Raithskar." He shook his head, pulled his torso forward, and poured some more faen. "When I saw Raithskar, so shiny and clean and cool, I knew I had to stay. There's no prettier place in this world, son. I know; I've been near everywhere you can go."

"You won't get any argument from me," I said, and we drank together in a toast to Raithskar.

"There was only one thing I could do well, so I went to the Chief of Peace and Security and asked him to hire me. He laughed in my face, and put me in a clerk's job. Best thing ever happened to me. I learned more about the job in that one year than I'd have gotten out of five years of standard guard duty. Oh, I got to do that after a while, too—old Yolim must have felt sorry for me or somethin', because he kinda took charge of my training himself."

"He recognized potential when he saw it," I said.

"Well, anyway, by the time he retired, I'd been working for him some fifteen years, and I knew his job inside out. He had a lot of respect in that city, especially from the people who worked for him. Everybody knew I was supposed to take his place. Everybody but one Supervisor, that is."

Ligor paused, so I said what he expected me to say: "Ferrathyn."

Ligor nodded.

"Then your—um—disagreement with him after he became Chief Supervisor wasn't the first one you'd had."

"Hardly. First, I could not stand to be around the man; just standing next to him made the fur on the back of my neck crawl up. Never understood that reaction—everybody else seemed to like him. He kind of reminded me of the people who travel *with* a caravan. They always kinda think they're better than the folks who belong there. . . ." He paused, searching for more words.

"I know what you mean, Ligor. Was that the only reason you didn't like Ferrathyn?"

"Not on your life," he said. "Like I said, being around him kinda scared me. And I didn't like what I saw him doin' to other people. The man has an absolute genius for persuasion, son," Ligor said, shaking his head. "And I fell for it just like everybody else. Until one time he came into our office wanting something that was downright illegal. I started to do it, too— but all of a sudden it dawned on me that this little guy was pushin' me around, just as if he were one of the big guards on the caravan. I'd come to Raithskar to get out of that, and I was fleabitten if I'd stand for it!"

He sipped his faen.

"I told Supervisor Ferrathyn what he could do with his special request. He was mad—so mad his eyes kinda glowed. But he left, and he never asked me for that kind of thing again." Ligor stared at the wall. "Made me wonder if Yolim woulda done it."

"Done what?" I asked, and Ligor laughed bitterly.

"Now, there's another reason the man spooked me. When he walked out of the office, I was furious. I was ready to go to Yolim and tell him what had happened. I wanted to know if 'special favors' for Ferrathyn were so common that he had expected me to go along with him.

"I went to Yolim's house, practically busted the door down, and when we were face-to-face . . .

"I couldn't remember what Ferrathyn had asked me to do."

"You don't have *any* idea?" I prompted.

Ligor shrugged. "It needed writing, that's all I remember— and *that* only because I still had the writing brush in my hand." He looked at me sharply. "Do *you* know, son?"

"We may be able to figure it out," I said, "but right now, let's get back to when you became Chief of Peace and Security. What reason did Ferrathyn give for not wanting to follow Yolim's wishes?"

"He made up a new rule that the Chief had to be a native of Raithskar. I—uh—think he had his own idea of who to appoint. The rest of the Council didn't support him then, but by the time I quit two years later, they had come around to his way of thinking."

"Ferrathyn was *pushing* for Zaddorn?" I asked, thinking of the conflict I had seen between the two men.

*Could that all be just an act?* I wondered.

Ligor must have noticed my alarm, but he answered calmly. "Yeah, he wanted Zaddorn in that spot. I remember thinking—" He frowned.

"What's the matter?" I asked.

"I just put some things together for the first time, that's all. When I heard Zaddorn was going to be Chief, I remember thinking he was being repaid for past favors."

"And?" I prompted.

"The day Ferrathyn tried to make me do something to our records, I was just filling in. The regular clerk, who was out that day, was Zaddorn."

"Are you saying that Zaddorn *did* whatever Ferrathyn had wanted you to do?" I demanded. "That he owes his position as Chief to that one thing?"

*Could Zaddorn be so easily controlled?* I thought. *No, I won't believe it. Ferrathyn was clumsy enough to try to control Ligor; he might have installed Zaddorn on the assumption that the younger man would be easier to manipulate.*

*He might have been surprised, too—and finally wise enough to stick with that mistake instead of trying out a new one.*

Ligor slammed his bowl down on the table, chipping its bottom yet again on the sharp, uneven marble mosaic.

"Fleas, man," he said. "I'm saying that whole incident is like an itch I can't scratch. I've been worrying at it for ten years or more, now. I didn't know half of what I just told you, right after it happened. I've been digging it out, little by little—but the final piece still will not come. What *was* it Ferrathyn wanted me to do?"

His eyes narrowed. "And when are you gonna tell me what this is all about?"

"As soon as you tell me why you quit your job," I said.

"I quit because I couldn't get anything done," he said. "Everything I did was criticized by Ferrathyn before the Council. They supported me—I suppose they knew how little we liked each other—but I expect they were relieved when I submitted my resignation.

"Now," he said, leaning back in his chair, "it's your turn."

"This story, too, starts outside of Raithskar. In fact," I said, and took a deep breath, "it begins half a lifetime ago, in Eddarta . . ."

By the time I had finished telling Ligor the truth about the Ra'ira, Ligor was on his feet, pacing and angry.

"All right," he said, "all right. I don't wanna seem unconcerned about the state of things in Raithskar now—to tell you the truth, it's gonna take me a little while to absorb that—but I wanna know what this means to that fleabitten itch. Are you saying that Ferrathyn used his mindpower on me?"

"Twice," I agreed. "Once to try to make you *do*—whatever it was. Again to make you *forget*—whatever it was."

"Why didn't I do it?" he asked me.

"How can you be sure you *didn't* do it?"

Ligor said, "Now, just a minute—" He stopped, staring at me. He started to pace the tiny room again, muttering to himself. After a while, he sank back down on the bench beside the table.

"I guess," he said with a sigh, "there's no way to believe only half of this. You're right, son—if he could make me forget, he could make me believe anything. I'm fleabitten, though, if I can figure any reason for him to do it that way."

"I have the same question," I said. "I don't think I have it clear about the timing. Was Ferrathyn already a Supervisor when this happened?"

"No, but he was already well known to the Supervisors. Even before I arrived in Raithskar, Ferrathyn had volunteered for service to the Council. By the time that—thing—happened, he was kind of a general assistant. He worked in the Council building, and everything. Most folks gave him what he wanted just because he generally represented the wishes of the Council."

I rubbed my headfur, remembering Zaddorn's scroll-laden desk. "What kinds of records does your office keep?"

Ligor shrugged. "Work histories of the officers, details of anything we get involved in—"

"What is it?" I asked when he paused. "Have you remembered something?"

"Yeah," he said excitedly. "It seems to me that I had just filed a decision with the Council on the death of a Supervisor."

"Decision?" I echoed.

"When somebody dies suddenly, the Peace division gets notified. If it was a violent death, we try to find out what happened."

"The dead Supervisor—did he occupy the place that Ferrathyn took on the Council?"

"No, Ferrathyn didn't become a Supervisor until a couple of years later—" He stood up slowly. "After *another* sudden death. Boy, are you telling me that Ferrathyn killed those men, that I knew he had done one murder, and he made me forget it?"

"Hold on, one thing at a time," I said. "First tell me how the first Supervisor died."

"The man died with a dagger in his heart; he had left a note saying . . ."

"That he had chosen to die?" I prompted. Ligor nodded and swallowed hard.

"Yolim wouldn't believe it. The man had been a close friend, and he felt he would have known if the man had been that . . . unbalanced.

"So he reported the death as a possible murder, presently unanswerable, but still open." Suddenly Ligor slammed his fist on the table. "I remember!" he said. "Ferrathyn wanted me to change the record to show self-inflicted death." His eyes narrowed. "That fleason Ferrathyn killed the Supervisor, didn't he?"

"I think it's very likely."

"Then why didn't he move right into that position? Why did he wait for another Supervisor to die?"

"I think that's the answer you're really looking for, Ligor—because you *didn't* falsify that record. People respond differently to mindpower, and some people seem better able to resist it than others. Ferrathyn may never have run into someone with a will as strong as yours before. He had to realize that if you could resist his compulsion, you might break free of the forgetfulness command. *You* stopped him from becoming a Supervisor then because he was afraid you would expose him. He had to wait until another Supervisor died—how?"

"The healer ruled it was some illness he had never seen before," Ligor said. "I saw the body; it looked like the man had been choked to death, but there wasn't a mark on his body. Could Ferrathyn have done that?"

I remembered the fierceness on Tarani's face, and the terror in Molik's, in that moment when Tarani had almost killed the roguelord by immobilizing his lungs with her mindpower.

"He could have done it," I said. "He must have figured enough time had passed that you wouldn't connect him with the earlier death. But he couldn't rest easy as long as you were in Raithskar. He couldn't kill you outright, either—you had proved you had substantial resistance to his power. I suspect he wasn't ready, yet, to use the Ra'ira overtly. So he used more ordinary tactics—political pressure and harassment—to drive you out."

"And now he's finally got what he wanted all along," Ligor said.

I sat up straighter. "What do you mean?"

Ligor's jaw tightened. "His first motion to the Council, as a Supervisor, was to disband the Security force. He said that if vineh could be trained to clean streets, they could be trained to fight—and would be totally loyal and beyond corruption." He laughed bitterly. "I thought it was a crazy idea—but I didn't know about the Ra'ira. Fortunately, the Council turned him down, but he brought it up every now and then. Now—Council or no Council—he's got his army of vineh."

# 10

"You mean you had heard nothing about what's going on in Raithskar?" I asked Ligor.

We had left Krasa behind us several minutes ago, and were making our way through the rocky brush of the hillside above the town. It had taken very little to convince Ligor to go back to Raithskar with me, even though neither one of us had a clear idea what help he might be. He had succeeded in resisting Ferrathyn's power once—but a power unaided by the Ra'ira and wielded by a much younger and less subtle Ferrathyn. There was no real reason to suspect he could resist Ferrathyn completely now.

I believed Ligor was coming with me out of a sense of responsibility to Raithskar for having "run out" when things became uncomfortable for him. There was no doubt he was angry on a personal basis, too, after learning that the mind puzzle that had tormented him had been set deliberately by Ferrathyn. I wanted him to come for a very different, very selfish reason. I trusted him, and he was on our side. I had a strong feeling that we would need every ally we could get before this was over.

"You got to remember, son," Ligor said, holding aside the tangled branches of a bush so that I could pass through, "Krasa ain't on the main road to anywhere. Caravans come here, they're generally *just* coming here, from Grevor or Dyskornis, and they ain't too frequent. We got one strange old maufel who sometimes takes it in his head not to talk to nobody, and he's in one of them spells right now. He gets and gives messages when he's asked—and paid—but he don't inquire about the contents and he *don't* share news.

"As Peace and Security in Krasa," Ligor added, "I expect I'd have made him keep shut about the vineh, anyway. These folks don't know about the way Raithskar used vineh. They'd have taken the news of a vineh sickness to mean that the ones near here, which are none too easy to get along with, might catch it and make even more trouble. I wouldn't have wanted that kind of panic."

We had struggled through a snarl of underbrush and come out onto a large, flat area of nearly smooth stone. We paused to catch our breath, and I called to Keeshah.

*Here we are, Keeshah. Ready to go?*

I had already talked to Keeshah about accepting Ligor as a second rider, and he had agreed. I knew he was nearby, but even I was surprised when he came up out of the brush nearly at Ligor's right elbow. He was yawning, and the impressive tusks—along with the other less spectacular but equally threatening teeth—were in full view.

"Yi-i-!" Ligor yelped, and jumped aside.

I heard Keeshah's mind chuckle, and I fought to hide my own smile.

The big cat took his time coming into the clearing, stretching out each foreleg and clenching the stone with his long claws, then drawing his body forward until his back legs were fully stretched, his tail extended and fluffed. Then he stepped over the bordering brush with his hind legs and was fully present in the rock-floored clearing.

He filled it up.

"I'd forgotten how big he is," Ligor said, looking slightly embarrassed.

*Keeshah, quit trying to scare him, and make friends,* I said.

*Already friends,* Keeshah said.

He moved as far away from us as he could and still remain in the clearing. Then he lay down, rolled over, and came to rest belly-up with his side leaning against Ligor's legs.

Ligor staggered against the impact, but kept his balance. He laughed uproariously.

"Hey, there, you haven't forgotten me, eh?" He glanced at me and chuckled at the look on my face. "You say you have Markasset's memories?" he asked.

"I have them," I answered shortly, "and he doesn't remember *ever* seeing Keeshah do that with you."

"That's because he never saw it happen," Ligor said, and leaned over to stroke the fur on Keeshah's chest and belly. A very special feeling of contentment came from Keeshah's mind, and something of a cherished memory. "He still had school a couple of years after he brought Keeshah out of the Valley, and I—um—I dropped by his house now and again during the day. Keeshah was big enough to scare the fleas off me, even then, but there was something *young* about him, and I played with him some."

That seemed to be an understatement. Keeshah's attitude toward Ligor gave me the impression that he was a long-standing, trusted, and much-missed friend. Before I could ask more questions, though, Ligor stood up.

"Good thing I made friends with him when he was younger," he said, as Keeshah rolled back over and stood up again. "But scratching his belly and climbing on his back are real different propositions. Wanna give me a clue about how to do this?"

We were busy, then, for a while, replaying a scene which had occurred once before with Zaddorn in Ligor's role. While Ligor's nervousness was lessened somewhat by his familiarity with Keeshah as a friend, he suffered the same cultural inhibition that had troubled Zaddorn. Since birth, Ligor and Zaddorn had expected to walk wherever they needed to go. There were no riding-sized animals in Gandalara except the sha'um, and their friendship was reserved for the Sharith—and the male descendants of Serkajon, who had separated himself from the Sharith at the end of the Kingdom. Ligor had never before trusted his weight and well-being to another living creature.

Eventually, however, Ligor was secure and reasonably comfortable with his body resting along Keeshah's back, his knees tucked up just forward of Keeshah's hind legs. I mounted the crouching cat behind Ligor, using pressure from my legs and hands to keep the full force of my weight off the cat's hips.

*Okay, Keeshah,* I said. *Stand up—slowly, please.*

To my surprise, he obeyed. With Zaddorn, Keeshah had taken no trouble to be gentle; he had surged up and started his run with no warning.

*I guess he knows Ligor better,* I thought. *Or maybe I don't have the history of rivalry with Ligor that Markasset had with Zaddorn.*

*Okay?* I asked Keeshah. *Is he pinching you anywhere?*
*No. Comfortable.*
*Then let's go,* I said.

The more time I spent with Ligor, the more he impressed me. Considering what he had told me of his life in Raithskar and his pride in his role as Chief of Peace and Security, I would have been the last person to blame him for settling into a comfortable berth in a small town and letting his life slide into idleness. But he had carried his job in Krasa with as much pride as in Raithskar, and his stocky body was muscular and fit. He had to be as old as—if not a bit older than—Markasset's father, but he made no complaint of the rigorous journey.

As far as supplies went, we were traveling as lightly as possible, carrying very little food and the minimum supply of water. Keeshah had hunted and fed well, and would wait until we reached the Refreshment House at Inid before eating again, and he shared our water sparingly. We adopted a familiar travel pattern: run for three hours, rest for one. Ligor became adept at riding second, so we alternated places. The one who rode in first position could doze while Keeshah's furry back hunched and flexed with his long stride.

We traveled along the western edge of the Strofaan Desert, where sand and rock cliffs offered little shelter from the heat and dryness. At the end of our second day of travel, we stood outside the gates of the Refreshment House at Inid. Fatigue was an everywhere ache; Ligor staggered beside me; Keeshah had dropped into a crouch and was panting heavily. My voice was sand-hoarse and barely louder than a whisper as I called out the formula request for entry.

At the first sound, the gatecloth dropped, and several people rushed out to support Ligor and me. One young man carried a haunch of glith. A slightly bigger girl brought out a skin of water and poured it into the freshly swept ceramic trough that rested against the outside wall. The Elder himself greeted us, hurrying through the formula and signaling for others to take our weapons without waiting for us to surrender them, and he provided a quick explanation for our reception: "The High Lord told us to expect you tonight or tomorrow."

"Wait," I said, and pulled myself free of the two young people on either side of me. I looked around to find Keeshah nearer the water trough but still resting in a crouch.

*Thank you for waiting, Keeshah,* I said, and walked over to the water trough. I scooped up a double handful of water and offered it to him. He lapped up the water, and nuzzled my open hands. *And thank you, as always, for letting us ride.*

*Friend,* he said, with more meaning than the word can convey. He pressed his forehead into my midriff and then shoved me gently aside. *Thirsty.*

I directed the Fa'aldu to leave the meat in the other, empty trough, and we all went inside. I declined the Elder's discreet offer of an inner apartment, and joined Ligor in one of the travelers' cubicles. In the brief moments before I drifted into a solid, refreshing sleep, I reached out for the cubs.

They were struggling, along with their mother and Tarani, through the blinding dust storm that always prevailed in the highest reaches of the Zantil Pass. The cubs had made it through that nasty trip once, on the way *to* Eddarta, and I was glad to see that they were not afraid, now that the sand and wind were more familiar. They were no more comfortable now than on that first trip, however, and when they sensed my contact, their minds were full of complaint and restlessness and undirected anger. I soothed them as best I could, and promised we would all be together again soon.

Then I wished Keeshah good night, and slept.

Ligor and I roused ourselves in time to share the stew-and-bread luncheon meal that was served to all the travelers. The Elder came to us in the late afternoon to assure us that Keeshah had been given more meat and water (a formality, since the Elder probably realized that Keeshah himself had already let me know), and to bring a message their maufel had just received from Relenor. It was for me, from Tarani.

"I insist that you and your friend join the family for dinner, Captain," the Elder said when he had handed me the folded parchment. I accepted the offer for both of us and, after the

Elder had left the cubicle, said to Ligor: "I hope you didn't mind my speaking for you."

"No—that is, you eat with the Fa'aldu? And what did he call you—'Captain'?"

"Yes—" I began, puzzled. Then I realized what the problem was. "Oh. I guess I skipped a few details when I told you about the Ra'ira."

"I guess you did," he responded crustily. "The Fa'aldu?"

I shrugged. "To tell you the truth, I can't account for it. One Elder helped me shortly after I—uh—became Markasset, and the Fa'aldu have taken an interest in me ever since. Another one now knows the whole story, and the Fa'aldu have agreed to handle messages for us and forward any information they think we can use."

"The Fa'aldu . . . have agreed . . ." Ligor said, then shook his head. "Let that go for now. What about this 'Captain' business?"

"I told you about Thymas."

"Yeah, he's the son of the Sharith leader, right?"

"Right," I said, "and wrong. At his father's insistence, I was—um—installed as Captain of the Sharith before we left Thagorn."

"Uh-huh," he said, after a moment. "Got any more surprises?"

I laughed. "Not that I know of," I said. "But, then, I haven't read this letter yet."

"Well, get on with it," he grumbled.

I unfolded the parchment and read the graceful characters of Tarani's cursive script.

> *Dearest, I am sure you know that we made the Chizan crossing with much effort but little incident. As I write this, we prepare to depart for Thagorn. Come as quickly as you can, but beware Chizan. Worfit grows ever stronger. With love—Tarani.*

"Tarani wrote this from Relenor," I said to Ligor. "She'll probably be in Thagorn by tonight."

"I can hardly wait to meet this lady of yours," Ligor said, then stopped and frowned. "As I recall, Relenor and Thagorn ain't that close together. How can she make the trip that fast?"

"I *must* have left out a lot," I said, and told him about Tarani, and Yayshah, and the two remaining cubs. He grew increasingly restless as I talked, and suddenly jumped up and paced the length of the small cubicle.

"What's wrong?" I asked him. "Believe me, I wasn't trying to hide anything—"

He waved his hand sharply, interrupting me. "I know that. I just don't like what I'm feeling right now. Like I bought my way into a friendly *mondea* game and suddenly somebody upped the stakes. Like I thought we were playing for coins, and now I find out my life's on the line."

I looked him in the eye. "It always was, Ligor. I'm sorry if I didn't make that clear. You can still drop out if you like."

He snorted and slapped the wall.

"That ain't what I mean, son. Sure, I knew it was gonna come to a fight. But I thought, you and me and the lady and maybe that Thymas fellow against Ferrathyn. Rough enough prospect just like that. But now I see you"—he spread his hands—"you're more than just you, son. You got the friendship of the Fa'aldu—I ain't never heard of that happening before—and the leadership of the Sharith. Your lady's special, too, what with the sha'um and the Eddarta business, and the mindgift you say is so strong.

"What I'm trying to say is, I thought I was heading for a *fight*. I'm beginning to think of a word this world hasn't heard for generations, son. I'm beginning to think this fight is a fleabitten *war*."

He leaned against the wall, pushing at it with his arms. I stood up and put my hand on his shoulder, and he turned around.

"I ain't blaming you, son. Now I look at it clear, I should have understood it from the beginning. It just didn't hit me true before now."

"And now?" I asked, my voice rough. In the few short days I had been in Ligor's company, I had come to rely on him as a friend. I knew what he was suffering—he was confronting and resisting the same sense of destiny, the feeling of being part of something larger, that had followed me all through this world. I could not let myself persuade him to go on with me. I could not force myself to want him to quit. It was his decision. I waited for it.

"Now?" he echoed, and rubbed his face with one big hand. "Now I'm more scared, and Ferrathyn is more dangerous, and

what you're trying to do is more important. If you still want me
with you, considering how dumb I been about this whole
thing, I'm on your side till it's over."

I grinned and grabbed his arms. "Best news I've had in a
long time, Ligor. How about some dinner?"

# 11

I would have preferred to allow Keeshah to rest longer, but I
was beginning to feel the pressure of time again. The longer
Ferrathyn remained in Raithskar unchallenged, the more
thoroughly the influence of his mind would alter the attitudes
of the people of Raithskar. Our trek through the Zantro Pass
was all the harder for our being already weary when we
started.

The Zantil and Zantro passes were high mountain crossings.
With the dry valley which contained Chizan, they constituted
the only link between the eastern and western halves of
Gandalara. They formed a nearly straight line between the
Korchi Mountains to the north and an unnamed range to the
south.

It was my opinion that the Korchis were called "mountains"
simply by convention. As far as practicality was concerned, the
northern border of the passes might just as easily have been
construed to be a southerly extension of the Great Wall. I
supposed, because Gandalara existed on both sides of the
Korchis but Gandalarans had no knowledge of what lay beyond
their Walls, that the impassable areas of the Korchis had to be
something besides a Wall, and so were named mountains.

I had Markasset's memories to tell me that no one in
Gandalaran memory had tried to surmount the Walls. The
Ricardo part of my personality rebelled at that, and argued
that some areas of the southern Wall rose gradually enough to
permit some high exploration. The Markasset part saw the
steepness of the northern Wall and the dryness of the southern
Wall as impassable barriers. As Rikardon, I had Markasset's
memory of the fourteen-year-old boy crossing the Khumbar

Pass, and my own experience with the Zantil and Zantro, to confirm the suffering encountered at high altitudes.

*All in all*, I decided, as I trudged along beside Ligor and Keeshah in the Zantro, keeping my face covered with a dampened scarf, *it's no wonder Gandalarans have never tried to climb their Walls*.

Though winds were rare elsewhere in Gandalara, they were constant companions in the high crossings around Chizan. Each pass was a narrow, shallow valley with high points at either end. Once across the first high ridge, travelers walked through a continuous storm of sand and small rocks. The wind seemed to suck away what little air there was at that altitude, and air inhaled without some sort of filter made the lungs burn and labor even harder.

We were approaching the second high ridge, and beginning to relax in the knowledge that this part of the trip, at least, was almost over. Keeshah's mouth and nose were wrapped with a scarf, and he walked with his head down and his eyes closed. Ligor and I did the same. If the high passes had any redeeming feature, it was that there was little chance of getting lost in them. The ground fell and rose so steeply on either side that we could literally feel our way through without risking our eyes more than necessary. It was only when we encountered someone coming from the other direction that we needed our sight.

Keeshah did not waste energy on a growl; it was his mind that alerted me to the approaching party. I opened my eyes to mere slits and peered ahead. In the dusty murk, I could see the outlines of several people, wrapped against the whipping sand just as we were. They were already within ten feet of us; Keeshah's sense of smell was all but incapacitated by the atmosphere of the pass.

As custom dictated, I edged to the right side of the narrow channel, pushing at Keeshah's side and pulling at Ligor's arm. Instead of moving to the other side, as I expected, the shadowy figures veered toward us. This time Keeshah growled; his mind warned: *Danger.*

I reached for my sword, but I wasn't fast enough. Two men grabbed me, wrapping length after length of rope around me, immobilizing my arms. Muffled yelling beside me told me Ligor was being treated the same. A scream rang in my ear, and one of the men who held me jerked backward. I steeled myself against the ecstasy of the kill that washed over me from Keeshah's mind, and twisted frantically against the ropes that bound me.

Another pair of hands whirled me around and pushed me to my knees. A third person came up behind me, grabbed my chin, and pulled my head up. I felt the sharp chill of a knife blade against the skin of my throat.

"Tell him to leave us alone, or you're a dead man, Rikardon," said a voice I recognized.

"Worfit," I said, gasping. "You don't know what you're asking. Look at him! I can't control him now!"

Not even the swirling dust could hide the menace that was Keeshah. He crouched on the northern slope, a dark, still figure. The sinuous motion of his tail created small eddies of dust with and against the wind. A tattered tan scarf hung from his muzzle. Through it, his lips curled back to expose tusks and teeth. A low, skin-stirring sound came from him as he gathered himself.

Worfit moved the knife. I felt a sharp pain, and a warm trickle of blood. Almost immediately, the small wound began to sting from the scouring sand. "Suppose you try real hard."

Keeshah's growl became a roar as he shared the pain of the knife wound. I felt his rage, tasted his anticipation, shared his pleasure in letting the man's fear build.

I reached out to Keeshah with my mind, seeking the blended contact we had achieved often before. I pushed through the animal fury to touch Keeshah's intelligent consciousness. I was nearly too late; even as I reached him, the tensed muscles along the cat's haunches were on the brink of launching his mass at Worfit.

But I *did* reach him in time. We were together.

Keeshah understood.

The big cat settled into a wary crouch, his tail still lashing.

Worfit laughed, and snatched away the knife. The two men who held me pulled me to my feet and jerked me around to face Worfit. Behind him, I saw Ligor, held by two others, only his eyes visible through the scarf wrapping his face.

I shook my head from side to side, dislodging my own scarf. I shouted to make myself heard above the whining wind.

"Worfit, you've been nothing but trouble for me since the day we met," I roared at him. "What do you want? What drives you?"

"What drives me?" he shouted back, coming closer. "Let's just say you're a symbol, Rikardon." He stressed the name sarcastically. "You're a symbol of the so-called honest wealth that will flow across my gaming tables but won't invite me to its dinner table."

"And you couldn't get your usual revenge with me, is that it?" I shouted, a small part of me registering the absurdity of trying to hold a conversation in the Zantro Pass. "I never caught the gaming fever, and I paid my debts. And you couldn't touch me because of Keeshah."

"Not until I figured out how to use you against him," Worfit said, and laughed again. "But I have you now, Markasset or Rikardon or whatever fancy name you carry. Your sha'um may kill me eventually, but not until you're dead. And, my friend," he said, coming even closer, "your death will not come easily."

I could see his face clearly now. I looked into his eyes and found the real answer: obsession. Worfit was as obsessed with killing me as Obilin had been with sick desire for Tarani. What he was saying was absolutely true. It was worth his own death to see me die.

"You're insane," I said.

Worfit's face went grim, and he stabbed toward my side, the dagger in his right hand. I brought my knee up sharply against his wrist and sent the dagger flying. In the brief instant of his surprise, I threw my weight away from him, against the man on my right.

*Now, Keeshah,* I called.

I went down dragging both of my captors with me. Keeshah dragged off one of the men; I got to my feet and aimed a kick at the second man's head. He dodged, and scrambled, giving me time to shrug free of the ropes and draw Rika. He quavered a moment, then turned and ran eastward into the swirling dust.

Worfit had dived after his dagger and now leaped toward Ligor, with the obvious intent of setting up the same sort of bribe, based on Ligor's life.

Keeshah got there first, his bulk and his bloody muzzle between the roguelord and Ligor, who was still held by two of Worfit's men. Everyone became very still for a moment. Then Keeshah turned his head toward one of Worfit's men.

"No!" one of them shouted. "He's right, Worfit. You *are* crazy!"

"We can't spend your gold in the All-Mind," the other added.

They threw Ligor to the ground, turned, and followed the other rogue.

Worfit slowly, deliberately turned his back on Keeshah.

"I still win," he shouted. "You couldn't have done it without that sha'um. I figure that shows me to be the better man."

"How do you figure that?" I asked, circling down from the slope to face Worfit on the relatively even floor of the pass. "You couldn't have done it without—what? Five men?"

He made no answer.

"You think I stopped Keeshah because I was afraid for my life?" I yelled. "If you knew him, you'd know better than that. There's only one kind of logic that could have stopped him. He held back because he knew—

"He knew that I wanted you for myself.

"There are no extra men now," I said, moving toward him. "Keeshah won't interfere, no matter what—he has agreed to that." I drew my dagger, sheathed Rika, then drew the baldric over my head and tossed it toward Ligor. "The odds are even, Worfit. You against me." I had kept it in check all this time, the anger I felt because of the people who had died as a result of Worfit's persecution and petty envy. I let it surface now, and I believe Worfit saw it in my face, a look such as a sha'um might wear. "You're the one who set the stakes, Worfit. Now roll your mondeana in a fair game for a change."

Worfit grinned, and settled his thick body into a fighting crouch.

"You're a fool," he yelled. "It's still my game."

I saw what he meant immediately. Markasset had trained in fighting with all weapons, but he had excelled in sword work. Worfit, on the other hand, had learned his skills under life-and-death circumstances, and it was clear that the dagger was his chosen weapon. Only the element of surprise had allowed me to disarm him so easily.

Worfit tossed the dagger between his hands, feinting at me even as he grasped its hilt. His speed, the whirling sand, and the blurring tears stimulated by the sand all made it difficult to keep track of his movements.

None of that mattered. I was ready for the end of it, consumed with a rage that matched the roguelord's obsession. I *wanted* Worfit's life, even if it cost me my own.

We circled slowly, feinting and dodging, each gauging the other's skills. Suddenly Worfit lunged forward, his right hand drawn back for a killing body thrust, his free hand ready to grab my dagger wrist.

I threw myself under his rush, slamming my body against his legs and tumbling him. Through the noise of the wind, I heard him grunt as he fell, but he rolled and was up again before I could grab him.

Worfit shifted the knife to his left hand. I waited for him, and caught the blade of his dagger against my own. His right hand found my throat and squeezed, and for a moment I was eye-to-eye with his grimace of hatred. Then I brought my left arm up sharply and knocked aside the hand at my throat. Before he could reclaim the hold, I doubled my fist and delivered three short jabs into the side of his broad face.

The blows surprised him rather than hurt him. He jumped away, then darted back, caught my dagger wrist, and twisted my right arm over his shoulder. I saw the dagger in his left hand, ready to stab backward. I kicked at his heel, knocked him off balance, and fell over with him.

We hit the rough stone hard. Worfit dropped his dagger and grabbed my knife wrist with both hands. He slammed the back of my hand against the rock, over and over, until that spot of rock was dark with my blood and the pain forced my fingers open.

Worfit caught up my dagger and rolled his body over mine, forcing me to my back. He pinned my wrists momentarily with his powerful arms. He ducked his head toward my chest, then snapped it up. The crown of his skull crashed into my chin, jolting my head against stone. I felt myself start to go limp.

Worfit rolled off me and came up again quickly. He had a dagger in each hand and a knee across my throat. He was grinning.

*Help,* Keeshah offered, his eagerness and fear a living presence in my mind.

*No!* I ordered. *Leave him alone, whatever happens, understand?*

*Don't like,* his mind grumbled, the emotion far more powerful than its expression. *Agree.* Then he added a plea that gave me almost as much strength as our joining might have done: *Don't die.*

I lay there, panting, eyes and lungs stinging, and waited for the right moment. It came when Worfit lifted the daggers for the killing thrust.

I curled my lower body and slammed my knees into his side. Thrown off balance, he still executed the double knife stroke. One blade shrieked harmlessly against the stone. The other caught the side of my thigh in a long, deep gash that sent waves of pain through my body and a wave of fear—not mine—through my mind.

*Hurt? Help? We come?*

The cubs also sensed the pain caused by Worfit's dagger. Their mindvoices roiled and shouted in my mind. I fought against their fear. I pushed through it to achieve, with each of them, the momentary bond of deep understanding I shared occasionally with their father. They saw that their fear endangered me, and they withdrew to the edges of my consciousness. Their concern gave me new strength.

Worfit still had the daggers, but my hands held his wrists. We thrashed back and forth on the ground. The movement scraped and battered the wound in my leg. I let the pain feed my anger.

I allowed Worfit to push me to my back and sit astride me. He leaned his weight and aimed his strength against my braced arms. He was panting heavily, but grinning with triumph. His burly arms and wide shoulders gave him the advantage in a contest of strength.

Instead of trying to force his arms—and the daggers—out away from our bodies, I began to draw them down and in, toward the few inches of dust-blown space that separated our stomachs.

Worfit's grin faded, and mine grew, as he realized his mistake. By committing his weight against my arms, he had granted me control. Dropping the daggers would release any hope of advantage. Now he was the one who had to resist—not only my strength, great already in Markasset's young body and freshly honed by recent hardship, but the burden of his own weight.

"You thought Keeshah was my only strength," I said with a sneer. Our arms trembled in the space between our bodies. I twisted his wrists slowly.

"You bet on the wrong player, Worfit."

The daggers pointed at his belly. At the last moment, he tried to release the hilts—but it was too late. I bucked my body, jarred his tenuous balance, and drove the daggers hilt-deep into Worfit's belly.

## 12

Worfit's body slumped down on me, and I felt the heat of his blood on my belly. All my anger and all my strength drained away. I suddenly felt the pain of my wound, exposed to the scouring sand. My eyes, my skin, my body—and my mind—ached from the ordeal. I closed my eyes against the sand, but I knew I could never hide from the memory of the killing hate I had felt toward Worfit.

*First Obilin, and now Worfit,* I thought, grieving not for them, but for myself. *Will it be this way when I face Ferrathyn—no thought given to the greater good, to destiny, to self-defense? Only private, selfish anger?*

*Or is the anger part of the destiny?* I wondered. *Ricardo killed often during the war, but those people were faceless. With every mechanized means at their command, they were trying to kill me and my companions. There were ideals, true—but that was the business of the politicians. In the front lines, it came right down to numbers: every enemy soldier who died was one less rifle firing at me. The men beside me were my friends; the men opposing us were strangers.*

*In Gandalara, killing is more personal. Maybe the Ricardo part of me needs the anger to make it easier—even to make it possible. Maybe Rikardon should be grateful that it's necessary.*

Worfit, alone, felt as heavy as had the pile of vineh that had threatened to suffocate me outside of Raithskar. Lack of air and loss of blood made me light-headed, and in the darkness behind my eyes, it felt as if the ground trembled and reeled beneath me.

The weight vanished from my chest, and I opened bleary

eyes to see Ligor stooping over Worfit's body, which was rolling
limply away from me. I took a deep breath, and the searing
pain of the sand in my nose and throat jarred me back to
wakefulness.

Yet the world was still reeling.

In fact, Worfit's body was not rolling at all, but was resting on
its side. Blood was leaking out around the two dagger hilts,
and his high shoulder was rocking back and forth. The arm and
hand which were balanced across his torso were flapping
slightly.

Ligor was not stooping, but crouching and staggering, trying
to keep his feet.

I could not see his face clearly through the sand haze, but I
knew he was terrified. I knew, because Keeshah's terror was so
intense that, as if he were a child running to a parent's arms for
protection, his mind slammed into mine with thoughtless
force, and Keeshah and I blended.

*Powerful muscles, bunched at shoulders and haunches.
Claws out, can't hold, scraping across rock. Fur lifting, ears
pulled tight against head. Sand hurts, can't smell, can't see.
Ground moves. Shift one way, need to shift again. No control.
Nothing the same. Nothing sure. Danger. Can't protect.
Danger. DANGER!*

I fought Keeshah for control of our blended thoughts and
emotions, but I made slow headway. His panic had brought me
understanding, and with it came a panic with a different
basis—which restimulated his.

*Earthquake. Bad one. We're in a steep-sided, rocky valley.
There'll be avalanches, new chasms. Even if we survive the
quake itself, the passes could fill in and we might be trapped
here for good. We could die here. We've got to get out. WE'VE
GOT TO GET OUT!*

*Can't move. Ground crazy. Afraid.*

*Got to move. Save us!*

*Can't.*

*Have to.*

*Afraid.*

*Me too. Help . . .*

*Yes.*

Keeshah's teeth closed on the cloth of my tunic. He hauled
me up to my feet. It was an odd, surrealistic sensation, being
physically separate but mentally together. We felt, equally, the

pain of our gashed leg muscle trying to support our weight and the airy, exposed sensation along the length of our fur-fluffed tail. Panic chittered away inside us.

I fell across Keeshah's back as he crouched. He surged to his feet as I struggled to straighten myself around. He/we were on the verge of taking off when I/we remembered Ligor.

I wrenched myself free of the blend and said: *Wait.*

Now I could feel Keeshah's panic both through our link—thankfully, not as intensely as when we had been blended—and from the tension and trembling in his body. But he held his place, and I looked around, blinking against the sand, for Ligor.

Just as I spotted him, another tremor shook the ground. The valley floor cracked right down the middle from the strain, and with a tooth-tormenting shriek of stone grinding against itself, the side of the valley on which we stood shivered upward, rising several inches above its previous level.

Keeshah and I rode out the upheaval in terror. Ligor was closer to the edge of the shelf, and the violence of the splitting rock knocked him over. He landed on his back and went limp.

Another shock hit, and the other half of the valley floor moved away from us, groaning like a million creatures in pain. On both sides of the valley, large chunks of rock were shaken loose and began to bounce down the walls.

*Now, Keeshah. We've got to get out of here NOW!*

Somehow, we made it to Ligor and got his unconscious body face-down across Keeshah's shoulders. Then Keeshah ran as he had never done before. Laboring for his every breath at this high altitude, dodging a veritable avalanche, stumbling and staggering when the ground shifted, he carried both of us over the high crossing—what remained of it on our side of the still-growing chasm—into the Chizan Valley.

It looked as if the entire Chizan passage were splitting apart. The break seemed to be a little south of center. We had been fortunate to be on the northern, larger side in the narrow Zantro Pass. On the wider floor of the Chizan Valley, as the aftershocks diminished in strength, we were relatively safe from the falling rocks that rained over the area closer to the northern wall.

Keeshah's mind was still in a panic when his body started to give out. He slowed and staggered, gasping for air with a horrible rattling sound in his chest. My own panic eased up as I felt the strain he was suffering, and I ordered him to stop. He stumbled on. I slid my leg over his hindquarters and slumped off his back, dragging Ligor with me. When the weight left his back, Keeshah surfaced from the fog of fear, paused and turned back.

*You have to rest,* I told him. *We're as safe as we can be, right here. Rest.*

I had the feeling that he complied more out of necessity than choice, but I could also feel his trust in me overcoming his fear as he collapsed to the rocky valley floor. The awful sound of his panting eased, even as I lowered Ligor to the ground and flung myself down beside him.

I could feel the ground shivering underneath me. It seemed less an aftershock of an earthquake than a human reaction to the quivering pain that follows recognition of a severe injury. As Keeshah's breathing slowed, I felt the turmoil in my mind recede, and calmness crept in with an irresistible coolness. It was not that I felt safe. It was only that I felt *safer* than I had a few moments earlier, and that small sense of security was enough to let my battered body claim its turn for attention. I tied my desert scarf over the bloody gash in my leg. Then I passed out.

I woke with a start that set the pain in my leg ringing. I groaned and sat up, looking around for Keeshah and Ligor. They had not moved, and I wondered how long I had been out. I rolled over and examined Ligor. He had a lump on his head, but he was breathing all right, and there seemed to be no bones broken. As far as I could see he and Keeshah were just resting.

*Like I should be doing,* I thought. *The ground's quiet; even the avalanches seem to have stopped. What woke me?*

As there seemed to be nothing in the physical environment that would have disturbed me, I looked inward—and found the awareness of the cubs crouching and whimpering in distress.

*Koshah, Yoshah,* I called to them. There was no reaction.

*Damn!* I swore to myself. *I never gave a thought to them or how they would be affected by my panic. I must have given them a hell of a scare.*

I forced myself to be calm as I reached out to them again.

*Kids? I'm here, I'm okay. Answer me—Koshah? Yoshah? Hey, it's all right.*

Only it was very much *not* all right, as I learned when I finally broke through the wall of fear that surrounded them. I was touched by their joy as they became aware of me. There was also a sense of relief, but not, as I had expected, from terror *I* had inspired. They were suffering from their own terror, which had been compounded as they had reached to me for comfort and had found me inaccessible and as frightened as they were.

I learned all this in the moment it took for us to reopen our conscious link, and I was busy for the next few minutes trying to calm them. I felt from them the same kind of all-consuming doubt of their environment that had swept through Keeshah during the earthquake.

*All of Gandalara probably felt that shock,* part of my mind thought, while I was soothing the cubs and trying to explain what they had experienced. *And as far as I can tell from Markasset's memories, it's a new experience for everybody.*

*Better now?* I asked the cubs, and received a shaky affirmative from the male. *Yoshah?* I prompted, and finally let myself ask the questions I had been holding back until they were calmer. *Is your mother all right? Is Tarani all right? Where are you?*

*In house,* she answered, meaning the house specially built outside Thagorn for Tarani and me. *Woman, mother gone. Mother said stay.*

Along with the concept of "stay" came a flash of memory: Yayshah, with Tarani riding, whirled back from the edge of the clearing which surrounded the house. The brindled female snarled and slapped Yoshah clawlessly, driving her and her brother back into the clearing. With a final growling comment, the female had carried Tarani off toward Thagorn.

*I may not be a sha'um,* I thought, *but I think I'd get the message to "stay" too.*

*Go after?* Koshah asked hopefully.

*No, you follow your mother's orders and stay near the house. Understood?*

*How long?* asked Koshah's mindvoice, sounding petulant. It was hard to imagine the fear I had sensed from him only moments before.

*They don't really understand what I've told them about the earthquake*, I thought. *They just know that I understand it, and that's enough for them. That means they either trust me completely, or they figure anything I can understand can't really be worth worrying about.*

\*Trust,\* came Koshah's mindvoice, surprising me. I had not realized that I was developing the same quality of rapport with them as Keeshah and I shared, and that they could occasionally follow my thoughts when we were in close contact.

\*Thank you, Koshah,\* I said. \*Trust me now, and stay near the house. Hunt if you get hungry, but don't—I mean this—do not go into the main valley unless Tarani and Yayshah come back for you. I think they'll probably be back soon.\*

\*You come?\* Yoshah asked. \*Father come?\*

I started to reassure them, but hesitated when it occurred to me that the other end of the Chizan passage had probably been badly hit by the quake, and I had no guarantee we could get through it. As I thought about the possibility, I sat up and looked westward as if I might be able to see, from a distance of some six mandays, whether the Zantil Pass was clear.

The horizons in Gandalara were strange in the high passes. The grayish rock edged upward until it met the grayish cloud cover, so that the demarcation was often more a matter of visible texture, rather than a color difference.

Not today.

North and west of us, the gray of the rocks stood out starkly against a black stain in the sky. The edges of the stain were leaking dark trailers into the soft gray of the cloud cover. At its center—as much as I could see above the high horizon—it rolled and tumbled like a storm cloud. I was sure that, from the right vantage point, I would see a column of the blackness rising straight up into the center of the stain. I leaped to my feet, fear driving out the pain of my wound for the moment.

I had walked in that cloud. Was it memory only, or newly created winds that brought me that sulfurous smell? I had come near to dying in it while it lay, idle and isolated, in the Well of Darkness.

The volcano had been rumbling then. Had it erupted because of the earthquake, or had its eruption *caused* the earthquake? Either way, the force of its eruption was spewing forth ash and noxious gases.

# 13

Somewhere to my left, Ligor stirred and moaned. I tore my eyes from the high darkness to the west, and stumbled to where he lay. I was relieved to see him come to full consciousness quickly.

"Got a fleason of a pain in my head," he growled, rubbing his neck lightly. "And a mighty thirst for a cool faen." He looked at me sharply. "Looks like you're the one needs help, my friend."

He tugged lightly at an end of the scarf, hanging free from the knot at my thigh. Pain shot through my leg, hip to ankle, and I dropped to the ground, feeling faint. Ligor pushed at me until I was lying flat and straight.

"I'd kill that fleason Worfit myself, if you hadn't done the job already," Ligor muttered. He removed the soiled scarf as gently as he could, but his every touch sent stinging fire through my leg. The word *infection* lodged in my mind, then *gangrene*, then *amputation*.

I passed out again.

I was alone when I woke up, with a nearly empty waterskin close to my right hand. Just seeing it made me thirsty, and I sat up.

At least, my mind did.

My body lifted head and shoulders, got very dizzy, and lay back down.

I struggled for a few seconds to get hold of the water pouch, then brought it to my lips and drank from it, lying down. The cool liquid cleared my head and, after a minute or two, I was really able to sit up.

The wound in my thigh was neatly bandaged. A length of cloth had been folded into a narrow pad and placed against the wound, then another had been tied, smooth and flat, around the thigh to hold the pad in place. My thigh ached dully and twinged when I moved about, but there was no more of the searing, stinging pain.

I sighed with relief.

Then I looked at the sky.

The black spot was spreading.

I began to feel faint again, looking at it. I lay back down.

*Keeshah, where are you?* I demanded frantically.

*Close,* he responded instantly and anxiously. *Well?*

*I feel better,* I told him. *Do you know where Ligor is?*

*Yes.*

I waited about fifteen seconds, and in spite of the fear and pain I felt, I was laughing to myself as I gave in: *Well? Where is he?*

Keeshah's response surprised me. It was . . . guilty.

*Man rides,* he said, *You need water, help. Man rode to city. Comes back. All right?*

A sha'um has only one Rider. Others may ride with the tolerance—and in the company—of the Rider. For the sake of my health, Keeshah had violated a trust to which he had been committed since Markasset had brought him out of the Valley of the Sha'um. Clearly, it was a possibility in his mind that I might be angry.

I was not angry.

I was amazed.

*Of course it's all right,* I told Keeshah. *I know it was a hard decision. I'm proud of you for it. Thank you.*

I felt Keeshah's relief just as he and Ligor appeared at the crest of one of the stony mounds that marked the center route of the Chizan passage. In a few seconds, they were beside me. Keeshah crouched, and Ligor stepped off his back to stand on the ground. As the sha'um stood up again to his full height, Ligor, who had half-turned in my direction, turned back to Keeshah. Hesitantly, he put his hand on the cat's jaw and stroked the fur back along the thickly muscled neck.

"Thanks, my friend."

Keeshah moved past the man, letting Ligor's hand trail along the whole length of his side. Then he moved off, jumped to the top of a miniature mesa of stone, and lay down.

"He says 'You're welcome,'" I said.

Ligor whirled around, then came over to me, grinning.

"Say, I'm glad to see you looking so alive," he said. "I was some worried about you." He knelt beside me and set down a packet wrapped in his neckscarf. The lower edge of his tunic was ragged and unhemmed—the source for my bandage. He helped me drink from his water pouch, then untied his scarf.

There was a fresh loaf of the nutty-tasting bread of Gandalara, some fruit, and a few strips of dried meat.

"Thank you," I said fervently, after I had eaten half of what he had brought. As he started in on the rest of the provisions, I looked at him carefully. His tunic was torn in several places besides its hem, and his face was bruised. "Wasn't easy to get, was it?"

Ligor paused in his eating, and looked suddenly afraid. He focused his attention on the food, and said: "Yeah, there was a bit of a fuss."

"Ligor," I said, "listen to me."

He looked up, alerted by the tone of my voice.

"I know how you found Chizan. Most of the city was built of clay brick; the earth movement must have shaken it apart. That means the water reservoirs are all broken, lots of people are dead or buried in rubble, and the unhurt ones are fighting for the food and water that can still be used."

Ligor looked startled, then glanced at Keeshah.

I shook my head. "No, I didn't see it through Keeshah's eyes—I was unconscious until just before you got back. I just know that Chizan is in total chaos because I've—well, it's logical."

I had been on the brink of saying that I had seen it before— but I had caught myself in time. *It would have been a lie, anyway,* I comforted myself. *Earthquakes may be a common part of Ricardo's history, but not of my personal experience. I lived in California and felt the earth shiver now and then, and I watched the television coverage of major earthquakes, but I was never actually exposed to the aftermath of a big one.*

*Well,* I thought, *it looks like I get my chance now.*

"Ligor, you know how important Chizan is to the people who need to cross through here. And you know the character of the people who settled here. Not exactly your natural leaders, would you say?"

Ligor snorted. "Not exactly your natural followers, either, I'd say. Folks looking out for themselves, mostly. It took somebody like Molik or Worfit to convince them that they could make more by working together than by cutting each other's throats." He took a drink of water, swallowed the mouthful of food he had been talking around, and squinted at me. "What are you getting at, son?"

"I want you to stay in Chizan," I said.

He was silent for a moment. "Me?" he asked. "Not us? You want a natural leader? I'd say you're it, boy."

"Have you looked at the sky lately?" I asked.

Ligor was sitting with his back to the east. I knew by the way he turned around immediately that he had already noticed the dark anomaly. With his back half-turned toward me, he said: "I should have guessed you'd know what that is. Just looking at it scares the fleas off me. I ain't sure I want to know any more about it." He turned back to me. "But then again, I ain't sure I just want to wonder, either."

I struggled for a way to present concepts which were totally alien to this man's—this race's—experience.

"It's poisoned air," I said at last. "It used to be in the Well of Darkness."

"Now, that's one place I never been, and never wanted to go." He paused, trying to understand. "You mean to tell me that the ground-shaking we felt went all the way over there and shook the 'darkness' into the sky?"

"I'd guess everybody felt that shaking, from Raithskar to Eddarta," I said. The words struck a chord somewhere in the depths of my mind, but the thought was ephemeral and vanished before I could grasp it. "It was more than just the shaking that drove the 'darkness' into the sky, but the shaking caused it."

Ligor twisted around to look at the eastern sky, and spoke with his back to me. "The shaking threw it up," he said. "But it ain't going to stay there, right?" He turned back to me. "And it ain't going to settle all peaceful back into the Well, right? Will it come over here?"

I shook my head, thinking: *Not unless there'll be a whole lot of shaking going on.*

The phrase was straight out of Ricardo's past, and I felt a wild urge to laugh.

*This is no time to get hysterical,* I told myself sternly. *The sooner you convince Ligor to stay in Chizan, the sooner you can let that responsibility go, and be on your way to Thagorn, and Tarani and Yayshah and the cubs.* Another inner voice said: *You don't even know if the Zantil is passable after the earthquake.* I took a deep breath and clamped down on the anxiety rising in me.

"That stuff is too heavy to go very far," I said. "But you're right—it won't settle back where it was. It will probably come down all around the Well—and bring a lot of smoke and ash and new poisons with it."

Ligor relaxed visibly. "Well, that's a relief, anyway. There ain't nothing around the Well to get hurt by it."

At first, I was appalled by the man's callousness. Then I realized that, unlike the Sharith, the minds of most Gandalarans did not turn first to the well-being of sha'um.

"The Valley of the Sha'um is close by the Well of Darkness," I said quietly. "I don't know how much danger the sha'um are in, but I've got to get over there and find out."

"You don't look real confident that they're safe."

"I'm not," I said. "In fact, I think they're all going to die—if not from breathing that stuff, then from starvation, because the animals they eat will die."

I had not tried to hide the thought from Keeshah. First, it would have taken a lot of effort. Second, it was not fair for the truth to be hidden from him. Third, it would not have worked, anyway.

Keeshah sensed my concern about his reaction, but he did not move from where he rested.

*Know already,* he assured me, with a calmness that puzzled me. *Ready to go.*

Ligor was staring at me, horrified. "But—son, what can you do about it?"

"Roughly a third of the Sharith sha'um are in the Valley right now. Normally they wouldn't come out for the better part of a year. But Keeshah left the Valley early for my sake. I'm hoping that other Riders will be able to call their sha'um out of the Valley. If some come out, maybe others will follow. But I can't be sure the Sharith recognize the danger. I've *got* to get over there—or at least try."

Ligor nodded sharply, signaling a decision. "And you don't need extra weight to hold you back. I understand, son—I'll stay behind."

I slapped my hand against the ground beside me, stirring up dust and provoking a satisfying sting in my palm. "Will you tell me," I nearly shouted, "why a man as competent and capable as you are would be ready to believe he's worthless?" Ligor stammered and scooted back from me, astonished by the outburst.

"Fleabite it, man," I said. "Don't you see that I can't leave Chizan in that state with a clear conscience? This passage is a river of life for both sides of Gandalara. Somebody has to take charge, get everybody to work together, clear the passes, salvage what water there is, arrange to get more. Sure, these people are rough. You know that better than I do—you know *them* better than I do. I could stay—yes, I could get the work done. But my heart wouldn't be in it, and it wouldn't be as easy for me as it will be for you.

"You came from among them, Ligor." I saw him flinch, and I hurried on. "As a vlek handler, you were part of the force that built Chizan and made it prosper. But you stepped out of that, and you've gained the habit and the manner of authority. Ligor, you can win these people, lead them, convince them that it's not just Chizan—all of Gandalara needs their help now."

Ligor stood up, walked away, came back and stood over me. "I got two questions," he said.

"So ask," I told him.

"You wanted me to come with you because of that fleason Ferrathyn. What help can I be if I'm in Chizan?"

"If you remember, I wasn't all that sure you could help in Raithskar," I reminded him. "There just seemed to be a chance. I don't think that chance outweighs the crisis in Chizan. If somebody with more on his mind than profit doesn't take charge here soon, the city will never function the same way it did before—as a supply source for travelers. Worse, the people may just fight over the remaining water and then die of thirst. I need you here, Ligor."

He nodded. "All right, you've got me convinced. Now you want to tell me how to convince them?"

I grinned. For that, I had an answer.

"Help me up," I said, offering my hand.

Chizan was even worse than I had expected. The upheaval in the earth had shaken most of the structures apart— including the top-of-building tanks that had held the only water available in the Chizan crossing. The water had drenched the city streets, reliquefying the crystalline deposits of vlek urine which lingered everywhere.

Keeshah balked at the outskirts of the city, his sensitive nose in mortal rebellion against the stink. I was catching it only lightly, but it wasn't just Keeshah's violent disgust that made my stomach want to roll over. The stink itself affected me, but not as much as the noise. We could *hear* the confusion in the city: voices crying out in search or pain or grief; vleks running, bawling, being cursed for being underfoot; bricks crashing from still-collapsing buildings or being thrown from piles of debris; and the solemn, firm sound of bronze blades clashing against each other.

Keeshah crouched; Ligor got down, and then took my arm to help me dismount. I wet my headscarf and tied it around Keeshah's muzzle. *Try to breathe through your mouth,* I told him. *I promise, we'll do this as quickly as possible.*

Ligor watched me work with the headscarf and then spend a few seconds scratching Keeshah's ears and stroking his neckfur.

"If I was a sha'um," Ligor said, "I'd be fleabitten before I'd take another step into that mess."

"He feels pretty much the same way," I said. "It's only his loyalty to me that makes him do something so much against his natural wishes." I looked over my shoulder at Ligor, and realized that I had never *spoken* the thought that had come so often to mind. "It's enough to make a man feel rich."

"Yeah," Ligor said, and I felt he really did understand what I meant.

"Let's go," I urged, and Keeshah crouched for us to mount.

Ligor and I rode Keeshah into the chaos that was Chizan. I think all three of us held our breath until we got dizzy. As people took notice of us, a crowd began to follow along behind Keeshah.

The people looked hurt in an especially moving way. Whether or not they carried bruises or bloody scrapes, there was a look of loss and fear in their faces that I will never forget. In the space of a few minutes, they had lost a way of life. They probably felt they had lost *everything* of value to them—and that's why they needed Ligor.

Chizan had formed a rough semicircle against the steep wall of the valley in which it lay. We moved through its perimeter toward the rich district that would have been the center of the full circle. We were fully prepared to break up fights and, if necessary, drive everyone we met toward the area in front of what had once been the seat of power in Chizan—a large gaming house that also contained the residence of the current roguelord—now the *late* roguelord. The wide avenue in front of that building offered the only possibility of addressing a large group of people.

The avenue was less wide now. The building had collapsed, its brick and wood debris covering a larger ground area than its original foundations.

Little persuasion was necessary. Most people followed us merely because there seemed nothing else of interest to do. Two men on a sha'um were an effective distraction. Fights quit as we passed by, and we led most of the living population of Chizan into the gaming district. Keeshah climbed an unappealing pile of rubble. I brought my right leg over Keeshah's neck and slid off to unsteady footing beside him, leaving Ligor mounted.

His speech was short.

"So you folks want to keep on fighting each other and getting nothing done, or you want to start to clean up this mess?"

From somewhere to our right, we heard the coarse voice of a woman. "For what?" she shouted. "So you can take over for Worfit? I say, fleabite this place. I'm going home to Dyskornis!"

There was a chorus of sounds, both in agreement and in scorn, from the rest of the crowd. I made a quick effort to count heads and came up with a rough estimate of three to four hundred people. I was sure I had heard no more than twenty voices. But as I looked, the vague expressions were leaving the faces of the people around me. The discussion was capturing their attention, forcing them to react.

"What makes you think Dyskornis is in any better shape?" Ligor shouted over the murmuring voices. "Or that you could get there if you tried? We were in the Zantro Pass when the shaking started: the Zantro split plain in half, and the walls collapsed inward. It will be gamer's luck whether anybody gets through there, ever again."

He paused, waiting for the murmur to crescendo into a roar of fear and confusion. It seemed that I had called it right—these people, totally ignorant of the real nature of this calamity, had assumed that only Chizan had been hurt by it.

There were no more vague faces now—just scared ones. Ligor lifted both arms, and the crowd gradually quieted.

"There's nothing we can do about the Zantro now," Ligor said. "Our business is to save what we can out of the buildings, help those who are hurt, and see about sharing the food and water we do have. Then we can send our strongest to the Zantro to find out if it's passable."

"What about the Zantil?" somebody shouted.

"Probably in the same shape," Ligor answered. "But we'll know soon enough if anybody can get through it." Because he couldn't ask Keeshah to crouch, he swung his leg across the cat's back, and slid down beside me. The rubble gave a little, and I caught his arm to steady him. "What are you doing?" I whispered.

"You want me to lead these folks?" he demanded in a whisper. I nodded. "Then give me room to do it my own way, son. If I need a sha'um to bring them into line, I ain't going to lead them for long."

He moved cautiously around me, to stand in front of Keeshah and face the crowd. "This here is Rikardon," he said.

I groaned inwardly, closed my eyes, and laid my head against Keeshah's side.

"I know you know the name, because Worfit would have moved the Walls to find this man and kill him. Worfit *found* Rikardon," Ligor said, and paused for emphasis, "in the Zantro Pass. Worfit's dead—as dead as the past of Chizan. I tell you that in case there's somebody out there thinks Worfit's reward still stands, and is stupid enough to value gold above water.

"Rikardon and his sha'um have to go west, through the Zantil. He'll be leaving just as soon as we quit this talking and start working to put things back together. If we see him again in a couple of days, we'll know the Zantil's blocked too. If we don't, we'll know it's clear.

"Now, you all understand that? Worfit's dead, Rikardon and Keeshah are leaving, and I'm staying. My name's Ligor."

The way he said his name, it was a blatant challenge, and it was a sure bet somebody would take him up on it. From close to the front of the crowd, a man shouldered his way out into the open. He was a big man, hard, with a sword scar where his right eye should have been.

"What makes you think you deserve to say what's what in Chizan?" he said. "Seems like one of our own ought to be the one who gives the orders."

"Seems to me one of your own should have been doing it already," he said, and stared the man down. For a heart-stopping few seconds, I thought the man was going to attack Ligor, but just as his arm twitched toward his sword, a scream rang out from the back of the crowd.

"Help, please help!" the voice cried. "My little boy—I found him, but he's trapped under all that brick. Somebody help me, please!"

Ligor looked at the man and pointed in the direction of the voice.

"There's your first assignment," he said. "Pick six men, tell them each to find five others, and spread your teams over the city to search the rubble for people who may still be trapped." The man hesitated, and the distraught mother wailed again. "What's your name?" Ligor asked.

"Hiben," the man growled.

"Do it, Hiben," Ligor said. "You got a quarrel with me, we'll settle it when things are back in order."

Hiben decided. He slapped his half-drawn sword back through his baldric, turned, and marched through the crowd, calling names as he went. The crowd closed in behind him and the men he took with him, and people came forward eagerly, asking for help or direction. In the space of a bare half hour, Ligor set up teams to build a water reservoir, locate and gather food, set up a first-aid station, corral the vleks, and begin clearing streets. Then he told the rest of the people to go to their own homes, salvage what they could, and come back in two hours to take a turn on one of the teams.

When everything had been set in motion, he turned to me. I reached out and took his hand in both mine. "I'm sorry to leave you like this, Ligor. There's no telling what your resources are—"

"We'll manage," he said. "And for what it's worth, Rikardon—thanks for convincing me. Feels like I'm doing good here."

"Better than I could, my friend," I said.

He grinned. "I know better than that, my friend, but thank you all the same. Keep that wound clean, and take care of yourself."

# 14

When Keeshah and I had escaped the revolting miasma of Chizan, I dismounted and rested while Keeshah did his own version of rounding up vleks. I lifted the water pouch beside me and wondered, suddenly, where Ligor had found water to fill the pouch on his earlier visit to Chizan.

*I didn't see a single reservoir intact*, I thought. *But he must have found one, at least, not entirely shattered.* I hefted the water pouch. *I wouldn't wonder that I have a majority of Chizan's water supply with me*, I thought, and felt a twinge of guilt. Then I saw Keeshah on a rise of land some hundred yards from me, running with a long, loping stride, stretching himself easily to cross a gap or mount a ridge in the rocky ground.

He was scouting, not yet hunting, and the sight of him stirred a tactile memory in chest and thigh of being astride him while he ran. A deeper memory stirred, and I slipped into a daydream version of *sharing* such a run with the big cat, our minds blended so that I felt his strength and sureness, and my pleasure compounded his joy.

I might have reached out for Keeshah then, for a true sharing rather than merely the memory, but I resisted. Instead, I cast my thoughts back to the time when I had been without him, when he had answered the call of his instincts and returned to the Valley to mate and continue his species. Until now, I had avoided any close examination of that time, for I remembered only a shadow of the pain—confusion, loss, grief, loneliness. I let it sweep over me to drive away the guilt, and prepare me for what, even at best, would be an ordeal.

*Of all the beautiful things in Gandalara*, I thought, *the exquisite glass, the gifts of the maufel and the Recorder, the intricate dancing, the detail of parquetry and mosaic, the simple and basic dignity of these people—of all these, there is nothing more precious than the partnership of a Gandalaran and a sha'um. Ricardo had much in common with these people, but the friendship I've found with Keeshah is outside Ricardo's experience, unique to Gandalara.*

*I've got the feeling in my gut that Tarani hasn't seen the danger, even though she has Antonia's memory and knowledge. If I can't get to Thagorn, the sha'um in the Valley will die. The Riders linked to those sha'um will suffer worse than I suffered in Keeshah's absence. Even though our link seemed broken to me, Keeshah had submerged that conscious connection under an overwhelming weight of animal instinct. The Riders will truly lose their sha'um—* I shuddered. *I don't even want to think about it.*

*Nor do I want to think about the other sha'um who will have no Valley and no families to return to—no females. . . .*

I paused, stunned by a new and terrifying thought. *There are two females outside the Valley,* I reminded myself, *Yayshah and Yoshah. How often have I felt—have Tarani and I discussed—the sense of destiny we feel about Yayshah coming out of the Valley with us? Don't tell me—please, God, don't tell me—that part of that destiny was to ensure the survival of the sha'um after this disaster.*

I reached out for Keeshah. I sensed a mood of satisfaction, an aftertaste of both the hunt and the vlek—not Keeshah's favorite meal, but adequate when we both knew that food of any kind was the main necessity.

*Ready soon,* he told me.

I realized my heart was racing, and I was clenching the ground with my hands. I tried to relax.

*Sorry,* I said. *I didn't mean to rush you, Keeshah. I'm just . . .*

*Worried,* the sha'um finished for me, when I hesitated. *For others like me. Why?*

*The poison—* I began, then stopped to consider. Keeshah could, if he wished, share all my knowledge and understanding. Surely he knew what I feared, the consequences of the volcanic eruption so close to the Valley. *Why what?* I asked him.

*Why worry about others?*

I was still confused, so I went back to the beginning.

*Keeshah, you know the sha'um in the Valley may be in danger?*

*Know,* he answered, a little impatiently.

*Then why aren't you worried about them?*

*Female, cubs—not in Valley.*

*Wait a minute,* I exclaimed. *Is that what you were asking me—why should I care about the other sha'um when you and your family are safe?*

*Yes,* he answered simply, then paused for a moment. *Angry?* he asked. *Why?*

*I'm not angry, Keeshah—I mean, of course I'm angry, you couldn't be fooled about that, but I'm more surprised than anything. You share many of my thoughts and most of my emotions. I thought you would understand how I felt—why I feel that way—without asking.

*No,* I corrected myself. *That's wrong. What I thought— what I assumed—was that you feel the same way. But you don't.*

Somehow, that revelation hurt me terribly.

*If you don't care about the other sha'um,* I began, *why do you think I care about the other people? Why am I trying to keep Ferrathyn from hurting them?*

*Don't know,* he answered.

I did feel anger rising then. I recognized that it was a useless and an unfair anger, that the betrayal I felt was nothing more than the truth shining through false conclusions, but I felt it just the same.

*Then why have you helped me, carried me, followed me all this way?* I demanded.

*You want it,* he answered. *I help.*

*But you don't care about what I'm doing?* I demanded. *You don't believe that it is right, and necessary? You don't feel that it's our destiny to be doing this?*

*You want it,* he repeated, sounding confused. He obviously sensed that I also wanted him to say something he could not say.

I broke off our conversational contact and tried to calm the anger and indignation I felt. I struggled to set aside my misconceptions and see things from Keeshah's viewpoint in an unbiased way. The first puzzle that came to mind was—why was I so upset?

*Keeshah hasn't failed in his loyalty to me,* I reminded myself. *He has given me all the support I've asked for—far beyond what most sha'um are asked to give. What he hasn't given me is his approval.*

*Is it important for the general to have the approval of his troops?* I wondered. *Or is obedience far more important? Logic says the latter—but Ricardo remembers jungles and bullets and terror and death, and a churning despair over the value of it all.*

There was a turning point for Ricardo—me—in the early days of that war, a time when fear of the enemy outweighed fear of my own commanders. I had settled into a stinking piece of swamp with every intention of not moving until the war was over.

A Lieutenant, a boy not much older than I, found me in my funk and pulled me out of it. He told me what the unit was doing, and why—how it fit into the strategy of this attack, the entire Pacific war. I understood for the first time that other troops, on other islands, depended on our performance there—on my active participation in this battle. I got up, and I followed that man.

The area I had chosen for my stand had been overrun by the enemy less than an hour later. Had I stayed there, a bullet or a bayonet would have ended my indecision. No mere command could have moved me from that inertia, but the understanding given to me by that young officer was enough to get me going again. I followed him until a land mine killed him, and then I followed other officers. The vision he gave me of myself as a moving and important cog in the machine of strategy never left me.

*I guess that Lieutenant,* I thought, *has been sort of a model of leadership for me ever since. He may have been a kid, but he knew that men would fight harder, be less afraid, and be more likely to survive if they were treated like men instead of chess pieces.*

*I think that's what scared me when Dharak wanted to make me Captain of the Sharith,* I realized. *My image of good leadership is a man who knows, leading men who believe in and agree with him. At the "installation" ceremony, I felt that commitment from the Sharith with some embarrassment, because I had no clear purpose in accepting the position. Dharak would continue to perform the daily functions of leadership. I felt as if I were cheating and deceiving the Sharith. Even now, when my position makes it convenient for me to lead the Sharith against Ferrathyn, if necessary, I feel as if I would be using, not leading, them.*

It was like being struck by lightning.

*This is what it's all about!* I realized. *Not Ferrathyn—or, at least, not only Ferrathyn. It's the sha'um too. I'm meant to try to save them, I feel it as strongly as if someone had told me so.*

I looked up toward the Zantil, and remembered the falling rock and shaking ground from the Zantro.

*Try to save them,* I repeated. *Nature might have her own ideas.*

I could no longer see Keeshah, but I looked off in his direction, anyway.

*Keeshah, do you remember the day we rode through the Hall, with the Sharith saluting us?*

*Remember,* he confirmed.

*I remember it too,* I said. *The people were calling out to me, but the sha'um were roaring for you. The sha'um were responding to the feelings of their Riders, but they were showing their respect for you, not for me. You felt it then; I want you to remember how it felt.*

*Remember,* he said again. *Why?*

*I'm trying to explain why I feel a commitment to do what I've been doing.*

*Not need,* he said, puzzled, then repeated his earlier comment: *You want it.*

*It is necessary, Keeshah,* I insisted. *That's part of the explanation, anyway, to show you why I feel you have to understand. Will you listen, and try?*

*Yes,* he said, and I felt him decide to come back to me.

*No, Keeshah, stay there.*

*Why?*

*Because this is something I want you to learn and decide about with only your mind. If you come back here, close, I won't be able to keep from touching you, and then I'll never be sure whether you were persuaded by my reasoning or my ear-scratching.*

*Silly,* he said, but I sensed him settling to the ground on the other side of the low ridge that separated us.

*Thank you, Keeshah. Now keep in mind what you felt in the Hall, all right?*

*Yes.*

*I want you to think back to Dyskornis the first time we were there. Ronar came up to you, lay down, and exposed his throat.*

I felt the surge of savage joy that came to him with the memory.

*Yes, you felt victorious then, didn't you? Were you proud?*

*Yes,* he said, without hesitation.

*Did it feel the same as when the Sharith sha'um saluted you?*

He hesitated. *Not same,* he said, after a moment.

*What was the difference?* I asked.

Keeshah was quiet for a long while, struggling with the task I had given him. I felt a moment's fear that I was asking too much of him. His rationality had always expressed itself on a very real and literal level.

*One sha'um,* he began at last, *was beaten. Keeshah won honor. Other sha'um gave honor.*

*Very good, Keeshah,* I said, excited. *I'd say it a little differently, though. I'd say that the sha'um in the Hall did give you honor but that you won obedience from Ronar. Do you agree with that?*

*Yes,* he said. *Says better.*

Before this, he had been complying with my requests with a spirit of tolerance. I sensed from him now a genuine interest in what we were doing.

*Let's call what you felt with Ronar the pride of victory, and what you felt in the Hall in Thagorn the pride of respect. Okay?* He agreed. *Which kind of pride felt better?* I asked.

*Both good,* he answered immediately.

I groaned inwardly, and felt a desperate temptation to tell him the conclusions I was trying to make him find for himself. I resisted.

*You can tell that there is a difference between them,* I said. *Try to explain the difference, and one may seem to be better than the other.*

He spent a few seconds in thought, then reached out for me again. *Pride of victory easier to get,* he said.

It was my turn to be puzzled. I felt he was going in the right direction, but I'd lost track of the roadway.

*I don't understand what you mean,* I said.

*Fought one sha'um,* Keeshah said. *Proved better. Other sha'um—no fight, respect anyway.*

*That's called faith, Keeshah. The sha'um in Thagorn respect you because they believe—without your having to fight them to prove it—that you deserve their respect.*

*No,* he disagreed. *Respect me because Riders respect you.*

I couldn't argue with that. Instead, I went straight for the point I had been trying to make.

*Do you respect me, Keeshah?* I asked.

I was very pleased that he started to answer me with an "of course" kind of response, but then stopped to think about it more before he said anything.

*I know you love me, Keeshah,* I said gently. *But it's very important to me that you understand what I'm trying to do, and that you come with me because you believe in that—not just because you're loyal to me. Let me put it this way: if you help me just because you love me, it's like feeling the pride of victory, but if you help me because you believe in what I'm doing, it's like feeling the pride of respect.*

It was a lot to take in all at once, and I gave the cat some quiet time to consider. When Keeshah was ready, he spoke to me again. To my surprise, he challenged the analogy.

*Riders respect you,* he said. *Riders not here, never with you. They know what you do?*

*They know about it in concept, Keeshah, even though they haven't been with me all the way, like you have.*

*Concept,* he repeated, not referring to the word, but to the amalgam of impression and feeling that he got from me when I "spoke" the word to him. *What is concept?*

I was suddenly conscious of my hurt leg feeling stiff and sore. It gave me both physical and psychological relief to stand up and begin to walk at a slow and limping pace. I marked a fairly level path around a clump of boulders, put one hand on them for safety's sake, then put my body on "automatic" while I concentrated on Keeshah's question.

*Concept is a general idea for a specific thing,* I said, and searched for an analogy within the cat's experience. *You and I can talk, mind to mind. That's a specific thing. Because we can do it, we understand that other Riders can talk to their sha'um the same way. That's a concept.*

I rushed on, in anticipation of the very literal cat's next question.

*It can work the other way too,* I said. *Thanasset taught Markasset the concept of the Rider-sha'um link before Markasset had actually experienced it. Markasset had the concept and went to the Valley to get the specific thing.*

He was silent.

*Can you think of another example?* I asked.

*Went to Valley wanting any female,* he answered promptly, surprising me. *Concept. Found female, cubs born. Specific thing.*

*Exactly right,* I said, excited by sharing Keeshah's struggle to master some very difficult ideas.

*Riders know concept of what you do, not specific things,* he said. *Keeshah knows specific things, not concept. Must learn,* he said emphatically, but I was not sure whether he meant he was insatiably curious about it, or he was rephrasing what I had said—that I needed for him to understand. *What is concept of what you do?*

Oboy, I thought. I asked for this.

*When you went back to the Valley, Keeshah,* I began, *you felt a drive to find a female, mate, produce young sha'um.*

*True,* he acknowledged.

*That's something called 'instinct,'* I explained. *Every creature has it, an inborn need to continue his own species. He doesn't think about it or plan it, he doesn't make a decision that his kind is worth preserving—the instinct is just there, and he follows it. He preserves the existence of his species.*

*Among men, there is another level of existence—not just living, but a way of living together. It's called 'society.'*

My foot came down on a slant-topped rock and slipped. I caught myself, cursed inwardly at the pain, but hardly noticed what I was doing.

*Most of the time, a man doesn't choose his society, any more than he chooses that he will be born a man and not a sha'um. As he grows, he learns about his society and how to survive in it. It is an important part of his life—so important, in fact, that he begins to feel something like his instinct to preserve his species. The continuation of his society is almost as important to him—with a difference.*

*Birth is the only way to continue a species,* I said to Keeshah, sensing that his attention was still totally focused on the effort to understand. *But society is a complex, intricate structure, formed and preserved by mutual need and human choice.*

*A man may look at the society into which he was born, and decide that the best way to preserve it is to change it. If other *people agree, the society changes. If they do not agree, a man either learns to live with it, or leaves that society for a different one. That is another way of change, but it works only for that one man. I believe that every man has a right to be part of a society, and an obligation to think about it and try to change it if he thinks it needs changing.**

I paused. *Keeshah, are you understanding this?**

*Think so,* he replied. *Keeshah left Valley with Markasset. Did last thing.**

Keeshah's already using example and analogy like a pro, I thought. As much as I respect and admire him, I think I've been underestimating his intelligence. The thought sent a thrill of hope through me. Maybe the sha'um in the Valley really do have a chance.

*That's right, Keeshah,* I encouraged him. *The sha'um have a society too. It's centered around the instinctive need to preserve the species. You and Yayshah both made the choice to leave sha'um society and join ours—for which Tarani and I are very, very grateful.**

*Glad too,* he said. *You want to change society?**

Back to the original question, I thought. What the hell am I really trying to do?

I discovered my leg was hurting, so I leaned against one of the boulders and let myself slide down it into a sitting position, sighing as I went.

*This part is harder to explain, Keeshah,* I said. *A man in Raithskar is trying to change society, and I don't agree with the change he wants to make. I'm trying to stop him, to keep things as they are.**

Not precisely correct, I realized. Tarani and I have already wrought considerable change. But—for the purpose of this discussion—close enough.

*Said any man can change,* Keeshah reminded me. *Why not him?**

*This is where the faith comes in, Keeshah,* I said. *When I talked about changing society before, I meant a man telling people his ideas, getting them to agree with him and to work with him to change things. Any man has the right to expose people to new ideas and invite them to choose his idea over another one.

*The man in Raithskar isn't offering people any choice, Keeshah. He is using a special power to force people to make *the changes he wants, to trick them into thinking they have chosen his way over their own. I think that's wrong, and I think the changes he wants to make are wrong. Everything I have done—even though I didn't know it myself for a long time—has been aimed at preserving for the people of Gandalara the right to choose their own society.*

*The Sharith didn't know that when they agreed to follow me,* I admitted. *But they knew that some kind of change was beginning to happen, and not knowing what it was made them nervous. I was already investigating that change, and they essentially said, "Do it for us too." They have faith that whatever I've done or plan to do is something they will agree with.*

Just expressing that to Keeshah made me feel the complicated mixture of pride and humility I had felt on the day the Riders had acclaimed me Captain.

*Pride of respect,* Keeshah said, as much responding to the feelings he had sensed in me as to the logical connection throughout our conversation.

*Understand what you do for men,* Keeshah said. *Sha'um not your society. Why worried?*

*You are a part of my society,* I said. *You, and all the other sha'um in Thagorn, have chosen the society of men over that of sha'um. You and Yayshah have proved that sha'um can survive entirely in the society of men, but right now you have the Valley, and the sha'um there, as an alternative society if you want it.*

*Consider, Keeshah—if all the sha'um in the Valley are destroyed, Yayshah and Yoshah will be the only female sha'um alive. Your species will survive, through them—but two societies will suffer. The sha'um will lose their first society, the one they were born to and still feel called to. The Riders will lose the sha'um.*

*Now any Sharith boy of a certain age who wants to, can try to find a sha'um friend, as Markasset found you, because many cubs are born each year. If the Valley sha'um are destroyed, there will be no new cubs until Yayshah has more and Yoshah is of mating age.*

*The Sharith have built their society around the sha'um, Keeshah,* I said. *And the Sharith society is part of the greater society of Gandalara. I know how much a man gains by sharing his life with a sha'um. I want to make sure other men have a chance at this special kind of friendship.*

*Sha'um need too,* Keeshah said. *Society of men different. More. Friendship good.* He thought a moment. *Sha'um stay in Valley. Society dies,* he said. *Take sha'um from Valley. Society dies too.*

*You're probably right,* I said. *Part of the basis for the society in the Valley is its isolation, plentiful hunting, and probably, after so long a habit, the periodic return of the Thagorn sha'um. There is no other place like the Valley in Gandalara. Moving the sha'um may save the individuals, but it will change the society, and effectively destroy the society of the sha'um.*

*So, why not direct that change toward something we already know is good, and workable? I want to take the sha'um to Thagorn, Keeshah. Family units can settle in the hills around Thagorn, if there isn't enough room in the Valley with the Sharith. The two sha'um societies can blend into one, and the Sharith can be part of it.*

*But I do need your help, Keeshah. Not just getting me to Thagorn in time to help the sha'um, but understanding and agreeing. It's not fair for a man to make a decision for the sha'um.*

*You were right when you said the Thagorn sha'um honored you because their Riders were honoring me. I happen to know that you deserve that respect on your own merits, but I can't say for sure that they understand that. But no matter how it got started, the fact remains that those sha'um do feel a special respect for you. In my book, that makes you Captain of the sha'um, and gives you the same kind of decision power and approval that I have.*

*On behalf of the society of men in Thagorn, I want to save the sha'um in the Valley. I know that, as my friend, you would take me to the Valley and let me try. I can't accept that, because I have no right to make that decision alone. The only way this will work is if you, on behalf of the society of sha'um in Thagorn, go with me to the Valley and help me because you believe we're doing the right thing.*

I felt exhausted. *I wasn't this tired after running across the Strofaan Desert,* I thought. *Thinking is hard work.*

*Well, Keeshah?* I prompted, feeling a tremor of fear. *What do you think?*

I heard the scratch of claws against rock above me, and the boulder against which I was sitting vibrated slightly. That was the only warning I had that Keeshah was so close before he jumped down to the ground in front of me. Was it my imagination, or was there a new expression on his furred muzzle, a difference in the way he held his head? I would have sworn that the gold-flecked gray eyes held a new depth, a more expressive warmth.

*Save Valley sha'um,* he said, lowering his lean but massive body into the mounting crouch. *Hurry.*

# 15

The trip through the Zantil was a nightmare of pain and frustration. Like the Zantro, it had been split in half, and rock had rained down from the walls into rubbly mounds that needed to be climbed or cleared away. The wind picked up the smallest rocks to make the scouring sand more potent. The footing was unrelievedly treacherous, the wind blinding, the clearing work exhausting in the thin air.

I rode when the pain in my leg demanded it, but I was always fearful that Keeshah would misjudge his footing and hurt himself falling into the rubble. So I walked as much as I could, testing the mounds for stability myself before I would allow Keeshah to follow me. He resented my caution, but acceded when I pointed out that *he* could carry *me* if *I* got hurt.

It was a long, long eighteen hours before we reached Relenor, the Refreshment House that rested at the foot of the western entrance to the Zantil. I could not even call out the formal request for shelter, but I discovered I had no need to. Tarani had asked the Fa'aldu to watch for me. The cloth barrier had fallen, and the Elder and several young men were rushing out the gate, before I had even let myself roll off Keeshah's back to the ground. Strong hands caught me up; concerned faces swam before my draining consciousness. I had time to

say only one thing: "Don't let me sleep more than four hours."
Then I let myself pass out.

When I first became aware of Lussim's hand on my shoulder,
my inner awareness told me that the Elder had followed my
instructions; it was just four hours since I had arrived. I knew
by the feel of the pallet beneath me that I was in the part of the
Refreshment House reserved for the Fa'aldu themselves.
Something was different, though—and I finally identified what
it was. It did not feel as cool as usual.

Lussim's hand shook me again, and I opened my eyes. Part
of the roof was missing, and heat streamed into the room,
diminishing the insulation provided by the salt-block walls of
the compound.

"Forgive me, Rikardon," he said as he helped me sit up,
"but you did say—"

"I know, Lussim. Thank you." I looked at him closely. He
seemed older, and very tired. "Was there much damage?" I
asked.

"This room," he said, "is the only one with any roof
remaining. Some of the walls have fallen too. But we are
managing," he said, and reached behind him to a small table.
He handed me a ceramic bowl, its workmanship damaged by
ugly chips but its contents giving off the wonderful smell of
*rafel*, the porridgelike stew that was a staple Gandalaran dish.
"Eat, my friend," he said, even as I was taking the bowl from
him. An eating utensil—a cross between a fork and a spoon—
was standing in the thick stew, and I began to eat hungrily.
Lussim turned back to the table, unstoppered a pitcher, and
poured water into a drinking cup. He set the filled cup back on
the table, out of my easy reach, and put the pitcher down
beside it, looking embarrassed.

"I hesitate to ask, Rikardon, for I know your need is great,
but I would ask that you take no more water than you truly
need. Our reserve of water is lost, and our production slow."

"Of course, Lussim," I agreed. "I would ask Keeshah the
same," I said, smiling, "but it is never his habit to take more
than he needs."

"His need was so great that he accepted water from us," the
Elder said. "He sleeps now in the shadow of the gate." He took
something from his pocket, and laid it beside the drinking cup.
"From the lady Tarani," he said. "It came with her warning to
watch carefully for you." Then he turned and left the room.

He was barely out the door before I snatched up the folded paper and opened it. It was scrawled, written hurriedly. It said:

> *Rikardon—*
>
> *If you read this in good health, then I beg you to come to Thagorn as quickly as you can. The Riders are plagued by an illness which finds no cure in my healing skills. Thymas is leading the Sharith toward restoring the fallen buildings, but is helpless against this strange malady.*
>
> *You are needed here, my love, for the sake of the Sharith and for the comfort of the High Lord. I shall not rest well until I know that you have survived this calamity.*
>
> > *Love,*
> > *Tarani*

The note both warmed and chilled me. Tarani's expression of concern was like a caress, and I became conscious of every single one of the days which had passed since we last had been together. Her brief mention of Thymas brought me relief from a worry I had not recognized. I was glad to know he had not been hurt by the upheaval, and more glad to hear that he had taken charge in Thagorn.

Taking charge was the duty of the leader of the Sharith, but Thymas had come only lately to the role of Lieutenant, and in a somewhat unnatural way. His father, Dharak, had been shocked into a catatonic state by the early, unexpected departure of his sha'um, Doral, for the Valley. I felt some responsibility for Thymas's position because Doral's leaving had been stimulated by the presence of Yayshah in Thagorn.

Though Thymas was young, and he and I had started out with enmity between us, I had come to respect his strength and basic goodness. Yet I knew he had private doubts about his own ability to lead, and the knowledge had translated into a subconscious fear that he would collapse in the crisis of the earthquake.

I felt better knowing he was handling the normal by-products—damage, confusion, shock—of the earthquake.

I felt worse knowing that all the by-products were not normal. *Illness?* I wondered. *And she said, specifically, "Riders"—not "Sharith." It has to be connected to the sha'um.*

*Ah, Tarani, forgive me for feeling smug, in the past, over my bond to Yoshah and Koshah. I'd give the world, right now, if they could speak to you, too, so that we could talk to each other through them.*

There was no sense in wishing for something I could not change, so I finished the bowl of food, drank only the cup of water Lussim had poured for me, then stood up and tested my leg. The Fa'aldu had cleaned and dressed the wound while I slept, and had left me wearing only a pair of the drawstring undershorts. Fresh clothes were laid out for me on a shelf, however, and resting on the floor were my own soft leather boots, dusted and brushed. Putting on the clean clothes helped to dispel the deep weariness that had settled in my shoulders and back, and I left the room feeling more refreshed than I would have thought possible.

This room, like the one Tarani and I had occupied at Iribos, opened directly into the family courtyard. I stepped out into the light, and stopped, staring. I had always been aware that the walls of a Refreshment House encompassed much more area than I had seen from inside, and I had always understood, implicitly, that the area hidden from me contained the secret of the Fa'aldu, the way they produced water, seemingly from the desert itself. The shaking earth had destroyed three rooms in the center of the innermost courtyard wall, and through the gap I saw their closely guarded secret.

I saw flashes of movement as men passed across the breached wall, stretching and tying a huge, semirigid sheet made of tanned and closely stitched hide. It filled an area nearly as large as the courtyard itself, and formed a tentlike structure, slanting from a rounded high point about ceiling-high to salt-block anchors the height of a man's waist.

*Well, I'll be damned,* I thought. *A still. That explains a lot of things. Why the Fa'aldu compounds, both the family and the visitor courtyards, are always so clean. The vlek waste gets dumped into the bottom of that still with all the Gandalaran-produced garbage—and body waste, too, I'd imagine. The last drop of moisture is baked out of it, rises with the hot air into that domed area, condenses, and drips into some kind of cistern. Slow—but steady enough, I guess. Lomir said they had reserves set aside, so they must gain back slightly more water from their visitors than they serve.*

A man moved away from the opening in the wall, and a flash

of pale green caught my eye. *Grain?* I wondered. *In the middle of the desert? Oh—of course, that dehydrated waste would be perfect compost. After years of tilling and mixing, the once-sandy ground around the still is probably ideal growing soil by now. They give the grain just enough water to grow, grow and harvest just enough grain to feed the family, and then contribute the husks and stalks to the still. Neat,* I thought, appreciating the cleanness and wastelessness of the cycle.

A hand touched my shoulder, and I turned to find Lussim beside me. He peered at me narrowly. "I believe you understand what you are seeing, Rikardon." There seemed little point in denying it, so I nodded. "I—I would like—May I know?"

He was struggling mightily against the ages-long, mind-your-own-business tradition of the Fa'aldu, but he was losing the battle. I helped him as best I could.

"No Fa'aldu has shared your secret with me, Lussim," I answered his unspoken question. "You know that I . . ." It was my turn to hesitate, but he only watched me expectantly. For some reason, I was reluctant to speak the lie again that I was a Visitor from an earlier time in this world. Yet I was not ready to confront this crisis-weary man with the truth, either. "I have not always lived in this time," I said, finally. "I have memories, and knowledge that I can't quite account for."

His hand tightened on my shoulder. "I had no fear of your silence, my friend. But I am relieved to know that no one here was so distressed by this disaster as to forget himself entirely. Come, I have your provisions ready."

I resisted taking the half-filled water pouch, but Lomir insisted. Keeshah had eaten well, and was deeply asleep when I reached out for his mind. He roused quickly, however, and was waiting for me outside the Refreshment House gate. Lussim returned Rika to me with as much ceremony as he had done before falling salt blocks had left the top of the compound wall looking like an irregular sine wave. I accepted it in the same manner.

*After all,* I thought, *it's not the home that makes the man.*

The path from Relenor to Thagorn took us south of the Well of Darkness, and in the flat bed of this desert, the column of blackness that fed the gray stain was clearly visible. I had hoped that the volcano would be content with one explosive cough, and that the poison inside it would rise once, settle again, and be done with it.

I had known it was a slim hope. The violence of the quake had been evidence that the volcano was doing more than throwing a quick tantrum. The curling black column confirmed my worst suspicions. I knew what must be happening at the bottom of what had once been called the Well of Darkness. A fissure had opened, and molten rock was forcing its way out, releasing a noxious mixture of gases. However, the pressure pushing those gases seemed less; the column rose to a height, now, that I was sure I would not be able to see from the Chizan Valley.

That was the good news.

The high cloud I had first seen had mostly dispersed; only a small amount of the airborne sediment could have been carried across the high mountains which cupped the Well of Darkness against the Great Wall. This lower cloud would spread no farther than those mountains, and settle in a relatively contained area.

That was the bad news.

The Valley of the Sha'um lay well within the area I guessed would be affected by the volcanic fallout. I had a queasy feeling such as might be caused by breathing air infected by the cloud north of us. But I knew what caused it. Dread.

Keeshah felt it, too—not just my fear but his own. Our conversation in the Chizan Valley had changed something essential about the big cat. I felt him questioning, as well as sensing. I felt him actively probing to find the reasons for my concern, to touch my mind as well as my feelings.

And I felt him understand.

It was night when we reached Thagorn. The flat desert, though cracked and humped by the force of the earthquake, presented much easier terrain for Keeshah than we had found in the high crossings. He had run from Relenor at a steady pace about one notch higher than was comfortable for him, so that he was panting heavily as we approached the little house, south of Thagorn, which Thymas had built for Tarani and me.

I had called ahead to the cubs, and had been surprised by their joy at hearing me so close. They had seen neither Tarani nor Yayshah since their mother had given them such explicit orders to stay put, just after the earthquake. They had obeyed her—and my—instructions and stayed near the house, venturing only far enough to hunt. The stream had provided them water, and they had suffered nothing but loneliness in the interim.

As Keeshah stepped from the narrow pathway into the cleared area around the house, Koshah appeared from behind a hidden corner, stretching his forelegs, pulling his torso forward, then stretching his hind legs and tail until they quivered. Yoshah appeared from the bushes at the edge of the clearing, turned aside to the small stream, and drank.

Their minds, however, belied their lazy show of indifference. The cubs were angry and haughty, affronted that they had been left alone so long, and they were ignoring us to prove they did not care. Yet curiosity and loneliness bubbled just below the surface of their masquerade, so that when I slid down from Keeshah's back and called to them with my voice, they abandoned all pretense.

Koshah hit me first, his weight slamming me to the ground. Yoshah was right behind him, and the two of them dragged and wrestled me around until I cried for mercy. I hugged and petted them for a while, enjoying their company and our bond as never before. Then I sat with my back propped against the house, Koshah's head across my knees, Yoshah curled up against my side. Keeshah lay in the center of the clearing, resting. All of us were dozing, contented, bathed in the silvery glow of the cloud-covered moon.

It was a moment of pure peace in a world full of upheaval and fear. It is a memory I treasure.

It was interrupted by another memory I treasure. One minute I heard the crashing sounds of a sha'um moving fast through thick undergrowth, and in the next moment Yayshah had appeared in the clearing, leaping out from a newly made pathway.

Tarani nearly fell from Yayshah's back, and was on the ground before the sleepy cubs had barely raised their heads. They came alert instantly and bolted for their mother, their claws kicking dirt into my face. I was still spluttering and wiping my face, trying to stand up, when Tarani pulled me upright and threw her arms around me so tightly I had trouble breathing.

Not that I minded.

I hugged her for a long time, both of us leaning against the wall of the house. She was breathing in little gasping sobs. Had

Tarani been human and not a Gandalaran, with a physiology that permitted no unnecessary water loss, she would have been weeping. I felt sort of the same way myself—I had been too busy to realize, consciously, how much I had missed the woman. The truth hit me now, as I held Tarani and rubbed my cheek against her dark headfur. We belonged together.

At last Tarani unclenched her arms and looked up at me. "When Yayshah told she scented Keeshah, I—I could not quite believe it. It seems as if we have been apart for lifetimes, my love. Let us never suffer such distance between us again." She touched my face, her long fingers tracing the line of my jaw. "I have been afraid for my sanity these past days, out of worry for you."

"Relenor was in such disarray, I didn't feel right asking them to send a message to you," I said. "A maufa couldn't have reached you much before we got here, anyway."

"You look weary," she said, moving back to look me up and down. She saw the bandage on my thigh, and stretched out her hand. "Oh, no—you must rest, my love, and let me help you heal."

I caught her hand, and brought it to my lips to kiss it. "Time enough for that later," I said. "I stopped here to see Koshah and Yoshah and give Keeshah a rest, but I need to get to Thagorn, to talk to Thymas and the Riders."

She looked at me intently.

"The illness," she said. "You know what it is?"

"I think so," I said. "The Riders who are stricken—their sha'um are in the Valley, aren't they?"

"Why—yes. But how did you—oh!" She stopped herself, and whirled to look in the direction of the Well of Darkness. The dark cloud was totally invisible against the starless Gandalaran sky. "Antonia knew of this, Rikardon. The gases and debris given off by the eruption." The Gandalaran word she used was not quite *eruption*, but I understood what she meant. She looked back at me, and I saw the horror of realization in her moonlit face. "The darkness is falling in the Valley of the Sha'um," she whispered. "The Riders are sick because their sha'um are breathing poisoned air."

# 16

Miraculously, the high stone wall which filled the narrow mouth to Thagorn's valley had escaped the earthquake virtually unharmed. So had the routines of the Sharith—the big double gate was closed when Tarani and I rode up to it. The guard on top of the wall could not have recognized us in the dimness, but the outline of sha'um was all the identification he needed. The gates swung open, and it was only after we had ridden through, into the bright circle of lamplight, that someone shouted my name.

"Rikardon!" said a gruff, familiar voice. Bareff, the veteran Rider who had been my first enemy—and then my first friend—among the Sharith, came down the narrow climbing ledges at breakneck speed, jumping the last ten feet to the ground. "By the First King, Captain," he said, coming to Keeshah's side and extending his hand with a grin for the handshake greeting he had learned from me, "we've had some bad moments wondering where you were when the ground started dancing."

I shook his hand warmly. "The worry was mutual, my friend. Tarani tells me that no one was badly hurt—I'm so glad."

"No. There were some close calls with collapsing walls, but no one was hurt—at least, not while stones were falling."

He frowned and sighed, and I said: "I know about that, too. Where's Thymas? I need to talk to him right away."

"I'll send someone," Bareff began, looking around.

"No, don't," I urged him, before he had located a messenger. "I'll go to him—where is he?"

"In what's left of the Great Hall," Bareff said.

"They have made that a care center for the Riders affected by the—for the ill Riders," Tarani said.

"That's perfect," I said, and began to turn away from Bareff. But the scar-faced man had noticed Tarani's hesitation. "What is it?" he asked. "What's happening to them?"

"I want to talk to the sick men first," I said. "Then I want to

118

talk to all the Sharith. Spread the word, Bareff. Ask everyone
to gather outside the Great Hall in a quarter hour."

"I'll do it, Captain," Bareff said, stepping back from
Keeshah. "See you then."

I nodded, and directed Keeshah toward the huge building
to the left of the road. Tarani rode beside me, and, even
though the doorways had been designed to admit a man riding
a sha'um, we left Keeshah and Yayshah outside.

We entered through the south doorway, which had been
thrown so badly out of plumb that one of its double doors had
come completely off and lay on the ground outside. The other
door had been jammed into place by the shifting stone; we
passed through the remaining opening, out of moonlight and
into lamplight.

The walls of the Great Hall had survived the upheaval, but
the floor had suffered greatly. Green marble tiles, perfectly
fitted and aligned, had formed a smooth, cool pavement for the
huge Hall. The earthquake had rippled across the floor, lifting
the tiles out of place, and had done a less than perfect job of
putting them back. In some places the floor was at least flat;
either those tiles had been lucky, or the Sharith had done some
restoration. In other spots, the tiles were piled and propped at
such crazy angles that walking across those areas might be
hazardous.

The usable areas of the floor were filled with men stretched
out on pallets, and a soft murmur of distress filled the echoing
vastness of the Hall. There were several people attending the
sick men, moving with the disturbing quiet of people awaiting
death to end their duties.

A laugh rang out suddenly in the quiet, and I saw Thymas
standing beside a pallet. He reached back down to take and
press the forearm the sick man lifted to him, then he moved to
the next bed.

"He is nearly finished," Tarani said. "Can we not wait a
moment more?"

I nodded and watched the young Lieutenant move from
man to man, speaking to and touching each man. He was not
aware of us until he moved away from the last pallet in the
irregular pattern, paused, and stretched his back. We were far
enough outside the circle of lamps that he must have been able
to see only our silhouettes, for he said: "Tarani? What are you
doing back here?" He came toward us, and sounded more

weary than angry. "You must rest, Tarani—who is that with you?"

The lamplight behind him glowed through his pure-white hair, giving him a halo and throwing his features into shadow.

"I am not the only one who requires rest," Tarani said, "but time will permit that later. Rikardon has returned."

"Ri—" he began, then rushed forward, grabbed my shoulders, and turned us both so we could see each other's faces. The boy's expression went quickly from disbelief to relief to a grin of pure joy. He hesitated, but I decided for him and pulled him into a rough and pounding hug.

The noise of our meeting attracted the attention of the man on the nearest pallet, who raised himself on one elbow to peer at us. "Captain?" he called weakly, and I waved. His voice came more strongly then, echoing low across the tile. "The Captain's back!" he called. All the attendants turned toward us, and heads lifted from pallets, and the sad murmur was transformed, briefly, into a pitiful cheer.

Thymas stepped back, still gripping my upper arms. His grin had faded to a weary smile. "They—and I—are glad you are well, Captain. Beyond that, I have encouraged the men to believe that you would find the means to make them well. If you cannot, then tell me now. I will tell them the truth, and beg your forgiveness." He paused, groping for words, and finally released me with a shrug. "We have found no way to give comfort to their bodies," he said, "so I tried to give comfort to their thoughts. It was all I could do."

"It was the best thing you could have done," I said. "Because, for one thing, it's true—I *do* know what their problem is. And for another thing, their illness is centered in their thoughts, not their bodies. May I speak to them?"

"You do not need *my* permission," he said, with a bitter laugh, and waved me toward the pallets.

I did not move. After a moment, surprised, he turned back to me.

"I'll say this one time, Thymas," I began, speaking quietly so that the nearest men could not hear me. "You are the Lieutenant. I am Captain by circumstance and necessity, and I guess right now it helps the Sharith to have someone extra, a symbol to cling to during a time of frightening change. I do have some special knowledge—information you could not possibly have—that will help in this crisis. But the Lieutenants have led the Sharith for generations, and you, Thymas, are not the least of them.

"Tarani told me how you pulled everyone together after the disaster, and just now I watched you talking to the Riders. I saw what you were feeling, saw the way they feel about you. You are Lieutenant by right, by training, and by instinct, Thymas. I couldn't take your place, even if I wanted to. So quit acting like you're 'standing in' for someone else. That attitude will only make you uncomfortable and less effective."

"That attitude," he said, "may be my only comfort—the belief that I will not be required to carry this responsibility forever."

"Or the belief that the responsibility is really Dharak's, and he will return to reclaim it?" I asked.

He shook his head. "In the beginning, perhaps," he admitted. "But not now." Thymas waved his arm toward the pallets. "He is not here—the only empty Rider not to be touched by this . . . malady. He is still exactly as he was when you left—quiet and compliant and unseeing. I believe he is gone forever.

"So you," he said, smiling sadly, "were my only hope for relief. And you are denying it to me."

"Yes," I said, unwilling to be less blunt. "But you'll feel less need for relief, once you've accepted it." I put my hand on his shoulder. "You are leading the Sharith more capably than I could," I said, "and fully as well as Dharak would have done. I'm sorry about your father," I said, sincerely.

*I would have sworn he was coming back, the last time I saw him,* I thought. *He looked straight at me, and I'm sure I saw awareness burning in those empty eyes. Perhaps he realized that Thymas needed permanence before he could find his full potential as a leader, and he consciously chose to go away again.*

"Now, *Lieutenant*, may I speak to your people?"

"I will say it again, Captain—though I thank you for your words and I understand your message—you do *not* need my permission." But the bitterness was gone, and I felt I saw a new confidence beginning in the boy.

In roughly the center of the huge room, the massive block of marble which had served as a speaking platform was still there, if slightly canted. It was close enough to the "hospital" area that it seemed the logical place to begin. Thymas and Tarani each took a lamp—candles mounted on tiles, with faceted glass chimneys—and stood at either side of the platform to light it while I stepped up.

When I turned back to face the men, I saw even the weakest of them struggle to raise head and shoulders to look at me.

"Please, rest yourselves," I said. I was gratified that the disruption of the Great Hall had not totally destroyed the acoustics. I spoke in a normal voice, yet the farthest man heard me, and lay back with a sigh of relief.

"I want you to listen carefully, and believe what I tell you. Not just because I am your Captain, but because I have experienced something like what you are feeling now. Like you, I thought that my sha'um had returned to the Valley and abandoned me totally. I could not reach him, speak to him, feel with him. At least, I thought I couldn't.

"But you know, too, that when I needed Keeshah, he came out of the Valley to help me. He *knew* I needed help. The instincts of the sha'um demanded that his conscious awareness of me be forgotten—but nothing could truly break that bond. It was there when we needed it, when it was important enough."

I could not prevent the flash of memory: hiding in a damp earthen cellar with Tarani, our coming together in something more than love, something animalistic, freeing and frightening. Only later had we realized that something in Tarani's special powers had allowed her to begin a bonding, long distance, to the female Keeshah had chosen as mate, and that our physical experience had been changed and enhanced by a concurrent experience between the sha'um. I felt the rushing thrill of the memory, then set it aside.

"In much the same way, each of you still has a bond with your sha'um. The illness proves it."

I heard Thymas gasp beside me, and knew he had understood the implication. From several pallets, however, heads lifted and I saw only expressions of puzzlement.

"Surely you have wondered why there is no physical reason for your illness," I said. "*You* are not ill—but your sha'um are. You are feeling what they feel."

One man tried to sit up, but had to fall back to a propped elbow.

"It *is* real," he gasped.

"Of course it's real," I replied grimly. "The sha'um are in terrible danger—and so are you. If they die, you may be released from the illness—or you may die with them."

A wordless clamor rose around me, and I knew what was running through their minds. I would have the same thought—that death might be preferable to living on without the friendship bond of a sha'um.

A hand gripped my arm, and I looked down to see Thymas climbing up beside me.

"Silence!" he commanded, and obedience was startlingly immediate. "The Captain brings us understanding, but he has brought hope, as well. If there is such danger, then there is no time to waste in worry. Listen to him, help him, obey him."

The boy stepped back down, and everyone in the room looked at me expectantly. As always, their trust frightened me. But this time, as never before, I realized that I represented their only hope of help, and the cost of failure could be no worse than the cost of failing to try.

"Bareff!" I called. "Are the others out there?"

A silhouette appeared in the doorway through which Tarani and I had entered what was left of the Great Hall.

"We're all here, Captain," Bareff assured me, in his deep voice.

"Ask them to come in—warn them of the uncertain footing."

While the others filed into the Hall and stepped carefully over the irregular floor to distribute themselves around the marble dais, I squatted down and spoke quietly to Thymas. He, in turn, spoke quietly to one of the Riders, then returned to the dais to report.

"Dharak is here," the boy told me, nodding to the left. I looked, and saw Shola, Thymas's mother, moving slowly and leading a man with thick white hair and a totally blank expression. When I looked back at Thymas, the boy asked me: "Is Doral already dead?"

"I have no way of knowing about Dharak's sha'um," I answered. "Have you seen any change at all in your father since the—" Not for the first time, I stumbled over the Ricardo concept for which there was no word in Rikardon's language. "Since the ground shook?"

Thymas shook his head. "There is no difference that I can see," he said.

"Then there is no reason to believe that Doral is dead," I answered.

"Can you help Dharak?" Thymas asked, glancing at me only briefly before staring off in the direction of the door.

"I don't know whether he is still within reach." I put my hand on the young Lieutenant's shoulder. "You know I'll do whatever I can." He nodded, and I stood up.

With the entire contingent of Sharith occupying it, the big room was only about a quarter full. The Hall had been built to accommodate sha'um as well as men, but only people were attending this meeting. Everyone fell silent as I stood up.

Briefly, I explained to the people who had just arrived what I had already said to the ill Riders—that the sha'um were in danger, and that their danger was causing the illness. There was fear in the faces I could see in the flickering lamplight as I finished the briefing.

"I want you to understand this clearly," I said. "These men are suffering because a few sha'um are ill—but *all* the sha'um are in danger. The poison in the air is a temporary thing, and even the sick sha'um may recover. But the ash and dust that are drifting into the Valley will destroy the plants and small animals, which will mean that the animals hunted by the sha'um will not be able to survive. In a very short time, the sha'um will have no food, no shelter, most likely poisoned water. There will be no more Valley. There will be no more sha'um, except those which are living here, with us.

"The solution is obvious—the sha'um need to abandon their Valley and live somewhere else. Here. If not with us, then in the hills around us. But the sha'um don't understand their danger, they only know they are ill. If you don't feel well, what do you do? You go home, to your own bed, and find some comfort in familiar surroundings.

"The sha'um will cling to the Valley in their illness, and that clinging will destroy them. *We* know the truth. *We* have to help them."

I held out my hand to Tarani. She hesitated only a moment before handing her lantern to someone close by and climbing up to stand beside me on the marble block.

"In the past, only one thing has persuaded a sha'um to leave the Valley—a bond between a male sha'um cub and a Sharith boy. It is my feeling that the most effective means of persuasion is for as many of us to attempt bonding with sha'um as can be done. Tarani's bond to Yayshah has proved two things. First, adults—both sha'um and Sharith—can achieve a bond. Second, those adults do not have to be male."

# 17

I did nothing to forestall the murmur of response to that statement, which quickly grew to a roar. I heard, and could sense, in that response a rich mixture of attitude and mood: question, challenge, denial, fear, acceptance, bewilderment, approval. It was the sound of people accepting paradox, and learning that the only way to maintain a cherished custom— more than that, the only way to continue their way of life—was to change it, utterly and permanently.

After a moment, I lifted my hand, and the Sharith quieted.

"Do you believe what I have told you?" I asked.

"The danger, yes!" someone called out.

"But not the solution?" I demanded. "Because you don't think it's possible? Or," I added with emphasis, "because you don't think it's *right*?"

Tarani's hand tightened on mine. I took the signal, and stepped aside to allow her to take the center place on the dais.

"Or because half of you are afraid?" she asked, her voice ringing out. "Not of being killed, but of becoming different, of changing from what you have been?"

Some people moved, and a woman stepped out into the cleared area in front of the gathered Sharith.

"You were able to bond with Yayshah because you are mindgifted," the young woman said. "I have no such gift." The words were more a question than a challenge, the girl's whole attitude more hopeful than despairing.

"Ulla, is it?" Tarani asked. The girl nodded. "Are you not wed to a Rider, Ulla?"

"Yes," Ulla said, reaching back into the crowd and dragging out a man in Sharith uniform, a young man. "Virram and I are wed, and . . ."

"And?" Tarani prompted.

"And . . . our child grows within me."

I almost burst out laughing at the double take the boy did at that announcement. The crowd did laugh, and both Virram and Ulla blushed. Virram stepped closer to Ulla, and put his arm around her.

"Then she must take more care of this new life," he said, with a serious firmness, "and not take the risk you propose."

"Is that not her own choice, Virram?" Tarani asked, but did not wait for an answer. "And what of your child, a son perhaps? Would you deny him the chance to bond to a sha'um of his own?"

It was Tarani's turn to reach out to me, and I took her hand and came closer.

"You are right, Ulla, in saying that my bond with Yayshah was achieved because I have a special gift. Yet it was not mindgift that brought me Yayshah's trust. It was the caring and trust and experience of this man, whose bond to Yayshah's mate insured my protection against physical assault. It was that which gave me the opportunity, and the time, to win Yayshah's regard. Look at Virram. Has he any mindgift?"

"Not a trace," she answered promptly, bringing another ripple of laughter from his fellow Riders.

"If a man needs no mindgift to bond with a sha'um," Tarani asked, "then why should a woman have need of one?"

Tarani's explanation of her own bonding had surprised me, but it made a lot of sense. I felt sure her mindgift *had* been involved during the at-a-distance, subconscious bonding she had experienced, but there was a lot of logic to the idea that a female would bond more readily to the mate of her own mate's Rider.

*Keeshah, are you close by?*

*Yes.*

*Come to the north door, and wait for me to call.*

*Yes.*

Tarani had paused to allow the Sharith to consider her question, and I spoke into that pause.

"The sha'um are *in* danger, but they also *are* a danger—to us. Those of you who have been to the Valley know what I'm saying." Heads—riding above tan Sharith uniforms—nodded agreement. "The sha'um protect their territory fiercely. They are ill now, but no less dangerous. They are afraid, and will react more quickly to anything they perceive as danger. There *will be* fighting in the Valley. But, for the most part, it will not be Sharith fighting sha'um—except in the sense that sha'um who have Riders are, themselves, Sharith."

There was a stunned silence. Then a Rider's voice echoed forward from somewhere near the door. "They will not do it," the Rider said.

"Not what?" I asked. "Not take us there? Or not fight the others?" I held up my hand. "It doesn't matter which you meant," I said. "Because they *will* do both things.

"It is essential that you stop thinking about yourselves and your sha'um as you 'have always been,'" I urged. "Dharak talked of change; you have felt it; it is happening. This is part of it."

"With respect, Captain," called the same voice, "how can *you* promise what *my sha'um* will or will not do?"

I let myself smile. "I have it," I said, "on the best authority."

I gestured toward the huge north doorway; unlike the northern entrance, both north doors stood open to let the air in.

*Come in, Keeshah.*

The big cat appeared in the doorway and paused to look around. I choked back a laugh. He knew exactly where I was, but he stood there anyway, his massive body silhouetted against the gray of the doorway, reflection of lamplight winking on one gleaming tusk and glinting from the heart of one gray-green eye.

*Great entrance, Keeshah,* I told him. *You're turning into quite a showman.*

*Important,* he said gravely, almost scolding me.

I accepted the scolding meekly, and turned my attention back to the Sharith, every one of whom was watching Keeshah. "Keeshah understands. He has made the same commitment I am asking of you—to go into the Valley and, if there is no other way, to *drive* the sha'um out. He does this for our sake—so that our children may Ride. He does it, also, for the sake of the sha'um—so that sha'um children may share a bond with Riders.

"Are you listening, my friends? Keeshah *understands*. So will your sha'um understand, and accept this need, if *you* can make that commitment."

Keeshah moved into the room and, to my surprise, Yayshah

stepped in right behind him. The two sha'um stepped carefully over the men on the pallets and waited for people to move aside, so that they could crouch down on either side of the dais. Thymas stepped up on the marble slab behind Tarani and me, to give the sha'um equal places at our sides.

"Yayshah," Tarani said, "also understands, and accepts. I will go to the Valley, as must all Riders. She commits not only her strength and will to this task, but consents to taking her cubs, as well."

I controlled my start of surprise. Tarani and I had not discussed this, and my first instinct was to leave the cubs behind. As soon as the thought crossed my mind, however, two voices were there to protest it.

*Want to go!* Yoshah said.

*Important!* said Koshah, in much the same tones his father had used.

I had never fathered children, but I suddenly felt a wave of sympathy for the fathers I had known. I had few real facts about the lifecycle of the sha'um, but I was beginning to suspect that Koshah and Yoshah were about to enter the equivalent of their teenage years, even though they were only a few months old.

It was sign enough of their growing up that their verbal and mind skills had developed to the point that they could hover unnoticed at the edge of my consciousness, listen to my speech and thought, and understand content as well as emotion. There was further confirmation in the sense of resolution I got from them. More than stubbornness or eagerness for a new adventure, I felt that they did, truly, understand, and would not be denied the opportunity to make a contribution. I could tell them to stay behind, but even if Yayshah tried to give them the same orders, it would never work. They would be eyesight-distance behind us (or ahead of us) all the way to the Valley.

*Yes, you may come with us,* I said, conscious of the irony of giving permission where denying it would be pointless. *Now let me concentrate here, please.*

"Tell your sha'um what is happening," I urged the Riders. "Tell them what we have to do, and why. If they continue to hesitate, tell them—" I bent over slightly, and smoothed the short fur between Keeshah's eyes and ears with my hand. "Tell them that Keeshah understands, and agrees."

There was a moment in which voices were quiet but there was a lot of foot-shuffling, as the Riders in the group spoke mind-to-mind to their sha'um, and the people around them turned to watch the outward sign of the several, separate communions. Bodies grew still, eyes went out of focus, expressions went lax. The few seconds seemed to be an hour, and I jumped as if I had been shot when a hand clamped down on my shoulder.

Thymas pushed me aside, breaking my hold on Tarani's hand, and leaped forward.

"Ronar will come," Thymas cried triumphantly. "Who else?"

Suddenly the Hall was filled with male voices shouting out names as each Rider confirmed the agreement of his sha'um. When the babel had died down, Thymas whirled to face me.

"All the sha'um are with us," he said, his eyes glowing with pride. "But the illness will grow worse with time, will it not?" I nodded. "Then we must travel quickly—which means we must Ride." He gestured to the people in the room. "Not all the Sharith may come. Will you choose?"

"I will not choose," I said. "The choice is dictated by the situation. First, the Riders whose sha'um are in the Valley must come, for they already have a bond. It will be easier, I think, to awaken a sleeping bond than to establish a new one."

"I would give my life to go," said an older man, lying in the row of pallets nearest me. "But I—I am so weak."

"And reluctant, perhaps, to ride another man's sha'um?" I asked gently.

He started to say something, then looked away and nodded.

"I believe your weakness can be helped, and that your sha'um's life is more important than your pride," I said. "However many of the ill Riders are able *must* come. All others should be women."

Again the front edge of the crowd was jostled from behind, and a boy of ten or eleven shoved his way out. Ulla and Virram, who still stood a bit forward of the mass of people, looked at him curiously.

"I am of the age to go to the Valley," he said, "and there are others like me. Let us go."

"No," I said firmly, to a chorus of objections from both young voices and the older voices of Riders. "We are not going to the Valley to bring out as many *bonded* sha'um as possible," I explained. "We will try to bring *all* of them out. Yayshah left the Valley because of *two* bonds—one to Tarani, and one to her mate. If there had been only one of those bonds, I wonder whether she would have had the courage to leave."

Tarani spoke up.

"Keeshah and Yayshah and their cubs will be an example for the Valley sha'um, but more than one example will be needed," she explained. "The more family units which agree, of their own will, to follow us from the Valley, the less resistance the others will have."

"First choice of the women to go will be those who are married to the Riders whose sha'um are already there," I said. "If our sha'um can carry more than those two groups of people, then women who are married to the unaffected Riders may come."

A voice called out from the crowd. "My sha'um has consented to carry three; he is strong enough."

I shook my head. "To get there, perhaps," I said, "but not to go quickly and arrive with most of his strength. No more than two per sha'um; that will give us the best balance between speed and people."

"And the Riders who are ill?" Thymas prompted. "You said they might be helped."

I stepped down from the dais, waited for Tarani to join me, and walked into the midst of the pallets. "Your bonds to your sha'um are buried deeply in your minds, and in theirs. I know what you are feeling; I have been through it. My bond was brought back to the surface because I felt such fear and need and loneliness for Keeshah that he could sense it through that unfelt link.

"I had held the small hope that once you accepted that your sha'um are sick, you could break the bad part of the bond, and make yourselves well. I see that it hasn't worked that way.

"I propose a gamble, and I won't hide the stakes from you. If it works the way I think it will, you will reach your sha'um, free your bodies of their pain, reestablish your bond as it was before the sha'um left, and send them a warning of their danger. Their instincts will still rule, and you won't be able merely to call them out of the Valley. But I think you *can* tell them to find some high ground, and move as little as possible before we get there. They will be stronger, then, and less ill than the rest, so that if they can be persuaded, they can help us with the others."

"And if it—whatever it is—does not work the way you expect, Captain?" asked a man lying in the corner.

"Then your bodies will be free of the pain you share with the sha'um—but you will also destroy the bond altogether."

I heard the Riders in the crowd utter a gasp of fear, almost in unison, but I ignored them. These men on the floor all around me were the key to the entire plan—unless they could persuade at least some of the sha'um *in* the Valley to come out of their own free will, I doubted that the Thagorn sha'um were powerful enough, in themselves, to force the colony of sha'um out of the Valley.

I waited. At last the man closest to my feet put out a trembling hand and touched my leg.

"I will try, Captain. What must I do?"

A chorus of voices rose then, asking the same question. I took a deep breath and hoped my relief wasn't visible in my face.

"Tarani has told me that all her healing skills have availed nothing against your illness," I said, "but I think they can help you now. Her gift reaches into the part of your mind you never think about using, a part that does things automatically most of the time. She lets that powerful part of your mind free to do its work more quickly, and part of its work is healing damaged areas of the body.

"She could not help you before now because there was no real damage to be healed. It's that same part of your mind, bonded to the sick sha'um, that is *causing* the symptoms you are feeling. Now that you know the truth of what has been happening, I believe that Tarani's healing sleep will stimulate that hidden mind to a different activity. Because you understand, and you are afraid—for yourself, and your sha'um—in the healing sleep, your healing mind will call out and shock the sha'um into a thinking bond again, and they will understand what you want them to do.

"Do *you* understand—the risks as well as the possible gains?"

Many men nodded, a few calling out affirmatives.

"Any man who does not want to do this may decline without embarrassment," I said sincerely. "I know how strange this must seem to you, and how frightening is the idea of the totally broken bond. Anyone who wishes to leave, raise your arm and someone will help you to your home."

Not a single arm came up from the pallets, and I felt a swelling pride in the men, in their faith in me, and—momentarily—in my own strength. I was more afraid than they were because, in spite of their willingness to believe me, they still did not understand the stakes in the same way I did. That I could recognize their ignorance, and take advantage of it, seemed to be exactly the opposite of what I had felt about Keeshah in the Chizan passage. Yet it was only time, now, that kept them ignorant. Their understanding had begun, and would grow as we proceeded with the plan. I was willing to take advantage of their obedience on those terms.

I turned to the standing crowd and said: "Please leave the Hall now, and prepare provisions for the journey. Thymas, will you, Bareff, and Shola figure out how many can go, and make a list of the women, in priority order? This may not work for all the Riders, and any who remain ill or—" I could not say it, could not propose the horror of a fully broken bond.

"When it is over," Thymas said, with full understanding of my omission, "we will see how much room there is." Turning suddenly formal, he offered me his hand. "Captain, thank you."

I took it, and pressed it hard. "Thank me when it's over," I said.

The people began to file out of the half-open door, and I moved among the men, speaking to the ones I knew best, trying to be encouraging. When the Hall was nearly empty of healthy Sharith, I looked up to see a shock of white hair near the doorway. Shola and Dharak had been near the door, but not the first ones out—and so had been pressed back out of the flow of people. It was now nearly possible for them to leave.

"Shola, wait," I said, standing up and hurrying over to them. When I got close enough to see her face, the only thing I could do was gather her into my arms and hold her. She sank against me briefly, and shook with the dry gasps that served the Gandalarans as weeping. After a moment, she let me push her away and turn her face toward the light. I tried to smile, but found that I could not. "I'm sorry this has been so hard for you, Shola," I said.

"You are not at fault, Captain," she replied. "It is only that his—" She gestured toward the pallets. "This has convinced me that Dharak is—will not—"

"Thymas said as much to me," I admitted, looking over her

shoulder to the man who merely stood where he had been when Shola's hand had left his arm. "May I speak to him?"

"Of course," she said, and stepped away.

I put my hands on the old man's shoulders and pulled him closer to the doorway, where the lamplight and the gray nightglow combined to illuminate his face. "Dharak, it is Rikardon. Please listen to me, try to hear and understand what I am saying. Tarani and I are going to try to help the men who have lost their sha'um get them back. We think it's possible, Dharak. It might help you too. But what Tarani does can only be done with the person's *consent*—his full agreement.

"Dharak," I continued in a soft voice, very much aware of Shola standing just behind me, "I know that you don't have full control of yourself right now. But I will accept anything, any voluntary movement, as a signal that you *can* give consent to this. If you can give me some sign of consent, I feel sure that this will help you and Doral too. Please, my friend, you don't need to take the effort to speak. Raise your hand, nod your head, blink your eyes twice quickly. Dharak, Lieutenant, my good friend—let us help you."

I waited, holding my breath and watching Dharak's face. Though deeply lined, it was passive now, its blankness more terrible than the fiercest frown.

I waited.

Something happened—an eye movement. The eyelids closed, and opened again, and Dharak's dark eyes were no longer unfocused. They were looking at me, seeing me, studying me—it was as if Dharak had never seen me before. The old man's face almost had a real expression on it, one I could not identify because it was only a fleeting impression.

The expression faded, the eyes went vacant.

After a few more seconds, Shola and I let out our held breath almost simultaneously. The second eyeblink never happened.

I stepped away from the old Lieutenant, and Shola moved into my place, taking his arm in her hand.

"Thank you for trying, Captain," she said. "I hope your effort is successful." She led Dharak out of the Hall.

Tarani began the odd, tuneless humming that was part and parcel of her healing skill. Her power of compulsion could affect the autonomous nervous system of Gandalarans. Her mindgift could affect the conscious mind too—it was the conscious mind she tricked when she cast her illusions. The healing gift combined those two powers, lulling the conscious mind into peace and comfort and withdrawal, and stimulating the autonomous body functions to accelerate their healing processes.

Neither areas, of course, equated to the subconscious mind. I was guessing that it was connected, though. After some discussion, Tarani and I had agreed on a technique. She would call the men into a trance state just short of the deep sleep required of self-healing, then would direct them to do as I instructed. I was hoping that the result would be something close to true hypnosis, so that the conscious minds of the men would touch and control the subconscious link with the sha'um.

I had to force myself to keep still as Tarani's voice filled the cavernous room with low-pitched echoes. Her power affected me only if I wished it, but I had always found it so pleasant that now I felt a tugging from my own subconscious, a latent wish for the peaceful state her voice invited. In other circumstances, I would move and distract myself while she worked. But I *had* to be here, and any movement might distract the Riders and make her job more difficult. So I sat still upon the edge of the big center marble block, willing myself to stay awake.

Tarani moved, walking soundlessly along the rows of pallets, her touch helping to focus their minds and complete the entrancement. She came to me quietly and said: "I believe they are ready." She drew me into the center of the pallet grouping again, and spoke in a clear, vibrant voice.

"Of your own will have you come to this place, between sleeping and waking. You have given consent to be guided by Rikardon, your Captain. As he speaks now, listen and obey." She stepped aside, with a small, unconscious bowing movement.

I began to talk quietly. My voice, though deeper in pitch than Tarani's, seemed to echo harshly in comparison to Tarani's rich tones. "Reach out to the sha'um whose mind you have touched," I directed. "You will find him as an animal, an unthinking being, a presence whose thoughts are so limited that you have been unable to detect them since he left for the Valley. Find that presence, follow it, touch your sha'um again. Wake him and touch him fully again. When you find him, when you can speak to him, let him see your fear and your need, and tell him that he must do this: *Find the high ground and sleep. We will be together soon*. Repeat this message: *Find the high ground and sleep. We will be together soon.*"

I walked among the pallets, repeating that statement over and over again, for about fifteen minutes. There was no visible change in the men during that time—no one stirred, no one spoke. Without exception, they lay with their eyes closed, breathing deeply as if asleep.

At last I stopped, and shrugged to Tarani. She came into the center again, and her voice rolled out softly. "You have done what was agreed," she said. "Wake now, slowly. Remember all that happened, and awaken with new strength."

As one, the men moved in small ways—stretching, rubbing their eyes, yawning. They blinked and stared upward, and I could not stand the suspense. I knelt down beside Liden, the Sharith who had been with Bareff at our first encounter, and who had also become a close friend. I had last seen Liden just after his sha'um had left him. He had been lying face-down in the main road through Thagorn, having drunk himself into a stupor in defiance of his self-preserving "inner awareness."

Now Liden lay on his back, staring at the ceiling. He looked at me when I touched his arm. He blinked, and then he grinned.

"Poltar is back, Captain. I reached him. Even now, he is climbing into the hills on the side of the Valley farthest from the Well of Darkness." He rolled up to brace himself on one elbow, and pressed my shoulder with his other hand. "And I am well, Captain. The debt I owe you can never be paid."

I put my hand over his and pressed it. The stress had been so intense, and the relief was so sudden, that I felt giddy. I grinned at the snaggle-toothed man and said: "A game of mondea, double or nothing?"

He blinked at me, then slapped my shoulder and burst out laughing. It seemed to be a cue of some sort. All around me, men started to talk and laugh and sit up. After a confused and tumultuous few minutes, it became clear that Tarani's power and the Riders' courage had worked a miracle. Every single one of them had recovered their bond—even the Riders whose sha'um were in the Valley during their natural cycle.

Tarani and I joined in the wild, slightly frantic laughter. Some of the other Sharith had lingered outside. When they heard the happy noise, they rushed in and became part of it. I saw Bareff talking to Liden, and their roar of laughter told me that Liden had quoted my first remark to him. I looked around for Thymas, but did not see him.

He showed up later, when the rush of joy had settled into the need for action, and everyone was leaving the Hall.

"The provisions and the chosen Sharith are ready, Captain," he said. "We leave at your command."

# 18

One hundred and forty-four people and seventy-four sha'um left Thagorn that night, traveling north. Koshah and Yoshah had offered, tentatively, to let someone ride, but I had seen too much uncertainty in their mindvoices to allow it. They were large enough by now, certainly, to carry smallish people, but they knew through me that a sha'um normally carried only the person to whom he or she was bonded. Keeshah had carried Ligor alone to Chizan and back, but that, too, had been a service to me. The cubs made their offer because they sensed my need to take as many people as possible, and I could sense their relief when I turned it down.

We left in the first hours after midnight, Keeshah and Yayshah and the cubs leading. I felt that the timing was fortunate. Guided by the more sensitive sight and smell of the sha'um even through the darkest part of the night, we would reach the Valley area at midmorning, and have the daylight hours to accomplish whatever we could. I was grateful, too, that the night diminished the visual impact of the volcanic cloud. It could still be detected as an area of the sky blacker than the moon-grayed cloud cover, but its presence was not as overwhelming as it would have been had we ridden toward it in daylight.

In the darkness, then, my mind was free enough to plan, instead of merely worry. By the time dawn streaked through the cloud cover to our right, I had formulated several strategies for approaching the Valley sha'um, and I called a halt. We all needed time to rest and eat.

Dawn stopped just this side of the Korchi mountain range. The beautiful, streaking shades of orange and red simply vanished at the edge of the blackness, which was now overhead as well as ahead of us. We ate a nervous meal as absolute darkness transformed into a weird twilight, and in the half hour or so we rested, our clothes collected a fine, dark dust.

Before we had left Thagorn, Thymas had organized all of us into several smaller groups, each with an active Rider for its leader. While we were eating, I called a meeting of those leaders, and I went into more detail about the cloud and what it was doing.

The Valley of the Sha'um was not a true valley, but merely a triangular area bounded by the Morkadahls on the west and the northern mountains which, by Gandalaran convention, were considered to be part of the Great Wall. Its mountain borders provided several cascading streams and, I guessed, an underground water table of considerable size, judging from the quantity of plant life supported in the area. Ordinarily, it was a fortunate place, ideally suited for the support of the large cats and all the other biological entities that supported them and their food chain.

Now, however, those same mountain borders were collecting and bouncing back the ash and gas expelled by the volcano, so that the Valley area would soon be totally unlivable. The poisonous gases would disperse eventually, now that they had been freed of the relatively confined space inside the Well of Darkness. But the ash would settle, and destroy.

I had explained this once to the Sharith, and they had believed me. Hearing it again while the powdery stuff was darkening their blondish headfur, accumulating on their sleeves, and settling on their food as they ate it, they began to really understand, and their fear mounted.

We had three objectives. One, call the bonded sha'um out of the Valley. Two, create bonds with as many other sha'um as we had people, and convince those sha'um to leave the Valley. Three, bring as many others out as possible.

The "priority order" of these objectives was also an advancing degree of personal danger, but the Sharith had passed the point of any hesitation. The group leaders stood up, a few of

them brushing the ash from their sleeves in disgust, and
departed to deliver the same instructions to their groups.
Thymas paused to clap me on the shoulder, then left for his
own group.

It was only to Tarani, who had stayed beside me silently
throughout the briefing, that I could voice my doubts.

"They won't all come," I said.

"The Sharith know that," she said.

"No matter how many are saved, they'll never forget how
many they lose," I said. "Neither will I."

"Yet each one saved, my love," Tarani said, "will be
remembered with joy, and in tribute to you." She put her arm
around my neck and pressed her cheek to mine, briefly and
warmly, then rocked back to look directly into my eyes.

"You have not said it, Rikardon, but I cannot believe that
you have not thought, as I am thinking, that this may be our
destiny. Can it be that the safety of the sha'um, not the Ra'ira,
is the goal to which we have been driven these past days?"

I shrugged. "The thought *has* crossed my mind," I said.
"But there's only one way to tell, isn't there?"

She returned my smile, and even laughed a little. "Yes—as
always, we will not see the next task until this one is done."
She stood up, and offered me both her hands. "Shall we
begin?"


Nearly single file, the sha'um moved carefully through the
Morkadahl foothills, as high as they could get without laboring
for breath. The terrain was rocky and treacherous, far above
the edge of the greenery that marked the boundary of the
Valley. Both sha'um and Sharith wore dampened headscarves
wrapped over nose and mouth, but still the air we breathed
carried an ominous, unhealthy odor.

When we had formed a ragged line through the hills above
what I judged to be the western edge of the Valley's triangle, I
raised my arm; signal shouts ran down the column, and our
sha'um turned eastward and began to pick their way carefully,
heading downslope. We moved through a thickening twilight,
drifting ash creating a dark haze under a darkened sky. When I
heard coughing start, and felt the tickle in my own throat, I
signaled a halt, and the sha'um backed up to a position where
breathing was possible, if not comfortable. The sha'um were
both advantaged and disadvantaged by their size. On the one

hand, the quantity of air they breathed assured a greater percentage of useful air with every breath, which meant that they might be able to go more deeply into the smog than Gandalarans could manage. On the other hand, they were taking a greater absolute quantity of pollutants into their bodies with every breath.

"Now," I called. "Riders, summon your sha'um!"

We all dismounted. Most of us found secure places within the line, where we would neither hamper the movement of the sha'um nor be likely to lose our footing and slip noisily at a crucial moment. Two groups of people moved forward, about thirty of the first Riders who had been ill, then a much smaller group of women—wives—of those Riders. A third group formed, but did not move forward yet. These were the other women, wives of the Riders whose sha'um had brought us here. I had insisted that the women come only voluntarily, and a few had been too afraid—with what consequence to their marriages, only time would tell. Still others had been very pregnant, so that the trip itself was a danger the Riders would not allow.

Thirty or so men, and no more than ten women, faced the huge shapes that we now spotted moving slowly uphill through the haze.

The men walked forward to meet their sha'um, and I felt my heart go out to them for their gladness and their distress. The beautiful cats, gray or tan or some combination, were uniformly sooty, their eyes sunken, their bodies thin, their steps uncertain. I saw Liden reach up to Poltar's neck, hesitate, then wrap his arms around the cat in a way that would support, rather than lean on, him.

So far, things had happened as they had been planned. I was just thinking that it was all going too smoothly when I heard the roar of challenge from just downslope. Another sounded, and another, and before we had time to react, a second line of sha'um appeared behind the first. These were narrow-shouldered females, the striping in their darker coats obscured by the settled ash their fur had collected.

"They are frightened," Tarani whispered to me. "Their dens are corrupted, the only security that remains to them is their mates. And they see that the Riders have changed the attitudes of the males, turned them away from den and family."

"Is Yayshah telling you this?" I asked.

"She sees it," Tarani admitted. "But I interpret it. Rikardon, they are terrified and angry. There is more risk for the women than I imagined."

The women themselves saw it, and were moving cautiously backward.

"Yet they *must* try," Tarani said. Her hand, clenched into a fist, struck the boulder on which we were leaning. "And now is the moment, their only chance."

She stood up. I grabbed for her, panicked, and sprawled out on the dusty ground as she dashed forward, running down the hill. *This isn't in the plan!* I thought desperately. *Keeshah, Yoshah, Koshah, protect her!*

The attention of all the sha'um was drawn to the noise of Tarani's skidding and running. Three of the closest females edged around their mates to face the woman, their neckfur lifted and their tails thickening. Their tusks were exposed, and a low menacing sound rolled out of their throats as they spaced themselves and held their ground.

But Tarani did not run to meet them. Instead, she angled off to her right, toward the main body of the column. She grabbed the arm of one of the women, and dragged her back toward the three female sha'um. One of the Riders—her husband, I supposed—caught the woman's other arm and yelled something. The woman, not young by any means, argued for a moment with the man, then freed her arm from Tarani's grasp and swung it full-force at the Rider, knocking him loose and sending him sprawling. She paused a moment, looking remorseful, then turned back to Tarani, who hugged her briefly. The two women ran toward the females, who had watched all this with growing suspicion. On the hillside above, Keeshah, Yayshah, and the two cubs were arranging themselves for battle.

*Don't fight unless you have to,* I ordered my three sha'um. *Try to follow what Tarani wants you to do.*

I considered joining the mess, and was ready to launch myself downhill, when I spotted Thymas—much closer—doing the same thing. He ran and slid down until he collided with the Rider who had just gotten up, nearly knocking him flat again. Thymas grabbed him, talking earnestly, then he turned and shouted to Tarani.

"The one in the center," he said, and we all knew what he meant. Thymas had asked the Rider to find out from his

sha'um which of these females was his mate. The man's sha'um
moved slowly toward his Rider, pressed his forehead into the
man's chest, then with a spurt of energy climbed the hill to join
Keeshah and his family.

Later, I wondered whether Tarani really did have some
element of telepathy in her mindpower, because the next few
minutes saw a degree of teamwork that seemed impossible
without some such unifying factor. Five sha'um faced the three
females. Four of them were *not* bonded to Tarani, but they did
the right thing at the right time. I directed three of them, and
I was sure the Rider-husband of the woman was directing his
male. There was no way for Tarani to tell us—or even to speak
to the sha'um directly to tell them—what she wanted the
sha'um to do, but we all worked together as if we had practiced
it a hundred times.

The female sha'um in the center of the group lunged
forward, not so much attacking the two women as challenging
and questioning her mate behind them. But the movement
brought her much nearer the women than the other two, and I
said: *Koshah, Yoshah, get down there on either side of the
center female.*

They obeyed immediately, and the sudden arrival of the
young sha'um set all three females to sidestepping and
growling. Apparently because these sha'um were cubs, the
females saw no threat in them, so Koshah and Yoshah were
able to get into place without causing an uproar.

Her mate moved forward then, forcing the women to step
aside to give him room. He touched noses with the female,
uttered a low sound from his throat, and rubbed the side of his
face along her jaw. Her ears twitched forward, and she raised
her head slightly so the male could lick the lighter fur of her
throat. I saw her close her eyes as she relaxed and crouched
down, offering the back of her neck to the attentions of her
mate.

*Now,* I ordered the cubs. They darted closer to the female
and leaned their weight against her, effectively limiting her
mobility.

The female's eyes snapped open, and we could see her
muscles gathering for a lunge out of the trap, but her mate
swung around. Instead of licking the fur on the back of her
neck, he opened his jaws. He caught a fold of skin at the nape
of her neck in his teeth, and pressed the female down to

immobilize her. We could all see he was being careful not to hurt her. He lifted one heavy foreleg and laid it across Yoshah's hindquarters and his mate's shoulders.

The female roared; the male's jaws twitched; she fell silent. The other females, alarmed by what was going on, roared and paced, but now Keeshah entered the picture, taking a protective position behind the female.

Facing the big, healthy male sha'um was more than the two other females wanted to handle. They backed down the hillside, crouched and watched.

Gradually, as the female realized she was not being hurt and no one was threatening to hurt her, the wild look disappeared from her eyes, and she stopped trembling. Tarani lifted her arm, and Yayshah walked slowly down the hillside, passing under Tarani's arm, crouching slightly and rippling fur and muscle, obviously enjoying the body-long caress.

Yayshah stopped close to the trapped female and crouched down. Both women went forward then, stopping on either side of Yayshah. Tarani mounted Yayshah, who stood up and carried Tarani off a short distance. The other woman walked forward boldly, and knelt in front of the furry head with its heavy teeth and silver-gray, suspicious eyes.

The woman seemed very small in comparison with the mass of sha'um around her, but she moved with deliberation and courage. *Please,* I prayed—to the woman, or to the God of my grandmother Marie, I was not sure which—*this is the first one, the keystone. Please let this work.*

The woman reached toward the female, keeping her hand always in the sha'um's visual range. Even at this distance, I could see the male's head twist slightly, to watch the woman with as much care as the female was watching her. Either instinctively or at Tarani's earlier direction, the woman held her hand very still in front of the female's face. Carefully, the triangular furred head extended itself, sniffing. The woman's hand moved closer; the female's ears twitched back, forward, back. The hand touched fur between the female's eye and the top ridge of teeth. The female's whole body flinched, but she made no hostile move. Her eyes were on the woman before her, even her captors forgotten.

Another hand came forward, and both stroked fur. The dark ears came forward, the eyes half-closed. The woman stood up slowly.

*Koshah, get out of the way,* I ordered the male cub, who stood up cautiously. The dark sha'um made no attempt to break away. The woman moved to the sha'um's side, stroking fur along her jaw, across her head, down her shoulders—behind the jaws of the male, who still held his mate's skin in his teeth.

The male still watched the woman warily. The woman laughed softly, and spared a caressing stroke for his sloping forehead.

The male released his mate, and when Yoshah felt the weight of his foreleg go away, she, too, moved off. As if it were an ordinary, everyday sort of action, the woman slid a leg over the female's back and settled into a slightly awkward, but conceptually accurate, imitation of a Rider's position. The female stood up carefully, turned to touch noses with her mate, then moved to stand beside Yayshah.

Only seconds later, the female's mate—mounted by the new Rider's husband—joined the two females.

It had begun.

# 19

It was an inexpressible relief to lie down. The pallet beneath me was thickly padded with vlek hair and, while not the soft comfort of a feather mattress in Ricardo's world, it was more comfort than I had known since Ligor and I had left Inid. I thought of the tenacious old man, and resolved to send a message, telling him that I was all right. I had the feeling that in spite of having his hands full with rebuilding Chizan, he was worrying about me. He was that sort of a man.

Tarani lay beside me, sleeping. We had dismounted our sha'um in the clearing that was our home among the Sharith, and sent them into the surrounding forest for a well-deserved rest. Then with one mind, we had staggered toward the stream, stripping off clothes as we went. The clear, cool water had rinsed away the accumulation of soot and dust, and we had been able to walk with more control into the house.

Tarani had kissed me tentatively; I had responded tentatively; we had both laughed.

"One would think," she said, "that we had only just met,
since neither one of us is honest enough to plead fatigue."

"Every day with you," I had said, running my fingers across
the delicate bone beneath her left eye, "I seem to meet you for
the first time. And desire for you is always with me, even when
I'm too tired to demonstrate it."

She had drawn me down, then, to the pallet, to hold me
tenderly. "It is decided, is it not, my love, that we shall never
be parted again?"

"Never," I had promised, and then I had held her until her
breathing slowed and she slept.

But I was in that state of utter fatigue that defied sleep. We
had stayed the rest of that day and part of the night in and near
the Valley. As I had hoped, that first bonding had been a
breakthrough. It had convinced the Riders that it could be
done, and their sha'um in turn had encouraged their own
mates into similar bondings.

When the wives of the Riders of the Valley sha'um had
achieved their bonds, every one of them following the first
woman's careful approach, we were greeted with some surprises. The oldest Thagorn sha'um had left us one by one, to
return later with not only one, but three or four sha'um—his
mate, and the last batch of cubs, now grown. Where the wife
of an active Rider had been with us, the male had controlled
and threatened the cubs in order to give his mate the chance to
bond to his Rider's mate.

When all the bondings had been achieved—not totally
without damage, but at least with no sha'um or Sharith having
been killed—we had ridden back to our camping spot and
spent the night in the fresher air, allowing the Valley sha'um to
recover some of their strength.

On the following day, the bonded sha'um—males and
females, unbonded cubs accompanying them out of family
loyalty—had reentered the Valley and herded out all the
sha'um that could be found. Though it had hurt us to see them
so weak and ill, we had not hesitated to take advantage of their
condition. Mounted, the Sharith had herded the protesting
sha'um away from the place that had been their home. They
had begun to recover as soon as they reached clear air, and
though there had been a few breakneck attempts to circle back

to the Valley, for the most part they had seemed content to move along with us.

The Sharith had opened their confining circle of bonded sha'um just north of Thagorn, and the ex-Valley sha'um had bolted for the overgrown hillsides.

The mood of the Sharith had been subdued—due as much, I had suspected, from thoughtfulness as from fatigue. Their lives had changed—drastically, irreversibly. They had accepted the change without question for the sake of the sha'um, but had not yet taken the time to assess the nature of that change.

Tarani and I had left a weary Thymas at the gate of Thagorn, declining the offered hospitality of his own home. Now that Yayshah was not the only female outside the Valley of Sha'um, there was no reason to forbid her presence in Thagorn. But this house was the only real home Tarani and I had known together.

Sheltered by the warmth of Tarani's closeness, I closed my eyes and, at last, let myself feel the pain. Outside the Valley I had told Tarani that we would never forget the sha'um we lost. I had not foreseen how personal that sense of loss would be.

As we were gathering up the camp after making the painful decision that any sha'um left were beyond saving, something had drawn my gaze to the western hills.

Doral had been there, at a level above the worst of the haze, watching us. Dharak's sha'um had no distinguishing marks, and the sha'um crouching on the hillside might have been any sha'um—but I had known it was Doral. I had almost called to Keeshah, tempted to ride after him and corral him like a wild stallion, but Doral had stood up just at that moment, had issued a heart-rending cry of loneliness, and had jumped down to appear in flashes, running among the rocks of the hillside. Running away from us—not into the Valley but parallel to the line of haze.

*It was as if he knew the danger,* I thought now. *Maybe some part of Dharak understood what went on in the Hall, and was able to warn Doral. But that sound the cat made—it was good-bye to us, and good-bye to the Valley. If there were any trace of Dharak left, surely Doral would have come back with us.*

I squeezed my eyes shut, and became aware that I was physically shaking my head in denial of that vision. *Doral will be one who survives—for a while. He'll cling to the area until he starves, or becomes so weak that other survivors, driven mad by hunger and poison, gang up on him and kill him for food. I couldn't face Dharak tonight. I couldn't do it.*

I tried to dispel the vision of Doral with images of the females, the cubs, the families who had visibly healed as they had traveled southward with us. The sha'um had considerable native intelligence. Even unstimulated by a mindlink with a Gandalaran, they were capable, I was now convinced, of understanding that they had been sick in the Valley, and were well outside of it. We might lose a few whose instincts for home were paramount, but I felt confident that most of them would stay close by—some out of fatigue; some, perhaps, out of curiosity.

The good thoughts relaxed me, but just before I drifted into an exhausted sleep, I saw again a swift and fleeting vision of a tawny coat flashing into sight between rocks, of a beloved friend fleeing to his doom.

I woke suddenly, my heart pounding. Someone was squatting next to me, the barest silhouette visible in the darkness. A hand was touching my shoulder, and an almost inaudible voice whispered: "Come outside."

The shape stood up. I heard, rather than saw, it move through the bedroom doorway. I heard the difference in the step when he left the tiled floor of the house and stepped softly on the dirt.

*Whoever he is*, I thought, *he didn't alarm Keeshah, which means he's a friend. And if he had wanted Tarani awake, he would have woken both of us.* I listened for a moment to Tarani's even breathing, then made up my mind. I got up quietly, grabbed the light woven cover we seldom used, folded it and wrapped it around my waist. Then I went outside to see the person who had come to us with such an air of mystery.

The moon was setting, the silvery light that pervaded the Gandalaran night was fading swiftly. But I could see, from the doorway of the house, what I could not have sworn to from that brief whisper—my visitor was a man. He stood for a moment facing away from me, watching the tiny waterfall of the stream in which Tarani and I had bathed. Then he turned around.

It was Dharak.

And yet it was not Dharak. This was not the strong and gentle, privately uncertain Lieutenant I had known before Doral had left Thagorn. Nor was it the empty shell, the blank-faced body which had lived in silence in Shola's home for the past few months.

The man was giving off an aura that reminded me of the look I had seen so briefly in Dharak's eyes in the Great Hall. His posture, his positioning, the tension evident in his silhouette—I could almost smell his fear. He looked, for all the world, like a wild thing poised to bolt at the slightest sign of aggression.

I had not been wrong about seeing some intelligence in him before, and in the Great Hall. But I had assumed it was the old Dharak, trying to break out. *I was wrong, so wrong*, I thought pityingly. *The strain snapped him. Amnesia, insanity, something—he's not the Dharak I knew.*

*But he is still*, I thought with determination, *the Lieutenant's father, and he needs my help. For some reason—probably a lingering memory—he has let only me see the truth. I have to try not to scare him, to win his trust.*

My heart was grieving for the old man as I stepped cautiously out of the doorway, into the fading moonlight. "Your name is Dharak," I said quietly, "and mine is Rikardon. We are friends. Please, don't be afraid of me."

I extended my hand toward him—slowly, as the first woman had done toward the frightened female sha'um. He sidled away and I froze, unwilling to frighten him further. He hesitated, then seemed to come to a decision. In amazement I watched him straighten up and step toward me with a strong, confident bearing. He took my arm in a forearm-to-forearm grasp, and held it firmly.

"I know who you are, my friend, because those around me have spoken of you. I know, too, from the leadership you have offered the Sharith and from this personal demonstration of your kindness that you are a fine and good man. But I must tell you that your friend Dharak is no longer here. He has chosen to pass to a different existence, and in his absence I seem to be using his physical self—something that I believe you understand very well."

Shock held me silent for a moment, then in a wave of primordial panic, I let go the stranger's arm and fumbled for the scissor-shaped scrapers on the ledge above the chimneyed lamp mounted on the wall beside the door. Frantically, I snapped the tiny chip of iron against the flint until a spark ignited the candle wick; then I replaced the chimney, put the

sparker down, and pulled the man I had known as Dharak into
the circle of light around the lamp.

I stared into the man's eyes and knew that he meant nothing
so simple as schizophrenia. "You're a Visitor?" I whispered
incredulously, and his direct gaze began to waver.

"Are you not also? It is what I have heard, what Dharak
believed. Was he wrong?" I heard the unspoken, clearly
implied question: Had I lied to Dharak?

"I am a Visitor—of a sort," I admitted, astonished that I was
willing to admit that to a virtual stranger when I had not felt
able even to hint at the truth to any native of Gandalara—not
even to Tarani, before she had learned of and been reconciled
to her own "extra" personality, Antonia Alderuccio.

The man who had begun to look less and less like Dharak
as I concentrated on expression, rather than appearance,
frowned in puzzlement. "There are different kinds?" he asked.

"There are at least two," I answered obscurely, "but that
doesn't matter right now. You must tell me where you come
from."

He frowned again, and it impressed me that he picked up
the significance of my question. "You demand my origin, but
not my identity? Something is very strange about you, my
friend, but I will hide nothing from you. I come from . . .
Raithskar."

There was just the slightest hesitation before he spoke the
city's name. So slight as to be almost unnoticeable, but I
detected it, and it set into motion a rattle-crack chain of pieces
falling into place in my mind. The spooky fear I had felt that
yet someone else from Ricardo's world had been slammed
unprepared into Gandalara was gone. I had suffered through
that experience, and knew that the new person had not had
sufficient time, yet, to lie so nearly perfectly. Yet if this person
were a Gandalaran native from another time, why would he
hesitate to give the name of his home? I had the sense that he
had not lied, but that he had considered and chosen among
alternatives.

It was a hunch, all the way, but it felt so enormously *right*
that I could not, as much as I might have wanted to, refuse to
believe it. I dropped my hands from the man's shoulders and
backed away from him.

"You mean Kä," I said, barely able to whisper the words.
"Raithskar was only your first home. You're Zanek."

The distance growing between us was not only my fault. Dharak, too, took a step backward. "How do you *know* me?" he demanded in a whisper.

"He has touched you," said a voice to my left, "as have I. None who have done so could forget you, or fail to recognize you."

Tarani stepped out into the lamplight, her legs bare beneath a hastily donned desert tunic—mine, judging from its ill fit.

"I was sleeping, and I heard in your voice, in Dharak's tones, the essence of a different man. The difference woke me, and in Rikardon's recognition came my own. Zanek, First King," she said, and she faltered, for a moment showing the youth that was always hidden beneath her poise, "we are . . . honored."

"And I," said Zanek through Dharak's voice, stepping forward with obvious relief, "am bewildered. I have so many questions, such a need for knowledge." Suddenly, firmly, he grabbed one of my hands and one of Tarani's. "I must know this first, my friends. *Are you the ones who will save us all?*"

Tarani looked at me in amazement, and I said: "Uh . . ."

Tarani shifted her arm so that she was holding Zanek's hand. "Come inside," she said. "There are more questions than answers, I fear, and our discussion will take some time."

"Dharak was aware that you are a Visitor, Rikardon, but had no such knowledge about you, Tarani." We had just barely settled in wood-and-cloth armchairs around a small table, on which there was a lamp, a ceramic pitcher of faen, and three drinking cups. "If you recognized me so readily, I should think you would be familiar to me, yet I cannot place you. Who are—perhaps the better phrase is, who *were* you, and from where do you know me?"

"I knew it," I said, with real satisfaction, slapping the arm of my chair and startling the other two. "The All-Mind is *not* the surviving place of your people, Tarani, it is merely their memories. A recording of the lives they lived—not their personalities."

"That is the interpretation to which I have always leaned," Tarani admitted, "but this does, indeed, provide proof."

Zanek had followed our words, and proved his sharpness by his next comment. "You met my memories in the *All-Mind?*" he asked. "How is that possible?"

"I am a Recorder," Tarani said, but Zanek merely looked blank. "It is a version of the mindskill developed after your lifetime," she said, then added: "or Serkajon's."

The man seated across from me flinched violently. "You know that I was a Visitor to Serkajon?" he whispered. "Have I no secrets from you?"

"Lots," I broke in. "To begin with, if it wasn't really you we met in the All-Mind, but only your memories, where *have* you been? And why have you come back now?"

The white-haired old man looked at me sharply. "Would you ask me that," he wondered aloud, "if you had come from the same place as I? Would you not already know that it is a state of being, a place of contentment and peace, a place of oneness and individuality, no concerns and yet awareness?

"I came back, as I did with Serkajon, because I had a sense that I was needed. The difference, this time, lies in the nature of the vessel. Serkajon invited and welcomed me—it was his need, in fact, which drew me back into the world. Dharak, however, merely offered his consent. This time, the need to return was my own. I *have* to know what is happening."

"Could you not see it from your—from the other place?" Tarani asked.

Zanek shook his head.

"Not in detail. We can—the word is not *see*, you understand—" Tarani and I both nodded. "We can 'see' the All-Mind, but cannot touch it as the—'Recorder,' did you say?" Again, Tarani nodded. "We cannot touch and read and see into the All-Mind as you have done, as a Recorder can do. We *can* rejoin the ebb and flow of life that creates the memories which are stored there, but we cannot reach into past lives—not to read, not to change. Even if that were possible, it would have been no use to me. The All-Mind performed its service when it alerted me to the danger."

"What danger?" I demanded, leaning forward out of my chair. "Do you mean Ferrathyn? The Ra'ira? The sha'um? *What do you mean?*"

"I wish I knew," he shot back, angry and sincere. "The nature of the danger is what I hoped to learn from you. I only know of its consequences."

"What consequences?" I demanded.

He hesitated. "You must realize that there is no *time* in the place of my existence," he began. "And there is some part of me still there, which was never a part of this world, and does not return to it with me. As an entire being, I made the choice to return. But"—he gestured helplessly—"as merely Zanek, borrowing the body of Dharak, I do not have the knowledge or the memory of the entire being."

"What consequences?" I asked again, the kernel of a hunch gathering itself somewhere in my gut, getting ready to punch me in the stomach.

"I am trying to tell you that I do not know the full answer to that. When I awoke here, I had only two memories related to why I am here. First, there is an image of the All-Mind, growing and expanding from its beginning, spreading with the growth of Gandalara, always enlarging."

"Like a swelling sphere," Tarani said, her voice soft, her gaze unfocused, "surrounded by a formless, lightlike energy which coalesces into interconnected columns to hold the lifememories of those who have lived, and then their children, and then their grandchildren. The energy recedes as the process continues, and the sphere extends itself to the border of the energy."

"I would not have stated it so," Zanek said in a hushed voice, "but that describes it excellently. You have touched it indeed, my lady. I respect your skill, and would learn more of it."

Tarani's eyes focused on Dharak. "It was my skill," she said, "but not my vision. Rikardon saw it that way, and it seems the truest image I have encountered."

"And the second memory?" I interrupted, the hunch nagging me for more information. "You said you had two memories."

"I have not finished with the first, my friend," Zanek said. "Using your own image, I remembered watching the sphere grow, and I saw it stop growing. Abruptly. Completely." He rubbed a hand across his face. "Do you understand me, my friends?" he asked. "I saw the death of Gandalara. No more lifememories forming because no more lives were being created. Everything ended." He leaned forward, elbows on knees, to stare into the candle flame. "I have said that there is no sense of time in that other existence," he said, "and I have also said that we cannot touch or read the All-Mind. Yet both things are, in some ways, untrue.

"Did I not touch and influence Serkajon before his lifememory had been resigned to the All-Mind? Yet I could 'see' but *not* touch the completed, ended All-Mind, which contained Serkajon's lifememory, which in turn contained evidence of my touch." He shook his head. "It is a paradox which eludes me," he said, then sighed and sat back. "And it is happening again."

Tarani was quicker than I to see what he meant.

"You have seen Dharak's lifememory in the All-Mind," she said, "and yet you are part of it now. That must mean," she said eagerly, "that the ending you saw is beyond the end of Dharak's lifespan. Is that true?"

"True," he said, but his tone of voice was not encouraging. "That brings up the second memory I retain. I know that I have come back close to the end. There will be a sudden expansion of the All-Mind in this generation, and a consistent dwindling thereafter."

"An *expansion* of the All-Mind?" I asked. "Oh, no—the All-Mind grows only with the death of Gandalarans. You mean that a lot of people will die, don't you?" The hunch twisted restively, almost ready to cast its blow. I stood up, and began to pace around the room.

"That fits with Ferrathyn," I said. "Your being here fits with him having the Ra'ira—you've been connected with it from the beginning. But the death of the *race*? Surely that's not Ferrathyn's aim. How can an egomaniac have power if there is no one to control?"

"It *must* be connected," Tarani said. "Zanek, you are sure—it begins now?"

I whirled to look at the old man as he nodded, and the hunch clobbered me so hard that I reeled back physically.

"Your very first question," I reminded him, crossing the floor toward him in a stealthy crouch. I was barely breathing. "You wanted to know if *we* were 'the ones.'"

The man leaned back in his chair, lifting his arms in a gesture of warding off, of protecting.

"You didn't come back just to watch it all end, did you?" I said angrily. "You think there's hope, and you think so because you *did* something. You reached into another world, and you tore us loose, and you dragged us here, without warning us or telling us or helping us."

I leaned over the chair, just barely keeping my hands from closing on the man's throat, because some kernel of reason was whispering: *He made you young again. He gave you new life.*

"It's my turn for a question, Zanek, a question I've asked myself a thousand times in the past months. Why me? Why Ricardo Carillo, a teacher, and Antonia Alderuccio, a sweet, elegant young woman. Why us? *Why?*"

# 20

"I do not *know* why," he shouted back at me. "I do not *know* who you are, where you come from, how you came here." His words rang with such sincerity that I felt myself backing off. He came forward in his chair, speaking earnestly. "I only know that when I realized that what I was seeing was the death of Gandalara, of the people I cherished and protected, to whom I gave hope at the beginning of the Kingdom, who suffered from the corruption of that hope at the end of the Kingdom—when I saw that it was all for nothing, it would end in nothingness, that Gandalara would die . . ."

He closed his eyes briefly, and took a deep breath.

"I grieved. In that place of contentment, that existence of apartness, there was only restlessness and sadness. I could see the death, but not what caused it. I wanted desperately to be able to understand, to help, to prevent. It was a wish so strong, my friends"—he paused to breathe deeply again—"a wish so strong that it seemed to take form, and—yes, in reply to my wish, something happened. As you put it, I *did* something. I knew I had *done* something, but when I looked at the All-Mind, I saw no change.

"It was at that moment that I knew I must return," he said. "Dharak's illness was a convenience for me—I maintained the fiction of being stunned, and listened to everything."

"You heard Thymas wishing for his father's help," I said slowly. "Before we left Thagorn last time, you heard us talking—it was *you* who looked at me that day."

"It was I," Zanek admitted. "And that was the first day I began to understand that you were different from all others. I could not be sure, then, that you were the hope and not the cause. It is only now, after I have seen you struggle for the survival of the sha'um and, thus, for the Sharith, after I have seen your respect for life, your strength, your unusual knowledge—"

He stopped, struck by a thought.

"What did you say, earlier? You are from . . . 'another world'? How can that be? There is only Gandalara."

"How can you believe that?" Tarani asked. "That place where part of you continues to exist—can you not see all worlds, all time from that place?"

"Can I?" he asked, bewildered. "I—that knowledge did not return with me, if I have it." He stood up, suddenly excited. "But it makes perfect sense, and fits in with the few memories I have. I recall despairing as I looked on the immobile All-Mind. When Gandalara was divided by dispute and greed, I held in my hands the power to help. With the Ra'ira as my secret, my *benevolent* weapon, I brought people together, instructed them in the concept of sharing, and of the welfare of one being the concern of all. I devoted my first, only true lifetime to that task, and I saw it as nothing less than preservation of Gandalara.

"When Serkajon saw how my vision had failed the future generations, I knew that *I* had the knowledge, the power to be of service once again, and I took the action I *knew* to be right— again, with the goal of preserving something good and worth saving.

"But when I saw this new danger, I knew I was helpless to serve again in any meaningful way. I was plagued with doubt, in fact, that my earlier efforts had been in vain—or worse, that I had unknowingly created whatever situation would result in the utter destruction of Gandalara. When I wished for help, I wished for knowledge and insight beyond my own limits. I wanted something or someone to see everything clearly, to know what was happening, to know what to do about it.

"And I see, now, that I could not have wished for a Gandalaran, *any* Gandalaran." He offered me both his hands. "More than I can tell you, I regret that you were drawn here against your will, your own life destroyed," he said. "I tell you again, it was not my conscious choice, I would not have done this harm to you deliberately, even if it meant Gandalara must truly die. But I see the goodness of what you have done already, and I know that, however this occurred, you were well chosen for this task.

"*You* have the knowledge that is needed. Who else—what Gandalaran—could have seen the danger to the sha'um, and taken such quick action to prevent it?"

"He is right," Tarani said, standing up and extending her hands to touch our joined hands. "How often have we said that to one another, Rikardon—that it is our *difference* which is so important to our destiny?"

"Destiny?" Zanek repeated. "Then you know? You know what is to happen, why you are here?"

"We know some things," I admitted reluctantly, and pulled my hands from the three-way joining. I moved closer to the table and poured faen into the three drinking cups. I handed Tarani one, Zanek another, then took up the third as I sat back down in my chair. "Forgive me my anger," I said. "The few things we do know we have found out in small pieces, never enough to make sense. It *still* doesn't make sense," I said, letting my frustration show.

"Perhaps," Tarani said, taking her seat again, "our difference has been inhibiting our full understanding. Each of us," she said, gesturing in particular to Zanek/Dharak, "has a different kind of knowledge. Let us each share it, and perhaps together we can find the answers."

"Tell me first," Zanek said, "of the Ra'ira. You mentioned it, and a man's name—Ferra . . . ?"

"Ferrathyn," I said wearily. "Look, I'm having trouble trying to keep straight what you know as Zanek, and what you may know from Dharak's memories, and what I did or didn't have time to tell Dharak. It seems the long way around, I know, but why don't Tarani and I tell you our story, as it has happened from the start? Maybe you can find your answers along the way—and maybe the retelling will jar something loose we haven't seen before."

"That is an excellent plan," Zanek said, and raised his cup in a salute to each of us. "I will not interrupt with questions, unless I truly fail to understand your words. And I fully expect to be fascinated."

It was dawn, and I had walked outside the house to stretch, watch the brilliant colors seep across the unblackened part of the sky, and wonder if I had dreamed the events of the night. It seemed incredible that Tarani and I had spent the past several hours telling a man from the dawn of history about the immediate past history of his world.

I heard a rumbling to my right, and Keeshah came stretching out of the bushes, and stopped beside me. Without warning, he slammed his head into my stomach and levered me off the ground slightly, then he moved on past. I caught his tail as it slapped into my side and pulled lightly; he snatched it free and jumped ahead, looking back disdainfully.

*Look silly,* he said, then walked to the stream for a drink.

I looked down at myself, and realized that the action of his head against my midriff had broken loose the haphazard tucking of the bedcover I had continued to wear through the night. The cover had slipped off and puddled in a circle around my ankles. Otherwise, I was stark naked. I bent over to grab the cover, then jumped forward with a yelp as something cold touched my bare bottom. The cover caught my feet, and I sprawled face down in the dirt, my dignity badly damaged. A paw and a lot of weight slapped me down again as I tried to push my shoulders off the ground, and two young but well-grown sha'um used me for a doormat, ignoring the ungentle things I was calling out to them through our mindlink. The last paw left my back, and I rolled over furiously—only to see Yayshah looming over me, one paw lifted delicately.

"Not you too?" I groaned, and grabbed to protect the most vulnerable part of my anatomy. But Yayshah placed her paw delicately on the ground on the other side of me, and carefully stepped over my prostrate—and thoroughly dirty—body.

I sat up with every intention of yelling at the cubs, then I grabbed frantically for the bedcover. Tarani and Zanek were in the doorway, laughing like idiots.

*What the hell?* I thought grumpily.

I stood up, gathered the bedcover, and threw it to the ground. Then I took off for the stream at a run and, before the sha'um could catch my purpose and react, I vaulted over the cubs and landed painfully—but with a great deal of splashing and satisfaction—in the middle of the stream.

The cubs howled and backed away, shaking themselves. Yayshah looked mortally offended, so that I felt obliged to say: "Sorry—I know you didn't deserve that." Keeshah merely turned upstream to drink from the unmuddied water, but he had to have the last word.

*Still look silly,* he said.

I turned around to climb out of the stream, but found Tarani there, holding out a bar of scented soap. "As long as you've begun . . . ?" she said, and my grumpiness dissolved. I took the soap, laughing, and she laid a towel and a set of clothes across a twisting dakathrenil limb. "Breakfast will be ready, when you are dry."

Over breakfast—fruit and bread and a soft cheese—Tarani and I discussed how much we still did not know. We had overcome our disappointment over Zanek not having all the answers, but I, for one, felt the niggling frustration of having the answers within reach.

"All the pieces are here somewhere," I said, for probably the fourteenth time. "Why can't we see how they fit together?"

"I must repeat that I am not the one who is *capable* of assembling them," said Zanek, who had been silent and thoughtful through most of the meal. "There must be something that you two—no one else—know or can do."

"We have told you of Ferrathyn, and our resistance to his power," Tarani said. "Is that not unique in Gandalara?"

"It's unique," I said, "but—I know this sounds stupid, after all we've been doing—but it's not *important* enough. Ferrathyn *is* dangerous, he *will* corrupt and destroy the *societies* of Gandalara. But how and why would he deliberately destroy the people themselves? It just doesn't make sense."

"Perhaps Ferrathyn is only part of it," Zanek said. "He may be, in fact, the part of the puzzle which *I* detected—it might have been the misuse of the Ra'ira that caught my attention in the first place. There are other things you have done which have affected Gandalara profoundly. Perhaps it is only as a whole that it makes sense. Eddarta becoming more humane. The sha'um protected from destruction. The Sharith, for the first time in generations, with a Captain to lead them. The— What is it, my friend?"

I had caught Zanek's hand without realizing it. The fruit he held fell unnoticed to the floor. I was looking at him, but what I was seeing was something else. Hazy images were crystallizing, pieces were falling into place. A map. A volcano. Salty deserts. Copper. No iron.

The result was an answer that I believed and rejected in exactly the same thought.

"No!" I moaned. "That *can't* be it!"

But I knew it was true, and it raised a specter that terrified me so that I began to shake all over.

"Please, no," I said again, whispering now. I turned my eyes toward Tarani, who was watching me in alarm. "Not now, not ever, that's too much to ask."

"Rikardon, *tell* us," Tarani pleaded, sliding down from her chair to kneel beside me. I still clutched Zanek's hand fiercely.

"Get the map," I begged Tarani. "Hurry, get it, please." She rushed to hunt for it, and I looked down to find Zanek's fingers turning white in my grasp. I released his hand, mumbling "Sorry."

"You know, don't you?" he asked softly. "Is it so horrible? Can it be changed?"

"Changed?" I echoed. Tarani arrived, knocked the dishes aside, and, kneeling beside me, unfolded the map on the small table. "You were the one," I said to Tarani, "who first mentioned that the map looked familiar. Study it now, and try to figure out *why* it's so familiar."

She started to protest.

"Don't you understand?" I asked, nearly yelling. "I could be wrong, so wrong! I need you to figure it out on your own. Look at the map through Antonia's memories. Please, Tarani, do it."

With a puzzled frown, she did as I asked. Her fingers traced the lines of the Walls slowly, and her face was intent as she stared at the parchment. After a moment, she said, in a strained voice: "There is still a familiarity, but I cannot capture it. I *cannot*, my love. Please—just tell me."

"Try this," I said, and took the map. "Gandalaran map convention shows the Great Wall as the northern border of the world, right? But we both know that this line"—I pointed to the thick line that ran unevenly across the top of the map— "actually runs sort of northwest-southeast."

"Yes," she agreed, as I rotated the map to put the line into that position from her viewpoint. She frowned. "Yes, from that perspective, the feeling of familiarity is stronger."

"Then consider what the land is like," I went on. Zanek was leaning over the table, silent and tense. "There are few heavy metals, few metals at all, in fact, except east and north of Eddarta."

"In the copper mines," she said, "here." She put her finger on the map in the general area I had described, then she touched the area marked "Rikalara"—"the high place." "There is something about this positioning," she said, and moved her hand to Raithskar. "And the shape of this border . . . Ahh-h-h!"

She flew back from the map as if she had been stung.

She cowered away for a moment, then came back toward the table and put a trembling hand on the map. "It makes an insane sort of sense," she said. "But—I still do not see how . . ."

"What? What is it?" demanded Zanek, looking from one to the other of us.

I held my hand up to calm him. "Give me just one more minute," I begged. "Tarani, tell me. *Say it. Please.*"

She touched the area of the copper mines.

"This is Cyprus," she said, the non-Gandalaran word sounding odd but musical. She tapped the map southwest of the copper mines. "Eddarta—it must lie at the mouth of the Nile." Her finger moved west. "Rikalara—Crete." She skipped over to Raithskar and followed the line of the Great Wall with a gesture that was unconsciously caressing. "The Skarkel River—the Rhone?"

She looked up at me, her eyes hollow and still questioning. "The land masses seem very different, but the outline is recognizable. The Middle Sea, the Mediterranean. That is it, is it not, Rikardon? The sea has vanished, and Gandalarans walk its dry and salty floor?"

I saw panic start to form in the back of her dark eyes, and I took her hands. "What happened?" she wailed. "The sea, our world—what has happened to us?"

"Nothing," I shouted, slipping down to kneel beside her and hold her tightly against me. "Believe me, please. Our world is safe." She shivered so violently that we were both shaking. "You and I—that is, Antonia and Ricardo—we are the only ones affected by this."

"How do you *know*?" she demanded. "Where has the water *gone*? Surely this could not happen quickly—*Madre mia*," she whispered in Italian. "We have moved through time. A war? A holocaust? Devastation and a new evolution? Time, so much time—how much time? Ricardo, how *much* time?"

"Fifty million years," I said, "or thereabouts. But not forward, Tarani. *Back*. We are in our own earth's past."

She grew still, then drew away from me. "What?"

"Geology held a lot of interest for Ricardo. I read about the discoveries in the Mediterranean that proved it had been closed off and dried up at one time. The tectonic plates of Europe and Africa had shifted toward each other, and closed up the Straits of Gibraltar. Scientists found evidence of the evaporation on the ocean floor. Salt mounds. Like the up-and-down character of the Kapiral—rounded hills underneath a centuries-long buildup of drifting sand." I was speaking quickly, throwing in English words where Gandaresh was inadequate.

"The *past?*" Tarani whispered, and I nodded.

"My friends," Zanek said, his voice strained. "Your words are strange, but I gather that you have found the answer to the mystery. Please, I beg you, speak to me in words that I can understand. What is happening? Can you stop it?"

Tarani and I stared at one another. We were not ignoring Zanek purposely, but we were entirely caught up in a shared, awesome vision.

"It became a sea again," Tarani said.

"Yes, the plates shifted again; the straits reopened; the floor of the ocean filled with water. It took a long time," I said, thoughtfully. "Anything built of salt would have dissolved gradually. Stone and wood buildings would have rotted and shifted until they became part of the ocean floor, nothing more than starting places for coral colonies."

"We sailed upon that sea in our own time," Tarani said shakily. "Do you see what that means? We did not prevent it in our past. If we *could* prevent it—would that not destroy the present we knew, possibly prevent our existence? But . . ." She frowned. "If we did not exist, we would not have been called to Gandalara. We would not have had the opportunity to interfere."

"Hush," I said. "You're describing the classic paradox of time travel. We are here now," I said. "And I don't think we're intended to stop the Mediterranean from refilling. It's not possible—not even with the technology and explosives of our own time. The earth's might is too great to control."

"Then what?" Tarani asked. "What can we do? What *did* we do?"

"Stop thinking like that," I urged her. "What we *do* and what we *did* may not be the same thing."

The thought felt right, and I began to be excited.

"They may not be the same thing at all."

# 21

A knocking sounded from the doorway, making us all jump so violently that the table overturned and the map flew into Zanek's lap. A serving dish flipped up by the edge of the table, rocketed through the air, and shattered loudly against the stone of the wall.

Thymas rushed in, alarmed by the noise.

"Rikardon, Tarani, I did not mean to frighten you—" The boy stopped in his tracks when he noticed the white-haired man. "*Father?*" he asked. Thymas rushed over to crouch awkwardly beside the chair and throw his arms around the man he had known, all his life, as Dharak.

Tarani and I exchanged glances, then rose quietly and went outside. I looked back to see Zanek holding the boy tenderly. Over the shaking shoulders, he nodded to us, grimly agreeing that the boy deserved the consideration of privacy when he learned the truth.

Thymas's arrival—and our feelings about that—provided only a momentary distraction from the problem.

"In the world Rikardon and Antonia knew," Tarani said, "Gandalara died without a trace—vanished. How can we alter what was? And if we could . . ."

She frowned, and I saw that she was caught up again in the paradox. I took her shoulders and turned her to face me.

"We can't," I said. "We *can't* alter our own world. Accept that, and don't be afraid that what we do here will affect anything in the present which we knew—not the one we lived in."

"'The *one*'?" she quoted.

"There are as many theories about time as there are people who think about it seriously," I said. "One of them says that there are things called *timelines*, moving along parallel to one another. The theory goes that such timelines are created at a moment of choice somewhere in their common past. Some of them also say that, at that critical choice point—and most

theorists agree that it does have to be an event of some
significance—*all* possible alternatives are chosen, each one
developing an independent timeline."

She frowned again, thinking hard. "Do you mean that since
we *are* here, our mere presence has generated a new timeline,
and Gandalara will survive?" She pushed me away, and paced
off toward the stream. "How? We could not hold back the
water? What could we—" She whirled back. "We cannot save
this *world*," she said, "but we may be able to save the *people*.
That is it, am I right? It is the special knowledge Zanek wished
for. We *know*, we can tell them, we can save them!"

"Whoa," I said. "Wait a minute. You seem to be asking me
for an opinion, but you're not giving me a chance to answer.
Some of that, I think, is right. Some of it isn't."

"Which?" she demanded. "The use of our knowledge—that
is correct, it *must* be; there is no other way in which we *might*
help."

"I think you're absolutely right about that. It *is* the 'bottom
line.' It's why we're here," I said. "But it's not as simple as it
sounds, and there is more to it. How can that knowledge help
Gandalara in and of itself, Tarani? We start now, and tell
everyone that the earthquake and the volcano are symptoms of
the end of their world? The Great Pleth is coming back, a lot
faster than it left, and if they don't hurry, they're going to
drown in it? Think like *only* Tarani for a moment, darling. How
would she react to such an announcement?"

The girl stared at the wall of the house, thinking, and then
her shoulders sagged.

"I see," she said. "No one will believe. They do not have the
*concepts* to believe." There was sadness, fear, and confusion in
her eyes as she turned to me. "Have we come to Gandalara
only to die in its death throes?" she asked. "And what of your
all-possible-choices theory? We *are* here—will we not, merely
by that truth, contribute some change?"

"We have the opportunity to contribute change," I said.
"That is what Zanek wished for, and what he got. I think I said
that the all-possible-choices theory is only one line of thought
in the area. Others say that people are the key, that which
timelines develop depends on the actions or merely the
existence of people in a position to make those choices. There
must be a timeline, for instance, in which Adolf Hitler died

during one of his childhood illnesses, and the Third Reich never happened.

"We can be that key here, Tarani," I said, "but not just by telling the truth." I took a deep breath. For the first time since I had arrived in Gandalara it all did, truly, *finally* make sense to me. There was a residual, continuous "Why me?" sort of feeling, but all the whats and whys were at last coming to light.

"It will take years to refill the basin," I said. "What did Zanek say? Three to five generations? But remember, he saw the All-Mind as it was *before* you and I came.

"Try to look at today's Gandalara as it would have been without us, Tarani. Ferrathyn unchallenged, probably already in control of Raithskar. The sha'um dead or dying. The Chizan crossing impassable because Chizan itself had been destroyed and abandoned. Eddarta with the Lords still thinking only of their own welfare, living enclosed and isolated. They would notice the lack of trade from the western side, of course, but their response would be to drain their landservants of the luxuries they were missing, until revolution took hold and the whole society of Eddarta was reduced to a disorganized mob. Under those conditions, I can readily see the end of life in Gandalara within five generations.

"But the government of Eddarta has been awakened, and the life-supporting corridor between Raithskar and Eddarta is still open, thanks to Ligor. Already, we have bought more time for the people of Gandalara.

"We can't change the physical truth, Tarani, but we have already changed the social character of Gandalara, and we need to make more changes. The only chance these people have is to recognize their danger *now* and begin to do something *now*. While Ferrathyn's around and contributing disorder and chaos, everyone will be too preoccupied to notice what's happening until it's too late—even if they *could* understand it."

"Are you saying," Tarani asked slowly, "that our destiny remains, partly at least, what we thought it to be—Ferrathyn's defeat? What of the Ra'ira?" She looked at me sharply, struck by a sudden thought. "Rikardon, could the Ra'ira be a *weapon* against this disaster? Might the flooding be stopped, or contained, through some property of the stone?"

"I doubt it," I said, frowning. "I think our role with respect to the Ra'ira is defensive, as it has always been. Get it away from Ferrathyn and protect it from madmen like him in the future."

She made a gesture of exasperation. "Then I still do not see, my love, anything we might *do* to prevent the calamity. Delay, yes, I accept that we have accomplished at least that much. But not prevention. Have we come here for a futile purpose?"

I took her shoulders and turned her toward me. "You're thinking totally like Tarani," I said, "like a native of Gandalara who believes that the World between the Walls is all the world there is."

She gasped. "You would have us *leave* Gandalara? But that is not—" She stopped to think a moment. "I see that it is physically possible," she admitted, "in one way. That is, there are some areas of the Walls which might be climbable. Yet recall how difficult it is to breathe in the high places. We would have no strength—to climb the Walls would be as sure a death as to walk into the growing Pleth and drown."

"That's true now," I agreed, "because we're adapted to the air pressure and altitude of the *floor* of Gandalara. We—our Gandalaran bodies—were born here. But we—our other bodies—were born with the top of the Walls as the floor of our world, and we survived there pretty easily. As nearly as I can figure it, the Khumbar Pass is almost at a height which Ricardo and Antonia thought of as 'sea level.' In their world, it would be the narrow channel between Corsica and Sardinia. I've crossed that pass, Tarani—Keeshah and I both made it. That tells me that Gandalarans have the basic lung power to survive on the—let's call it the 'surface.' A person born on the floor of Gandalara would not be comfortable on the surface, because it is too much a change from the metabolism, lung and heart speed that his body has trained itself to. But a person born and raised on the Walls of Gandalara—say half a mile below the surface—could make that climb and live reasonably comfortably on the surface."

"Born on the Walls?" Tarani echoed, looking puzzled.

"Specifically," I said, "the River Wall."

Suddenly, the expression of confusion vanished and Tarani grabbed my arms in an excited, almost painful grip. "I see it. Yes, I see your vision now, Rikardon. The River Wall climbs gradually to the surface, and provides a ready source of fresh water. It is as far as possible from the area which is refilling, which would grant us even more time.

"For the climb must be slow, am I right?" she asked, then hurried on without waiting for an answer. Her eyes were looking over my shoulder, into the future—a possible future. "Each generation would climb to a level at which their breathing discomfort is tolerable, so that their children would grow to it naturally, and lead the next generation even higher."

"It *is* possible," I said. "It will take a lot of faith and commitment for a group of people to start and continue a journey like that, generation after generation."

"It would require peace, as well," Tarani said thoughtfully. "The business of relocating and surviving would require all the attention the people could spare. Harassment by Ferrathyn or others who might disrupt the journey for private gain—a continual possibility while the Ra'ira is open to abuse—would be fatal to the purpose."

"It's important to take Ferrathyn out of the picture for another reason too," I said. "As High Lord, you might be able to convince the Eddartans to undertake the journey. As Captain, I could probably persuade the Sharith to join us. But climbing the Wall is only part of the story, Tarani," I said. "At the top, Gandalarans will have an entirely different climate, a new environment to cope with.

"Gandalaran society won't survive up there unless it changes, and change is always promoted by cross-fertilizing different attitudes, viewpoints, skills. The more of 'old' Gandalara that reaches the surface, the better chance for a healthy 'new' Gandalara. 'New' Gandalara will need what Raithskar has—the concept of elected officials, a knowledge of how to mine and work iron, skill with irrigation and ceramics. It will need the glassmakers of Dyskornis, and those who quarry and mason Omergol's green marble. The journey up the River Wall must be undertaken by *all* of Gandalara—not just parts of it. And as long as Ferrathyn has the Ra'ira and control of Raithskar and the vineh, there is no hope of that kind of unity."

"An excellent analysis, Rikardon," said Zanek from the doorway. He glanced quickly at Thymas, who had stepped out in front of him and stood a little way behind me. The boy looked confused and sad, but he smiled slightly in response to my nod of greeting.

"I have given the Lieutenant a far too brief summary of what we have learned of one another during the night, my friends,"

Zanek said. "At this point, he understands even less than I do of this discussion, to which we have been listening unashamed for the past few moments. I do see, however, that you both believe you have found the answer for which I wished so deeply, and I am profoundly grateful. Anything that I can do to aid you, you may ask of me."

"I may ask a great deal," I said grimly, looking into the old man's eyes.

He looked at me questioningly.

"You heard what I said—that the journey we plan must be undertaken by *all* of Gandalara?"

Zanek nodded.

"The first step is to defeat Ferrathyn. Your knowledge of the Ra'ira and your mindskill may help us."

A shadow fell into the old man's eyes, then passed on.

"It is not a welcome task, as I feel sure you already knew when you proposed it," Zanek said. "However, what I can do, I will."

"That's the easy part," I said, allowing myself a smile. "The hard part comes after Ferrathyn is beaten. It will be necessary to reunite the separate parts of Gandalara, to bring everyone together in a single purpose." Zanek's eyes widened, and his face turned pale. "I won't argue that you've already done more than your share for this world," I said softly. "But neither can you dispute the fact that the symbol of the First King, returned to found and lead a new Kingdom, is possibly the only thing that would draw Gandalara together after the damage wrought by the shaking earth and Ferrathyn's madness."

Before Zanek could reply, Thymas stepped forward and spoke.

"You are assuming," he said, "that everyone will believe, without question, that Zanek has returned. I have seen him and spoken to him, and it has not been easy for me to believe it."

Zanek found his voice.

"The Lieutenant makes a valid point," he said, "and so do you, Rikardon. I would ask your patience, and make no commitment just now. The prospect of accepting such responsibility again—it will take some consideration, not only of my feelings but of my capabilities. As you say, it is Ferrathyn's defeat which is the first step, though not, as you say"—he smiled—"the 'easy part.' Let us concentrate on that effort first, and delay this awkward choice until it is clearly needed."

"The defeat of Ferrathyn," Tarani said suddenly. "Rikardon, you have not made it clear to me yet. In this time-changing theory you describe, is our victory over Ferrathyn assured merely through our presence?"

"I wish I could say yes to that, Tarani," I answered, "but I can't. If our continued presence in our own world had made a difference there, I'd say, logically, that our arrival here makes change inevitable. But Antonia and Ricardo both had such a short time left to live, I doubt their sudden absence created an event significant enough to alter *that* timeline."

"Then . . . in our own 'timeline' we might have been called back in just this way, and still—and still failed," she said.

"There is no way to know," I said. "All I know, what I *believe*, is that Ferrathyn and the geologic changes are part of the same world-changing event which is capable of generating *two* timelines. In one, Gandalara disappears from the earth's memory and is never known to the future. In the other, Gandalara survives to climb over its own Walls, and humanity—if not strictly *Homo sapiens*—walks the surface of the earth fifty million years early.

"I don't think merely our being here is enough to guarantee success," I said. "But I also know that if we fail, it won't be because we didn't try. Agreed?" I asked, looking around.

The four of us came together in a massive hug that carried with it the special sweetness of hope.

# 22

"How likely is it," I asked Zanek, "that Ferrathyn knows what we know?"

Zanek looked up from the map on the table to frown at me. "Did you not say that you and Tarani are resistant to his power?" he asked.

"*We* are," I said slowly. Thymas had left us less than an hour ago, and would return as soon as he felt able to leave his mother.

*That's a hard message to carry,* I thought to myself. *"Dharak's body is alive, but my father doesn't live there anymore." I'm glad Thymas is not here now, though, because this is a tough question, and one he would be especially sensitive to.*

"I guess I'm really asking about the power of the Ra'ira. We feel sure that Ferrathyn's power reached all the way to Eddarta, to help Gharlas when he fought Tarani, me, and Thymas. Can't he reach into Thagorn, to a mind that he *can* read, and learn all our plans as quickly as we make them?"

Zanek nodded. "I see your concern," he said, "but it is unfounded." He smiled. "It surprises me that you do not already have that answer, from our 'meeting' in the All-Mind."

"Those meetings were very brief," I said, "too brief. In case I haven't mentioned it, I feel very honored to have the opportunity to really know you, Zanek."

He shifted his weight in the armchair, and seemed at a loss for anything to say. Tarani chose that moment to come inside again, having gone out to the stream to fill a water pitcher. She looked from one to the other of us as she gathered drinking cups from a high shelf and set them on the table. "What have I missed?" she asked, pouring water into the cups.

"I was only thinking," I said, "that we still don't know much about Ferrathyn, and even less about his powers, with and without the Ra'ira. I'd say our experience has proved that he can't read our minds, though his compulsion power does have a limited effect on us. But what's to keep him from watching our movements through the other people in Thagorn? Or does he not even know we're in Thagorn?" I threw up my hands. "How can we *fight* somebody if we don't know *anything* about his capabilities?"

"We *do* know about his capabilities," Zanek assured me, taking one of the cups from Tarani. "At least, as far as the Ra'ira is concerned. To answer your earlier question about seeing thoughts at a distance, that can be done only under specific conditions and at the cost of a great deal of physical strain."

"What are the conditions?" Tarani asked.

"In concept, it is rather like the way a maufel guides a maufa," he said, sipping thoughtfully at his water. "The linking element is not a place, however, but a person."

Tarani was quick to grasp the point Zanek was making.

"A bird cannot be sent to a place his handler has not seen," she said, "and Ferrathyn cannot see the thoughts of people at a distance unless . . ." She paused, thinking. "There must be someone present at that distant place," she said, turning to me suddenly, "someone like Gharlas who has been—" She turned back to Zanek. "What would you call it?" she asked him. "Touched? Marked?"

Zanek shrugged. "Either term would do, I should think. What happens is that once you—meaning someone who is using the Ra'ira—have contacted a person's mind frequently, a sort of bond is established. You can create such a bond deliberately; I did it, myself, with anyone who was going somewhere to speak for the Kingdom.

"That bond survives any distance, but the effort of reaching it increases with the distance between you and the familiar mind."

Thinking of Gharlas, I asked: "Is it possible for you to use the, um, familiar mind as a channel for your own mindgifts?"

"Such as?" he returned.

"Such as," I said, "using that familiar mind as a—a distant base from which you can see what's going on, cast compulsions, read other people's thoughts, or—uh—create another familiar bond."

Tarani gasped, but said nothing. Zanek looked from one to the other of us, then leaned forward in his chair, elbows on knees.

"I see this has a special meaning for you," he said. "No, it is not possible—at least, I never did it."

"What about the people who 'spoke for the Kingdom'?" I asked. "This occurred to me when you said that, because I thought you meant you could exercise all your power through them."

Zanek shook his head. "No, I saw only their circumstances through their own minds. If they could not handle a situation, I ordered them to return to Kä and I journeyed to the place myself."

"Were any of your 'speakers' mindgifted?" Tarani asked.

"Some, I'm sure," Zanek said. "Why?"

"Tarani is thinking," I said, standing up and stretching, "that through Gharlas, Ferrathyn has twice touched Thymas's mind. You say you never tried it, Zanek, and I also know that mindgifts were not as widespread, nor people as familiar with them, as they are now. Gharlas had a considerable native gift which Ferrathyn was able to use. Possibly, he used it only by suggestion or compulsion, and it was only Gharlas's own strength we felt.

"Possibly, however, Gharlas's mindpower made him an especially effective familiar, and allowed Ferrathyn's strength and skills to work through him—at a distance."

"I agree that my experience does not preclude that possibility," Zanek said after a moment, "but my memory is very clear on the amount of effort it required merely to contact someone I knew a great distance away. If such a thing is possible, I feel strongly that it would be practical only if the familiar mind stayed fairly close to the person using the Ra'ira."

"Practical," I echoed, thinking: *He's said it probably couldn't happen, and he's the most valid authority we have. Why won't I believe him? Why is this idea bugging me so?* "But possible at the longer distances?"

"Yes, *possible*," he emphasized, moving impatiently in his chair.

"I don't mean to doubt your opinion," I said, "but—"

"You know how this conversation would hurt Thymas, if he heard it," Tarani interrupted, looking at the cup in her hands.

"Yes, I do know," I said quietly. She turned the empty cup in her hands, still not looking at me. "I also know how he would feel if it were true, and we ignored the possibility."

"Thymas?" Zanek said, with genuine surprise. "You suspect Thymas of being such a second-stage familiar mind?"

"Twice he was exposed, for a prolonged period of time, to compulsion control by Gharlas, and to some extent, we're sure, by Ferrathyn *through* Gharlas. It might have been enough time, given Gharlas's usability as a channel, for Ferrathyn to make such a bond."

"Twice Thymas threw off Gharlas's control," Tarani said, beginning to sound angry. She put her cup down on the table and stood up. "How can you suspect he would allow such an abomination?"

"Of course he wouldn't allow it—if he knew about it," I said. I stood up, too, and put my hands on Tarani's shoulders. "I saw how he hated being controlled, Tarani. But this may be a completely different feeling, one he can't detect. I don't want to believe it—I *don't* believe it. But I don't think we have room for even the slightest error about this sort of thing."

"You want to exclude Thymas from our plans?" she said, and I nodded miserably.

"I know it will hurt Thymas terribly," I said. "But I think he will understand. I think, in my place, he would do the same thing."

"Personal considerations aside," Zanek said, so that I released Tarani and we both turned toward him, "and looking at it from a purely practical point of view, how can the Captain of the Sharith exclude the Lieutenant from plans which may include the Sharith?"

I started pacing, thoughts which had been floating around in my head beginning to coalesce into an idea. "For a while," I said, "the Sharith will not be in any condition to sustain a fight. They're going to be busy incorporating the new population of sha'um, getting accustomed to women being Riders, sorting out what that means to the sha'um and their own lifestyle. Thymas has every practical need to concentrate on guiding the Sharith through this period of confusion. We only need to tell him the truth," I said decisively, "that Tarani and I are going into Raithskar to see what's happening, and will send for the Sharith when they are needed."

Zanek sat up, a shocked look on his face.

"You would face Ferrathyn alone?" he asked.

"Not *face* him," I assured the old man, "but, as I said, *scout* him. How often have we said that we know too little about him, and about his plans? And we certainly know too little of what is really happening in Raithskar.

"Tarani and I have the best chance to get into Raithskar undetected," I said. "And that's about as far as we can plan right now, because our next actions will depend on what we find there."

"But you do mean to send for the Sharith?" Zanek said.

"If they are needed," I said. "I have a feeling that they will be needed badly."

Zanek shook his head. "If the Lieutenant is an information source for Ferrathyn," he said, "I see no substantial difference between his knowing your full plans and his knowing that you are in Raithskar, attempting to learn Ferrathyn's plans."

"You're right," I admitted. "So we may have to lie to him by omission—he won't know we're in Raithskar. He may come to suspect it, but if Ferrathyn is 'listening in,' that can only serve to keep him nervous."

"How can we hide our going?" Tarani demanded.

"Zanek," I said, "will you go back to Thagorn immediately? Keeshah will take you, in fact, if—" I stopped at the look on Zanek's face, and remembered that he had once been a Rider, but his sha'um had left him voluntarily, to allow him to concentrate on the serious and time-consuming business of the new Kingdom.

"It's only to be sure you reach Thymas before he returns here," I said, "and Keeshah's presence will lend credence to what you'll tell Thymas."

"Which will be . . . ?"

"Part of what we've mentioned—that the Sharith need some time to get acclimated to the new circumstances, and that Tarani and I will be resting and"—I took her hand; she pressed mine and flashed me a quick smile—"getting reacquainted after our long separation. He'll respect that, and leave us alone for a few days."

Now Zanek stood up, and he paced around the room, out the door, came back in. "I must say I have somewhat more regard, now," he said, "for the people who followed my orders without question. I do not wish to remain behind, Rikardon."

I put my hand on his shoulder. "I'd like to have you with us, Zanek," I said sincerely. "But here again, I'm trying to play the odds. If Thymas is *not* connected to Ferrathyn, then Ferrathyn has no idea that you're back, and it would be to our advantage to keep that a surprise as long as possible. If you go to Raithskar with us, you'll be going into range to be contacted directly by Ferrathyn."

Finally, he nodded and sighed. "Yes, I see the sense of it," he agreed. "But I have one more question," he said, and I waited. "Assume—as we all truly believe—that Thymas is *not* Ferrathyn's channel. In Raithskar, you feel the need to summon the Sharith, so you visit a maufel, who sends a message to Thagorn—despite the fact that the Fa'aldu would be violating their own taboo against visiting the stronghold of the Sharith. Ferrathyn catches the thought and the message from the maufel, and is warned of our movement. Will not all your effort toward surprise be wasted?"

"It would be," I agreed, "if we planned to send a message

with a maufa. The cubs will be with us; one of them will carry messages for you, and only you. Not as fast as a message bird, of course, but fast enough."

"Then you have satisfied all my practical objections," Zanek said, "even though my feelings still want to go with you." He slapped my shoulder, his hand lingering to squeeze it for a moment. There was a rough affection and respect in the gesture that caused my throat to tighten up. "I shall do my best with Thymas—deceive him when I must, help him where I can. If you will call Keeshah and direct him, I will be on my way."

He turned to Tarani and held out his other hand, which she took. "Care for yourselves well, my friends. I regret the pain I have caused you, but I cannot regret that you are here. I hope we shall be together again soon."

"In a world free of Ferrathyn's threat," Tarani added. She looked odd and awkward for a moment, then dropped Zanek's hand and threw her arms around his neck. He staggered back a step, caught his balance, and returned the hug with as much force as it was given.

After a moment, Tarani stepped back, and said in a shaky voice: "Waste no time in regret, King Zanek," she said. "Both Antonia and Tarani have gained more than any cost, past or future, can match. I am content."

Zanek nodded sharply once, then again, and finally turned away from Tarani to go outside. I followed him out, and was standing beside him when Keeshah bounded from the edge of the clearing to crouch in front of us. Zanek walked toward the big cat, his hands clenched into fists, his arms trembling. He stopped, just before mounting.

I had already asked Keeshah about taking Zanek into Thagorn, and he had agreed.

*Man coming?* Keeshah wondered, turning his head as far as he could to watch Zanek. *Hurry.*

*Give him a moment, Keeshah. This is hard for him.*

*Boring,* Keeshah snorted, and turned forward, stretched his neck, and laid his head on his forepaws. The muscles of his legs and along his flank relaxed, and his body settled to the ground.

*Keeshah, don't—do you want to insult him?* I demanded

in a panic. But Zanek only laughed, and some of the tension in *his* body seemed to leave with Keeshah's.

"Sometimes it is easy to guess what a sha'um is thinking," he said. "I apologize for the delay, but . . ."

His voice trailed off, and I said: "I think I understand. You once gave up a sha'um."

"No," he said in a soft, almost guilty voice. "I gave up *two*."

"Doral?" I asked. "I saw him in the Valley, but he was out of reach. When I found out Dharak was really gone, I figured Doral had sensed his passing, even through the instinctive barrier. I don't know it, of course, but I would suspect that a sha'um who loses his or her Rider would be more stubbornly wild thereafter than those who had never been bonded."

"I suspect you are right," Zanek said. "As you were right about the bond continuing, even though contact seemed to be broken. I did . . . feel Doral. The shock of Dharak's leaving restimulated the contact, and he was . . . inquiring and curious. Grieving, yes—but I believe he would have been willing to accept me in Dharak's place."

He held his arms in a pained-looking huddle.

"I could not accept, Rikardon. I may not be King now, but the situation is the same—I need my full attention for this task. I knew that, long before I knew what the task was. I could not accept Doral's friendship. Once before, a sha'um had stayed in the Valley. This time is worse, much worse. Because of me, Doral will die."

*What can I do?* I asked myself, hurting for the man standing beside me. *Give him time. That's all.*

He straightened himself suddenly, and took a deep breath.

"Doral will remain a treasured and sad memory," he said, "but dwelling on the past has no profit for me now. Please tell Keeshah that I am grateful for his service, and will try to ride smoothly."

I told him. He lifted his head and tightened his muscles in preparation, and Zanek mounted expertly. Keeshah rose, walked a few cautious steps to become accustomed to the slightly different weight pattern, then set off down the pathway that had been cut to our house from the caravan road.

*Come back as quickly as you can,* I told the big cat. *We need to start for Raithskar soon.*

*Home?* Keeshah asked me as he disappeared from sight on the twisty path. *Glad. Back soon.*

I stood there for a moment, staring at the edge of the clearing, wondering what Zanek was feeling, and wondering what we would find when we got "home."

# 23

In spite of the fact that neither Tarani nor I had benefited from much sleep the night before, we set out for Raithskar with a renewed energy. The sha'um had rested well, and we were able to nap through the first day as Keeshah and Yayshah carried us north.

As on our most recent trip to Raithskar—during which Yayshah had been heavily pregnant—we followed the green fringe of land around the Kapiral Desert, north through the Morkadahl foothills, then west toward Raithskar. While we did not have Yayshah's temporary disability to contend with, we did have four sha'um mouths to feed, and the only practical solution was to remain in areas where they could hunt for themselves.

Tarani and I talked frequently during our traveling breaks, trying to decide on a plan for when we reached Raithskar. In the final analysis, however, we could make no definite decisions until we got there.

One thing we could agree on readily: we could not take the chance of the presence of the sha'um provoking another attack by the vineh. Ferrathyn may have directed the massive attack of the apelike creatures outside Raithskar's gates that had taken the life of one of Yayshah's newborn cubs. But it seemed unlikely that Ferrathyn had been responsible for our encounter with wild vineh on the eastern side of Gandalara, between Grevor and Sulis. The vineh seemed to have an instinctive dislike for sha'um—probably left over from a time when the two had been natural enemies, when the slow evaporation of the Mediterranean had made the floor of Gandalara green with salt-adapted vegetation.

If the Raithskar vineh caught scent of the sha'um, not only would there be a ruckus that could easily endanger our friends, but whatever hope we had of visiting Raithskar undetected would be destroyed.

When we were still a full day's ride from the city, Tarani and I dismounted in an abandoned dakathrenil orchard and prepared to walk the rest of the way to Raithskar. It was *not* a popular idea.

*Danger. I come,* Keeshah said stubbornly.

The cubs were a perfect echo of their father.

*Don't leave,* Yoshah pleaded.

*Go with!* insisted Koshah.

*Be reasonable,* I said, speaking simultaneously to all three of them. *You'll just increase the danger by alerting the vineh.*

Wrong move. All I got from that was a surge of savage joy at the prospect of battle. And for these sha'um, it was more than an age-old instinctive hatred.

*Killed other cub,* Keeshah said. *Fight.*

*No—* I tried to argue.

*Grown now,* Koshah boasted. *Stronger. Not get hurt.*

*Hurt me!* Yoshah chorused. *Fight!*

All four of the sha'um paced around us, their tails thickening and their neckfur rising. Yayshah seemed as active and eager as the others, and Tarani turned to me with panic in her eyes.

"I tried to explain about the vineh," she said. "Rikardon, she *wants* to fight them." I only gestured toward the pacing cats; her gaze followed the direction of my arm, and she gasped. "All of them? Look at them—they want to *attack*." Her mouth tightened. "And I understand how Yayshah feels. I fear my arguments carry too little sincerity to be convincing."

I reached out with my mind toward Keeshah, seeking the blended understanding we had shared so often. I was shocked when he avoided my attempt, mentally backing away from me. Thinking he had misunderstood, I tried again. He dodged again.

*Do what I want,* he insisted resentfully. *Fight . . .* The sha'um did not use the word *vineh* to describe the creatures who had attacked Keeshah three different times, but the image he sent was powerful and real, and not the least self-deceptive about the strength and dangerousness of the vineh. It was blended with the trembling eagerness that made the sha'um such an effective fighter. Keeshah did not *care* about the danger to himself.

For the first time in our relationship, I made a deliberate effort to be scornful toward the big cat.

*I see,* I said. *You don't care about revenge for the dead cub. You're just spoiling for a good fight, no matter what that does to everybody else's plans. Well, go ahead,* I urged him. He stopped his pacing and stared at me, the silvery flecks in his eyes seeming to swirl as he considered. *Go on!* I said.

*Go,* he agreed abruptly, and leaped away. Yayshah and the cubs followed him.

"No!" Tarani cried. "Rikardon, stop them!"

"Wait," I whispered, barely able to spare her that much explanation. I was trying desperately to conceal my own dread from Keeshah, and let him see only anger and contempt in my mind. I took Tarani's hand and pulled her with me. We started walking east, back the way we had come.

Tarani walked with me, her head turned back to look over her shoulder. "Show anger, if you can," I told her, keeping my face firmly forward, looking away from Raithskar.

"What?" she stammered, then recovered. "Oh, yes—I think I see. Yayshah is asking me where *we* are going." She shuddered, but squared her shoulders forward. "A terrible risk," she said, and squeezed my hand. I knew she was frightened—not for any "destiny" or "mission," but, first and foremost, for the life and safety of her sha'um partner.

Tarani was right—it was a heart-hurting gamble. I kept my mind open to all three sha'um and tried to stay calm.

*Go where?* Koshah asked me.

*Back to Thagorn,* I snapped, and waited. Had my Gandalaran body been able to sweat, I would have been soaked by now.

*Just came,* Yoshah said. *Why go?*

*Because of you,* I said, again letting all three sha'um hear the comment, and hating myself for the whiny, resentful, blame-laying attitude I was portraying.

*It's for a good cause,* I told myself. *If it works, they'll understand why I'm doing it. If it doesn't—well, by God, the words are true!*

I chanced a "glance" along the links, and discovered that the sha'um, already out of eyesight distance from us, were no longer running. They were moving slowly, Yayshah in the lead, the cubs glancing back. Finally, Keeshah's curiosity got the better of his pride.

*Why go?* he asked.

*We can't possibly accomplish what we came for if you pick a fight with the vineh,* I said.

*Cub dead!* Keeshah shouted into my mind, outraged— with some justice, according to his logic—by the obstacle my uncooperative attitude was placing in the way of his instincts.

This time, I did not have to fake anger. *Do you think Tarani and I were not hurt by that too?* I demanded. *That's part of why we're here. The vineh did the actual killing, Keeshah, but it was Ferrathyn who directed them to attack, Ferrathyn who really is responsible for his death. If you and the others attack the vineh, we won't have a chance to make Ferrathyn pay for what he did.*

A long hesitation. Tarani was watching my face. "Yayshah complains that the others have stopped," she whispered, as if the sha'um could overhear us. I had the same skulky feeling. I nodded sharply, but kept on walking, drawing her with me. I was afraid that if we stopped, the sha'um would doubt our commitment and suspect I was trying to manipulate them.

Guide and protect, I corrected the thought. Not manipulate. Oh, please let this work.

Keeshah asked: *True?*

It was the first time Keeshah had ever accused me of lying, and it hurt. It hurt partly because it was true, in a way, and pushed all my guilt buttons. It also hurt because it was evidence of the degree to which, at this moment, Keeshah's instincts outweighed his reason. Under normal conditions, it was impossible for us to lie to each other, and absurd to consider that it might be possible. I let some of that hurt show.

*Why would I tell you something that I didn't believe to be true?* I asked him. *I don't care about the vineh—surely you can tell that's true—and have no reason to want to protect them.*

*Want to protect us,* Keeshah said, a bit more gently. A quick surge of emotion accompanied the thought, acknowledging my good motives, and I felt him gathering himself to explain.

That's it, Keeshah. Start to think again, and we'll get through this.

*Protection not important,* the sha'um said, that rage—

which had both an instinctive and a logical basis—boiling up
again, but in a more controlled way. *Killing vineh important.*

*Not as important as killing Ferrathyn,* I said.

I thought I used "killing" in place of "stopping" in order to
make the point with Keeshah, but as I sent the thought to
Keeshah, I had a chilling sense of its rightness. Ferrathyn was
fanatic and mad, beyond even the most elementary level of
reasoning. There was only one way to stop him.

*You'd know that, if we blended. I think that's precisely why
you refused to blend just now. You know I'm right, and
keeping words and distance between us gives you an excuse for
not really understanding.*

*No!* his mindvoice shouted. But after a moment, he spoke
more thoughtfully: *Yes.*

Another pause, during which I'm sure my heart stopped
beating, and he conceded.

*I will listen,* he said, and opened his mind to me.

My body went rigid, and part of me heard Tarani gasp.

I *was* Keeshah. I felt his fury at the vineh, the full force of
the paradox of his instincts. If his family were attacked, he
would defend them to the death. Yet he was willing to lead
them into a fight which would endanger them, to avenge the
lost cub. He was bonded to mate and cubs by instinct and
conscious affection, and he fully recognized that they—and
he—might die in a fight against the Raithskar vineh. He had an
eager image of the fight, a foretaste of the almost transcendent
state of fierceness he entered in an all-out battle. The image
included Yayshah and Koshah and Yoshah fighting beside him.
It accepted the possibility of their deaths, as well as his. And
what Keeshah felt was not sorrow, but an overwhelming pride.

Later, when I could think again, I would remember that
intense flash of feelings in connection with another event that
had occurred halfway across Gandalara. I would see Thymas
swinging his sword, killing a man I thought should live. I
would hear him recite, as justification, a traditional litany:
"Sharith kill their enemies." And I would see that event in a
more tolerant light, considering that the tradition might be
less a product of history than of a secondhand instinct.

Now, however, thinking was not possible. As I shared
Keeshah's character for that moment, so was Keeshah experi-
encing the feelings and thoughts uppermost in my mind. I
could exercise no control—shielding, choice, deception—in

that communication. Whatever was in me at that moment, Keeshah learned.

As always, the experience was too intense to be sustained. Keeshah and I withdrew from one another, and I took notice of my surroundings again. I was lying down, nearly buried in the narrow-leaved ground cover that floored most dakathrenil orchards. Tarani was kneeling beside me, and relief swept through her tense face when I opened my eyes to look at her.

"You stopped, and then collapsed," she explained. "It has not been like this before. What happened?"

"He *wants* the vineh," I said. "Intensely."

She worried her bottom lip, with one wide tusk. "Will they attack?"

"I don't know yet," I said to Tarani, then spoke to Keeshah. *What will you do?* I asked.

*Don't know!* he answered, with such anger that I flinched physically and startled Tarani.

*Keeshah, do you believe that Ferrathyn is really the one who killed your cub?* I asked.

*Believe,* he agreed, still seething with an anger I was at a loss to understand. *Can't hunt man,* he said. *Can hunt vineh. Vineh easier. Everything easier, before.*

*Before?* I asked.

*You don't want man because of cub,* he said. *You want man because of society.*

The tone in which his mindvoice carried the word *society* answered my question. I took Tarani's hand and used her weight as an anchor to pull myself into a sitting position. I stared at the green leaves between my knees and concentrated my attention on the sha'um.

*This is what I wanted, in the Chizan Valley,* I thought. *A rational, reasoning being inside the skin of a sha'um. But that rational sha'um—who understands that a man could murder his child through the agency of a vineh—is still at war with the instinctual one—who can remember the death cry of his son, and sha'um blood on vineh hands.*

*I admit it, Keeshah. I think that stopping Ferrathyn is more important than just avenging the cub, and I would think so even if I weren't absolutely sure—as I am—that Ferrathyn is responsible for that loss. And I see what you mean about things being easier 'before'—when you felt no responsibility to anyone besides me, yourself, and your family.*

*Believe me,* I said fervently, *I do understand what you're feeling. But the fact is, Keeshah, you have changed, you have accepted responsibility for your society—which is now, more than ever before, a part of mine—and there is no going back to the time before. You have to decide whether to attack the vineh on the basis of which responsibility is more important.*

He was silent for a moment, then burst out in a flash of rage. *HATE THIS!* his mind yelled at me. *WANT VINEH!* *THEN GO GET THEM!* my mind yelled back.

I heard a whimper beside me, and realized that I was crushing Tarani's hand as I clenched my fist. I released her, and spoke again to Keeshah. I was calmer, but no less angry. I let him see my anxiety and impatience.

*Do what you want, Keeshah, but make up your mind, so I'll know what to do next. If you aren't going after the vineh, we're wasting time we could use to go after Ferrathyn.*

Another moment of silence, then Keeshah's mindvoice came to me quietly and sadly.

*Decision hard,* he said, with characteristic understatement. *Help?*

*I wish I could help you,* I said. *But I remember what you said to me earlier—that you were going to do what you wanted. You didn't say 'for a change,' but I heard that part of it too. What happened near Chizan has transformed our friendship, Keeshah. More than ever before, we're partners now. I've told you what I want to do, and why. You have to decide for yourself if my reasons are good enough for you.*

## 24

I felt Keeshah's struggle like a pain in my gut. I knew this decision was only the first—and maybe the hardest—he would ever have to deal with.

"Keeshah is coming back to us!" Tarani said, confirming what I sensed from the big cat. She threw her arms around my neck. "Rikardon, you persuaded him." She grew very still, then pulled away abruptly. "Yayshah's furious," she said. "She still

hungers for revenge—Rikardon, she's heading for Raithskar
alone . . . no, not alone. The cubs are with her!"

While Tarani was reciting events happening half a mile away
from the viewpoint of the female sha'um, I was receiving three
other views of the same scene. Koshah and Yoshah were
following their mother because she was going the same way
their instincts led them, but they felt a puzzled sense of loss
and wrongness in Keeshah not being with them. They had
picked up enough of my feelings through my exchange with
Keeshah to be aware that there might be a reason not to do
what they were doing—but they had not achieved the
complete knowledge Keeshah could gain by our blending.

*I will stop,* he told me grimly.

Keeshah's actions now frightened me.

Frustrated in his need to fight the vineh, and now committed to the need to keep hidden from the apelike creatures,
he was venting all his pent-up anger toward his family, and was
racing after them with a stop-short-of-death intention of
violence, if necessary, to keep Yayshah and the cubs away from
the vineh.

*Wait, Keeshah, that's not the way to stop them,* I said. *If
you and I can convince the cubs to stay, the three of you can
keep Yayshah here without hurting her.*

*Make cubs stay?* he asked. *How?*

*I've blended with each of them on occasion,* I said. *I can
do it now, maybe with both of them at the same time.*

I had to take a second to think through the idea that had
come to mind. The cubs' battle mode was in control, and they
were in full stride in the wrong direction. There was too little
time, and too little thinking available, to make a long
explanation.

What am I thinking of? I wondered suddenly. They don't
need to make the same decision Keeshah did—they only have
to believe Keeshah made the right decision.

*Keeshah, I want you to blend with me, and then I'll blend
with the cubs.*

*May not work,* Keeshah said, and I sensed he was feeling
something similar to what had nearly overcome him before.
Keeshah's fighting rage had been stirred up. He wanted a fight,
even if it was his own family who had to provide it. Yet he did
not want his family hurt.

*Will try,* he said at last.

His presence surged into my mind with the keen poignancy of total sharing, and together, fighting to sustain the contact, we groped out in search of the cubs. Suddenly they were with us, two surprised presences who had an instant to express curiosity before they were melded into our union.

If I had found such a union with only Keeshah to be unbearably sweet and sharp, the experience of sharing the minds of three sha'um simultaneously was an exercise in wonder.

*Each mind similar, each mind unique. Variance in physical perceptions of sight and touch and smell. Identical reaction to the blending with other sha'um—total and unrestrained delight. An overwhelming sense of their regard for me and the unqualified assumption that I would always be part of their lives. Their response to my affection for them—Koshah taking it for granted, Yoshah returning it warmly, a new awareness of it taking shape in Keeshah. The cubs shyly recognizing something more in their father worth respecting than merely the fact of their relationship. Keeshah's discovery of the innocence and ignorance of their young minds, and the beginning of a deep tenderness to accompany the robust affection he had always expressed to them.*

One flashing instant of the four-way meld, then we could hold it no longer.

When it broke apart, I screamed.

Tarani caught me in her arms and held me with a fierce protectiveness while I shuddered and sobbed and clung to her. I hurt as if a piece of my brain had been sliced away. I felt it in my mind and heart and soul.

The mental wound had been sharp and real but clean, and even while I suffered I knew I would heal. The pain had begun to ease almost immediately, the cause of my emotional shock shifting from loss to wonder.

When I had calmed, Tarani pushed me away gently and looked into my face.

"You succeeded, my love," she said. "Yayshah is still angry, but she is yielding. Keeshah and Yoshah and Koshah are bringing her back here." She studied me. "What happened?"

Keeshah reached out for me tenderly. *Sorry hurt you,* he said.

*It wasn't your fault, Keeshah,* I assured him. *How do you like it?*

*Different,* he said, and I understood many things in that one word. *Glad.*

*Are they all right?* I asked.

Keeshah hesitated a moment, then said: *Yes. Confused. Miss you.*

*Tell them—* I felt my shaky emotional calm flaking away.

*Understand,* Keeshah assured me.

Only then could I look at Tarani and answer her question. "I've lost the cubs," I said. "The bond has transferred to Keeshah."

Tarani let out her breath slowly.

"Oh, my love," she said gently, and stroked my arm. "How sad for you. But it is sweet for Keeshah, is it not? What a wondrous, wondrous thing," she breathed. Then she shook her shoulders, and smiled shakily. "And you, Rikardon? Are you well?"

I nodded. "It hurts, but not like when Keeshah left. Koshah and Yoshah are still with us, after all, and I can sense them through him the same way the cubs knew him through me, before. I'll be all right."

"You were blended with Keeshah—and the cubs?" she asked. "As it was in the fight outside Raithskar, the first time you touched them?"

"Yes," I said. "Only it was a deeper, stronger blending—because they're older, I guess, and because we established the blend from desire, rather than life-and-death need. I don't know why it happened this way. Maybe it was the shock of actually *meeting* their father. Maybe it was only because Keeshah's mind is more like theirs."

*Like yours,* Keeshah corrected me.

*What?*

*Made me think like you,* he said, and I suddenly understood what he meant. The idea sent my head reeling. I clutched at the ground cover beside my feet.

"What is it?" Tarani asked.

"I told you about my conversation with Keeshah in Chizan," I said, and she nodded. "And we've talked before about the sha'um operating on a purely animal level, but possessing a latent intelligence. It's one of the logical arguments behind the bonding of a man and a sha'um—that the sha'um gains fuller use of its mind." Tarani nodded again.

"I think I helped Keeshah take another step in Chizan," I said. "From *just* thinking to *abstract* thinking. From *latent* intelligence to *active* intelligence.

"Think of an unbonded sha'um as first-stage, and Keeshah, now, as third-stage. His mind is more like ours, capable of contemplating as well as learning, speculating as well as understanding. And *he* can provide the stimulation needed by a second-stage sha'um: a bonded one. Or two."

Tarani stared into the distance for a few seconds. "I proved that women may bond and ride sha'um," she said, "and now there are many women Riders. Is Keeshah, too, the first of many?" She turned to me, and the look of seeing *elsewhere* vanished from her face.

"Your alertness to the danger in the Valley has made it possible for us to save the sha'um, if anything *can* be salvaged from the coming disaster," Tarani said. "In spite of my close contact with Yayshah, I saw the survival of the sha'um as desirable, but not essential; their loss as tragic, but not debilitating.

"I see my error now, Rikardon. The sha'um are not *species* but a *race*, capable of an even richer, more equal partnership with Gandalarans than they have yet achieved. They *must* be given time and means to wake fully to their potential," she said, pounding fist on thigh for emphasis. "We *must* save them."

"You'll get no argument from me," I said. "Let's get to it."

The sha'um arrived while Tarani and I were shuffling our swords back and forth on the ground, concealing them in the thick ground cover. We hoped to enter Raithskar with as little use of Tarani's illusion as possible—not only because it would tire her but because Ferrathyn might detect its use. So we hid the only two steel swords in Gandalara, and Tarani tied her desert scarf around her dark headfur.

Yayshah wrapped herself around a dakathrenil trunk and lay down, a growl of complaint rumbling in her throat. Tarani went over to her and stroked down the restive neckfur, humming as she worked to soothe the female with her thoughts.

Koshah and Yoshah came up to me slowly, almost shyly. I was startled to see how big they were. *I guess I've broken free of the parent's perspective*, I thought. *They're sha'um to me now, not just Keeshah's kids.*

I held out my hands, and the cubs sniffed tentatively, as if I were a stranger. Then the awkwardness passed, and Koshah punched me in the stomach with his nose. I grabbed his neck, both wrestling and hugging him, and reached out to scratch behind Yoshah's ear.

*Love you,* Keeshah said, and somehow I knew he was speaking for the cubs. *Don't want you to go alone to city. Me neither,* he added emphatically.

*I explained that, Keeshah.*

*Understand,* he said. *I stay. Cubs stay. Don't like.*

*Me neither,* I said, and I felt amusement from him. *We'll be careful, Keeshah. Try not to worry.*

"Are you ready, Tarani?" I asked.

She stood up and offered me her hand. We set out for Raithskar.

The countryside east of Raithskar had once been its most fertile area, a garden for the water-rich city. Now it lay in a state of devastation and abandonment. The grainfields were trampled and stripped. Dakathrenil orchards were threatening to go wild. Tall training nets that once supported rich berry harvests lay tangled in the dying vines.

Grain had been the major crop, and, as we moved toward Raithskar, Tarani and I saw several groups of vineh roaming about, efficiently stripping kernels from the few untouched grainfields with their large, strong hands.

Vineh were large animals that fit the ecological niche in Gandalara filled by apes in Ricardo's world. They had characteristics which resembled apes—great dexterity, highly pronounced supraorbital ridges, nearly erect posture. They were covered with coarse, curly hair, and adult male vineh were usually stronger than adult male Gandalarans. Tarani and I had never seen vineh acting "normally," and we watched them now with interest as well as with caution.

The moving clusters of vineh seemed to be family groups. There was usually at least one female with young vineh scampering along behind or clinging to a shoulder. Something in human—or Gandalaran—nature makes the young of any species appealing, and even with as much reason as we had to despise them, the vineh were no exception. The young animals watched us as we passed. One young female, about chest-tall, broke away from her group and followed us for a short way, comically burying herself in the broken grain stems whenever we turned to look directly at her. The mother was occupied with twin babies climbing about her head and shoulders. When she noticed her elder daughter was missing, she uttered a chattering call and clutched at her babies. The young female exploded out of her makeshift haystack and answered her mother's call. The mother dropped her babies on the ground and rushed toward us, screaming a challenge.

The challenge was answered from behind us. Three male vineh were coming through an untouched grainfield, sounding their high-pitched, hair-lifting battle call. One male jumped out into the roadway, shrieking and feinting toward us, shaking his hands overhead. The other two males crossed the road to join the female, who had stopped her rush to clutch and sniff at her daughter. The two males touched and examined the two females, then broke away to scream and lunge in our direction.

With as much caution and calmness as we could muster, Tarani and I backed away from the outraged group. The male in the roadway, biggest of the lot, kept challenging us aggressively, but stayed close to the others. I tried to see through the back of my head, to be alert for other vineh groups which might be attracted by the ruckus, but I was afraid to turn my head physically for fear that might be the thing to trigger the big male's attack. We moved a good hundred yards off before the male quit his noise and turned to check out the mother and daughter. We were another hundred yards away before we started to breathe again, and dared to walk facing frontward toward Raithskar.

## 25

"Why did they not attack?" Tarani asked.

"I've got a better question," I said. "Why don't they attack each other?"

She only looked at me, puzzled.

"In Raithskar, the male vineh were used to do some menial work; you knew that. Did you ever see them working?" She shook her head. "They wore short trousers to cover their genitals, and Markasset thought it was to prevent them from fighting among themselves. I hadn't thought of it before, but the groups which have attacked us have been mostly males fighting with good cooperation, stark naked."

"Then the clothing must have had some other purpose," Tarani said. "Or their continual subjection to control through the Ra'ira made them quarrelsome and the covering did, indeed, make the temptation to fight one another less strong." She shuddered. "They can find such control no more pleasant than a thinking person, perhaps less so," she said. "And they would have no outlet for their anger except toward one another."

"The shorts may really have been a control factor, making the other male vineh sort of neutral."

She was quiet for a moment as we walked, keeping more alert toward our horizons than before. "I cannot find anger for the vineh in myself," she said, "Fear, yes, and pity. There seem to be so many of them, and these have lost the skill to survive outside the society of men. Look what they have taken, and not replaced. What will they do when the easily available food is gone?"

I merely shook my head in answer. I was shocked and awed by the changes around Raithskar, and overwhelmed by the certainty that the intellect and ambition of one man had created this havoc. It would take years to restore Raithskar to beauty and plenty, even if Ferrathyn were defeated today. The oncoming calamity made an attempt at restoration pointless, of course, but somehow I still felt a sense of loss.

As we approached the city itself, we saw a different kind of destruction. The grain which grew on either side of the road into Raithskar had been burned off, to leave the area for five hundred yards around the walls of the city totally empty of anything except ankle-high, blackened stumps. We had seen that the grain stopped somewhere ahead, but the tall grain and the twists of the road had obscured our view until we were actually on the edge of that dark open area.

The sight of it stunned me. It called up memories from Ricardo's mind: scarred hillsides, defoliated forests, camps surrounded by barbed wire. I said nothing to Tarani, but she moved at the same time I did. We stepped off the roadway into the standing grain, and crouched down to look out over that devastation from concealment.

It felt as if we were acknowledging a declaration of war.

For centuries, Raithskar's walls of mortared stone had served only as a symbol of defense, its gates long ago discarded. The gateway had stood open to the rest of Gandalara for trade and travel and good will, guarded ceremoniously and needlessly by two Peace and Security men.

The gateway was barricaded now, and guards walked some kind of buttressing behind the wall, their shoulders visible above the gray stones. They were stationed about two hundred feet apart, and they paced continually, facing outward.

From where we crouched, we could hear the indistinct sound of a bustling, busy city, but the only people we could see were the guards on the walls. The area between us and them was utterly, desperately empty.

"I had no idea it would be this bad," I said.

"Nor I," Tarani said. "It seems incredible that one man, even with the help of the Ra'ira, could maintain control of an entire city."

"We still don't know what it's like inside," I reminded her. "Those guards could be keeping the people of Raithskar *in* as well as everyone else *out*."

"What purpose would that serve?"

I shrugged. "None that I can see," I said. "I'm simply making the point that Ferrathyn doesn't have to control *everyone* in that city. Just a few who control all the others."

"The Peace and Security forces?" Tarani suggested. "And—" She turned to me, and this time there was no question in her tone. "And the Council of Supervisors. Thanasset."

Tarani's gaze shifted over my shoulder, and her expression warned me before I heard her cry: "Look out!"

I dived and rolled, and came up in the open, facing back toward the grainfield. Three male vineh loomed head-and-shoulders above the tops of the stripped grain stems. One of them caught Tarani around the waist, pinning her arms. He held her suspended off the ground while she twisted and kicked.

The other two vineh had been a step behind the first, and now they had to come around him to get to me—a distance made longer by the furious struggle Tarani was making. The one who held her staggered back and forth with her weight, catching the attention and blocking the progress of the other two. They seemed slower, less active than in our other encounters with vineh.

One of Tarani's powerful kicks connected with the vineh's knee, and he howled in pain. I drew my dagger, jumped in, and stabbed at one muscular arm. He howled again, and I tugged Tarani out of his grasp. She landed on her feet with her dagger already drawn, whirled and slashed it across his throat. I pushed his collapsing body back against the others, grabbed Tarani's hand, and pulled her toward Raithskar.

We heard the two vineh snarling, then their battle challenge rang out as they started after us.

"Let us face them," Tarani urged, even while she ran beside me. "The city is no sanctuary for us."

"Think, Tarani! They came up on us without a sound."

"Ferrathyn?" she asked. "Still, why not face two enemies we know, rather than a city we cannot trust?"

"They're making noise now, aren't they? That means Ferrathyn's just letting their natural disposition bedevil us now. He's gone after reinforcements. We *may* have a chance in Raithskar, just because he can't control everybody at once. Out here—"

I glanced back. The vineh, free of Ferrathyn's control, had regained their full range of movement, and they were gaining on us. Another group of vineh—five adult males—had rounded the western edge of the wall and was cutting across the empty field to intercept us.

*We're only about a third of the way to the gateway,* I thought. *We're going to get caught between them. But—what's going on at the gate?*

Men were working at the barricade, which seemed to be an organized heap of carts and furniture and boxes. An opening appeared at its center, and a dozen men ran out, swords drawn and ready.

Tarani groaned, and the sound expressed my own sense of helplessness.

*I come,* Keeshah offered.

*No, Keeshah,* I ordered. *There isn't time.*

*Man knows you come,* the sha'um argued. *No need to hide now.*

*You can't do us any good, Keeshah. You'll just get your

*family hurt for nothing. Besides,\* I said, with growing hope,
\*it's looking better.\**

The men from the city had run out along the road in pairs.
One man from each pair was on either side of the road, and the
men stood back to back. They formed a protected corridor
straight into the city. Their position limited the threat of the
new vineh group, but could not protect us from the ones
behind us. If they caught us, the delay might give the other
vineh the chance to reach us before the guards could break
formation to help. Our only chance lay in reaching the near
end of that corridor first.

Tarani had seen the intent of the city guards, and with a cry
of hope, she summoned a burst of speed and raced ahead of
me. She ran between the first two men just as a big hand
brushed my shoulder and caught the back of my tunic. I broke
stride, and claws raked my back. Another hand caught my
bicep in a painful grip, and I felt the breath of the vineh on the
back of my neck as he prepared to sink his teeth there.

A sword blade was thrust over my shoulder, barely missing
my cheek. I heard a gurgling howl behind me, and the hand
let go. Tarani pulled me forward, and the two guards followed
us, backing up. The second group of vineh was leaping and
screaming, but they seemed to respect the bare swords facing
them. The corridor collapsed behind us as we moved to and
through the barricade.

Once we were inside the city walls, the guards who had
come out after us gathered around, uncomfortably close.
Another man pushed through them, a man with an air of
authority.

"Did you send them out?" I asked.

"I did," he admitted, standing in front of us with one hand
on his hip, the other on the hilt of his sword. He was tall, with
a hard face.

"Thank you," I said.

"My pleasure," he growled. He snatched at Tarani's headscarf. The scarf fell away, exposing the uncommon dark color.

"It might be fitting for the Raithskarian traitor and the
Eddartan whore to die at the hands of the vineh, but it would
be less satisfying." He took a step back. "You know the orders,"
he told the men. "Kill them now!"

Only Tarani's quick thinking—and her mindskill—saved us.
The men rushed toward us, then past us.

"What? Not me . . . Aahh!"

The cry came from one of the guards. Tarani's hand tugged at my arm, and I followed her through the crowd of armed men. When I looked at her, I saw her true shape and appearance through the transparent image of another soldier, and I realized she had given me the same disguising illusion. Two guards had been the unfortunate focus of a double illusion of Tarani and myself.

Down one of the streets leading from the gate was the large open area which had once been Raithskar's marketplace. As we approached we could see that it was full of more than the usual movement and bustle, and there was organization amid the chaos. Vleks were penned in a makeshift corral at one end of the area. The remainder of the space, stripped now of the colorful vendor tents which had been the common sight, was being filled by a continuous stream of people, each one bringing something to add to the compilation of . . .

War supplies.

Food. Extra clothes. Swords, daggers, baldrics. Closed containers that might be used for water. There were people working to sharpen swords, rebuild carts, inspect containers.

More frightening than the actual accumulation of the materials was the attitude that pervaded the activity. Raithskar had been a comfortable, generous, cheerful city. On my last visit here, uncertainty about the vineh had begun to undermine that pleasant mood. Now there was only a stern desperation. Lines creased the faces of the people we passed. Children accompanied parents to the marketplace storehouse, their arms carrying lighter burdens but their eyes haunted with fear and bewilderment.

"They're here," someone whispered harshly. "Markasset and that woman are in the city!"

"They say she forced the guards to kill one of their own," someone else said.

"What are they doing here?" a woman asked bitterly. "Haven't they done enough to us?"

As the column of people penetrated farther into the city, Tarani and I slipped down a side street. I pulled my headscarf out of the belt where it was hanging and gave it to Tarani. Once she had her telltale black headfur covered again, she let the illusion go. We continued walking, since everyone visible in the city seemed to be moving.

"He was expecting us," Tarani whispered. "Do you think that Thymas . . . ?"

I shrugged. "I don't think it matters much now," I said. "The point is, we're here, and we're in time."

"In time?" she echoed.

"I'm thinking of all that activity in the square," I said. "It looks to me like they're only a day or so away from being ready to move out of here. We would be forced to use the Sharith against them. Strung out in a line, every person seeing his own survival in the balance—there would be so much death . . ."

"How will that be different *inside* the city?" Tarani asked. "And what can we do to stop it, short of attacking Ferrathyn directly?"

"We can't attack him now; we need a diversion," I said. "We can't *prevent* the mobilization, but we may be able to delay it until the Sharith can provide that diversion."

"And what effect can we have, when we are to be killed on recognition?" Tarani demanded. She shook her head sadly, and lowered her voice.

"I find it hard to believe," she said, "that the friendly people who took such an interest in the young cubs could now be convinced that you and I are dangerous enemies."

"You're thinking of the people of Raithskar as individuals," I reminded Tarani gently.

"Given the time to think and remember and consider the matter logically, I doubt that any of them would believe Ferrathyn's lies. But Ferrathyn has not allowed the opportunity for that kind of critical examination. He's planting the kind of fear that needs a quick answer. The people are told that the vineh are dangerous and, in fact, the only vineh they are allowed to see *are* dangerous. Ferrathyn has provided a channel for their fear by setting us up as scapegoats. Of course they're grabbing at it—it's the only thing that even *starts* to make sense.

"These people are so scared that they're a mob, Tarani, and a mob is easy to direct."

"And difficult to stop," Tarani added.

"The *way* to stop it is to remind them of being individuals, and individually responsible for the action of the mob. Wake up their rational thinking."

"How?" she asked.

"By giving them something to *think* about," I said. I caught her arm, and we stopped walking. "Recognize where we are?"

She looked around. We were in a residential area, on a street corner.

"It does look familiar," she said. "We must be close—" She broke off. "Rikardon, you cannot be thinking of . . ."

"Surrendering." I finished the thought for her. "To Thanasset—and *only* to Thanasset."

"But he has to be one of those under close watch by Ferrathyn," she protested.

"He has also been a Supervisor for many years, and has a strong sense of law and rightness. I'll wager that Ferrathyn has used persuasion and peer pressure on Thanasset, more than compulsion. And no matter *what* he's been persuaded to believe, if we ask for a public hearing—a right of every Raithskarian accused of a crime—he will protect us until the hearing can be held."

"Thus causing the delay you seek, and capturing the attention of the unthinking mob." She thought about it, and finally nodded. "I can think of nothing less dangerous. I agree."

We stepped around the edge of the corner house, and jumped back again quickly. The cross street was the one on which Thanasset lived. It was about halfway down the block, on the other side of the street. Two guards stood in the street on this end of the block, two at the other end.

# 26

"We must first find a way to *reach* Thanasset undetected," Tarani said. "I will disguise us. . . . There." She had taken on the image of Illia, the young woman who had cared for Markasset, but whose affection had shifted to someone else.

"Am I Zaddorn?" I asked, and she nodded.

I had an uncomfortable feeling that I could not pin down. I

squeezed Tarani's hand, a warm pride spreading through my chest, followed closely by a chilling fear.

"Thank you for trusting me, High Lord."

She smiled up at me. "So far, Captain, even your ill advice has not been fatal. Let us hope to continue that good fortune."

It was just the right touch of lightness to send me around the corner. First, however, I reached out to Keeshah. *Send one of the cubs to Thagorn,* I said.

*All go,* he answered. *You say don't help. Too hard to wait.*

*Good idea,* I said. *Go to Zanek. And get back as fast as you can, okay?*

*Yes.*

"They're all going back after Sharith," I told Tarani.

"So Yayshah says," Tarani said. "Shall we begin *our* task?"

The instant we stepped out into the street, that funny feeling I had got worse. The guard nearest us took one look at us and bolted toward us, shouting to the others.

"What's wrong?" Tarani demanded.

"Don't ask," I said. "Just run—and *keep the illusion.*"

We ran back down the block we had just traversed, then cut sharply left. Two of the guards were behind us; the other two had run down the next intersecting block, and were coming toward us. I grabbed Tarani and slammed open a garden gate, dragging her through it. We ran through a backyard considerably smaller than Thanasset's. A woman emerged from the back door of the house just as Tarani vaulted the four-foot stone fence that separated this yard from the next. "Here they are!" the woman screamed, as I scrambled over the fence after Tarani.

In the next yard, a group of children were seated in a ring on a stone-laid patio. They looked up when Tarani landed in their yard, and started to get up from their circle when I appeared. They were directly between us and the gate that led into the next street—Thanasset's street, again—and Tarani and I ran right through the center of their circle.

I had judged we would come out fairly close to Thanasset's house. When we were directly in front of it, two more guards materialized—probably from inside the house.

I flew straight at one of them. He braced his feet and brought his sword up in his right hand. I swerved at the last minute, and he stepped out to follow me, lifting his sword slightly higher for a downstroke. I pivoted and threw my weight under the upraised sword, slamming his ribs with my shoulder. He staggered backward. I caught his sword wrist with both hands and fell backward, drawing the man with me and flipping him over my head. I heard him strike the cobbled street with a grunt of pain. I pulled out my dagger, and started to scramble to my feet . . .

The point of a sword stopped me.

I looked up to see another guard scowling down at me. Behind him stood Tarani, each of her arms held by one of the guards who had followed us. She was panting heavily, but I noticed that she still held the illusion.

"I don't know how you got out, Zaddorn," the guard said, "but you're going back. You know, I wasn't too sure you were as incompetent as the Council claimed, but this sure as Zanek proves it to me. Stupid to come walking right up to us!"

In spite of the danger in the situation, I felt something like gratification. *I knew Zaddorn wasn't a flunky for Ferrathyn,* I thought. *He knew the truth about the Ra'ira and was more opposition than Ferrathyn could handle. So Zaddorn got pressured out of office and locked up.*

The man turned partway around to look at Tarani—whom he thought was Illia—and I saw the change happen. Muscles tightened in his jaw; his eyes narrowed, and his lips pulled back from his teeth, exposing the wide tusks. "Wait a minute," he said, and his voice was different. "Zaddorn *wouldn't* have been that stupid."

"What are you saying, Omin?" one of the other guards demanded. "He's Zaddorn, and he did it, right?"

"Not right," the man said, nearly shouting. "Don't you ever listen to the Council? We've been asked to keep watch for a man and a woman together, and warned that they could do some strange things. If this *isn't* Zaddorn, then she's got to be that Eddartan witch. And this—" He turned back to me, and I saw triumph in his face, his eyes.

It was more than a guard's gladness to have been alert, or a citizen's pride in having captured a sought-after traitor. It was Ferrathyn. Gloating. "This has to be Markasset, disguised somehow to look like Zaddorn. And our orders are clear about Markasset."

I was still on the ground. In a leisurely way, keeping his gaze locked on mine, he put away his dagger and took the hilt of his sword in both hands. He lifted it, and prepared—eagerly—to bring the blade down across my neck.

"*No!*" Tarani screamed.

The man froze—all but his eyes. I saw shock and fury in them.

Tarani screamed again, this time a high wail of anguish. The guard—abandoned for the moment by Ferrathyn's dominating presence—lowered his sword slowly, looking confused.

The two guards who were holding Tarani were struggling to keep hold of her. She had gone rigid and stiff, her back arched, and her face a rictus of pain. Amazingly, she still held the illusion.

*Damn Ferrathyn!* I thought. *Tarani used a countercompulsion on this guy, and Ferrathyn is striking at her directly now. More than the illusion will break, if he keeps it up. I need to distract him. . . .*

The puzzled guard was the logical choice. I came up from the ground with the dagger in my hand, and almost succeeded in stabbing the man in the side before he noticed me. Notice me he did, however, and the live spark of Ferrathyn was once again in his eyes as he knocked aside my dagger, dropped his sword, and caught my throat in a strong, crushing grip. Dimly, I saw Tarani sag down from her stiff posture.

"Kill the girl," the guard ordered, through gritted teeth, and he applied more pressure to my throat, forcing me first to my knees and then into a strained backward bend.

Behind me, a door opened.

"What's the meaning of this?" demanded the familiar voice of Thanasset. "Release those people at once! When has it been the province of Peace and Security to execute without a hearing?" The guard's face turned almost feral as he looked up at Thanasset, and I heard the old man's step falter momentarily. Then he was hurrying over, his hands pulling at the arm that held me bent over backward, choking me. "In the name of the Council, release him," Thanasset said. "Do you hear me? Release Zaddorn."

"This is not Zaddorn," the man growled, then grinned savagely. "Don't you recognize your own son?"

Tarani must have been aware enough to hear the conversation, for I heard Thanasset gasp as the illusion vanished. I was on the brink of unconsciousness, and I had very little breath available, but I got out two words.

"Surrender," I whispered. "Hearing." Then my mind reeled toward blackness.

Pain drew me back, the pain of air passing through my bruised larynx. I found myself lying on the cobbled surface of the street, practically alone. Thanasset and the guard were faced off, arguing. I was relieved to see that the fierce, mad light was gone from the guard's face. Now he was just a guard, trying to do his job. On his own behalf, he was arguing for killing us outright.

"I do not care *who* issued the order," Thanasset was saying. "Every citizen of Raithskar is entitled to a hearing before the Council, and my son is no exception."

"All right, you made your point about Markasset," the man said. "But the girl's Eddartan. Raithskar's rules don't apply to her. You saw what she can do, too, with your own eyes. She's too dangerous to take chances with." He turned to the men who held her. "Kill her."

Before the two guards could act on the order, Thanasset was standing in front of them, their own daggers in his hands and pointing at their throats.

"Release her. Now."

They let her go, and she slipped under Thanasset's arm, backing away from the leader and toward me. Thanasset followed her, also backing, keeping both daggers at ready.

"They are in my custody," he said. "You have fulfilled your duty by capturing them, and I will commend you to the Council. Now, I feel sure you have other assignments . . ."

He stood there, waiting, protecting us, until they all accepted the situation and moved off down the street. The leader was the last to go, and he backed away. Only when they were out of sight did Thanasset turn to us.

"In the house, quickly," he said, and helped Tarani drag me to my feet. Once I was standing, my head cleared a little, and I was able to walk into the house under my own power.

When we were inside, I turned to Thanasset to thank him, but was cut off.

"Say nothing to me," he ordered coldly. "As a Supervisor, I granted your request for a hearing; it is fully within the law. Anything you have to say must wait for the formal hearing."

"You tried to save us before the request was made," Tarani said. She flinched back when Thanasset turned his gaze to her.

"I thought you were Zaddorn and Illia," he said.

"You knew about Ferrathyn's kill-on-sight orders for us, didn't you?"

"Yes," the old man said, "but they were less orders than official agreement with public intent. You brought a fine distinction to my family, Rikardon," he said bitterly. "In all the history of Raithskar, no one has been so hated as my son."

"Or so wronged," Tarani said quietly.

"Or *misled*," Thanasset snapped, staring at her coldly.

Tarani drew up to her full height and I could see that Thanasset was not immune to the dignity and force of her presence. He took a small step back from Tarani.

"When we met, Thanasset, you kissed my hand in tender welcome, and you opened your home to me," Tarani said, her voice trembling with emotion. "I saw the love you bore your son, and the respect you offered the man who had replaced him. I had comfort here, and a sense of goodness.

"When we arrived in Raithskar, and heard those ugly lies, Rikardon convinced me that only with your help did we have hope of being fairly heard. I heard his logic, and I heard his need to be able to trust you. I listened to my own memory, and longed for the warmth I remembered here.

"This is not the same place I remember so fondly," she said, and her voice turned stern and cold. "Your home, and your mind, have been corrupted by the same force that is destroying your city, and remaining here will corrupt the warm memory I cherish. I prefer to take my chances with the city guards."

She walked past him, and he caught her arm. "You are in my custody," he said.

"Take your hand from me," she demanded.

Thanasset looked uncertain, and removed his hand.

"I shall not force you to stay here," he said, "but I cannot allow you freedom—this for your own sake as much as for my guarantee. You may find a restriction cell much more to your liking, and your presence there places an obligation on the guard to protect your lives, rather than take them. For your safety, I will be pleased to escort you personally."

He opened the front door, and Tarani moved through it. Thanasset waited for me to go through, then he came out. There was a sudden, furtive movement down the street.

"You, there," Thanasset called, and one of the guards who had recently "left" came fully into view, looking a trifle embarrassed. "Go ahead to the warden and tell him to expect two prisoners shortly, and that he will be held personally accountable for their safety until the hearing is held. Go on!" he shouted, when the man did not move immediately. The guard did move then, running as if he had been stung.

The place where Thanasset took us was an extension of the building in which Zaddorn—or, rather, the current Chief of Peace and Security, whoever that might be—had his office. The building was made of fired clay brick, and the interiors of the cells resembled nothing so much as Keeshah's house on Thanasset's property.

Each cell had three walls with no windows, but with a regular pattern of missing bricks. The holes allowed air circulation, and those in the outside wall admitted dim light. The interior wall had a small doorway which was blocked by a frame of latticed wood, mounted in bronze clasps on either side of the opening—on the guard's side of the door, of course. Each cell had a pallet, a nightpail, and a pitcher of fresh water.

Thanasset stood by while Tarani was locked up in one cell, then he escorted me to the next one. As the door was fitted into place, I looked through the widely spaced slats at the man I respected as if he were my own father. His face was grim, and he lingered a moment, seemingly wanting to say something, but uncertain as to what.

I was feeling pretty much the same way. It was only when he started to turn away that I found my voice.

"Wait," I called. "Just one minute, please. I won't say anything to prejudice the hearing."

He faced me again, waiting.

"I want only one more thing from you," I said. "At the hearing, I want you to *truly listen* to what Tarani and I say. Listen with your whole being, Thanasset, and with an open mind. Only then will the truth be clear to you."

"I have guaranteed your presence to the Council," Thanasset said. "Now I offer you the guarantee of a fair hearing."

"That's beyond your power," I said flatly, and I saw lines of anger form across his brow. "All I want is for *you* to listen fairly—and maybe to wonder, between now and then, why I think it's even necessary to remind you of your duty to be impartial."

He looked at me for a moment longer, frowning. Then he turned and left.

A set of fingers appeared in the side wall opposite the one I shared with Tarani's cell. The open places left in the brick were not large enough to admit the whole hand, but I thought I recognized the strong, elegant fingers. I touchéd them, and the voice from beyond the wall confirmed my guess.

"Well, well," Zaddorn said with a chuckle. "Indestructible as always, I see."

"You knew about the kill-on-sight order?" I asked.

"*Objecting* to that order put me in here," he said. The fingers twisted slightly, so that they could grasp mine. He whispered: "It is the Ra'ira causing this madness, is it not?"

I had told Zaddorn about the true nature of the Ra'ira on our last visit to Raithskar. Zaddorn had been given the task of controlling the vineh—far less dangerous then than now—but he had been given the same lie as the rest of the city about *why* they were out of control. I had thought it only fair, and very much in the interest of protecting the city, that he be aware that the vineh had been suppressed and directed by the use of the Ra'ira and were now free of that direction. At the time, I had still believed that the Ra'ira had actually been taken out of Raithskar.

I squeezed his fingers. "That's exactly right, Zaddorn. Ferrathyn has had it all along. I didn't know—or, believe me, I would have told you."

"I do believe you," Zaddorn said bitterly. "We've all been taken for fools. The citizens, the Council—all of us. I began to realize it when Ferrathyn began giving orders as if he carried the authority of the entire Council. And no one else objected, Rikardon! Am I the only one who sees the man clearly?"

"There are others who know—"

"Caution, my love," Tarani warned. "Remember that Ferrathyn cannot see *our* thoughts."

"But they are all outside of Raithskar," I finished. "When we are heard in Council, more will know the truth."

Zaddorn was silent for a moment. "Do you really believe he will let you live to speak to the Council?"

*That depends on how confident he is,* I thought, *and on how much he is using his power directly. If he has merely guided the Council, then he still needs their goodwill. He wouldn't dare have us killed before Thanasset provides us the hearing he's promised us.*

"It's what we're counting on. Zaddorn, I'm afraid I can't tell you more than that."

"You can't—" he began angrily. "Oh. I see." His fingers withdrew, and I heard the sound of his fist striking the wall. "It is . . . degrading to know that my thoughts may not be my own," he said, "and that I might be a danger to my friends."

I knew Zaddorn's pride and sense of control, and I could hear in his voice the pain this situation was causing him. I had no comfort to offer him, but Tarani spoke up suddenly from the other cell.

"Zaddorn, can you hear me?" she asked, speaking in the same soft tones we had all adopted.

"Yes, Tarani, I hear you," Zaddorn answered.

"Then be encouraged," she said. "That we choose not to share our knowledge with you is merely a sensible precaution. It is my feeling that the true power of the Ra'ira lies in the secrecy of its nature, and in its use on those who do not suspect its power. Think—if Ferrathyn had such power over you, would he have allowed you to oppose him to the extent of public confrontation? There are others, obviously, whom he *does* control. The difference must lie in your knowledge, Zaddorn. You knew the Ra'ira's power, and suspected its use. You are a public figure, a man respected among the citizens of Raithskar. It would have been much to Ferrathyn's benefit to have you seem to support him. But such subtle control was beyond his power, so he chose to discredit you and isolate you physically. To me, that says he cannot reach you, use you, control you—*because you know it can be done, and would be alert to the intrusion of his mind.*"

"Thank you for saying that, High Lord," Zaddorn said. "Yet it is only speculation, is it not?"

"Speculation from one who has felt the force of his power directly," Tarani said quietly. "And—forgive me, Zaddorn—if you hear my words, Ferrathyn, hear this too: I am your equal in power and by far your superior in other ways. Your defeat is at hand."

I stared at the wall in shock, and Zaddorn was utterly silent for that same period. Suddenly, he laughed.

"Well done, Tarani. I know the Chief Supervisor very well, and he could not have restrained a reaction to that challenge. You have made your point—both points, in fact. I have renewed faith that I *can* resist the Ra'ira's power. But that I am doing it now is no certainty that I do it always. I consent, in better spirit, to being left ignorant of your plans. I wish you success, and would help if I were able."

"Thank you," I said, but was interrupted by a ruckus at the entrance to the wing of cells.

"I don't care what your orders are, or who they come from," a determined voice was saying. "You either let me in there to visit my nephew, or I'll disturb your precious Peace and Security until you'll have to let me in as a prisoner!"

# 27

I grinned and moved over to the latticed-wood barrier.

"Hit him, Milda!" I shouted through the door. "Then he'll have to arrest you!"

I heard the sound of a scuffle, then light footsteps, running, followed by a heavier tramping. "All right," said the voice of the guard as he opened the door into the narrow building, lined with cells. "But you can't stay long. When I say it's time, you come out of there, no argument. Right?"

"No, it's not right," Milda said. "But I agree. Now open the fleabitten door!"

I heard the latch pull up, and the door open, and then Milda's footsteps came hesitantly down the aisle between the opposing cells.

"Here, Milda," I called. "Next to the last, on your left."

Suddenly she was there in front of me, looking older and more frail than I remembered. She had gone nearly totally bald, but there was still a bright alertness in her eyes. Alertness—and doubt.

It hurt.

"You, too, Milda?" I said. "Why did you come, then?"

Like a rainbow following a storm, something beautiful swept into Milda's eyes. She came forward to where my hand was resting on one of the crosspieces of the door, and she touched my hand lightly at first, then more firmly. A soft sadness came into her face, and I ached to set the bars aside and hold her.

"Has the world gone mad, Rikardon? I came because I didn't

want to believe it, but I couldn't know for sure until I had seen you, heard your voice. I wasn't home when you came, or I would have seen the truth then, and Thanasset would never have sent you here."

"We left your home by choice, Milda," Tarani said from the next cell. "Without the love and welcome we shared there, it is as barren as this cell."

Milda left me a moment, and went out of my line of sight to speak through Tarani's cell door. "We've just put some of that love back, my girl, and Thanasset will add his share again, if I've anything to say about it. I don't know what has gotten into the man!"

*Ferrathyn's control,* I answered silently. *Tarani's right about knowledge making a difference. For Thanasset to be so mired in the public attitude, Ferrathyn must have been working on him slowly, for as long as he has been a Supervisor, to prepare him for this.*

"We do," I said, "and, Milda, you're not to try to change him, do you hear me? If you can keep him from knowing you've seen me, that would be even better."

The old lady came back to my cell and stared at me.

"You will only create danger for yourself and Thanasset," I said. "And you could make our situation worse, not better. We're being held for a Council hearing, and after that . . ."

"After that, things will be better?" she asked skeptically.

"Either better, or over," I said. "The point is, nothing can be done until then. Promise me you'll be patient."

She stared a moment longer, then nodded sharply. "I have to say, Rikardon, that I loved Markasset. He was a rogue in manner and a child at heart, and I was always in a turmoil over the misunderstandings he had with his father. But complicated as life was then, it's gotten worse since you arrived. It's certainly beyond this old mind to figure out what's going on. I'll keep still, as you ask."

"Thank you, darling," I said. "I think Markasset would say that the stakes are high in this game."

She pressed my hand again. "I just want you to know one thing," she said. "This change in Thanasset—it's not his fault. There was just so much public opinion that—" Her voice broke, and she paused for a moment. "He's fleabitten *blind*, that's what he is, or else he could see the goodness shine in you, as I do."

"Milda, darling," I said, and grasped her fingers. "It's not his fault. I do know that. Now—I think it's best you go, Milda. It would break my heart if you were hurt because of me."

"All right, Rikardon," she said. She sort of shook herself, and stepped away, but before she had actually started for the door, Zaddorn spoke up from the end cell.

"Milda, if you see Illia, tell her I am well."

"Zaddorn?" Milda exclaimed, and stalked down to look through his doorway. "In your own cell?" She came into view again as she took a huge step back from the door, her hands held up in front of her. "I won't ask, I suppose I really don't want to know. I'll give Illia the message, Zaddorn—message!"

She came toward me, fumbling with her tunic belt pouch.

"I almost forgot the reason—well, the excuse, anyway—for my visit," she said, as she pulled two folded papers, sealed with wax, out of the pouch. "The maufel came to the house the other day, ranting about duty only going so far. He said these had come for you two, and maybe he was obligated to deliver them, but he figured nothing forced him to deal directly with traitors. I was related to you, so he gave them to me. Thanasset, by the way, was not there at the time."

She handed one of the papers to me.

"This one is addressed to you." Then she moved to Tarani's cell and said: "And this one to the High Lord of Eddarta. I presume that's you, dear?"

"Yes, Milda, thank you. And thank you for coming."

"You take care," Milda said. "I hope you'll come home soon."

"I hope so too."

Milda walked to the end of the corridor and banged on the door, which opened almost immediately. "Where have you been?" she scolded the guard. "I've been twiddling my thumbs for the past five minutes, waiting for you to say 'time.'"

The door closed behind Milda, and Zaddorn said: "I think that guard will be delighted to see the last of your aunt, my friend."

"She's certainly one of a kind," I said.

"Your messages?" Zaddorn said. "I never realized how boring these cells can be. May I know what is in them?"

I opened mine just as I heard the snap of the wax seal from Tarani's cell. My letter was from Naddam, the man who had once been my supervisor at an Eddartan copper mine. The very fact that he had written to me was not encouraging, and I opened the letter with a sense of dread.

The letter was written in the neat handwriting that I had seen throughout the mine's bookkeeping records. It struck me again that there was nothing in the man's rough and burly appearance to hint at the precision of his handwriting, the clarity of his thinking, and the depth of his humanity.

"*You asked me to tell you if Indomel and Zefra were meeting their agreement with the High Lord,*" the letter began, with no salutation. "*The answer is no. Together, they have taken over control of Lord City. Hollin is dead, assassinated. All the High Lord's reforms have been reversed, and anyone from Lower Eddarta who dares to speak of the High Lord is enslaved and sent to the copper mines. They are saying it was too good to be true, that the High Lord has abandoned them. Anger is growing in the lower city, and guild groups are threatening to deny their product to the Lords, saying that if all guild members stand together, their power can equal that of Pylomel's wife and son. A few of the Lords continue to support the High Lord's policies, but Indomel has made it clear that the High Guard will act against anyone who dares to defy him in public.*

"*I have a few old friends among the High Guard, and there are a few young men who have the sense to see what fighting among the Lords will actually mean—the lower city will take advantage of the chaos to overwhelm the Lords. Some see that as wrong, and some merely wish to protect their jobs, but for whatever reason, a good portion of the High Guard will stand with me against any order to attack the guard of another Lord family.*

"*Everyone, Lord and craftsman alike, is saying that the only solution to this chaos is the return of the High Lord. I hope this letter will persuade you to assist her speedy return.*"

The letter was unsigned.

"At least something goes well," Tarani said. I heard the crackling as she refolded the thin parchment on which her letter was written. "My letter is from Hollin. The conversion of the copper mines is proceeding as planned. Lord City is prosperous and peaceful."

I stared at the cell wall, and then at the letter in my hand. *Logically*, I thought, *it ought to be a tossup which letter is lying, since either one could have been faked. But I think I'm the one who has the real McCoy. First, I saw a great deal of Naddam's handwriting, but Tarani saw only a few samples of Hollin's. It would be harder to fool me.*

*Second, more people have more reasons to lie to Tarani. The longer she's gone, the more deeply Indomel and Zefra can entrench their political control of the Lords. At least, they would believe that. I'll bet they don't have the faintest idea what might happen if Eddarta decides it has had enough, and rebels against Lord City.*

*So I believe I know the truth,* I thought. *The question now is, what do I tell Tarani?*

The question became suddenly urgent as Tarani said: "Your message, Rikardon? Who sent it?"

*There's nothing she can do about it now,* I reasoned. *Ferrathyn's our first priority. After that—if we're still here— then I'll let her worry about Eddarta.*

"Ligor," I said. "He says to tell Zaddorn hello for him."

"Ligor!" Zaddorn exclaimed. "I thought he was in Krasa. How is the old rascal?"

"Busy," I said, then stopped, struck by a new thought. *Unless Ferrathyn has a satellite spy in Chizan, he doesn't know the passes may be blocked. That might be a piece of information worth hoarding until the proper time.*

Zaddorn heard the sudden stop in my voice, and sighed.

"Not even news from an old friend, eh? But never mind— what you lack in conversation, you have provided in material for speculation."

"I'm sorry, Zaddorn," I said. "Really sorry."

"We can talk of other things," Tarani said. "How is Illia? I believe your wedding was scheduled for shortly after our departure. Did it go well? Who was there?"

Zaddorn chuckled. "Actually, it was something of a disaster. Illia, sweet as she is, may never forgive me. . . ."

I heard him settle to the floor near the wall, and he began to describe the day of the wedding. His duties had kept him out late the night before; he had been tired and clumsy, especially with the celebration feast. Zaddorn described every moment of the day, every person attending, their dress and manner, in such a wry, witty style that Tarani and I both laughed uproariously. At one point, the guard came in to check on us, moving with deliberate quietness. Of course, we knew he was there, incredulous that three people in our situation could laugh about anything, and his presence set us off again.

When the guard brought us our evening meal, he also brought some unwelcome news.

"Your hearing has been announced for noon tomorrow," he said. "And the Council has decided on a closed hearing."

When he had gone, Tarani said: "It's too soon!"

I said nothing, because of Zaddorn. But I had a sick feeling inside. I had not imagined the hearing could be arranged so quickly. It would take the sha'um three days, at a full run, to reach Thagorn.

Later that night, when Zaddorn had fallen asleep, I rolled over next to Tarani's cell and spoke through one of the lowest openings. "Tarani, are you awake?" I called softly.

"Yes," she answered immediately, from a point directly on the other side of the wall. A lamp had been set in the corridor to burn all night, but little of that light penetrated the latticed door. I could barely see the movement as her fingers appeared in one of the openings.

"Rikardon, I have been thinking. No matter what Thanasset has promised, Ferrathyn cannot afford for us to appear before the Council. He must keep the Ra'ira with him at all times; he would not risk my being in the same room with it."

"I've been thinking along those lines, myself," I said.

"He will try to have us killed."

"But not tonight," I added. "He's still trying to keep on Thanasset's good side, or we would already be dead. Thanasset offered us the protection of Council law, and he would suspect the coincidence of our getting killed by guards, no matter what excuse is offered. No, Ferrathyn will want to find a way to kill us by mandate of the citizenship."

"The mob," Tarani said.

"Exactly. There will be only one opportunity—when we're being escorted to the Council chambers."

"We must be ready," she said.

"No, *you* must be ready," I corrected her gently. "You can disguise *yourself* fairly easily. I will stay and be their target. Who knows, they may even let me talk, and listen to me."

"I would not leave you!" she said fiercely.

"Only to save me," I said.

"Listen to me, Tarani. Ferrathyn's taking a chance with this hearing. He wouldn't risk it at all if he weren't ready to make his final move. I think we've lost the chance to wait for the Sharith. We have to tackle him ourselves if we want even a slim hope of getting out of this mess alive.

"You have to get into operating range of the Ra'ira, Tarani. That's the only way we can be sure of breaking Ferrathyn's control of the city."

"I was boastful, earlier," she said. "What if I cannot break free of the mob, or I am too late to save you?" Her fingers stroked mine, very gently.

"We can only do what feels most right, Tarani," I said. "Your boast was true; you *can* beat him, I know it. Something else you said earlier is true too. This is the final battle; we can't hold anything back." She was silent for a long time. "You once said you have no regrets," I reminded her. "Is that still true, Tarani?"

"With one exception," she said. "I deeply regret that we must spend this night with a wall of brick between us."

We lay silently, together but separate, our hands barely touching through the wall. I sent a sleepy thought toward Keeshah, and received a sense of his total concentration on running. He was moving by scent through the darkest part of the night, and I shared his awareness of other sha'um moving around him.

*I won't disturb your concentration, Keeshah*, I thought to myself. *It would only upset you, anyway, to know that you'll get here too late to help. I don't see a chance in the world of my surviving—all I want to do is buy Tarani the time she needs. You'll know when it happens*, I thought, with a sensation of writing a letter I knew would never get mailed. *But now you won't be so alone, Keeshah. You'll have Koshah and Yoshah. I'm glad that happened.*

Tarani and I were awake at first light, having slept only fitfully. A different guard brought us a breakfast of water and porridge, and a bowl of water to use in washing. Time passed slowly. It was Zaddorn who put into words what was on all our minds. "I have an uneasy feeling about your leaving these protected, if uncomfortable, walls," he said, just before we heard the corridor door clang open.

"They will be safe," said Thanasset. "I have promised they will be heard."

The lattice door across my cell was lifted away, and I stepped out into the hallway to face Thanasset. The guard moved to

Tarani's cell and began opening the bronze fastenings into which her door was mounted. Thanasset misread the look on my face.

"Are you so surprised that I should keep my word, Rikardon?" he asked bitterly.

"Don't come with us," I urged him. "There's going to be trouble, Father, and I'm sure Ferrathyn would jump at the chance to see you dead."

He drew back in shock, and for just a moment, he seemed on the point of asking me to explain. Then his face closed up again. "I told you yesterday," he said angrily, "to save your comments for the hearing."

"We will never *reach* the hearing," I said.

"That's enough!" He turned on his heel and walked toward the door. The guard waited for Tarani and me to follow him, then came out. He closed and locked the door.

"Keep safe!" Zaddorn shouted after us.

Outside, the cloud-diffused sunlight seemed terribly bright after the dimness of the cells, and Tarani and I could only stand and blink for a moment. By the time we could see clearly, we were surrounded by a squad of guards. One of them was the man who had been in front of Thanasset's house, the one through whom I had looked into the eyes of Ferrathyn.

The eight men formed a marching group around Tarani and me, and Thanasset moved out in front of the group.

I felt the keen edge of energy that was, by now, familiar and welcome—it marked the shift from waiting to doing. It was both like and unlike the other times—when I had decided to enter Lord City and contact Tarani's mother, when I had finally made the commitment to search for Kä and the second steel sword. The relief of action after inactivity was there, but there was also a greater weight of fear, and awareness of the consequences of failure.

Always before, I had defined success partly in terms of my own survival. That was not the case now. During the night, I had considered the possibility that I had already accomplished all that I was meant to do in Gandalara. I had been the mechanism by which the sha'um had been saved. I had been the first to comprehend the significance of the earthquake and volcanic eruption. I had brought Tarani, integrated with Antonia and somewhat protected from Ferrathyn's power, to a place where she had a fair chance to defeat Ferrathyn. Zanek had come back. He could be the one meant to lead Gandalara into a new life, beyond the borders it had always known. For the first time since my arrival in Gandalara, I felt a deep sense of having fulfilled my destiny.

Once again, I had come to terms with imminent death.

*Just don't bet I'll go quietly,* I said to myself, aiming the thought at Ferrathyn, *or that I'll be alone when I go.*

The Council offices—and the vault where the Ra'ira had been kept—were in the building directly opposite the confinement center, but the Council met, officially, in a large building at the edge of the largest city square. It was a distance of some ten blocks, and my nerves were on edge as we passed each side street. I noticed that our "friend" from the day before had taken up a position directly behind Thanasset, and that only made me more sure that an attack was planned. Tarani looked back at me once, tilting her head slightly in Thanasset's direction, and I nodded.

Apparently, no attempt had been made to keep our capture a secret. From the moment we left the jail, a crowd of people had gathered to follow us, calling out angrily. More people joined them from the side streets as we moved along the wide avenue. Thanasset turned to talk to one of the guards, and our escort spread out to keep as much distance as possible between us and the crowd, and still form a containment ring around us.

We were nearly in the square when it happened. Tarani, as she had promised, was ready for it.

Out of the side street ahead of us ran a group of armed men, not in uniform but moving with an air of trained precision. At the exact moment they appeared, someone in the crowd behind us yelled: "Kill the traitors!" The crowd surged forward from behind, forcing the rear guards to whirl around to face them. Thanasset had drawn his sword and was standing his ground against the oncoming group. Behind him, the guard drew back the hand which held his dagger.

I slammed my shoulder into the guard on my right, snatching the man's dagger from its sheath as he fell away from me. Then I leaped forward.

The guard, and the men in front of us, were staring in confusion at Thanasset, who had taken on the appearance of Milda.

*Thank you, Tarani,* I thought fervently.

The High Lord herself was nowhere to be seen.

I wrapped my left arm around the neck of the guard behind Thanasset and buried my dagger in his right side. The men in front yelled, and Thanasset whirled around. The half-image of Milda—transparent only to me, I was sure—wavered and faded, and it was clearly Thanasset who stared at me, the guard, our positions, and the dagger clutched in the man's hand.

Something changed in Thanasset's eyes.

"I don't have time to explain now," I said. "Defend yourself!"

Apparently, Ferrathyn had assigned the guard to Thanasset specifically, and was counting on the distraction of the mob and the efficiency of the armed group to finish off Tarani and me. All our original guards were defending their own lives against the angry mob, which left Thanasset and me to hold our own against the armed squad which had appeared so suddenly. Wordlessly, Thanasset tossed me his own dagger to supplement the one I had stolen, and he faced the attackers with only his sword. With our former guards, we formed a shoulder-to-shoulder circle of defense—nine men against nearly a hundred wild-eyed, frantic people caught up in a mob mentality.

I steeled myself against sympathy for them, and fought hard beside Thanasset. There were too many for us. A sword slashed into Thanasset's side, and he fell beside me. I killed the man who had hurt him, then I pulled Markasset's father into the center of the circle of guards. I cradled his shoulders in my arms and hugged his head to my chest.

"Rikardon," he said, gasping for breath. "What happened? Tell me, what happened?"

"The Ra'ira never left Raithskar," I said. "Ferrathyn has had it all along. The vineh are under his control."

"Ferrathyn?" Thanasset demanded, and then coughed painfully. "The Council has to know!" He struggled to stand up.

"The Council *will* know," I assured him, gently forcing him back. His tunic was soaked with blood around the ugly slash in his side, and blood was pooling on the cobbled street beneath him. "Tarani is on her way there now. She can use the Ra'ira, Thanasset. She'll beat him."

The old man looked up at me. The small scar on his brow looked dark against the stark, sudden paleness of his face. "So many lies," he said. "And I believed him. I let him use me. I betrayed you. Forgive me, son."

I squeezed his shoulder. "You saved us, too," I said, "and Ferrathyn deceived us all. But listen to me, Thanasset," I urged him. "It's all more important than just Ferrathyn, just the Ra'ira, just Raithskar. The life of Gandalara itself is at stake. We're going to win, Father, and you've helped us win." I groped for something more to say. "Markasset would have been very proud of you."

The old man smiled at that. He seemed to have passed the point of pain from the wound in his side; I knew he could not last much longer.

"Markasset proud?" Thanasset said. "And what does *Rikardon* think of Thanasset?"

"I—I love you . . . Father."

He smiled more broadly, and brought a weak hand up to cover mine and squeeze it. He nodded slightly, and then his eyes went out of focus and his hand fell away, limp as the rest of his body.

# 28

I clutched at the old man's body, kneeling in the eye of a hurricane of strife, and I screamed inside my head. The battle, Ferrathyn, the danger Tarani faced—all were momentarily forgotten in the grief I felt for the kind man who had done nothing but want the best for his family and his city.

It was only when I noticed the cessation of movement around me that I realized what had caused it—my silent scream of grief, voiced in the throats of three sha'um. I laid Thanasset's head on the ground as gently as I could, then leaped to my feet.

*Keeshah!*

*Stay,* Keeshah said. *Coming.*

And come he did, straight down the main avenue of Raithskar, scattering people every which way. The fight around me had stopped at the chilling, unrepeated sound of the sha'um cry, and everyone was milling about uncertainly. In the square west of me, Keeshah leaped into view and waited. He was joined, a moment later, by the cubs, and the three sha'um crouched and began a menacing advance toward the crowd.

The crowd disappeared into the side streets.

Quickly.

The cubs rubbed against me on either side, and Keeshah lowered his head to nudge Thanasset with his muzzle. Keeshah's mind was so full of sympathy and personal loss that I had to resist letting grief recapture me.

Another sha'um appeared in the square, this one carrying a Rider. He waved and rode over to us, then jumped down and hugged me. It was Thymas. When he released me, he saw the body, and looked at me curiously.

"Thanasset," I said. "My father."

"Oh," he said, and pressed my shoulder. "I am sorry, Captain."

I nodded, then asked: "How did you get here so fast?"

"We were barely a half-day behind you all the way," Thymas answered, and grinned. "Zanek told me what you had planned, and also that you had given him full authority to use his own judgment. His *judgment* dictated that we not allow you the opportunity to face Ferrathyn alone."

"Where *is* Zanek?" I asked.

Thymas shrugged. "We encountered several large groups of vineh—some of us are still fighting them. After your sha'um met us last night, Zanek rode Yayshah. We got separated during one of the battles. I have not seen him since." He looked around. "For that matter," he said in a worried voice, "where is Tarani?"

I went cold inside. "She was trying to reach the Council chamber," I said, pointing across the square, "to face Ferrathyn alone."

We could have *run* across the square in only a short time, but our sense of urgency was such that Thymas and I both leaped on the sha'um to ride to the Council chamber. We dismounted running, and crashed through the double doors of the high-ceilinged room together.

Tarani was not there. No one was there—no one alive, that is. Seated and lying on the benches that ringed the floor of the room were the torn and bloody bodies of the other Supervisors.

"Who did *this*?" I wondered.

"Are you sure he was here?" Thymas demanded.

"Wait," I said, catching Thymas's arm. "If this was to be a *closed* Council hearing, then only Council members should have been here. Without Thanasset, that would only be eleven people, and there are—" I counted. "Twelve." I blinked, and looked carefully at the bodies. The room was a horseshoe-shaped amphitheater, with its only opening at the door through which Thymas and I had come. Near the far end of the room, two of the bodies were close together, one half-sitting, the other sprawled face-down across a bench. As I concentrated, their outlines blurred.

"There!" I shouted, and jumped farther into the room.

The seated figure moved and changed, and became a thin old man, standing beside the prostrate figure. Gone was any vestige of weakness or kindness. The wrinkled face was like chiseled stone, the slim body wiry with health.

"You are too late," Ferrathyn said in a cold, powerful voice. "Too late for anything. The people of Raithskar have joined with the vineh; already the Sharith are beginning to falter. And as for this—this *nuisance* . . ."

The old man reached to the body before him, lifted the face, and turned it toward us. Thymas yelled, and I went speechless with pain. The body was Tarani's. Her throat had been cut.

Ferrathyn saw us hurting, and he laughed—a low, hollow, infuriating sound. Together, deliberately, Thymas and I stepped together toward the evil old man.

Something struck my shoulder, knocking me forward, and I glimpsed Thymas falling beside me. I heard a swishing sound, and then a clatter. A dagger had struck the brick wall point first, then bounced to the tiled floor. I rolled over to see one of the "dead" Supervisors leaping over benches, a sword ready in his hand. His face was a terrifying blankness.

Purely by reflex, I drew back my right hand and threw my dagger like a javelin. It struck the man squarely in the stomach. He staggered, but his momentum carried him into the open area, where he collapsed to the floor. I looked around. Thymas was on his back, pressed there by another of the Supervisors, and all around us, the "dead" men were rising, their wounds still seeming to bleed.

It was so eerie and unnatural that, for a moment, I merely

crouched where I was, staring in shock. Then I heard a sharp, skittering sound, and the hilt of Rika appeared near my hand.

"Pull yourself together," said a voice from behind us. "They are illusions, and illusion is not Ferrathyn's skill but Tarani's. The High Lord must still live, or her skill directed under compulsion by this . . . *abomination*."

I put my hand on Rika's hilt, and looked back at the doorway. Dharak/Zanek stood there, holding the other steel sword. His presence, and the familiar weight of Rika in my hand, brought me out of my half-trance.

Thymas had rolled to the top of the struggle, and was ending it. The other Supervisors moved toward us as I stood up. There were eight of them left, and three of us. Considering that they were moving under compulsion, with less agility and force than *thinking* fighters, the odds were not overwhelming. But fighting them would keep us distracted, and give Ferrathyn time to summon more help.

"Supervisors, I claim the right of a fair hearing," I called, and the formula was so familiar and so traditional, so highly respected, that it made even the madman-dominated minds of the Council pause.

"You know the power of the Ra'ira," I said. "It is being used against you by one whom you trusted, one who has used and manipulated the entire city to achieve his own gains. Resist it—"

An invisible hand seemed to close around my throat, and my brain seemed to catch fire. Thymas gasped, and I knew he must be suffering similar pain. I would have closed my eyes—I wanted to close my mind—against it, but I had virtually no control over my own body.

Thymas and I had faced this danger before, but we had been half a world away at the time. This was more proof that it had not been Gharlas's native power which had threatened us then. It had been Ferrathyn, using the Ra'ira to reach out to and through his satellite to strike at us. Even then, we had not been able to break free unaided—it had taken the sudden distraction of Tarani's appearance, and the surging presence of Keeshah in my mind, to shatter that control.

*I'm not as vulnerable as Thymas*, I thought, fighting against the searing pain. *But half of me is Gandalaran, and I'm not totally immune. It's always taken time to counteract his compulsions. He's learned from those earlier encounters, and the closer we are, the stronger he seems to be. Even these illusions were fully effective for me, at first. There isn't any time!*

The pain had been clenching my throat ever tighter and increasing in intensity in my head. Suddenly it hesitated, and I was able to gulp in a mouthful of air.

It pained me to move my eyes, but I could do it. The Supervisors had resumed their advance when Ferrathyn had attacked us directly. They paused now, and the image of blood and death wavered around them. The fire in my mind pushed forward again, seemed to vibrate. It withdrew slightly, then advanced again in a rush. It was like nothing so much as a reverse tug-of-war, and it was no child's game.

I was facing the rounded end of the horseshoe-shaped room, and I had a clear view of Ferrathyn, standing beside what I hoped was only the image of Tarani's corpse. Ferrathyn stood squarely, slightly taller than the image in my memory, and for a moment I doubted Zanek's comment about the illusion skill being entirely Tarani's. Then I recalled how much of Tarani's dance illusions had been merely dance, and realized that this powerful man had wrought the image of the frail and kindly Ferrathyn with gifted acting skills, not mindpower.

Thymas coughed beside me, and I took another breath. Ferrathyn stared at Thymas, then glanced down at Tarani's limp form, frowning. *Ferrathyn thought I was holding back his power,* I realized, *until he sensed the resistance in Thymas too. He must be remembering that Tarani helped Thymas break free of the compulsion in Dyskornis.*

The voice of Dharak, speaking from behind me, caught Ferrathyn's attention.

"Tarani was right," the voice said. "Mindskills have grown since my last time in this world. I can oppose you, Tinis, but I cannot defeat you—not alone. And hear me clearly—your victory will mark the *end* of Gandalara. I ask you, in the name of the Kingdom, to set aside your ambition and aid a greater cause—the salvation of our world."

"In the name of the *Kingdom*?" Ferrathyn said, sneering. "I take it you mean the First Kingdom, for *I* am the new Kingdom! *This begins it!*"

"What will you gain in ruling a world that is doomed?" Zanek said.

"Do you think to frighten me with your nonsense?" Ferrathyn shouted. "And if you know the name 'Tinis,' then you *know* what I seek to gain. Those who despised and scorned me, who sought to destroy me, will see my power. Their fear created me from an innocent child, and they will be ruled by their own creation."

If I had not already had trouble breathing, I would have choked on that. *Innocent?* I wondered. *In a fit of pique, that kid forced three men to kill themselves. It's true they were cheating him, and his anger was probably justified, but not his actions. Not murder!*

Zanek spoke again, his voice vibrant with a power that came from Zanek's mind, not Dharak's body.

"Tarani," the voice called. Dharak took a step into the room. "I need your help, woman of two worlds. This man controls you only because he has learned well the use of the Ra'ira. It adds to his power, and you have no *experience* to counteract it. The experience is mine, Tarani, and the strength is yours. Join with me. Resist him."

Zanek was moving forward carefully now, edging past me into my line of sight. The wall of flame shivered in my mind and began to inch backward. Almost in echo of that movement, Ferrathyn stepped back.

"Hear the truth of the words you admire, Tarani," Zanek said. "They speak not of the past but of the present. They have meaning for each one of us, today. They were a prophecy toward this moment.

"'I greet thee in the name of the new Kingdom,'" Zanek said. He took another step. "'From chaos have we created order. From strife have we enabled peace. From greed have we encouraged sharing.' What is there in Raithskar now but chaos, strife, and greed?" Zanek asked, still moving cautiously.

The bloody corpse beside Ferrathyn stirred slightly. The old man's gaze flickered toward it, but he returned his concentration to the man who was advancing, slowly but inexorably, toward him.

"*Listen to my words, Tarani,*" Zanek said. "'Not I alone, but the Sharith have done this.' Is that not true? Would you and I be here, if not for the Riders who are even now struggling against the vineh? 'Not we alone, but the Ra'ira has done this.' *This* is the task before us now, Tarani. With the Ra'ira working *against* us, we are lost. *We* must control the stone. Resist

Tinis. Fight him. Help me claim the Ra'ira for the *future* of this world, not its destruction.

"The Ra'ira is our goal, Tarani. It is our destiny."

Ferrathyn gasped and staggered backward, clutching his chest. Beneath the bench where Tarani lay, the pools of blood began to fade.

"'I greet thee in the name of the new Kingdom,' Tarani," Zanek quoted. "'And I charge thee: *care for it well.*'"

The blood vanished altogether, and Tarani, beautifully clean but deathly pale from the strain of the effort she was making, struggled into a sitting position.

Ferrathyn staggered again. His back was against the chamber wall. He reached into a concealed pouch and pulled out the Ra'ira. As if it were a defense in itself, he held the stone tightly, his hand extended toward Zanek, who was very close now.

"Who—Who *are* you?" Ferrathyn whispered.

"'I am Zanek, King of Gandalara.'"

A cry of shock was wrenched from Ferrathyn. The pain in my mind had receded. I was breathing easily now, but I was hypnotized by Zanek's rich voice, immobilized by the pulsing aura of power in the room.

Zanek was right in front of Ferrathyn. Gently, but inexorably, Zanek pried open Ferrathyn's fingers, and lifted free the blue gem. He turned to Tarani, caught her wrist, and placed the Ra'ira in her open palm. Her fingers closed around it, and, with his own hand enclosing stone and fingers both, Zanek helped Tarani stand up.

"It is not hers," Ferrathyn said, in a stunned and desperate whisper. "It belongs to me."

Zanek, half-supporting Tarani, looked over his shoulder at Ferrathyn and answered quietly: "It belongs to Gandalara."

For a moment they stared at each other, the two old men, and the contrast between them was crystal clear. It was not merely that one stood straight and confident, and the other cringed back against the wall. Nor was it so subtle a thing as the fact that Zanek had been given charge of Tarani's power, as well as his own, and he overshadowed the older man in a psychic sense. The two men were Promise and Failure, Hope and Despair. Zanek, the man from Gandalara's past, was now its future; Ferrathyn was merely its fading present, and both men knew it.

It was over.

Zanek turned his back on Ferrathyn, and he and Tarani came slowly down the steps. In silence, they moved across the floor.

The Supervisors, released from the compulsion which had held them, were looking generally confused, but one or two of them had figured out some of what was going on. "The Ra'ira?" one of them wondered aloud. "Ferrathyn had it?"

"Ferrathyn *used* it," another man said. "On *us.*"

"You there," one man called to Tarani and Zanek, "you stopped him? Why are you leaving him, untouched? Why don't you *finish* it?"

Tarani and Zanek did not answer, but walked between me and Thymas toward the door. Tarani did no more than glance at me, but I knew we had the same thought.

"Get out," I told the Supervisors, my voice husky from the strain of the compulsion on my throat. "Now."

One or two—the more aware, and more angry—hesitated, but the rest obeyed my tone of voice and headed for the door. Ferrathyn came away from the wall and pulled himself to his full height. "I have one consolation, *High Lord,*" he said scathingly to Tarani's back. "If Eddarta will not be mine, it is at least no longer yours. Gharlas was mine, and through him, I brought Indomel under my control. I have worked in Eddarta as well as Raithskar to bring chaos and disorder. I had thought it would make me more welcome there, but I take pleasure from the thought that *your* efforts have been wasted. Both cities will lie in ruins."

Tarani hesitated at the open doorway, and I saw the muscles of her neck tighten as she fought the impulse to turn and question the vicious old man. After only a moment, however, she walked on through the door.

When the room was empty except for Thymas, Ferrathyn, and me, Ferrathyn spoke again.

"It has come to the final moment," he said, staring proudly down from the place of the Chief Supervisor. "I had thought our positions would be reversed, Rikardon. It would be so, now, except for Zanek. I must admit your strangeness and Tarani's power interrupted and changed my plans, but I would have prevailed in the end. If the truth be known, these fools in Raithskar were easily led, and those other fools in Eddarta, fat and complacent and unsuspecting, offered me no prospect of a challenge. You brought new interest to the game."

"Game?" Thymas cried, stepping forward. "Your 'game' has cost the lives of men and sha'um, you piece of filth!"

I caught Thymas's arm, and he glared at me. "You can't mean to let him live?" the Lieutenant demanded.

"Of course I must die," Ferrathyn agreed. "But not at the hand of a mewling boy. No matter what other help was given him, it is essentially Rikardon who has beaten me. He will kill me himself," Ferrathyn said grandly, "and I shall accept death more easily, knowing that the one who strikes has *proved* himself my better. There was a time," he added, almost wistfully, "when I thought none existed."

A tremor shook Thymas, and my own rage echoed his impulse, but I checked it.

"There was a time," I said to Ferrathyn, "when I thought you might have some justice on your side, Tinis. I see now that I was wrong. Long ago, you lost any real interest in ruling Eddarta. You got caught up in the plotting, the intrigue, the manipulation of people who were unaware of your power—the 'game.'

"I *would* kill you myself, and gladly," I said, and he quavered back from the hatred that rang in my voice. "Thanasset is dead, a victim of your 'game.' But there was another, earlier casualty, and a claim of vengeance that takes priority over mine."

I started backing toward the door. Thymas resisted until he saw my face, then his own went pale and he moved with me.

Ferrathyn stared at us. "What?" he asked, his voice faltering. "What are you doing?"

"It must be hard for you, after all this time with the Ra'ira, to try to *guess* what people are thinking. Don't worry," I said, putting my hand on the door. "You won't have long to wait."

Thymas and I stepped out into the bright day, and I dragged the boy aside. Yoshah and Koshah shouldered past us, squeezing together through the double doorway. We heard a sharp intake of breath from Ferrathyn, a shout of "*No!*", and then his screaming mingled with the roar and growl of the cats.

# 29

Tarani and Zanek were standing to one side, their hands joined between them. Tarani was hunched and tense, and Zanek was talking to her, very quietly. Thymas and I approached them, and Tarani looked up at me with a haggard face.

"Rikardon, I cannot bear it. The images, the feelings—the beauty of people, and their inner torment."

Her face was so drawn that I was afraid for her.

"Look away," I said urgently. "The Ra'ira won't work unless you ask it to. All you have to do is *not* use it."

"But that is the horror of it!" she cried. "I *could* turn away, but I cannot. It is so alluring, so fascinating, to look into the mind. The—the *discovery* is addictive. Rikardon, help me!"

"Zanek?"

The man holding Tarani's hands so fiercely shook his head.

"I have tried, my friend. Her strength is too great; I can do nothing."

"And he does *want* to help," Tarani said, her voice falling into a sing-song rhythm that sent chills along my spine. "I see him, you know. A good man who has accepted both triumph and defeat, who mourns for two sha'um and a love lost long ago. The Kingdom took their place. It was his lover, his friend, the object of all his caring . . ."

Zanek flinched. The effort he made to keep his hands touching the girl was visible. He frowned in concentration. In pain.

I started to put my hands on Tarani's shoulders, but hesitated. Tarani caught the movement, and stared toward me; her eyes were unfocused, glazed.

"How odd that you are the one I would most like to see, Rikardon, and yet you are closed to me. It is as if there are windows into all men, but your window is shuttered. Open it for me, Rikardon. Let me see who you are truly."

I felt a probing sensation in my mind, like an insect crawling somewhere inside my clothes. It terrified me. I closed my hands on Tarani's shoulders, applying pressure. I may have imagined it, but I would swear I felt something from her, a mild but tingling shock.

"Think of Antonia," I told her. "You can't see my mind because I'm not entirely Gandalaran—use the non-Gandalaran part of yourself to shut off the Ra'ira. You can do it, Tarani, I know you *want* to do it. Remember Volitar's abhorrence of this very thing, the exercise of power over people who can't resist it? Fight the temptation, Tarani. If you can't control it, Ferrathyn has won, after all."

I was babbling, saying anything that seemed as if it might convince her. Something of what I said reached her. She twitched; her head lifted and her shoulders straightened; she took a deep breath. Then she snatched her hands out of Zanek's grasp and threw herself against me, sobbing. I hugged her tightly. The Ra'ira had been inside Tarani's hands, and the violence of her rejection had let the stone drop and skitter across the brick pavement of the square.

Zanek followed it, picked it up, and went over to the group of men hovering in confusion nearby.

"You are what remains of the Council of Supervisors of Raithskar," he said to them. "In the past, your families have known me as Zanek, and as Serkajon. Do you accept that?"

They nodded—ready, I felt sure, to believe anything after the events of the past few minutes.

"As Serkajon, I gave the Council charge to keep the Ra'ira idle," he said, "and you have failed that charge. Take the stone now, and do what you can to mend the error. Stop the fighting. Send the vineh west, to a land where they can learn to live naturally again, at least for all the time that is left to them."

The men hovered around Zanek's outstretched hand. Impatiently, Zanek took one man's hand and put the Ra'ira in it— but he kept his own hand closed around it too.

"I have no skill with the vineh," he said scornfully. "This is yours to do, and every moment you fail to act is costing lives."

The man Zanek was touching swallowed and nodded, and the Supervisors formed a group around Zanek. Around the city, the noise of battle underwent a subtle change, but did not stop.

"Thymas," I said, but the boy was already mounting Ronar.

"There has been death enough even to satisfy the sha'um,"

he said. "I will call them back, and let the vineh go." Ronar carried him off toward the main gate of the city.

Tarani's trembling had stilled, finally, and she pushed at me. I let her pull away, and was glad to see that the deep lines in her face had smoothed. She continued to seem troubled, but not in that strained, unnatural, half-hysterical way.

"I do not believe that will happen again, Rikardon," she said. "It was only—" She shivered. "What I felt, it was the way Ferrathyn lived. It was his mind I first touched through the Ra'ira, and the shock of it—" She shivered again, then looked off to the east. "How ironic that we feared Thymas so bitterly," she said, "when it was Indomel whom Ferrathyn chose to corrupt through Gharlas. What Ferrathyn said of Eddarta—it is true. I saw it in his mind."

"He believed it was true," I said. "He knew Indomel is working toward that ruin. But it may not be fact, not yet."

She looked back at me. "What do you know of this?" she asked. I pulled out Naddam's letter and handed it to her.

"I don't think Ferrathyn made any allowance for a continuing loyalty to you," I said. "The date on this letter tells me that Eddarta may still be holding fast against chaos. So there is still time."

"To reach Eddarta?" she asked. "We have no idea if the Chizan crossings are passable—" She caught her breath, then crumpled the letter in her fist and stared at the bricks underfoot. "You mean for me to use the Ra'ira."

"It ought to work," I said awkwardly. "Even if the connection between you wasn't formed originally with the assistance of the Ra'ira, your mind has touched both Indomel and Zefra."

I let my voice trail off, but the silence was unbearable, and I stumbled along again.

"Ferrathyn wanted a civil war in Eddarta that would destroy everything," I said. "The city, the buildings—they're dispensable; they'd have to be abandoned, anyway. But the crops, the livestock, the wrought goods—Eddarta has to bear the brunt of support for the first stage of the journey, Tarani. Gandalara can't afford to lose those supplies."

She nodded, still staring at the pavement, and I wanted to hold her again, but I kept my place.

*This must be what she felt for me when Keeshah left us,* I thought. *I would suffer this for her, if I could.*

Zanek walked up, and was surprised when Tarani held out

her hand for the Ra'ira. But he gave it to her readily. Because she flinched when it neared her skin, the stone dropped a few inches before her hand caught it. Zanek would have walked away, but Tarani stopped him.

"Stay with me, Zanek," she said. "I must reach to Eddarta, but the Ra'ira continues to frighten me. I shall do this alone," she said firmly, "but your presence will be a comfort to me."

"I will stay, gladly," he said, "and I offer you this much advice, High Lord. Find a place of comfort before you begin; it will cost you great effort."

"Come home, Tarani," I said. "It would please Thanasset, and I—I need to tell Milda."

"Tell her what?" Tarani asked, and I am sure she had no need of the Ra'ira to see what I was thinking. "No," she said. "Oh, no, not Thanasset. And the last words he heard from me were so harsh, Rikardon."

"Your words shocked him, and helped him look at things differently," I said. "At the last, he understood."

She put her hand on my arm. "Thank you for saying that," she said. "Yes, I would like to go . . . home."

The sha'um settled happily around Keeshah's house, alternately competing for and peacefully sharing space in its shaded interior. Milda was unsurprised by the news of Thanasset's death. She claimed she had sensed it when it happened.

The people of Ricardo's world would have called that "intuition." Gandalarans would have explained it in terms of the All-Mind, saying Milda had sensed Thanasset's arrival there through her own connection with it. It was the same phenomenon, no matter how it seemed to work; people who care deeply for one another establish connections, and can sense when those connections are severed.

By the time we reached the house, Milda had suffered through the first rush of grief and was ready for the distraction of preparing refreshments. Zanek, Tarani, and I ate Milda's dinner gratefully, then Tarani insisted on using the sitting room at the front of the house as the place from which she would try to extend her consciousness toward Eddarta. The four of us—Tarani asked Milda to stay, too—arranged ourselves in the armchairs, and Tarani held the Ra'ira in both hands, laid her hands in her lap, and sort of slumped down.

After a moment, she opened her eyes.

"I feel nothing," she said, and turned to Zanek. "In trying to shut off that rush of thought, have I destroyed my ability to use the stone?"

"That is unlikely," Zanek said. "Perhaps the difficulty lies in the distance involved, and you have too little practice with shorter distances. Reach out to someone closer, first."

"I—who? It is an . . . invasion. Who could I . . . ?"

"You will see," Zanek said, "that it is less intimate, and more controlled, than what you felt before. Do not choose one of us, simply because your concern for our privacy may hold you back. Reach for someone else, someone you know—and only see what they see."

"I will try," she said, a little uncertainly, and closed her eyes again.

We all waited a moment, then Milda, who was sitting opposite Tarani, jumped out of her chair. "Zaddorn," she scolded, "you scared me out of my tusks. I didn't hear you—oh!"

Milda's outburst had drawn our attention to the area of the room behind Tarani's chair. I had only a glimpse of a transparent figure—the image of Zaddorn—before Tarani's eyes snapped open and the image faded.

"I—that—it was Zaddorn. He was *real*," Milda said. "Wasn't he?"

"He was one of Tarani's illusions," I said. "He looked solid to you, I'm sure, but I could see through him."

Zanek looked shaken. "The mindskills have certainly changed since my time," he said. "Tarani—what did *you* see?"

"As you suggested," she said, "I tried to look through his eyes. He has been released, and is reorganizing the Peace and Security forces. Just now, he is supervising the disposition of the dead vineh which virtually surround the city."

Her face brightened. "You were right, Zanek—this touching of minds can be as deep or as limited as one wishes. This time, it was similar to what I have felt as a Recorder. Contact with the thoughts, but not necessarily the person."

"Were you seeking Zaddorn, in particular?" I asked.

"Yes, but I thought I might find him still in his cell; I could not remember anyone specifically ordering his release."

"I expect he did that for himself, once he realized what was going on," I said.

"The important thing is," Zanek said, "you found him because you knew him. I believe it will work the same way for the people in Eddarta, Tarani, though it may require considerably more effort."

"I will try again," Tarani said, then smiled at Milda. "I'm sorry to have frightened you," she said. "I did not consciously cast Zaddorn's image, but I was aware of it. I believe it helped me locate him. There may be others, as I make this search."

"I'll keep quiet this time," Milda said. "It just surprised me, is all."

Once again, Tarani's head slumped slowly forward over her folded hands. She was the only one who seemed relaxed, in spite of the effort we knew she was applying. The rest of us were leaning forward in our chairs, tense and anxious.

For just a moment, there was a change in the air behind Tarani, but it was no more than a flash of white, and it was gone. Tarani sighed, and stretched out her arms and legs, rolling her head to unkink her neck. "I believe I found Indomel," she said. "But I could not hold him. The distance is too far."

She put the Ra'ira down on the small table beside the chair and stood up, stretching and bending at the waist. "It is indeed an effort," she said. "Zanek, we used the Ra'ira together against Ferrathyn. Can you help me in this?"

"I might be able to help," he said thoughtfully, "but you must remember that only today, out of three different lives, have I *shared* the use of the Ra'ira. As I have no experience from which to draw, I must advise you out of logic.

"I think you would do better to ask the aid of someone who also knows the one you seek. You would have not only the extra . . . reach, for want of a better word, but greater chance of forming that bond.

"I see, also, that you are already weary, Tarani, and I would advise only one more effort. If the matter is as urgent as it seems, then in order to give that effort the highest possible likelihood of success, I would suggest you and Rikardon work together."

"Rikardon?"

"Me?"

Tarani and I had spoken at the same time, with the same air of disbelief. I had jumped to my feet in shock, and now I walked over to the tall, latticed windows, and looked out at the sha'um. Yayshah was cleaning herself in front of the house, and Keeshah had claimed the roof for his own. "I haven't a grain of mindpower," I said, "and the non-Gandalaran half of me won't *connect* with mindpower. It's what makes me half-immune to compulsion."

"Did it keep you from seeking out my lifememory in the All-Mind?" Zanek asked. "Did it prevent you from forming your own bond with Keeshah? Does it make you totally blind to Tarani's illusions?"

"No, but those are different—" I began.

"It may work," Tarani interrupted excitedly. "Think, Rikardon—I can help you heal, when you allow it. As Zanek says, you are able to enter the All-Mind easily. You need only wish it, and we may be able to reach together to Eddarta. It would be fitting, as well, for us both—Captain and High Lord—to speak."

"But—" I protested, and they waited.

"But—" I said again, and they only looked at me expectantly.

"But—the Ra'ira scares me blind," I admitted at last. "I don't want any part of it. I don't want to be *able* to use it." I could not look at Tarani. "I know it's not fair."

Milda's voice cut into the silence.

"I thought Markasset was dead."

"What?" I asked, turning to look at her.

"You heard me," she said. "You sound just like Markasset. He wanted to be a Supervisor, but he didn't want to learn anything or work at anything or take any responsibility for anything. He just wanted people to look up to him."

"Now *that*," I said, gritting my teeth, "is *not* fair. I've done nothing for the past months but work and worry and do things that frightened me."

"And done them how well?" Milda challenged, standing up and putting her fists on her hips. "Zanek and I had a talk before dinner, and he told me that *he's* the one who brought the Sharith today, directly disobeying the orders of the 'Captain.' If the 'Captain' had brought the Sharith with him, maybe Thanasset would still be alive."

"And maybe," I shouted, stepping toward her to lean on the back of the armchair, "this entire city would be torn up and ruined because Ferrathyn would have been *ready*, instead of distracted by the need to kill Tarani and me *and* Thanasset." I did not even try to hold in the anger. "How can you stand there, Milda—you who have been in Raithskar while I've been enslaved and insane and forced into responsibilities I never wanted—and tell me that *I* made the *wrong* decision?"

"And how can *you* stand there," Milda shouted back, "you who have been through so much already, and imagine that you're not strong enough to use the Ra'ira without being hurt by it?"

I was ready to yell at the old woman again when the meaning of her words sank in. I gaped at her, opened and closed my mouth a couple of times, and finally said: "You could have done that more gently, Milda."

"Would you have listened?"

I shook my head, sat down in the armchair again, and gingerly picked up the Ra'ira. I realized that the reproductions Volitar had made for Gharlas had been true works of art—by sight, they had been identical to this stone, even down to the uneven lines deep inside it, the merest suggestion of a crystalline formation. The color, pale blue when you looked through the edge, deeper as you looked into the center of the gem, had been perfect.

There was, however, a tactile difference between the Ra'ira and its replicas. The surface was as smooth and cool, the shape as irregular, as the duplicates. But this stone, the true Ra'ira, had slightly more weight and a—a sensation to it. I felt from it the same odd tingling as when I had touched Tarani earlier. I really wanted to drop the thing, but I closed my hand around it.

"You'll have to tell me what to do," I said.


## 30


It was an experience not unlike my visits to the All-Mind. Tarani was the one who actually planned and executed what we did together, and I was merely present, like a passenger in an automobile. There was a similarity, too, in the spirit of seeking with which we began. But there were other, significant differences.

The All-Mind imagery of the interlocking cylinders or tubes

of golden energy, each tube representing the lifememory of a single individual, was not there. Instead, Indomel's consciousness was only one among uncountable, separate sparks, and Tarani sought the spark which was uniquely his.

In the All-Mind there had been some sense of distance, because we had arrived near the outer arc of the sphere and moved toward the center. We had been aware that our bodies' energy was being used to maintain the link with the All-Mind, but there had been no sensation of effort. We had been concerned with how "far" we went only as it related to how long it would take us to get back to our entry point and, ultimately, to our physical bodies.

Now we *felt* the distance across which our consciousness stretched. I had halfway expected a visual overview of the land itself, but it was nothing so understandable. Where the All-Mind had seemed to me to be a sphere, the—for want of a better term, I thought of it as the "mind level"—was a flat plane, with sparks scattered throughout it. We did not have a visual overview of the mind level, because we were imbedded in it. Yet we could "see" it all in some sense, as if a map and a marking on the map were, in concept, the exact same thing.

Where there were cities in the physical world, there were clusters of sparks on the mind level. Just as Raithskar and Eddarta were at opposite corners of the Walled World, we knew we would find Indomel on the far side of the mind level. The direction and distance seemed very clear, but not the pathway. The All-Mind had been a pathway in itself; on the mind level, the sparks seemed isolated in empty darkness.

But Tarani's unsuccessful attempts had taught her that there lay, invisible within the darkness, a network of interlocking lines of force which could be sensed—with effort—and crossed—with effort. She had exerted the small effort of reaching out to me, had enveloped my mindpresence, and eased it free of my physical presence. The first touch had been alarming, a more pure version of the tingle my body had felt when I had touched the Ra'ira. But once established, the contact between Tarani's mind and mine was as effortless and comfortable as the experience we had shared in the All-Mind.

Tarani set out across the dark void between us and the Eddartan minds very carefully, and there was a definite feeling of *pushing* ourselves off from our physical anchors. She never became confident, even though it was clear to us both that there was no risk of "falling through" the plane; we were inextricably part of it. The risk lay in misjudging the path and wasting energy by backtracking. The risk lay in not being able to find our way back, or in not having sufficient strength left to *come* back.

The risk lay in the possibility of being lost and stranded on this plane until our bodies died. Then, presumably, our memories would join the All-Mind, and we—well, we would see for ourselves what Zanek had not been able to remember.

"Tarani, if I had known you were taking this kind of chance, I—"

"You would have been more concerned," she interrupted. "You would not have prevented it, Rikardon. The risk is the price of the power, and the power is necessary, for now. Please allow me to concentrate."

I kept silent as she guided us through the darkness. In some way, she had linked us so that she was using my strength equally with her own, and the drain was less for both of us. Yet we both felt the cost of the effort by the time—subjective time; I had no idea how much real time had passed—we approached Eddarta. Only then did I speak again.

"How will you recognize Indomel?" I asked her. "Every one of these—minds—looks identical to me."

"I see differences," she said. "I cannot explain why you do not see them, as well. Here, look *with* me—"

She seemed to wrap more closely around me, and it was only then that I realized Tarani had gone to some lengths to minimize the contact between our minds. Tarani and I suddenly achieved a closeness very like the blending that Keeshah and I sometimes shared. She and I became a single entity for a brilliant, searing instant, and we shared ourselves totally. Our emotions, our memories, our private fears and hidden shames . . . what we believed, our attitudes and logic patterns, our experience and everything our experience had taught us . . . our *selves*.

It was wondrous and terrifying and unbearable and beautiful. Tarani broke the contact almost instantly and, for the moment, we paused in our journey merely to rest. The moment was part of our memories now, and we would be able to sort through what we had learned of each other at some later time. For now, there were two immediate by-products of that union.

First, I could now see what Tarani saw—each spark was surrounded by something not really visible. Each mindpresence emitted an aura which was unique to itself, made up of patterns and pulses of different energies. A spectrum of colors is an appropriate analogy for the range of energies, but the quality of the energy itself was more akin to the lines of force in the mindplane than to anything in the physical world.

It was the other effect of our brief union that made us pause. In a way which had never before been possible, I *knew* what Tarani thought of me. What's more, I *knew* how her feelings had changed as she had been exposed to all of me, all of my very private, innermost me. That was what kept me silent and shocked. She had seen all the filth and self-hatred and unwanted memories resting at the bottom of my soul, and she had come away with more love for me than she had felt before.

Yet, how did her reaction differ from my own? I had looked into the depths of Tarani, too, at the things she was hiding from herself. The way a sixteen-year-old girl, caught between Volitar's abhorrence of control and Antonia's sensual maturity, had been frightened and fascinated and exalted by exercising the sexual and mental power Molik had craved. The guilt she carried for every moment of enjoyment she had reaped from their warped relationship. The self-loathing and self-doubt stimulated by meeting and being disgusted by her natural father, Pylomel. Other things, childhood horrors from both Antonia and Tarani.

I had seen all that, yes. And I had seen her tenderness for the sha'um cubs, the sense of peace and goodness that entered her when she cast her healing sleep, her determination to make life better for the Eddartans. The net effect of all that deep learning was to make me *appreciate* Tarani more.

I realized that Tarani was not merely an individual who had been born. Nor could her specialness be explained by the invasion of Antonia's personality. Tarani had made herself what she was through a constant struggle, a continual need to make choices. Most of what was locked away in the dark closet which had opened to me were choices she regretted. But she had emerged from the struggle whole and good, with an awareness that there would never be an end to doubt, but with an established habit of making right choices. She was committed to values I respected and—more importantly—she herself respected.

The weakness I had seen only made her strength more impressive. Her doubt called out to my sheltering and protecting instincts, and I made a fierce resolution that her choice to love me would never have to be relegated to that ugly closet.

If I came away from that encounter with new commitment to and a stronger love for Tarani, why did it surprise me so that Tarani could have the same reaction toward me?

As I recovered from the intensity of our blending experience, I found the answer—an answer I had given to Shola and Dharak and Thymas in Thagorn. It is always easier to forgive another than it is to forgive yourself.

Tarani's guilts and fears seemed only natural to me, some of them even inconsequential. But my own were real and terrifying and, certainly, much worse than everyone else's. At least, I had thought they were, until Tarani had touched them. She was not disgusted and repelled—because, as I had done with her, she had touched the good things in me, too, and found them to be more important.

Knowing that she could tolerate the awfulness inside me diminished it, and made me feel more positive, more complete. It seemed as if I had been loving her imperfectly, drawing limits just short of the closets of my mind. Something in me had been freed when those boundaries had vanished. I loved Tarani with more confidence that my love had value.

"I did not know that would happen," Tarani's mind said at last, "and if warned, I would have resisted it. I am glad we had no warning, for it is a memory I shall treasure forever." She paused. "Tell me—the clearer sight which was the reason for our joining—do you have it?"

"I see the auras," I said. "But I still don't feel sure I can help you find Indomel."

"I found him before, and will recognize him again," she said. "It is a different sort of sensing—I believe you will recognize him too. We should begin the search."

As I agreed, I noticed that I was no longer enclosed within Tarani. If the word *touch* has any meaning in this purely nonphysical sense, we were barely "touching," yet the mind-to-mind communication was as easy as it had been before. Now she did not carry me, but led the way, and I was able to follow.

We seemed to flow from one mindpresence to another, moving swiftly. Tarani's prediction proved to be correct. As we approached each mindpresence, I *knew* whether or not we were approaching Indomel. Eventually, we found him—one presence in a cluster of others, the patterns surrounding him erratic but strong. There was another, nearby, which issued similar patterns, but in a forced, unnatural way. In the minor differences of its pattern we recognized Zefra.

"He must be keeping her under compulsion," I said, knowing that Tarani, too, had recognized her brother and mother.

"As horrible as that must be for her," Tarani said, "I am glad that she is not helping him willingly."

"What now?" I asked.

"Now, my love, we announce our presence."

She swept toward Zefra's mindpresence and . . . replaced it. Two patterns were visible to my heightened senses: Tarani's strong and balanced pulsing and, underneath, a weaker pattern which shifted uncertainly as Zefra's mind threw off Indomel's control.

So suddenly had Indomel's compulsion been broken that I sensed him reeling from the shock. I took advantage of his imbalance, and I . . . became Indomel.

I had a moment's shock, myself, as the "normal" world screamed into my senses again. I was in the central meeting room of Lord Hall, seated in the chair on the dais reserved for the High Lord. Six other Lords were present, all of them right now staring at Zefra, who was reeling back toward the door that led to the main area of Lord Hall. The man nearest the outer door was half out of his chair, his hand extended toward Zefra.

"Wait," I said, and all the heads snapped in my direction. "Wait a moment. She is all right."

"Indomel," said the man in the chair which represented the Rusal family. He was the only Lord I remembered. The other five men were young, new. "You may force me to call you High Lord in public and accede to policies which violate my sense of values, but I beg you again to release the lady Zefra from your domination. Her statements in support of you have served their purpose; what more use can she be? We have seen her body fail under your continuing compulsion. Would you destroy her utterly?"

Inside me, Indomel, I felt something utterly surprising. Regret. Shame. Love. All from Indomel for his mother. Just as Tarani's presence had released Zefra from Indomel, my arrival had destroyed the—literal—mindset which Ferrathyn had established in Indomel.

He *was* still Indomel. There was ambition and greed and the excessive self-interest that Pylomel had instilled in his son, but there was also the pitiful cry of an abandoned child, the anger of a boy against a mother not strong enough to claim him, the love that had never been given an opportunity for expression.

Indomel's mind was free of the superimposed madness of Ferrathyn's manipulation, but the boy was left with the memory of what he had done and—worse—the memory of having enjoyed the domination of his mother, enjoyed it to the point where he had employed it unnecessarily, enjoyed it to the point where he had literally endangered her life. Even for Indomel's decadent, self-serving spirit, that truth made him ashamed.

"I am not Indomel," I said, and in the wake of the Lords' shocked expressions, I stood up and moved away from the high-backed chair. "And the true High Lord is here to claim her place."

Zefra/Tarani had recovered her balance, and Zefra walked the length of the room, to climb to the dais and stand beside me. There were murmurs from the Lords as Zefra moved—the way she walked betrayed the difference.

"Your kindness," Tarani said to the Rusal Lord, "is deeply appreciated, by Zefra and by me." She looked around the room at the faces reflecting bewilderment and realization.

"Does anyone doubt that I am Tarani, and rightful High Lord?" she demanded, "or that the man beside me is not Indomel at the moment, but Rikardon, Captain of the Sharith?"

Those who could find the strength to move at all shook their heads in silence.

"Good," she said, and moved to sit down. "Indomel's dominance is at an end, and work must begin immediately to repair the damage he has done. Our time here is short, so listen carefully. First, I see Indomel has replaced nearly everyone. I see no need to create further distress by recasting the Council of Lords, provided you follow my instructions explicitly."

They all nodded.

"Good. Now, if you will please introduce yourselves . . ."

# 31

The first thing I was conscious of, when I awoke again in my own body, was a burning sensation in my left hand. I jerked my hand away, and Tarani echoed the gesture at almost the same time. The Ra'ira rolled across the floor between us, turning clumsily. It was pervaded with a glow that seemed to be fading.

That initial, startled movement sent tremors of weakness shooting through my body. The elbow that propped me started to shake, and gave way. I flopped back down, my head reeling.

I heard Zanek speak from the other side of Tarani. "Lie quietly, please—you have used too much energy. It will take you quite some time to recover."

"Successful," Tarani said, her rich voice thick now with fatigue.

"We know," Milda's voice said, sounding none too steady. "Your . . . illusions—we saw it all, heard it all." Suddenly the old voice broke. "I wish Thanasset had been here."

Tarani's hand crept across the space between us and pressed weakly on my arm. "It was a . . . special experience," she said.

"Well, rest now," Zanek said, and Milda came around to me and began to touch my face with a dampened cloth. "When you are feeling stronger, food will help. Just rest now."

We stayed on the parlor floor for several hours, and were finally able to struggle to a sitting position. Milda descended on us with an enormous spread of food, and we ate voraciously. From there, we staggered upstairs to share Markasset's bedroom and sleep, exhausted, for nearly a full day. Then we rose, and bathed, and visited the sha'um. Finally, we felt ready to be in touch with the world again.

Neither one of us had worried about the Ra'ira, and we were not surprised to find that Zanek had ordered the glass display case moved from the government house to Thanasset's midhall, and had stored the gem in plain sight of anyone who came into the house. It made sense and seemed an appropriate reaction against the way the stone had been handled for so many centuries. Secrecy had not really been a protection; perhaps public awareness would do more to keep the stone's power controlled.

When Tarani and I came in from our baths, Zaddorn was standing near the case, staring at the stone. He turned around when we entered, produced a smile which, I was glad to see, had a faint echo of his old wryness, and gallantly bowed to us both. In contrast to the efficient, elegant gray outfit he had worn on our first meeting, he wore a ragtag mess of torn but clean clothes, and he looked weary. Yet the composure and presence which had always impressed me were still there.

"The outskirts of the city have been cleaned up, and the vineh show few signs of continuing interest in Raithskar," he said. "Work parties have been organized to clean up the city's interior, and that project is progressing. Having put all this in motion, the Council of Supervisors has voluntarily—with some relief and a lot of embarrassment, to my view—dissolved. As much as Raithskar has a government now, my friend, you two are its government. I have come to report progress and get further instructions."

I went over to Zaddorn and clapped my hand on his shoulder. "I think that 'honor' goes to you, my friend, at least for as long as Raithskar continues. Tarani and I will rely on you to keep things organized here, and to supervise preparations for the move."

"What?" he demanded, his face darkening. "What move?"

Tarani came up and took Zaddorn's hands. "Come and sit down," she invited. "When you understand, I think you will agree."

He did, but it took a lot of talking. Finally, he said: "All right, I believe you. But remember that I *know* you—as much as you *can* be known by a . . . Gandalaran. The citizens of this city are already feeling betrayed and bewildered. They have just reclaimed Raithskar; I doubt they will abandon it readily, and then their agreement will depend on being *convinced* that what you've just told me is true. Will you spend this much time talking to each citizen of Raithskar?"

Tarani and I looked at one another uncertainly. It was a phase of our planning we had not thought through clearly.

Milda came into the parlor just then. She greeted Zaddorn warmly, then handed us several messages which the maufel had just delivered. Tarani had three from Eddarta. One was from the Rusal Lord, confirming that everything was being handled according to her instructions. Zefra's note thanked Tarani for freeing her from Indomel's compulsion, but admitted that her own ambition had paved the way for it by not resisting too strongly. It was an apology, and what sounded like the first sincere expression of love for Tarani that Zefra had ever given her daughter. Tarani read that letter aloud, folded it, and tucked it inside her tunic, smiling to herself.

The third letter was from Indomel himself, its tone predictably defiant. It promised Tarani his cooperation and, in plain terms, acknowledged his defeat. And it asked a question similar to Zaddorn's.

I had been present in Indomel's body when he had heard Tarani speak of the upcoming disaster and the preparation required. Because of that, Indomel knew it was true. But he said that under Tarani's instructions, the Lords were giving Lower Eddarta back to the people who lived there. How did Tarani expect to persuade them to give it up again?

I had a most welcome message from Ligor in Chizan, announcing that both passes were open again. Supplies were still very limited in the city, he warned, and anyone attempting to make the crossing should carry extra water. As Tarani had done with hers, I read the letter aloud—the final line with some surprise. *Give Milda my very best regards*, Ligor said, *and tell her I may be ready to settle down, finally, if she hasn't made other plans*.

I looked at Milda, whose face was blushing furiously.

"Ligor told me he saw a lot of Keeshah while he was barely a kitten," I said. "Now I know Keeshah wasn't the only attraction he found in Thanasset's house."

"The silly old rogue!" Milda exploded. "If he thinks I've waited all this time for him, well—well—" She shrugged, and smiled wryly. "Well, he may be right, is all. When it comes time to head for Chizan, Rikardon—I'd be obliged if I could travel with you."

I got up and hugged her, laughing. "That's one reunion I wouldn't miss," I said.

Zaddorn left shortly after that, and Tarani and I discussed the problem he had brought to us. It was later that evening, when we walked in Thanasset's garden—now thoroughly ruined by the four large sha'um presences—that we stumbled on the answer.

"They will never believe," Tarani said. "Their existence is too solidly tied with the value of water. How can we make them believe that water can be harmful—even if they would believe in the concept of the Pleth refilling?"

"I wish I knew," I said fervently. "I wish we could give them what we feel, the sense of change, the certainty of the consequences, the awareness that we have to start to work together *now* to avoid disaster."

She thought a moment. "But what *has* changed?" she asked. "I mean, physically, observably. The earthquake startled everyone, but the damage was done and people are already beginning to cope. Certainly there have been social changes, but none of them are directly a sign of the disaster to come."

I stopped moving.

"What?" Tarani demanded. "What is it?"

"I think I know how to do it, Tarani."

Some four weeks later, Keeshah and Yayshah were wet and miserable, and Tarani and I had to shout at each other in order to be heard. The sha'um, over their own substantial protests and in an act of pure loyalty to us, were picking their way fussily across the spray-slick surface of what had recently been a dry and rocky plain. For generations of Gandalarans, this place had been no more than a marking on a map: the Valley of Mists. Now it was growing—or shrinking, depending on one's point of view—and it was creating the future of Gandalara—or destroying it, depending on one's point of view.

Tarani and I had little to say to each other, even if we had been able to converse normally. We had made our plans before leaving Raithskar, and had reviewed them the night before, at our camp at the edge of the mists. We had wakened this morning soaked to the skin, with two very unhappy sha'um on our hands. Only the promise that we would complete our mission today and start back for Thagorn tomorrow appeased them.

In one sense, we had known what to expect when we penetrated the wall of fog. We knew that the rolling clouds of condensation were the product of spray from a waterfall meeting the hot, arid air of the Gandalaran desert.

The waterfall had been here throughout Gandalaran history. It was the product of the Atlantic Ocean pushing its way through what remained of the Gibraltar Straits, after a geological cataclysm had smashed the African continent into the edge of Europe. The volume of water had not been great enough to compensate for evaporation across the tremendous surface of the Mediterranean basin, and the sea—known to the Gandalarans as the Great and Lesser Pleth—had shrunk down until it was little more than a wide pool at the base of the Atlantic waterfall.

Knowing what to expect, and truly expecting it, are two very different things. The land masses had separated, and what had been a narrow waterfall now stretched a quarter mile wide and loomed impossibly high. The Skarkel Falls in Raithskar disappeared into the cloud cover, but here the force of rushing water generated a turbulence that drove Gandalara's heat upward and dissipated the clouds—which, at least in part, must have been a phenomenon not unlike the wall of fog. Any rain or moisture which fell into the basin area became vapor when it encountered the tremendous heat radiating from the salt-sand floor of the basin.

Tarani and I urged the sha'um along the southern slope beside the waterfall, to a vantage point which was high enough that we were clear of the main force of spray from the thundering falls. Above the rushing water, we could see a stark and ragged outline of rock, and I fancied I saw a resemblance to the Gibraltar I had seen from the deck of a cruise ship. Below us, salty spray burst up from the agitated surface of the rapidly enlarging pool at the base of the falls.

The ledge we had chosen was wide enough, and slightly tilted, so that we could sit with our backs braced and legs extended without much fear of sliding off the slippery stone. The sha'um moved off and crouched behind a group of small boulders, their ears flattened and eyes half-closed. I could sense Keeshah's discomfort. The only thing he hated worse than wet fur was the reflex which tried to fluff it—which let the moisture in next to his skin.

*It won't take long,* I assured Keeshah. *Thank you for going through this.*

*Important,* he admitted grudgingly, but then grumbled: *Not fun.*

Tarani had opened her soggy belt pouch, and she barely hesitated as she reached in and brought out the Ra'ira. Neither one of us had wanted to touch it again, after the burning sensation we had felt at the end of our Eddartan mindjourney. Whatever had emanated from the Ra'ira, it had not been conventional heat; there had been no mark on my hand or on Tarani's. For me at least, that made me all the more reluctant to touch the strange blue gem.

I took it now, however, as Tarani and I settled back against the smooth rock and joined hands around the Ra'ira. This time the shock was one of sudden silence, as I found myself on the mindplane once again, and the noisy waterfall had vanished from my perceptions. Tarani and I were together, but individual.

"As I thought," Tarani said, "you are as skilled as I, Rikardon. That will make it much easier. Shall we begin?"

Together, we set out across the network of force, moving slowly at first, and then more confidently—but never without caution. Raithskar, physically closer to us, was also closer on the mindplane, so we touched there first. Zanek was easy to find, the pulsing of his aura clear and steady. He became aware of us instantly, and there was warm greeting in his mindvoice.

"All is ready here, my friends," he said. "Most of Raithskar is gathered in the square, awaiting the event."

"We will touch the other locations, then begin," Tarani told him.

We moved off once more, and located Indomel in Dyskornis. His mind jumped when we touched him. "I am here, as you *requested*, Sister," he said. "I remain uncertain about the feasibility of this plan."

"Only try, Indomel," Tarani said. "The Sharith have alerted every city in Gandalara to expect our message. The mind of every Gandalaran should be open to us. All I ask is that you channel our message clearly, with no coloration of your own."

"I have already agreed to that," he said, sulkily. "Let's get on with it."

"In a moment," Tarani said. "We must connect with Zefra, first."

We moved once more, gliding through the darkness toward the cluster of mindpresences that was Eddarta. There, Zefra responded immediately to the touch of Tarani's mind. "All is ready here, Daughter," she said.

"Something is wrong, Mother," Tarani said. "What is it?"

"Nothing," Zefra protested, but she must have realized how futile a lie was in this close contact, mind to mind. "I fear I am not strong enough," she admitted quietly.

"You are strong enough," Tarani assured her, and I sensed Zefra's mood lightening.


# 32


Tarani and I returned to the waterfall, and I let my consciousness return to my body. As we had planned, Tarani remained in trance, and maintained her link with me as I woke. The close connection with her mind overlaid my perceptions, making everything seem slow and dreamlike. It was not inappropriate, for we had come here to dream.

"I am Tarani, and I speak to everyone in Gandalara," Tarani's mindvoice said.

I knew that it was reaching out to Zanek, Indomel, and Zefra, and through their mindpower was being broadcast through the length and breadth of the World between the Walls.

"You have been told how this is being done, but not why. A time of change has come upon Gandalara," she said. "The shaking of the earth marked its beginning. I wish to tell you of this change, and what it means to each person, each city, each place in Gandalara. But I, myself, understand it only imperfectly.

"I will therefore serve only as a channel for the memories, the knowledge, and the understanding of the man some of you know as Rikardon, Captain of the Sharith. First, look upon what lies inside the Valley of the Mists. . . ."

I turned my eyes toward the majestic waterfall, and kept them focused on the rushing water. The thundering noise reached me faintly, as if we were much farther from the falls. Through the link with Tarani, who was receiving secondhand feedback through her links with the three other mindskilled people, I sensed the wave of reaction from the Gandalarans who were seeing their very first waterfall. It varied from awe to disbelief to simply lack of comprehension.

"To explain this, we must begin far, far in the past . . ." Tarani began, and I let my mind visualize everything I now understood to be the history of Gandalara. I saw the earth's surface as it must have been: rich vegetation; land and sea and air teeming with life. In my mind's vision, I focused on the Mèditerranean area as the massive tectonic shifts began. The huge southern continent edged northward and choked off the opening between the Atlantic and the Mediterranean, and the sea began to shrink.

As the water level fell, the Chizan passage rose up, making the eastern half of the sea little more than a big, stagnant pool which evaporated rapidly. The western half, receiving some replenishment from the narrow falls, lasted longer. Into my vision came bipedal, apelike creatures, foraging down the drying slopes and gradually migrating and adapting to the higher air pressure on the floor of the vanishing sea.

From the sky, a meteor rocketed into view and smashed into a cliff, trailing hard radiation that wrought a highly viable evolutionary change in the social creatures who had been wandering near the collision site. A pool of knowledge, accessible to all individuals, was formed subconsciously by the progeny of the affected survivors; later, that pool of memory would be called the All-Mind. With this storehouse of learning, the products of that first change rapidly advanced and multiplied into the first Gandalarans, while others, unaffected by the radiation, evolved into vineh.

The society of Gandalarans grew and advanced in knowledge. Specialized skills were passed down within families, and in a remarkably short time, a rich culture prospered around the edges of the two Pleths. Yet, within generations of that prosperity, strife between cities and individuals had become a common occurrence, as the Great Pleth shrank away from the walls and arable land became concentrated around the rivers which flowed down from mountain and wall.

One man had seen the danger of the continuous strife, and had acted to unite the efforts of all Gandalarans for the benefit of everyone. Yet even as wise as he had been, he had not seen the truth, and his vision of a lasting cooperation among cities had died with Kä—built at the edge of the Great Pleth, marooned in desert when the Last King abandoned it.

The Pleth had all but vanished. What remained of it had lain hidden within the Valley of Mists, to confound the understanding and vision of Gandalarans. But the recent shaking of the earth had been a warning—the gate to the ocean, nearly closed for so long, was opening again.

I stared at the waterfall and watched it grow through the coming years. The opening was not wide enough yet; there would be more earth movement to ease it ever wider. The waterfall was pouring over rock and earth which had built up over the centuries, but the force of so much water would quickly break down that barrier, and the flood would begin.

I envisioned the Pleth growing again, and Gandalarans moving around its edges, first enjoying the new wealth of water, however salty, then retreating as the sea reclaimed its floor. Painfully, I drew the vision of Gandalarans retreating to the eastern basin, only to find themselves in the same situation after a few years. I imagined them recognizing the danger at last, and attempting to climb the walls.

I imagined their efforts to breathe at the higher altitudes. I imagined their failure.

In the end, I imagined the refilled Mediterranean, placid and peaceful, its waves and tides obscuring and destroying all that was Gandalara. It was a lonely, empty scene, and I pulled myself back into the present to sense a wave of sadness and shock flowing back to us from the people.

"What Rikardon has shown you of the past is true," Tarani said, "or as close to the truth as can be guessed. What he pictured for the future, however, need not be true. There is a way in which all the best of Gandalara can be saved. That, too, is Rikardon's vision, and I share it with you now. . . ."

Again I slipped into a daydream state, but this time I visualized the gathering of people and animals, goods and skills, into the area around and above Eddarta.

I pictured how it would be, each generation cultivating the rich land between the branches of the Tashal at one level, and preparing the next level for cultivation. It was a strong and moving image of people working together: parents suffering discomfort so that their children could breathe normally; all skills contributing support to all people; sha'um and Sharith working side by side with farmers and artisans; everyone clearly seeing an objective far beyond their own lifetimes, and the achievement of that objective the basis for law and government.

I tried to picture the reclamation of the sea, as well, so that the final generation climbed to what would be the surface of Ricardo's world as the sea rose to claim their most recent encampment.

"This is how it shall be, for those who have dedication and courage enough to claim a future for Gandalara," Tarani said, speaking over and through the vision. "In three moons, a meeting will be held in Eddarta to plan the first step in climbing the River Wall. In each city, choose a few trusted people to attend that meeting. They will return to you with a set of rules. You will be obliged to accept those rules for the duration of your own lifetime, and to encourage acceptance in your children.

"Your representatives will also bear instructions about preparing for the journey. Each of you who chooses to accept the rules will be welcomed, and will increase the chances of this second vision coming true.

"Our message ends here," Tarani said. "I urge you to consider this matter carefully, to believe what you have seen, and to join us at the River Wall when the great journey begins."

The dreamlike state eased, and I became more aware of my body, as Tarani dissolved the close connection between our minds. I was once more conscious of the cool dampness of the fall's spray, the pounding roar of water impacting water, and a fierce burning in my hand.

As had happened in Raithskar, Tarani and I both flinched away from the Ra'ira. The stone rolled unevenly along the sloping ledge, rambled up a slight rise of stone at the rim of the ledge, and teetered there precariously. A bright blue glow was fading at the center of the gem.

Tarani lunged for it and caught it just before it fell, scraping knee and elbow on the rough surface of the rock. In sudden panic, I grabbed for her legs, but my fear was unfounded; she was in no danger of falling. Nor was she looking at the Ra'ira as its glow faded completely. She was staring across the pool of water, toward rocky slopes which seemed steeper and more clifflike than on this side. Puzzled by her absorption, I crawled down beside her and followed her gaze.

I studied the clifflike rocks for a moment before I noticed the movement, but suddenly I could see them: big white birds, circling from nests in the cliff. As I watched them, one soared out over the pool, adjusted the position of its wings, and glided down toward us.

Tarani and I sat up as the bird drew near. It hovered before us, its big wings beating slowly. It opened its beak and made some sort of sound, but the roar of the falls drowned it out.

*So this is where Lonna came from,* I thought. *I wondered why we never saw any other birds of her species. How in the world did she manage to get trapped by a dralda, halfway across Gandalara, so that Tarani could rescue her? Another mark for "destiny," I suppose.*

Tarani reached out to stroke the breast feathers of the big bird, as she had done so many times with her close and deeply mourned friend. It happened, however, that the hand she extended still held the Ra'ira.

Only then did we notice that the Ra'ira was glowing again.

Tarani jerked her hand back, releasing the stone, and this time it did fall over the edge. The bird darted upward and headed for the cliff. Tarani had doubled her fists and was pounding the rock beside her knees, only the distorted grimace on her face evidence that she was screaming.

I tried to hold her, but she pushed me away roughly. We were too near the rim of the ledge, and she was too distraught, for me to try again. She jumped up suddenly, and began running back toward the sha'um, jumping recklessly from ledge to ledge. Beyond her, I could see Yayshah standing up, her neckfur lifted up in damp spikes.

Yayshah's movement had alerted Keeshah and he, too, got to his feet. It was strange to see him like that, with his fur slicked down. The true shape of his powerful body was visible without that shadowing cushion of fluffy fur. Even though it showed the massive lines of muscle, the great cat looked somehow naked and vulnerable.

*Go now?* Keeshah asked me.

*Very soon,* I said.

I crawled to the rim of the ledge and looked down. The

Ra'ira was resting in a small depression on the ledge below this one. It took a few minutes to get down there and back up, but when I mounted Keeshah, I had the Ra'ira. Tarani and Yayshah had already left.

We caught up with them just at nightfall. Tarani was sitting on a rock, and Yayshah was rolling in the sand, trying with small success to dry her fur. I dismounted and went to sit beside Tarani.

"You went back for it," she said quietly, staring at her hands.

"I had to," I said.

"It *belongs* at the bottom of the sea," she said.

"All of Gandalara knows what it can do," I answered. "If we left it, someone would come after it before the sea could cover it up. No, the only way to keep it safe is to keep control of it."

Her body jerked, and she looked up at me, a terrible fear in her eyes. "Are you so sure that it is safe with us?" she demanded. "I *called* that bird, Rikardon. I compelled it to come to me, because I was overcome with sadness for Lonna. If I used the Ra'ira for my own gain once, I will do it again. Leave it, I beg you."

I had put the blue stone in my belt pouch. I took it out now and stared at it, trying to decide.

*Why am I hesitating?* I wondered. *Is this just another version of what Tarani's feeling? A dependence? An addiction?*

I felt a chill born of more than the dampness. Even looking at the thing had a slightly hypnotic effect. The eye was caught by the beautiful blue at the outer surface of the gem. Then one noticed one of the crystalline lines, and tried to trace its twisting path toward the center. The original thread was lost, but another was taken up and followed inward, only to be lost once more.

I realized that I was caught in that loop and, with an effort of will, I put my other hand over the Ra'ira to block it from view.

"You see the danger too," Tarani said, with some relief. "Will you take it back, and throw it into the pool of the waterfall?"

"There may be a better way," I said, and caught her hand as she started to protest. "Believe me, Tarani, there may truly be a way to destroy the thing for good. I don't remember anything in Zanek's experience with the stone about that sensation of heat, do you?"

She shook her head. "No. In fact, I asked him about it in

Raithskar, and he said he suspected it was connected with the distance we were trying to encompass."

I shrugged. "That may be it," I said. "It could also be that the stone's just getting old—it's been around for centuries, after all. But I think there's another reason. Until now, the Ra'ira has never been used by more than one person at a time."

She frowned. "But the heat was not damaging," she said.

"Not to us," I admitted. "But look . . ." I uncovered the stone. "See the lines deep inside? What if the stone's power is somehow a product of vibration along those lines when mindpower is focused through it? The more mindpower, the more vibration."

She gasped. "Then with enough mindpower . . ."

I nodded. "I think it's worth a try. If it doesn't work, you have my promise I'll bring the fleabitten thing back here and dump it in the ocean."

# 33

The attempt to destroy the Ra'ira would have to wait for three months. As soon as we reached Eddarta, we began making plans to accommodate the representatives who would arrive for the meeting. We were hopeful that at least half of Gandalara's cities and towns would send spokesmen; we were grateful when people actually began to arrive; we were stunned when it became evident that every single social group in the Walled World had responded to Tarani's call for a united effort.

The Refreshment Houses had sent their Elders, so that there was a miniconvention of Fa'aldu being held in Eddarta. I was delighted to see Balgokh again, the Elder who had first befriended me in this world. I tried to thank him for all the help he had offered me then, and later, among the Fa'aldu, but he waved my thanks aside.

"Since the time of Harralen," he said, "the Fa'aldu have acted on behalf of all of Gandalara. Though we were not entirely aware of it at the time, any assistance our people have given you has been given in the same cause."

Tarani was surprised, one day, by a guard bearing a formal request to the High Lord for an audience. Tarani and I were in our sitting room, papers and plans spread out on a low table between us. Tarani frowned, obviously mystified by the message.

"Well, please escort the person back here," Tarani said, and the guard left.

We got little work done in the next few minutes; Tarani was concentrating more on speculation about her visitor than on calculating food requirements for the first movement stage. When we heard the guard's knock again, Tarani nearly jumped from her chair to open the door. I was seated on the hinge side of the door, so I saw only the door, not the visitor. I stood up in alarm, however, when I saw Tarani's reaction.

The color drained from Tarani's face, and she stepped back from the doorway slowly, as if hypnotized. Following her progress, at the same slow pace, first the hem of a gown and then the figure of a woman appeared past the edge of the door.

I thought, instantly, of Balgokh and the sense of presence and purpose he always conveyed. This woman was not tall, but she held herself rigidly erect, and seemed taller than her physical height. Her gown was blue, and flowed shapelessly from her shoulders to her ankles. The sleeves were full, but drawn up at the wrist. Only the thinness of her light-colored headfur and a slight hesitation in her walk betrayed her age.

Her face was expressionless, but her eyes were fastened on Tarani. This woman clearly frightened a person I knew to be capable of ruling a nation. I moved around the table, my hand unconsciously seeking the hilt of the sword I never wore "at home." My foot struck Tarani's chair, and the scraping sound of its movement seemed to set time moving again.

The woman stopped, and sighed deeply.

"I thought it must be you," she said, and there was something familiar about her voice. "My child, my child, what have you become?"

"Tarani?" I asked, getting clear of the table so that I could step between Tarani and the old woman, if it became necessary.

The old woman turned her eyes on me, and I was lost in confusion. Her eyes, too, made me think of my Fa'aldu friend.

They were eyes which reflected wisdom, and sureness. My every instinct told me this was a person to be respected, even revered. Yet my intellect said that Tarani was afraid of her; therefore, I should fear her too.

I feel sure my body posture conveyed more threat than trust, for it was to me that Tarani spoke.

"It is all right, Rikardon," she said, coming up to my elbow. "She is an old friend—but not forgotten," she added, for the woman's benefit. "If I may ask—I would like to speak to her privately."

Tarani's voice was subdued, and she was staring at the floor. I hesitated.

"Do not be alarmed by her first reaction," the old woman said to me. "When last I saw this child, she had reason to fear my displeasure, but that claim of authority was lost long ago." There was a bitterness in her words that brought the color back to Tarani's cheeks in force, and her head came up defiantly.

"It was my only choice at the time," she said, fiercely. "As it happens, it was the correct choice, as well."

Suddenly everything connected—the relative ages of the two women, Tarani's almost childlike apprehension at the other's sudden appearance, and the touch of familiarity in the older woman's voice. It had a timbre and a richness similar to Tarani's.

"You're a Recorder," I said.

"She is a Record Keeper," Tarani corrected me, "a teacher of Recorders. She was *my* teacher. Her name is Livia." For the first time since the woman had appeared, Tarani smiled. "Have you come to scold me in person, Livia, as you did in so many letters?"

Livia smiled back, and I felt the tension in the room evaporate.

"I might hope to reclaim you from a traveling show," she said, her tone still a bit sarcastic, "but I doubt I shall convince the High Lord of Eddarta to return to her studies." She turned to me. "She was the most promising of all the students who have passed through my school, and I fear I began to see her graduation as my own greatest triumph. When she chose to leave us, I reacted more like a parent than a teacher."

Tarani walked over to the old woman and took her hands. "Your affection was never unwelcome, Livia—only your insistence on my return." She stepped back, turning to me. "Allow me to present Rikardon."

Livia smiled, and I bowed slightly.

"Rikardon," I said, "who is now going to leave and let you 'forgotten friends' get reacquainted."

I was the forgotten one then; as I moved toward the door, Tarani asked: "Why *have* you come all this way, Livia?"

"I am in Eddarta to attend the meeting, representing the school," Livia said. "I am in your rooms to ask the questions I should have asked, rather than scolding as I did. Why did you leave? What has happened to you since? That message—it was . . . breathtaking. I came primarily to learn—but it did cross my mind that perhaps even the High Lord of Eddarta might have need of the counsel of an old friend."

"Yes to the last," Tarani said fervently, as I was closing the door. "As to my life since leaving you, that is a long tale. . . ."

It was early in the day. I took the interruption as a reprieve from work, and called Keeshah to meet me at the gate of Lord City. Eddartans were becoming accustomed to the sight of sha'um since Thymas had relocated the entire Thagorn settlement to a temporary encampment on the slopes above Lord City. The "extra" sha'um had come along as if it were the most natural thing in the world, and ranged wild on the higher slopes and in the thickly overgrown hills to the east of the city. But Keeshah still attracted considerable attention. The guards, the merchants at the gate, the people moving up the sloping road from Lower Eddarta—all of them stopped to watch as Keeshah came up and crouched for me to mount.

*Run?* Keeshah asked.

*Please,* I said, and he took off.

I leaned forward and hugged the furry back, delighting in the flow of muscle beneath my body. I let my mind slip into the quiet communion with the big cat which gave us both so much joy. I felt the satisfying thrust of his legs against the earth; he felt the sweep of wind across my hairless face, and my different sense of the motion of his own body. We were never so much *together* as we were during a run like this. Not even the brief, intense moments of blending could yield this sense of unity, of belonging. When it was nearly dark, I roused from that pleasant state, and asked Keeshah to take me back to Eddarta.

*Have to go?* Keeshah asked.

*I'm afraid so,* I said.

*Not afraid,* Keeshah said, with conviction and a little sadness. *Want to go.*

I was amazed—and somewhat embarrassed—to realize that, as usual, he had read my feelings more accurately than I could. I had, indeed, already turned my thoughts back toward Eddarta. I was wondering how Tarani's reunion was progressing. I was thinking about the planning which had been interrupted. As abruptly as if I had flipped an electrical switch, I had freed myself of my association with Keeshah and tuned into my association with the future of Gandalara.

*Yes, I do want to go back, Keeshah,* I admitted. *But it doesn't mean that our run is any less precious to me. Thank you.*

I was struck by a sudden, chilling thought, and Keeshah responded to my emotion by pulling up short, sidestepping, shaking his head so violently that his neckfur fluffed out next to my face and provoked a sneeze.

*No!* he said adamantly. *Different now. Sha'um society. Man society. Same. I will stay!*

I had recalled sharing Zanek's lifememory in the All-Mind when he had realized that his sha'um would not return from the Valley, for no other reason than the pressure of leadership. Zanek had not been able to spare time for his friend, and his friend had sensed the continual burden of guilt it placed on the King of Gandalara.

I had been thinking how long it had been since Keeshah and I had shared a run, and how long a time it might be before the next one, when the memory had surfaced. The burden seemed similar, and I had wondered if the outcome might be the same.

I no longer wondered.

*You're absolutely right, Keeshah,* I said. *It's different now. I'm not carrying that burden alone; I have Tarani, and Zanek, and Thymas to help. Thanks to the communication that occurred through the Ra'ira, everyone is working for the same thing, and my job is a lot easier than Zanek's was.*

Keeshah had started forward again, and was accelerating into his ground-covering stride when I added grimly: "Except for the paperwork."

The sudden distraction made him break stride, and I felt the jolt of mischief in his mind just before he veered into a dakathrenil orchard. I shouted with laughter, and bent my attention toward *not* getting scraped off Keeshah's back.

By the time we reached Eddarta, it was already night, and both moods—the tranquil pleasure of the run, and the sudden fear—had faded. In its place was a pleasant exhaustion that let me, thoughtlessly, open the door of our suite without knocking.

Livia was seated in a chair, and Tarani was sitting on the floor, her head resting on the older woman's knee.

"Oh—I'm sorry, Tarani, Livia. Forgive me for intruding."

"In your own home, young man?" Livia said. "Nonsense. We've finished our visit in any case; I'm just sitting here for the company and because my old bones take rest whenever they can get it."

Tarani stirred and shoved herself up to her knees. She put her hands on the old woman's arm, where it rested on the arm of the chair.

"Thank you for coming, Livia," she said.

The teacher patted Tarani's hand gently. "Do consider what I've said, won't you?"

Tarani nodded. "I promise."

Livia started to stand up, and was struggling so that Tarani got to her feet, and I moved closer to help, if needed. Livia nodded, chuckled, and said: "I never refuse help, young man. I find movement much more important than pride."

I took her arm, and together Tarani and I levered her up. She spent a few seconds getting her back straightened out, then she stood as regally as when she had stepped through the doorway.

"Tarani has told me a great deal about you, Rikardon," Livia said, "but there's one thing I won't believe until I hear it from you personally. How do you feel about Tarani?"

I smiled, and tried to catch the eye of the High Lord. I felt a twinge of uncertainty when Tarani refused to meet my gaze. I had been tempted to answer lightly, but I changed my mind and spoke sincerely.

"She is the grandest person I have ever known, Livia. She's strong, and good, and I love her deeply."

Tarani looked up at me then, with one of the rare smiles that lit her face, and made my heart jump.

"Thank you," she said.

Livia looked at Tarani, and then at me. "Well," she said, "that's that."

She walked out of the room, closing the door behind her.

I put my hands on my hips and looked at Tarani.

"What was that all about?"

Tarani laughed, but not easily enough to satisfy the twinge I was still feeling.

"It has to do with being a Recorder," she said. "Somil, you see, was an outstanding exception to the normal behavior of a Recorder."

Somil lived in Omergol. I had known he was something of a renegade because Markasset knew Recorders as quiet people who lived circumspect lives. But I realized that Tarani's comment related to one particular aspect of Somil's lifestyle.

"You mean Recorders are supposed to stay celibate?" I demanded, astonished.

"Not exactly," she said awkwardly. "But—um—physical closeness is not encouraged on a regular basis. The theory is, an emotional bond in the physical world diminishes a Recorder's bond to the All-Mind."

"The *theory*," I said. "You yourself have disproven that theory a number of times."

"I know," she said, and went into the other room.

I followed her and watched for a moment while she changed into the brief gown that was standard nightwear for both men and women.

"You told Livia you would 'consider' something," I said at last. "What?"

She shook her head. "Nothing we need to discuss at the moment," she said, smiling, and opened her arms. "Shall we not—um—indulge in some physical closeness?"

It was an obvious ploy to close off the conversation, and it worked.

The next morning, we began our planning again. The days flew by, and suddenly the day of the meeting arrived. There were hundreds of people—far too many to fit in any building in Eddarta—so the meeting was held outside the eastern wall of Lord City. While the intent was to leave the gate and road open to normal activity, almost everyone who climbed the road wandered around to see what was happening.

Tarani and I, and Zanek, had climbed to the top of the wall of Lord City, and it was from there that we presented our plan to the representatives of Gandalara's cities. There were a few questions, but it seemed clear that, rather than the people here requesting a commitment from their cities, their cities had already made that commitment and had sent their people for information and instructions.

We had gathered an unofficial audience *inside* Lord City, and when we had climbed down from the wall, Indomel came up to us. I could not restrain a small shudder. The boy might be Tarani's full brother, but he was as unlike her as a person could be. He had acknowldged defeat in words, but I had the feeling he was still watching for opportunities to strike back. I got fidgety in the same room with him, and I *never* let him get behind me.

Tarani was facing me, and did not see Indomel behind her. "Everyone displayed such discipline and cooperation, Rikardon," she was saying enthusiastically. "Dare we hope for things to go this smoothly throughout our effort?"

"Of course things will go well for you, Sister," Indomel said. I was gratified to see Tarani's shoulders twitch, as if her feelings about her brother were like mine. "Merely continue to use the Ra'ira . . ."

Wrong.

Tarani whirled on Indomel, her eyes flashing with anger. The boy shrank back, lifting his arm to ward off a blow, and I could see that Tarani was tempted.

"The Ra'ira never entered Lord City, *Brother*," she said. "What we have done is the product of truth and fairness." She turned to me. "Do you recall our discussion in the Valley of Mists?" she asked. "I believe this is an opportune time to make the trial."

I nodded. "I'll send for Thymas." We had entrusted the gem to the Lieutenant, who had hidden it somewhere in the hills—only he knew where.

Tarani turned back to Indomel. "In one hour, you are to call for Zefra and bring her to Lord Hall. Understood?"

Indomel, cowed by Tarani's fierceness, only nodded. Tarani stormed off. The small group of people who had witnessed the confrontation got out of her way, and began whispering questions back and forth when she had passed.

Zanek touched my arm, looking as puzzled as everyone else.

"I'll explain later," I said, and tried to move away.

"If it's Thymas you need," Zanek said, "you'll find him just outside the main gate."

It was my turn to be puzzled.

"But Thymas has been in on all the planning, and it was his

idea to send a cross section of the Sharith as representatives—
some Riders, some not, some men, some women, some of the
cubs." By Sharith convention, boys between fourteen and
sixteen who had bonded to sha'um were called cubs. "I
thought he hadn't planned to come himself."

"He did not come for the meeting," Zanek said. "He came
because I asked him."

"Why?"

Zanek waved his hand. "We can discuss that later, as well,"
he said. "Take your message to the Lieutenant."

## 34

I broke away, still wondering. I found Thymas—and Ronar—sitting against the wall of Lord City, surrounded by wide-
eyed Eddartan children. They touched and patted the big
sha'um, while Ronar closed his eyes and twitched his ears. He
lowered his head and pushed outward, lifting a smallish kid off
the ground. The little boy screamed with delight. He moved
away; a little girl took his place; Ronar gave her the same sort
of ride, to the same reception.

"This is a far cry," I said, "from the day when Ronar wouldn't
let Tarani anywhere near him."

Thymas grinned and stood up, dusting off the seat of his
trousers.

"It is a time of change," he said, and then grew serious.
"Children are more important than ever, now. They will be
around sha'um all the time; they must be taught to respect
their strength, but not to fear them."

I was quiet for a second. Then I said: "And this is the man
who doubted his leadership ability? His vision?" I put my hand
on his shoulder. "Thymas, you've grown so much since I've
known you. I know that seeing you now would fulfill every
hope Dharak had for you."

"I hope that is true," Thymas said, looking at me squarely,
"but I believe I have learned something both you and my
father tried to tell me. It is foolish to live by another's

standards. If I am true to myself, and do not willingly shirk responsibility, well, then"—he shrugged—"whatever I do is the best I can do, and is enough."

I was truly amazed by the insight of that remark, and for a moment I just stared at Thymas.

"What is wrong?" he asked, after a moment, with an unwelcome shadow of the sullen mood which used to be standard for him.

"I'm realizing how little contact we have had these past weeks," I said, "and how much I depend on you to handle the Sharith on your own. And I'm feeling very grateful that you're here to do it."

He accepted that with more poise than he had ever exhibited before, but he said: "Zanek has helped."

"Speaking of Zanek," the boy continued, "he asked me to come here today. Were you going to take me to him?"

"What?" I said, momentarily confused. "Oh—no, he said whatever he needed could wait. I've come to ask you to get the Ra'ira for us. Bring it to Lord Hall in an hour—well, less, now that I've delayed the message. Is it close enough to get it here in that time?"

The boy nodded, and gently disengaged the current rider from Ronar's head. I expected tantrums and wailing when Thymas stopped the game, but all it took was Ronar standing up with Thymas on his back to send the children scampering backward.

*Thymas is right in one way*, I thought. *All children will have to acquire a passing acquaintance with sha'um. But I doubt they'll ever stop being just a little bit afraid of them, unless they bond with one. And that's good. It's safer. Because I have good reason to know that even bonded sha'um never stop being just a little bit wild.*

Thymas walked into Lord Hall almost exactly at the appointed time. His step faltered briefly when he came into the room and saw Indomel and Zefra standing beside Tarani and Zanek, but he recovered, walked directly to the High Lord, and offered her a leather pouch.

Indomel seemed to sway forward, and Tarani must have noticed the movement from the corner of her eye.

"Thank you for coming so promptly, Thymas," she said. "Please take the stone out of the pouch and place it on that post." She pointed to one of several hip-high stone pillars that dotted this one area of the big room.

Lord Hall was really a wide corridor that ran inside the octagonal walls of the Hall, surrounding the central chamber which was the official meeting place of the Lords. In the chamber stood the Bronze, the engraved message written by Zanek and recently quoted to Tarani. Behind the ceiling-high panel that held the Bronze was the treasure vault of the High Lords, the avenue by which Tarani and I first had entered Lord Hall.

On that night, these pillars had been hidden by closely latticed wooden frames which had been positioned on the pillars, covered with cloths, and laden with food for the Celebration Dance. At the formal proclamation of Tarani's becoming High Lord, sturdier frames had provided a platform to support Hollin and Tarani during the ceremony. Now, however, only one pillar was in use: it supported an oddly shaped blue stone.

Tarani left Indomel and Zefra and walked around the pillar to stand beside me. Thymas had moved back, but I had the feeling he was still around, curious about what was going on.

*It's only fair,* I thought. *He's been involved since the beginning; he's entitled to be here at what I hope will be the end of the Ra'ira.*

"Indomel, move this way a little; Mother, go the other way. . . ."

She guided everyone until the stone was surrounded by a square of people, Tarani and I together marking one corner of the square. We had not discussed how to go about this, not once since that conversation three months ago. It felt right that Tarani and I were together. She seemed to be a catalyst through which I could have some effect on the Ra'ira. Her closeness comforted me for another reason. The Ra'ira still frightened me terribly.

*No, that's wrong,* I realized suddenly. *The stone doesn't frighten me; what I could do with its power, what I can feel myself wanting to do with its power—that's what frightens me. It's not that the Ra'ira's power is dangerous in the hands of evil men like Ferrathyn. The really scary thing is the temptation presented by that power. People with good intentions have little real use for something that can control and deceive other people. But people with good intentions are tempted. Every-*

*body has at least a few flawed and ugly places hidden away
inside themselves. Those places respond to the lure of the
Ra'ira, and the person suddenly becomes aware of them.*

*I've seen a few of mine. They are scary.*

When everyone was arranged to Tarani's satisfaction, she
said: "Rikardon, will you explain it?"

Roused from my fixation on the Ra'ira, I did explain, as best
I could, my theory about the way the Ra'ira actually worked.
Before I had gone very far, Indomel figured it out.

"You want us to destroy it!" he exclaimed. Zefra gasped, and
Zanek raised his eyebrows.

"Do you really think it can be done?" Zanek asked.

It was Tarani who answered.

"We have all been in contact through the Ra'ira before,"
Tarani said, "but only at great distances. It is my hope and
Rikardon's that the four of us—I count Rikardon with me," she
said, taking my hand, "can shatter the stone at close range and
with deliberate intent."

"I won't do it!" Indomel said, his voice low and fierce.

Tarani's hand tensed, and she grew very still.

"Indomel, I hoped you would cooperate in this without
coercion," she said.

"Coercion?" he echoed. "Do you mean compulsion? I doubt
you will do that, Sister, or that it would, in the end, work.
While you are controlling me, some of your own power is
diverted, so that the gain would be very little. And in any case,
you have proved that you can control my mind, but my skill is
a different matter altogether."

"Compulsion would, indeed, be profitless," Tarani responded. "It is not what I meant. I will give you what you
believe you want, Brother. I give you a taste of the Ra'ira's
power."

Now it was Tarani who leaned toward the stone, angling
toward the thinnish, mean-spirited young man some ten feet
away from her.

"Would you use the stone to see the thoughts of others,
Indomel? Then look into *my* mind. See *my* thoughts."

The boy's eyes grew wide. His muscles went taut so
suddenly that he staggered a step sideways, and groped
blindly for one of the pillars for support.

"It is not true," he whispered. "No—stop it, please."

But Tarani had let loose something she had suppressed for a

long time, and it snapped out of her with the force of a cracking whip.

"Anger and hatred," Tarani said. "I have seen you take pride in inspiring them, Indomel. But they are not so pleasant, are they, without a shield of distance? Imagine what it would be like to be surrounded by it, exposed to it like this every hour of every day. That is what the Ra'ira would bring you, my brother. Is it truly what you wish?"

"I—no," Indomel said, then seemed to recover a little. There was a stubborn certainty in his voice as he said: "This is not how it would be. *You* are doing this. If I used the Ra'ira, I could—I could—"

He stumbled, and it occurred to me that, probably, Indomel had never quite defined what he wanted in seeking the enigmatic power of the stone.

"You could look only for pleasant things," Tarani said scornfully, "such as . . . the love of a mother for her son."

Zefra started, and had enough time to say a few words before she, too, went rigidly tense: "No—I beg you, do not let him see—"

Whatever it was that Indomel and Zefra shared, it caused them both so much pain that both their voices blended in an anguished wail. The sound echoed in the big room, then stopped abruptly as Tarani released both Indomel and Zefra.

We were all quiet for a moment, then Zefra said: "That was cruel, Daughter—a cruelty I would not have expected from you."

"Agreed," Tarani said. "The Ra'ira encourages cruelty, Mother. It is because I find myself capable of doing such a thing that I am determined to see the stone destroyed. Listen, both of you," she commanded.

Indomel drew himself up straight and looked at Tarani. His face was haggard.

"If we cannot destroy the gem, it will be hidden far away from here. I trust Zanek to leave it be for the remainder of this lifetime, for he has proved himself to be trustworthy. I trust myself only because I am not alone," she said, squeezing my hand, "and someone of good sense has some control over my actions. But I know the Ra'ira will never cease to hold a fascination for the two of you, and I will be plagued constantly with worry that you will find a way to retrieve it.

"Rikardon and Zanek and I have a great task before us, and it is one to which we must apply every possible energy. I will not let simple respect for our blood ties force me to endure such a distraction."

Zefra quailed. "Tarani. You would have us killed? Me? Because of this—?"

Indomel said nothing, but the look in his eyes showed his absolute faith in Tarani's willingness to destroy him.

"The stone's power *must* be neutralized," Tarani said. "If it cannot be destroyed, then those who would *use* it must be destroyed. But—no, Zefra, I would not 'have you killed.' I bear you more regard than that, and I could not fairly assign that responsibility and guilt. I would kill you myself, with a sword or a dagger—cleanly, without the taint of the Ra'ira."

We all knew it was true.

Zefra turned to her son.

"Indomel, no matter what you saw in me, please believe this. I loved you as a child. I have hated what Pylomel made of you, but I would not, willingly, see you die. Do as Tarani asks; help her destroy the stone."

The boy stared at his mother without speaking, until Zefra could stand it no longer.

"Are—are you thinking that I beg for my own life?"

"No," he said. "I am—Mother, I do believe you. I saw it when Tarani brought us together. The hatred—yes, that was a bitter hurt. But—I saw your love too. You not only felt it then, there is still some affection for me, in spite of what my father did, in spite of what *I* have done to you. How can that be?"

"The quest for that answer," Tarani interrupted, "will wait until another time. If the Ra'ira can be destroyed, there will be enough time for you and Zefra to truly begin to know one another."

Indomel nodded, stood up straight, and stepped forward. "I am ready, Tarani. I will give you whatever strength I can command."

"Come closer," Tarani said, "and join hands."

I felt there was less logic in that command than a need for a physical confirmation of our united purpose. Zanek/Dharak's hand was strong and warm in mine.

No order was required from Tarani; we merely began, all of us, staring at the stone. A glow shimmered in its depths, and grew brighter. Even though I had associated the mindplane experience with communication across distances, as the feeling of power built, the room seemed to darken with the tangible nothingness of the mindplane, until I was seeing the room with all my senses. Zanek, Zefra, and Indomel were physically visible, but their bodies were cloaked in the auras of energy I had sensed before. Tarani's was not visible because, as in every earlier instance, we were together.

I felt that closeness now with hand and mind, and I had an awareness of the others. The room was pervaded with a sense of purpose that was as awesome as the force of mindpower at work.

Rather than focusing that power *through* the Ra'ira, it was, itself, the object of all that power. If my theory were correct, and vibration within the stone transmitted and amplified that energy, the vibration should be doubly intense if no outlet were provided.

The Ra'ira, too, had a double image. It shone with an ever brighter blue glow, and it struck my other senses as pulsing with the energy being applied to it. The effort we were making felt, to me, like applying steadily increasing pressure to a stone wall. I bore down, and I sensed the others pushing harder.

The images of the Ra'ira blended, and the pulsing psychic radiance seemed to turn to blue light. The pulsing became slower and stronger, and impacted our mindsight like the sound of a booming bass drum impacts the ear. Slower . . . stronger . . . brighter . . .

The radiance flared into an intolerable whiteness and vanished.

Instantly, all the connections between us vanished, and we snapped apart as if we were sections of a taut rubber band, sliced through at four points simultaneously.

Resting on the pillar was a tiny pile of lusterless blue chunks. I picked one up with a shaking hand, but I felt nothing from it. No tingle, no aura, nothing more meaningful than a shapeless and rather unattractive chunk of blue stuff.

# 35

Indomel and Zefra left Lord Hall together, caught up in a strained and uncertain silence. Only then did Thymas come forward from the corner he had sought while the rest of us were concentrating on the Ra'ira. He reached out toward the pile of fragments, but did not touch them.

"Amazing," he said. "The trouble that thing has caused, and now it is gone."

"I find only one sad thing in this," Zanek said. "Without the physical image as a reminder of the stone, it will be soon forgotten, and along with it, the lessons it taught about strength and power."

"What?" Thymas said. "I do not believe that anyone who heard Tarani's message, saw Rikardon's vision, could forget it, Zanek."

"Not they, certainly," Zanek agreed. "But their children will not have the experience. Their parents will recount these events, as is required in the rules we have set forth. But to children, they will be only stories. The movement up the River Wall—that will be real to them, and I do not doubt there will be a continued commitment to its purpose. But the Ra'ira will be far in the past by then."

"A legend," I said, feeling troubled. "Like all the inaccurate legends I have run into these past months. The few people in Raithskar who knew about the Ra'ira believed that only the last, harmful Kings had possessed and used the stone. With Serkajon's steel sword part of their everyday lives, carried by one of the Captain's descendants, no one remembered that another steel sword had existed during the time of the Kingdom. Only in Eddarta, where the Lords had settled and passed down the story of the twin swords, was there any knowledge of that second sword.

"It makes me wonder. There is still a lot to do, but I feel we have laid the foundation of a strong, shared vision. Each new generation will be instilled with a sense of responsibility to

continue the climb. But when they get to the top, will anyone
remember why it all happened?"

"I have a more serious question than that, my friend," Zanek
said. "It had not occurred to me before now, but—how will
that final generation *know* that they have reached the top?"

The question sent a chill down my spine. *Why haven't I*
*thought of that before?* I wondered. *Only Tarani and I have*
*any knowledge of what the terrain will look like. That's only a*
*guess, but it's more than anyone else has. By the time*
*Gandalarans reach the rim of the basin, nomadic movement*
*will have become a habit. Why should it matter that they start*
*moving on level ground, rather than on an incline?*

*That's not what we intended,* I thought. *Gandalara's culture*
*has developed in a geographically static—though environmen-*
*tally evolving—location. Our whole purpose is to preserve*
*that culture. The idea is to take it up the Wall, find a suitable*
*location, and settle down again.*

Aloud, I said: "You're right, Zanek. We have put a lot of
thought into starting the movement, and none at all into
stopping it when it's time." I shrugged, feeling unhappy. "As of
now, I don't have any ideas."

"I have one," Tarani said, "and I believe it will satisfy both
those questions of accurate remembrance."

I turned around to face Tarani. She had picked up a few of
the Ra'ira fragments in one hand, and was letting them drop,
one by one, into her other hand.

"You have seen only one side of the Recorder function,"
Tarani said. "It is possible to *add* information to the All-Mind,
as well as retrieve it."

In a long-ago conversation with Thanasset, this capability of
the Recorders had been mentioned. The information had
come in the flood of confusion that had beset me before the
integration of Ricardo and Markasset, and I had not thought of
it again, until now.

"*Add* a lifememory? Deliberately?" Zanek challenged, horrified.

"I did say 'information' and not 'memory,'" Tarani corrected
gently. "It is a regular practice of all Recorders—and has been,
since the first Recorder—to place in a specific location a
description of each question asked by a Seeker, the search path
and location of the answer, and what was discovered."

"An *index*?" I questioned, using Ricardo's word for the concept.

Tarani nodded. "It functions that way, yes," she said, and frowned. "In terms of your vision of the All-Mind, Rikardon, it would seem to be an extraordinarily long cylinder of light, attached at only one end."

"I have been to the All-Mind three times," I said. "Twice with you, once with Somil. Neither one of you touched something like that."

She smiled. "Do you recall the ritual of entry? The Recorder establishes the link with the All-Mind a few moments before the Seeker joins the Recorder. In that brief time, we consult the—index, as you name it.

"I *say* that the skill has not been used for any other purpose," Tarani continued. "That does not mean that it cannot have other uses. We have asked the people to tell their children of the events of these past weeks, and you have pointed out that, in the telling, the tale may become less real.

"I propose that we attempt to do exactly what Zanek imagined: create a special Record which, essentially, contains the lifememory of a living man. It would not *be* a lifememory, you understand, or even memory at all. It will be one person's recounting of the basis for the journey.

"I also propose that the education of our young include a Recorder as one of the teachers. We attempt a rigorous environmental change, and we are forced to expect that some of the adults will die during any given move. The lost ones may be of any craft, any skill, and not only their contribution will be lost, but the continuation of their skills through their children. By integrating Recorders into our regular education, we can guarantee that such lost skills can be partially replaced.

"It will be necessary," she said, turning to walk a few steps, turning back, "to seek out talented children to be trained as Recorders. A few have been sufficient until now; many more will be needed to make this plan effective. The teaching Recorders will serve to educate our children in their own history, and part of each child's education will be the sharing of the *constructed* lifememory about the beginning of the journey. Children will learn the general background from their parents, but in sharing the knowledge, the conviction, the present awareness of one person who lived through this beginning, the children will recover the *spirit* which pervades us now, the certainty of disaster, the grand purpose, which is nothing less than survival."

We were all silent a moment, caught up in Tarani's special vision. It was Thymas who finally spoke.

"I see the value of the plan, Tarani," he said. "But you have not spoken to Zanek's concern. How can such a memory assist our people in identifying the final destination?"

"It will serve that purpose, as well," Tarani said, "if the lifememory is Rikardon's."

I jumped, even though my mind instantly agreed with the logic of it. Another thought crossed my mind.

"Is this what Livia asked you to 'consider'?" I asked.

"Livia's visit was very helpful," Tarani said. "I had conceived of the idea of the special Recording, and of everyone sharing those memories, but I had not foreseen the need for more Recorders, and their value in other areas. Livia made that suggestion, and its value was obvious."

"If you accepted that, then what *were* you considering?"

Without fully realizing it, I had tensed up, and was leaning on one of the pillars, one hand on my hip. It was no wonder that Tarani reacted defensively.

"Her comment has nothing to do with the plan we are discussing," she snapped.

"I have no quarrel with the plan," I said. "I have some questions about its details, but I know they can be worked out. But this is the first time you've mentioned this plan to me, and I'd rather not be surprised by what else Livia suggested to you."

"If you must know," Tarani fumed, "she asked that I make provision for at least one of our children to become a Recorder!"

"Our . . . children?" I said.

"She asked it as a favor, a replacement for my departure. I told her such a choice would be made by us both, and not before our second child is born.

"Since you insist on discussing this now," she continued angrily, "would you not also like to know what her parting remark meant?"

"You mean, 'That's that,' after I told her I . . . love you?" Suddenly I felt embarrassed that such a small thing had almost built to a quarrel. I relaxed from my aggressive stance, and smiled. "You must know, by now, that I have a lot more love than tact—or timing."

To my great relief, she laughed.

"A highly pardonable failing, my love," she said. "So I *shall* tell you what Livia meant. I had told her that I shall be the Recorder who enters that special Record, and she had assumed I meant to take on the formal appearance and behavior of a Recorder—including a private, separate residence. I fear," Tarani said with a wry smile, "that I was rather blunt in my refusal."

"Good for you," I said. "She struck me as a tough old lady; I'm sure the bluntness didn't hurt her."

"As a matter of fact, she countered me with a wise caution against Recording while I carried a child, and used that as an argument for at least a temporary withdrawal until the Record was complete."

"I fear I do not understand the wisdom in that restriction," Zanek said. "Why should it matter if a woman were pregnant?"

"Only that the bodies of a child and its mother are in intimate contact," Tarani said, "and that no one can tell if their minds, too, are touching. It is possible that the child would suffer the strain imposed on the Recorder. I agreed to Livia's counsel willingly, but shared with her one of the tenets we are asking all of Gandalara to accept. A high birth rate is essential, to replenish our strength as we climb.

"The Record will be a difficult task for both of us, my love," she said, coming toward me with her hands outstretched. "We will need several sessions, I think, and considerable distance in time between those sessions." I took her hands. "My own desires, as well as our need to set an example, will not permit postponing our family."

I pulled her into my arms and hugged her, for the moment too moved to speak. After a moment, I stepped back.

"What solution have you found, then?" I asked. "To select someone else to create the Record?"

"Ah, no!" she exclaimed. "It is a privilege I claim for myself, and a task to which I believe my slightly different skills are particularly suited. I propose a compromise solution: that I shall not attempt to Record during pregnancy—which will certainly prolong the time it will take to complete the Record—and that, for several days before a session, I shall withdraw to solitude to achieve the tranquillity of mind and body which will, I believe, be necessary. Understand, Rikardon, for the purpose of the Record I shall have to abandon my other duties entirely for a time, and take on the formal aspect of a Recorder." She laughed. "That is, what I understand to be a traditional Recorder—*not* Somil."

I laughed too. "I can live with that," I said. "What did Livia say?"

"She acknowledged the fact that I had already decided, and she could not change my mind. But she refused to offer her support unless she could be convinced that my feelings for you were returned. Actually, the phrase she used was 'Is he worth all this concern?'"

Tarani smiled, but looked down at the floor as she said: "Obviously, your answer convinced her."

I touched her arm, and she looked up at me.

"The whole plan is inspired, Tarani. I support it fully, and I'm grateful for your 'concern'—for me and for our children. I think the Record should begin with my arrival here, and continue through these planning stages, don't you?"

I looked around at the others too. They all nodded.

"Then you are no longer angry that I made these plans independently?" Tarani asked.

"I was never angry, Tarani, and I think I trust your judgment even more than my own. I feel sure there will be occasion for each of us to make independent decisions in the coming years, even though we are, essentially, a ruling council of four."

"Rikardon," Zanek said, "may I interrupt a moment?"

"Of course," I said, turning to him.

"We have told the people that, when everyone who is coming has gathered here, they will be asked to approve an administration system which we have not yet thoroughly designed. I would ask a gift from you, my friends."

"After all you have done for us, Zanek," I said, "I'm sure I speak for Tarani and Thymas in saying you may ask anything of us."

Zanek smiled. "A rash statement, Rikardon, but I shall hold you to it. I would like to leave now."

"Well, certainly," I said. "The Ra'ira's destroyed—"

"Don't be such a *vlek*, Captain," Thymas interrupted. "He means to leave Dharak's body, not this hall."

# 36

"What?" I stammered, staring at Thymas.

"Zanek was kind enough to ask me about it a few days ago," Thymas said, "since, for me, he feared it would be like losing my father twice." He turned to Zanek. "I will say, before them, what I said to you then. It is *your* loss I'll feel, Zanek, but I would not hold you here for my sake. Dharak and I have been honored by your visit."

Zanek put his hand on my shoulder. "Do not look so horrified, Rikardon. In Thagorn, you merely assumed I would share the burden of leadership, but if you think back, I never promised such a thing."

He smiled, and though it still looked like Dharak's face to me, I knew it was Zanek who smiled. He looked sad, and tired. "I have done this before, you know—restructured the world. If you think to benefit from my experience, consider the final products of my work. They were hardly lasting successes. It could be argued that you will be better off without my advice."

"Do not say that," Tarani said. "Had you not established the Kingdom as Zanek, and then destroyed it as Serkajon, there would be nothing here today worth saving."

"She's right, Zanek," I said. "And though it causes me pain to say it, so are you. You have done more than your share already. You—you have my consent, if you feel you need it."

"I do need it," he said sincerely, "for without it, I would feel as if I am betraying you, and I could not go." His eyes went out of focus. "I have said there is no memory of that place in me, but there is a longing for it. It may be that I am being called. Tarani? Will you, too, give me your good wishes?"

Tarani moved past me and put her arms around Dharak/Zanek. Over her shoulder, I saw his eyes close as his arms tightened around her.

"If I feel any lack of contentment in that other place," Zanek said as Tarani withdrew, her breath coming in the sharp gasps

269

that was Gandalaran sobbing, "it shall be because I miss you, my friends."

"Before you go, Zanek," Tarani said, "can you tell us if we will succeed? The abrupt ending of the All-Mind—has it changed?"

Zanek laughed heartily, and it was that action that finally freed me of the worst of my grief. He had not been so lighthearted in months, and I felt sure it was the prospect of leaving—with our blessings—that cheered him so.

"I shall have that answer soon," he said. "But, of course, I shall not be able to tell you. Perhaps that is best, for the continued uncertainty will demand your best effort—and I feel sure it is only that which can change the dead future I saw from that other place."

Thymas put his hand on Zanek's arm.

"I have a favor to ask of *you*," he said, and looked around the stark, empty hall. "Don't leave Dharak's body in here."

"I'd say we could all use some air," I said, and Zanek nodded.

*Come, Keeshah,* I called.

Tarani paused at the pillar and swept the blue fragments into her pouch. Then we walked unhurriedly to the gates of Lord City. Ronar and Keeshah were there.

"I did not call Yayshah," Tarani said. "Will Keeshah mind carrying two?"

"Not at all," I said.

She and I mounted Keeshah, and Thymas and Zanek mounted Ronar. The two sha'um kept a close pace as we left Lord City and climbed the green hillside above it. Thymas seemed to be leading the way; we climbed to one of the stairstep levels of ground that kept the Tashal River from being one continuous waterfall.

We all dismounted, and Zanek stroked Ronar with unmistakable affection. He turned, with us, to look down at Gandalara.

Far to our left was the beginning of our first encampment. The Sharith had begun it; in the next few months the few hastily constructed tents would swell to hundreds, thousands. These first shelters would be little more than resting places for people who tilled land or tended crops at a higher level until their lungs burned. The people who moved to that level and began the next would really be taking the first *step* up the

River Wall. The first *action* step was to leave everything behind and turn our faces upward.

It would begin soon.

It was intimidating.

It was intoxicating.

It was, simply, our destiny.

The man who had set it all in motion drew a deep breath and said: "Captain, perhaps you and the Lieutenant would be kind enough to spare Dharak's body the indignity of falling?"

"Of course," I said.

Thymas and I each took one of the old man's arms. Zanek smiled once more, his face seeming to beam with a special radiance. Then Thymas and I caught the weight of Dharak's empty body.

Thymas shrugged off my hands and lifted his father's body in his arms, cradling the head on his shoulder. The boy was short, but strong; the old man was not an excessive burden for him.

"I'll miss him terribly," I said. "But he was right in thinking I would have leaned on him heavily, had he stayed. I am grateful to have both of you."

Thymas looked surprised. "Surely you don't think *I'm* going to be much help?"

"Of course I think so," I said. "The three of us—"

The boy was shaking his head. "I am Lieutenant of the Sharith," he said. "That's plenty to keep me busy. I finally believe I can handle it, Rikardon, but it's *all* I can handle. Call on me for advice in that area, if you like, but don't ask me to make decisions for anyone else."

Tarani spoke up, then. "I, too, will be concerned with special projects, my love. I did promise Livia to coordinate the new structure for Recorder schools, and I feel a special responsibility toward the Lords and Eddartans who will provide so much material and support for the rest of Gandalara during these first stages."

I stared from one to the other of them.

"Are you telling me that *I* am the administration plan we'll present to the people?" I asked.

"I believe we have already discussed the need to divide the people into distinct groups of some sort," Tarani said. "Whether those groups are to be skill-based, or structured around the source cities of the people, remains to be decided. Each separate group will have a leader or leaders, but someone must provide coordination among those leaders. Someone *must* have ultimate authority."

"From the beginning," Thymas said, "we have been guided by your vision, Rikardon. I see no reason to stop now."

I thought about that for a long minute. "All right," I said, at last. "As long as everybody understands that the decision of the 'ultimate authority' may be to put an issue to a vote, either among the leaders or the people themselves, and abide by the majority decision."

"That comment, Captain," Thymas said, "only confirms your value in that position. I—may I see to Dharak now?"

"Of course," I said. "If there is to be a ceremony—"

"There will," he said. "I will let you know when; it would dishonor Dharak's memory if you and Tarani were not present."

"Wait a moment, Thymas," Tarani said. She opened one of Thymas's hands, and placed the pouch full of Ra'ira fragments in his palm. "These are dead, as well. Perhaps Dharak's body will not mind sharing the ceremony."

Tarani and I and Keeshah lingered on the hillside. Eddarta had grown to nearly twice its size. To the east, west, and south there were clusters of people, makeshift corrals filled with vleks or glith, and piles of supplies. Sha'um with Riders appeared frequently, working as short-distance messengers.

Keeshah lay crouched between us, and Tarani and I absently stroked his fur.

"Why didn't you call Yayshah?" I asked.

She shrugged. "I wanted to ride Keeshah with you one more time," she said. "This seemed the *right* time. Also—I am truly sad to lose Zanek. I think I needed to be close to you."

I nodded, understanding.

I shielded my eyes and looked up into the gray cloud cover, seeking the brighter spot that was the sun.

"I've thought about the need to adapt to lower air pressure," I said, "but we must also consider the effect of less-shielded sunlight."

"Yes, eyes and skin must both be protected to some extent at each new stage," Tarani agreed.

We stopped and looked at one another.

"There is so *much* to think about," I said. "So *much* to do."

"It cannot all be considered or accomplished at one time," she said. "Deal with one thing at a time."

I smiled and reached for her hand.

"No matter what our 'official' roles are, Tarani, will you promise always to be my personal advisor?"

"Except as needed for the Record, I promise, my love."

"Ah—the Record. When would you like to begin?"

I felt a sudden tension in her hand, and I turned to face her.

"We *cannot* begin for at least nine moons," she said.

It took me a second, and then I felt my knees go weak.

"A baby?" I whispered. "Our child?"

"A son," she said, with knowledge born of the Gandalaran inner awareness. "The night of Livia's visit, I knew I was fertile. It was unfair not to ask you, Rikardon, but I wanted it so badly. Are you angry?"

"Angry?" I echoed. "Angry? I'm—" I laughed aloud, rose to my knees, and stretched across Keeshah's back to kiss her. "I'm delirious, that's what I am," I said. "A son, you say?"

*Keeshah, did you hear that? I'm going to have a son!*

I felt a strange wash of feeling from him: gladness that I was so happy, mingled with an uncertainty drawn from experience.

*Cubs fun,* he said. *Also nuisance. Nothing the same again. But good.*

I pulled away from Tarani, and saw a glow in her that was born of nothing more dangerous than a mother's joy.

I took her hand and settled back down. After a time, Yayshah joined us, stretching out beside Tarani, seemingly unresentful of Keeshah. Still later, Koshah and Yoshah sought us out, and curled up against their parents.

Tarani and I sat there until the light vanished, watching the future of Gandalara begin.

# END PROCEEDINGS:
# INPUT SESSION SEVEN

   —*I am withdrawing our minds from the All-Mind . . . and now your mind is separate from mine. Are you well, my love?*
   —*Physically very weak, Tarani, but food and time will ease*

*that. In spirit, however, I feel stronger for knowing the Record is complete.*

—It is only one of the many good things you have accomplished in the passing years. Did you find the younger Rikardon to be so different from the man you are now?

—Before I answer that, you promised you would give me your opinion.

—Very well. I believe that experience has made you stronger and more sure in your role, and that has made you a better man, not a lesser one. In your comments at the beginning of this session, I saw the same fear which was so clear in this Record: the fear that you would misuse the power the people have given you. As long as the fear exists, the possibility of misuse does not. And now . . . your judgment?

—Essentially the same, Tarani, but for a different reason. I'll take a lesson from Livia, and measure my value by the caring of my friends. As long as I remember that I must be "worthy of all this concern," I think I'll stay on the right track.

—It is an odd feeling, is it not? That the effort of many years is at an end?

—More so for you, I should think, than for me. Will you miss Recording?

—I shall not have the opportunity. Now that the Record is complete, I must begin training Recorders in its use.

—There is never an end to it, is there? Always something more to do.

—I remind you of something you said to me at Iribos, that we might wish for "a pleasant duty, and a peaceful destiny." There have been and will be exceptions, of course, but in general I feel we have found our wish. For me, it is enough.

—For me as well, Tarani. As long as I may share it with you and our children, and Keeshah and his family.

—Then call those who wait outside, so that we may renew our strength for the tasks to come.

## ABOUT THE AUTHORS

VICKI ANN HEYDRON met RANDALL GARRETT in 1975. In 1978, they were married, and also began planning the Gandalara Cycle. A broad outline for the entire Cycle had been completed, and a draft of *The Steel of Raithskar* nearly finished, when Randall suffered serious and permanent injury. Working from their outline, Vicki has completed the Cycle. Of all seven books, Vicki feels that *The River Wall* is most uniquely hers. The other titles in the Cycle are *The Glass of Dyskornis*, *The Bronze of Eddarta*, *The Well of Darkness*, *Return to Eddarta*, and *The Search for Kä*.

Vicki lives in Austin, Texas, and is currently working on *Bloodright*, an occult novel, and *Castle of Judgment*, a futuristic mystery.

# READ THESE OTHER
# ROUSING FANTASY NOVELS BY
# KENNETH C. FLINT

☐ **CHALLENGE OF THE CLANS** (25553-3 • $3.50 • $3.95 in Canada)—Flint's first tale of Finn MacCumhal, his birth, his long, arduous, enchanted apprenticeship and his rise to glory.

☐ **THE RIDERS OF THE SIDHE** (26606 • $3.50 • $3.95 in Canada)—The beginning of the saga of Lugh of the Long Arm, one of the greatest of all Celtic heroes. With the seagod Manannan (disguised as the jesting rogue Gilla) and Aine, a spirited warrior-woman, Lugh challenges the evil Fomor to restore the True King to the throne of Tara.

☐ **CHAMPIONS OF THE SIDHE** (24543-0 • $2.95 • $3.50 in Canada)—Lugh and his band of champions join together to defend their homeland from the Fomor Lord Balor and his stunning, unnatural power.

☐ **MASTER OF THE SIDHE** (25261-5 • $2.95 • $3.50 in Canada)—The final battle. Lugh and his cohorts must storm Balor's Glass Tower fortress in one last attempt to end the dread reign of the Dark Lord forever.

### AND LOOK FOR
### THE DARK DRUID
#### SEQUEL TO *STORM SHIELD*, COMING SOON

Buy these books wherever Bantam Spectra paperbacks are sold, or use the handy coupon below for ordering:

# RAYMOND E. FEIST'S
# EXTRAORDINARY
# RIFT WAR
# SAGA

Praised as a creation that "invites comparison with Tolkein's LORD OF THE RINGS" (*Best Sellers*), Raymond E. Feist's land of Midkemia is an enchanted realm of elves and dwarves, trolls and darker beings. Filled with high adventure, powerful magics and wondrous imagination, his epic *Rift War Saga* is a new masterpiece of heroic fantasy.

"TOTALLY GRIPPING ... A FANTASY OF EPIC SCOPE, FAST-MOVING ACTION AND VIVID IMAGINATION."
—*The Washington Post Book World*

☐ **MAGICIAN: APPRENTICE** (26760 • $3.95)
☐ **MAGICIAN: MASTER** (26761 • $3.95)
☐ **SILVERTHORN** (25928-8 • $3.50)
☐ **A DARKNESS AT SETHANON** (26328-5 • $3.95)

Buy all four volumes of the Rift War Saga wherever Bantam Spectra Books are sold, or use the handy coupon below for ordering:

**BANTAM**
SHOP·AT·HOME
C·A·T·A·L·O·G

# Special Offer
# Buy a Bantam Book
## *for only 50¢.*

*Now you can have Bantam's catalog filled with hundreds of titles plus take advantage of our unique and exciting bonus book offer. A special offer which gives you the opportunity to purchase a Bantam book for only 50¢. Here's how!*

*By ordering any five books at the regular price per order, you can also choose any other single book listed (up to a $4.95 value) for just 50¢. Some restrictions do apply, but for further details why not send for Bantam's catalog of titles today!*

*Just send us your name and address and we will send you a catalog!*